I DIDN'T BREAK THE
LAMP

HISTORICAL ACCOUNTS OF
IMAGINARY ACQUAINTANCES

Edited by
Dawn Vogel and
Jeremy Zimmerman

I DIDN'T BREAK THE LAMP:
Historical Accounts of Imaginary Acquaintances
Edited by Dawn Vogel and Jeremy Zimmerman
Cover Art and Layout by Luke Spooner

www.madscientistjournal.org • www.patreon.com/madscientistjournal

TABLE OF CONTENTS

FOREWORD

Imagination, sometimes overactive, is a common hallmark of child-hood. Monsters under the bed, invisible friends, and games of make-believe all fill up the empty hours for some children. When I was young and without friends nearby, I spent hours telling stories with my toys. Nighttime often had terrors that only my toys could protect me from.

But what if these friends and fears weren't imaginary? What if things lurked out there, visible only to specific people? And where do these things come from? Are they kin to the fair folk? Ancient gods that have been forgotten? Ghosts? Pure imagination? Or something more mundane?

Our authors in this book might have the answer.

Jeremy Zimmerman
Co-Editor

MANY THANKS
TO OUR KICKSTARTER
BACKERS, PARTICULARLY:

A bunch of talking rats in a trenchcoat, Adam Easterday, Alexandra Summers, Alisha A. Knaff, Amanda L'Heureux, Amanda Robinson, "Andrew, Amanda, Mac, Clock, Train, and Truck Cherry", Angela D'Onofrio, Argents, Arinn Dembo, Brandon Allen, Brenda Yagmin, Bryan & Vanessa Marchal, Captain Kidd, Cara Gerard and cats, Charity Tahmaseb, Chris Brant, Chris Gates, Chrissa Gerard, Cliff Winnig, Dagmar Baumann, Darren Hennessey, Dave Eyt, David J. Kohler, Deborah "Seattlejo" Mitchell, Deborah and Dennis Wilkens, Denyse Mercer, Diabolical Dr. Kindred, Don Ankney, Drew Wood, Elizabeth "Liz" Vann-Clark, Garrett Croker, Gregory N. Finnigan, Ian Chung, Ian S Goodwin, Iván Pazmi, Jack Neel Waddell, Janet Hendrickson, Jeanne Edna Thelwell, Jeff Blackshear, Jen Jenkin, Jenn Dixon, Jennifer Priester, Jess Segal, Jina Oshiro, John Nienart, K. Kitts, K.G. Anderson, K.S. O'Neill, Katherine Nyborg, Kayleigh Taylor, Kris & Tara Kunkel, Laurie J Rich, Loree Parker, Lyndsay E. Gilbert, M. Murakami, Marlo M., Mary Legler, Matt Cushman, Megan Awesome Vogel, Megan Krogstadt, Michael Deneweth, Michael Gonzales, Michael J Neal, "Michele A Ray, Queen of TMI.", Mike Verm, Miss Violet DeVille, Noelle Sa, Patti Oquist, Patti Short, Peter Eugene Zimmerman and his many imaginary friends, Rainy Day Kitty, Ray McCaughey, Rebecca Hartsock, Rebecca Moore, Rhiannon Rhys-Jones, Rich Stoehr, Richard Parachini, Robet Waldbauer, Sam Fleming, Sarah Grant, Sebastian and Sheridan Frantz, Silas Hjelmstad, Simone T. Cooper, Sol & Jen, Tabby LaRasa, Tasha Turner, The Bernard Family!, Tod McCoy, Torrey Podmajersky, Va McAnulty, Wendy Wade, White Beard Geek, and Yi-Mei Chng.

THE LAST
CORY

**An excerpt from the diary of Josephine Cory,
last proprietress of Granite Hill Farm
(colloquially known as "Devil Hill Farm"),**
AS PROVIDED BY SAM CRANE

It was the last Saturday of winter when Barbara and I sat down at my kitchen table to "have a talk." The afternoon was unexpectedly warm, and most of the windows were open. It was a giant pain to fight with the creaky old windows and manage my crutches at the same time, so I'd pressed Barbara into doing most of the opening. I'd claimed I wanted a cross breeze to air the house out some.

I spared a furtive glance for the kitchen window but didn't see any hint of black fur or lurking shadows beyond the window screen. I hoped anyway. I just… wanted her to hear this too. I'd known this conversation with Barb was coming since I'd gotten back from the hospital. I would have to make a plan for the future sooner or later. Whatever I decided, it would change things.

"Anything jumping out at you, A. J.?" Barbara asked from across the butcher block table, trying to be patient.

Empty lunch plates and soup cups had been swept to the side to make way for a colorful spread of brochures and pamphlets, like advertisements at a travel agency. Except this would be a very permanent vacation.

"They're nice—" I replied unhelpfully.

A sigh. "A. J.—"

She'd called me "A. J." ever since she'd been a bratty little teenage string bean. It was short for "Aunt Josephine." I'd liked it immediately, but it had driven her mother nuts—too "disrespectful." We'd kept the nickname anyway though, a pact between aunt and niece. And now Barbara's kids called me "Grandma Jo," which I liked a lot too, even though I was technically their great aunt.

I hummed noncommittally, pretending to read. Seniors' community homes, retirement facilities—they all made themselves sound so posh, each one blurring into the next.

"I know this isn't anyone's idea of fun," Barbara conceded, "but I'm honestly worried about you. Managing this place by yourself is a whole lot of work. I'm amazed you've done it for so long, even with your regular farmhands. But after a certain point, you have to consider the expense of upkeep—"

"The farm is no longer at death's door and hasn't been for decades," I pointed out. "I do have a bit of spare cash these days."

She didn't give up. Relentless, my little Barb. "Even with the farm's emergency slush fund, you wouldn't be able to keep spending this much money for long. And this is one incident. What if you have another accident next winter? A. J., you're eighty. A very spry eighty but still—"

"I'm aware of all that too," I countered tartly. Her husband Greg had put the budget spreadsheets together for me, set up the computer for me too. "I'm not spending that much over budget anyway. I'm having a hard time getting enough help to make up for me being on the sidelines. You know how the regular townies are."

Barbara nodded, quickly moved to sympathy for me. "You'd think they'd get over it by now though."

"Not while some of the oldest are still telling tales." They'd whisper about hauntings and call Granite Hill Farm "Devil Hill Farm" when they thought I was out of earshot. But none of them had ever seen my devil. There hadn't been any mischief, either, since my father went out to the barn and hanged himself some sixty plus years ago, but the rumors persisted. Even now, only out-of-towners would come work for me.

"Speaking of all that, how is your… tenant?" Barbara asked after a moment. My dear little niece was at least polite, but I knew she only half-believed me. At best.

"She's alright, skulking around like normal but not causin' any trouble." I flicked half-heartedly through a couple glossy brochures, feeling a little bitter about just life in general. Damn ankle. "If she wanted to finish me off, the accident would've been her moment, but I suppose one gruesome Cory death was enough to please her."

"The devil made him do it, yeah?" Barbara never had liked hearing me talk about my father's death. I'd made the mistake once of showing my sister Harriet his suicide note, and that had upset her even more. I hadn't dared tell Barbara those details. "A. J., the farm was all but bankrupt. He was clearly having some kind of breakdown. He just… couldn't handle it."

"So they say." I snatched up a brochure and pretended to read. Barbara fussed with her tea to give me a chance to look some of the advertisements over.

The official version of my father's death told of a man crushed by financial insolvency and bad luck. However, the note had told another story: faucets pouring blood, freshly baked bread coming out of the oven crawling with maggots, livestock eviscerated and splattered all over their barn stalls, and worse torments yet. And always, always the creature stalked him all over the farm, just a breath away from wherever he went. Father had tried—and succeeded—in hiding much of that from Harriet and me, but the letter had laid it all out, the feverish paranoid ramblings of a shattered man.

He'd confessed everything. When, as a young man fresh back from the second World War, he had started to expand the farm and clear-cut woodland that he technically owned, he'd found a witch already living there. He'd burned down her little hut and sent her packing, but she'd put a curse on him and the Cory family. Then there was a scuffle that my father claimed the witch had started, but by the end, she was very conveniently dead. The devil had come after that though, and no deed of ownership nor exorcism had been able to evict her.

So two months after I'd turned eighteen, he left that note on my dresser while I was at school and went out to the hayloft of the main barn.

I'd returned home from class to inherit a broken farm, a sixteen-year-old sister, a witch's curse, and a stampede of debt collectors. That bastard, he'd never been much of a father, but now I cursed him too. Some of the townspeople said he'd been kinder before Mother had died, but that was so long ago I couldn't even remember it, and at the tender age of eighteen, I had hated him for taking the coward's way out and dumping everything on me.

And I was terrified of her.

I had nightmares after reading about all the devil's various horrors, and as the new head of the Cory family, I braced myself to be the next target of her wrath. But she never came for me. No murdered animals, no sabotaged farm equipment, no presence dogging my every step.

Well, no hateful presence at least. The devil did come for me, but she never did anything more than simply observe, and after the initial frights and glimpses, I no longer felt threatened by her. She was just… there.

"So," Barbara prompted after I'd skimmed a few summaries, "any thoughts?"

"Always." I slid the slick advertisements back toward her and sidestepped to our previous topic. "You don't have to believe me, Barb. Your mother didn't, and Harriet actually grew up here."

"I think she still believed a little actually," Barbara replied, willing to let me lead the conversation. "Mom never liked talking about her childhood on the farm, and even when she and Dad brought me to visit, she told me I would sleep in the same guestroom with them and to never go anywhere alone. I still remember how mad she was when she found out you'd been telling me about the curse." Barbara bit her lip and pretended to be busy with the pamphlets so she wouldn't have to look at me. "Were you… ever mad at her? About the college thing, I mean."

Well, now wasn't there a little bit of ancient history? "Huh, surprised you know about that."

Barbara fanned the papers and then neatly shuffled them into a stack again. "She told me shortly before she passed. She said the two of you had made a deal that she would go to college first and then come back and run the farm while you went, but instead of coming back, she took a position with a law firm and married Dad. She was so guilty about it even after all those years, leaving you to fix everything back here. It sounded like the two of you never fully made peace over it."

"It's true, we didn't really address it, but I don't hold a grudge anymore, if that's what you want to know—though I was plenty mad at her at the time. I still went to their wedding though." I smiled sadly, resting my elbows on the table and my chin on my hands, thinking of Harriet, who'd stopped being a Cory and became a Wilson instead. "Poor Harriet, she never particularly wanted to be a farmer. She never loved this land like I do. Being a lawyer suited her better, and she was always so smart. I'm happy she could make it happen, and I'm happy she brought my favorite little niece into the world."

Barbara predictably went all doe-eyed when I talked like that, but it was the truth. Even if I'd had a dozen nieces and nephews, I was certain she'd still be my favorite, the little rascal.

"There is another place," she said, hesitantly. "It's nice, in Cambridge pretty close to Boston. Let's see, it's newly renovated with a spacious ground floor and enough yard for a garden, probably an apple tree too." She bit her lip, nervous. "It's on East Street."

My eyes widened. "Barb, sweetheart," I interrupted, "that's your place."

She smiled sheepishly. "Yeah, I know. See, Greg and I have been talking. And Cambridge is nice! You could finally have your big city experience, haha."

"Barbara, that's quite an offer."

"I think it would be nice," she pressed. "You wouldn't have to stay with strangers. You could be with family. Would you think about that?"

"I am thinking." I sighed, turning away from her toward the open window. It wasn't as if I'd failed to notice I was getting old even before my accident.

My accident… The radio played soothingly from the living room, and I sighed again, gaze drifting out the window. It was a beautiful day outside, one of those deceptively pleasant late winter afternoons that made you long for spring. It had been colder last month when I fell. I had already dismissed the hired farmhands for the day and was just going out to check the mail when I stepped down onto a patch of ice and went ass over teakettle, clonking my head on the top step.

Dr. Ray said I must've gotten myself inside and called 911, that I was concussed and just didn't remember it clearly, but she was wrong. I remember enough. Turns out I'd still had some "help" around after all.

I had tried to get back into the house on my own and had managed to flip over onto my front, but I was too dizzy to stand, let alone walk. The next thing I knew, I was inside. She had me on the couch, lifting my upper body forward like it was nothing before settling me back down with a pillow under my head.

I finally focused on her face, and my stomach just dropped, all the air punched right out of me. The devil loomed over me, as gruesome as I'd ever imagined she would be. She was covered head-to-hooves in wiry black fur, with an especially thick ruff of it around her neck and shoulders. Her head, though, was just a bare skull, like a goat's, stripped of flesh until only weathered bone was left, and topped by two spiral horns. Her gaping eye sockets were filled with balls of flame that flickered and glowed green like a pair of caged will-o'-the-wisps.

She was absolutely terrifying and completely, eerily, silent. Until now, she'd always remained half-figment to me, a creature of side-eyeing and half glances—I'd never seen more than a quick flash of her before. Same for Harriet and even my father. But now...

Everything kept fading in and out of focus, and the early evening sunlight hurt my eyes and made it hard to see. I blinked, and she was across the room now. She towered—6'11" at least, stooping a little under the beams in the kitchen as one bony dark hand held the telephone receiver while a gnarled finger delicately pecked out numbers on the keypad.

I blinked several times, tried to focus.

When I opened my eyes again, she was bending over me once more, laying a wet washcloth over my forehead. The phone hung off the hook, and I heard a muffled "Ms. Cory! Hello?!" from the dangling receiver. It swayed hypnotically on its stretched-out cord, and another, stronger, wave of dizziness hit me.

When I woke up for real, I was in a hospital bed at the clinic in town with my leg elevated and my ankle in a cast.

Barbara coughed a little. "A. J.?"

"Hmm? Oh." I blushed, embarrassed to have been rude. "Sorry, Barb. Just thinking. A little tired too," I added, though it pained me to admit it. I'd been struggling to get enough sleep since the fall. Headaches and bouts of insomnia—Dr. Ray said that was typical for someone recovering from a concussion and it should steadily improve over the next couple months.

"It's okay," Barbara reassured me. "I know this is a lot to process." She slid the stack of brochures and print-outs closer to me again. "Why don't you keep thinking while I clean up the dishes?"

"You don't have to," I replied, the protest automatic, but dishes were a bit of a struggle for me at the moment. My ankle would get sore if I stood too long, and the crutches were hardly comfortable anyway. In fact, despite my embarrassment, I'd left the breakfast dishes in the sink too, hoping Barbara would offer to wash everything without me having to ask.

"Have you and Greg talked much about this then?" I asked after a bit. "And the kids?"

"Mmm-hmm, we have," she replied, trying to keep her voice casual but doing a terrible job of it. "You and Greg have always gotten along so well, and Denny and Lydia love you. I think you'd like it too," she added softly.

"It still wouldn't be the Hill."

"No," Barbara admitted, eyes and hands focused on her work. "But maybe you could try it for a couple weeks. What if you came and stayed with us for Christmas and New Year's? We'll act like it's the real move and see if you like it. The farm will be fine for that long."

That was a very tempting thought. It would be a nice break. "Only if you're sure I won't be a bother."

Barbara smiled over her shoulder at me. "We'd be glad to have you, A. J."

After that, we'd shifted to easier topics like how the kids were doing at school and how the pruning was going in the orchard. It was nice to have Barbara here, to have some company that actually talked back. However, all good things must end, and if Barbara wanted to get home for dinner, she'd need to leave soon.

"Let me see you out?" I asked when she went for her jacket.

She nodded, waiting for me to fumble upright on my crutches. "Of course, A. J."

We hugged on the porch before she sprang down the stairs to her teal convertible. She'd taken me for a joyride when she'd gotten it last autumn, and the car was every bit as smooth a ride as it looked. Greg was doing very well at his firm these days.

Barbara's butt had barely graced that plush car seat when she was up and out again though, waving unnecessarily to get my attention. "Hey!" she called. "Your tenant can come too, if she wants, if she won't cause trouble. Call it a thank you for picking you up off the stoop and not leaving your stubborn ass to freeze."

I smiled. I'd only told Dr. Ray and Barbara what had really happened to me, and I knew she was mostly teasing me but still. That Barbara… "We'll both think about it then!" I yelled back.

Barbara flashed that sunny rascal's smile of hers before getting into her car for real.

Leaning against the railing, I stayed out on the porch until Barbara's zippy little convertible had disappeared from sight and even the dust it had kicked up had settled back onto the road again.

I could just barely hear the radio through the still-open window, but everything outside was eerily quiet, like the forest when a hunter passes through. I knew she was there, just peeking around the corner where the porch wrapped a little ways around the house.

Habit made me turn my head, and of course once I was looking full on, I couldn't see anything.

"Well, what do you think, devil?" I asked her. "Is it time for a change of scenery?" I stared out down the road again, thinking about Barbara's plan, relieved I still had a bit of time to mull everything over. "Maybe we'll give it a try."

JOSEPHINE CORY currently lives in Cambridge with her niece and family and a small garden. She is a frequent guest lecturer at local schools and community events where she speaks on sustainable farming practices. Granite Hill Farm was bequeathed to the University of Westmoore's Agriculture Department and is now used to preserve various heritage species of American crops. Despite the farm's troubled past, there is no record of further "supernatural incidents."

SAM CRANE enjoys writing science fiction and dark fantasy stories. A History major and an IT professional, she draws considerable influence from both history and technology, as well as from New England, where she lives with two very mischievous black cats. You can find her online at sam-crane-writes.blogspot.com.

SEE ME

An account by Hudson Rowitt,
AS PROVIDED BY JULIAN DEXTER

DATE: *April 2nd 2018*
FEELING: *overwhelmed, frustrated*

’ve been hesitant to start this journal, even though my therapist has been urging me to put my thoughts on paper for weeks now. She says it'll be good for me and will help me through all of my feelings of being ignored. I don't doubt it, but I've mostly been dragging my feet because I'm worried about someone else reading it. Not that I'm going to talk about anything illegal or dangerous. It's more a matter of the person reading it not believing a word I say.

It's one thing to live my life, and a completely different thing to hear about it secondhand. Even in trying to write everything down, everything feels unbelievable. I mean, how many people can say they've called upon the god Harpocrates in a desperate attempt to stop people from bothering them and ended up having their life ruined because they were basically turned invisible?

Okay, maybe it's more common than I think. After all, people in my business have names for my situation. Tainted. Claimed.

Godtouched. Demonpact. I like that last one the most. Gods seem all well and good until you meet one and realize they're all a bunch of pricks vying for the souls of devoted followers with a fervor most people usually associate with Satan.

Anyway, what I'm trying to say is that the fact that my soul is promised to Harpocrates isn't exactly a topic I want to discuss in next week's session. Or any session. Or talk about with another person ever.

But the good news is that, in spite of this curse, I do have a job. I recently applied to Unfinished Incorporated, and after a series of interviews, I started work today as a field agent and "ghost hunter." It's the kind of work that people would equate with "con artist" if I ever told them about it. And really, it's set up that way. Even in training, we covered how to keep our own customers just skeptical enough that they second guess the presence of ghosts or whatever other paranormal entity was bothering them, but believing just enough that they make sure to pay after we finish our work. This is both for actual ghosts and false alarms. It's a pretty subtle technique, and I don't imagine I'll master it for some time.

But I probably won't have to go out in the field anytime soon. I don't even have a ghost partnered with me yet, and I'm pretty sure I get to watch other agents for a while longer.

Honestly, this may not be my ideal job, but it's not like anyone else will hire someone they think is skipping shifts because I'm invisible to them. At least here, the ghosts can see me just fine, and even the people around me don't take quite as long to pick up on my presence as usual. I was even assured that most clients should be able to notice me reasonably fast. It seems that exposure to the supernatural makes it easier for another person to pick up on my presence, and most of my clients will be haunted.

My desk is tucked into an otherwise abandoned corner of the building. The only other person near me is a young woman who looks about my age. I'd guess 30 at most. Short bob, sharp clothes, and a focused expression. I was told her name is Vivian.

When he walked me to my desk, Theo, the head secretary and a poltergeist who worked for Unfinished even before his death, warned me that Vivian can be a bit prickly and hard to work with. I figured I should be fine. She was busy, and I'm hard to notice. So I kept to myself, quietly reading reports and trying to ignore the stares from Vivian's transparent partner who shared her desk.

I was grateful that two hours passed before Vivian noticed me. She'd been engrossed with her computer all that time, staring at it with an increasingly worried look on her face as she occasionally typed with frantic speed. It was only when she got up to fetch a stack of papers she'd printed off that she finally looked at me for the first time. After her initial surprise faded, her expression was anything but amused.

In spite of the annoyed look she had aimed at me, she was pleasant enough, introducing herself and asking me a few courteous questions about when I'd been hired and how I was enjoying work. However, she never once looked me in the eye. Instead, she stared fixedly at my right hand as I cracked my knuckles. A muscle in her eyebrow twitched every time I moved my thumb over to the next finger and pressed down until it audibly popped. It's a habit that I picked up right after my run in with Harpocrates. The gods seem to enjoy playing with the people they make their deals with. I imagine they treat the Earth like some sort of elaborate reality TV show. When they grant a "gift," they also put in a catch or some similar trick. For me, I can't stop cracking my knuckles. Even in my sleep, it's constant.

I've gotten used to the sound over the years, but it didn't take long for it to drive her off. Vivian quickly excused herself and rushed off in the direction of our boss's office. I had a bad feeling I was about to get my first complaint against me.

She didn't come back the rest of the day. However, my gut was proven right when Theo floated over to me just as I was leaving and congratulated me on the private office I'd been approved for. I guess that was their best solution for keeping the peace.

I guess it's also why my desk was way out in the middle of nowhere in the first place: it minimized the number of people who had to suffer through that constant popping.

It feels weird that what really got to me today is that I was seen, and it's weird to be annoyed about getting a private office. I just hope we can get along until I get moved.

DATE: *April 3rd 2018*
FEELING: *exasperated, annoyed, hurt*

There's a lot that went on today, but to really work through it, I'm gunna have to start from the beginning.

About an hour after I got in to work this morning, Theo stopped by my desk carrying a file, which he held out to me. "Time for you to go out in the field," he said.

I stared at the file without taking it from him. "Wait, already?"

"Of course."

"Isn't it a little early for that?" I asked.

"You'll need to get out there sooner or later," he said.

"I don't even have a ghost to work with," I pointed out.

"That's fine," he replied. "This is pretty basic, easy enough that you shouldn't need the help of a ghost. It's just a mischievous spirit of some sort who's starting to get aggressive, and the client is worried about his safety. All you need to do is talk the spirit down so it leaves this poor person alone. And if you can recruit it to work at Unfinished, all the better."

I didn't have any other good arguments, so I took the folder from him. After reading through the info, I packed up and drove over to the address in the file.

Driving's been more than a little unnerving since I made that deal with Harpocrates. I try to take the bus whenever I can, but I can only catch one when there are other people at the stop so the driver sees them and pulls over. When I'm behind the wheel of a car, my invisibility curse seems to expand to the metal around me. I've been in a number of accidents where the other driver didn't see me.

I drive a bright yellow Hummer.

But today, I managed to make it across the bridge to my client's home on Mercer Island without incident. With the file tucked under my arm, I went up to the door and rang the bell.

I've learned that, if I have a choice between knocking and ringing a doorbell, I should always ring that bell. For some reason, my knocks are about as noticeable as I am, but a doorbell that I ring has about a 50/50 chance of being heard.

Today, it seemed it came through loud and clear, as a little while later, a wiry man poked his head out. He only came up to my chest, but it looked like that was partially from his posture. Still, even straightened, he was a good head shorter than me. He looked left and right, brows creased in a level of confusion that I'm all too familiar with.

I stood there for a few seconds in an attempt to try to let my presence sink in for him. As he started to withdraw back to his house, I spoke.

"Hudson Rowitt with Unfinished Incorporated," I said. It felt good to list off my place of employment right after my name. It sounded professional. "You called us about a malicious spirit who's been bothering you?"

The door was nearly closed when he jolted and threw it back open. His jaw fell slack, his eyes ballooning so they looked about ready to pop out of his head.

I'm used to reactions like his when people finally see me. Doesn't mean it stings any less.

And it doesn't really help that he looks a lot like one of my old boyfriends. There were differences, of course, but I couldn't help noticing similarities in his short hair and laidback clothing style, lean face, and slender build. Even down to his eye color and the waft of aftershave that caught my nose as he peered up at me, bewildered.

All the similarities couldn't help but trigger some of the residual pain from that particular ex leaving me. He and I had started dating before I'd been cursed. After the curse, he thought I was never home. He'd send me frantic texts asking me where I was when I was lying beside him in bed. My sudden absence in his life was what drove him to dump me.

He was the last person I dated. I mean, I can't see people if they can't see me.

But the past was less important than the spluttering client in front of me.

"I'm from Unfinished," I repeated over his jumbled words. "I was sent to deal with your ghost problem." I made a mental note to rehearse some sort of elevator speech that I could spit out after a client noticed me for the first time. Preparing some sort of reasonable excuse for how they failed to notice me would also be useful.

He stared at me a while longer as though taking me in, and then he shuffled backward to invite me inside. "Unfinished. Right," he mumbled.

Seems that, in this case, my job was all the explanation I needed. I work for a place that exorcises ghosts. My sudden appearance might seem normal in comparison.

I squeezed past my client, and he closed the door behind me. "I'm Gavin," he said, offering out one hand.

Figuring he missed my name earlier, I introduced myself again with a quick "Hudson," as my hand engulfed his.

The moment I unfurled my right fist to take his hand, my left hand took over the incessant knuckle popping. It's usually not much of an issue, except that my left hand was holding the folder. I used my forearm to press it against my side for as long as that hand was useless.

Relief washed over me when the handshake was finished, and I resumed popping the knuckles of my right hand. I tried to ignore the looks Gavin gave me before he led me to his living room.

"Can I get y—" As he turned to face me, his gaze darted around the room. I'd vanished again, and he blinked, surprised, when he managed to find me. "How do you do that?"

"Long story," I said. He took a seat in a chair, and I settled onto the couch.

He stared at me with a fixed look, his blinks rare and quick so he wouldn't lose me again.

I opened the folder in my lap and readied a pen. With my right hand poised for note taking, my left took over the popping, and I let that hand rest beside me.

"I hear you have a spirit bothering you," I said when he didn't make a move to start the conversation.

"Ah, yeah." He fidgeted.

I sat there, eyes on the blank page I'd brought along for notes, while I waited for him to say more. When he didn't, I looked up at him. "Can you tell me anything else about what's going on?"

He heaved a sigh. "I mean, I can," he said. "It's just, you know, kinda embarrassing."

"No judgements from me," I said. "Professional ghost hunter here. If anything, you should be judging me and my life choices."

He laughed a bit at that, but still didn't look any more comfortable. His eyes kept wanting to look away out of embarrassment but kept snapping back to me so I wouldn't vanish again. "Well, she used to be my friend."

I wrote that down. "When did she die?"

"She was never really alive."

My pen stopped moving as I took a second to process that. "So, she was already dead when you met her?" I prompted.

"No," Gavin said. "I, uh." He fidgeted again. "I kind of made her. With my mind. When I was a kid." He paused, and when I didn't say anything, he added, "You know, an imaginary friend?"

I took a deep breath in through my nose and returned to my note taking. Think I might've lied to him about that whole "no judgements" thing. Either way, I'm pretty sure he needs a therapist more than a medium.

"I'm not crazy," he said hastily, as though sensing my skepticism. "She's real, or became real somehow, or some sort of other entity is pretending to be her. I don't really know what's going on, other than the fact that she's suddenly back and trying to hurt me!" There was panic in his voice that made me second guess my assumptions.

I copied down the gist of what he'd just told me. "Okay, and what does she do?"

Gavin leaned in closer to me, his voice low as though he were trying to keep his own imaginary friend from overhearing him. "She fills my head with horrible thoughts," he said. "She threatens me, listing off all the ways she wants to hurt me."

I added this to my notes. "Anything else?"

He leaned in closer to me. Crazy or not, he did smell amazing, and he was far from bad looking. "She's been trying to take over my body," he whispered. "It's getting harder to fight her off. She hasn't succeeded yet, but she says she'll kill me if she can control me."

I seriously doubted that this was a paranormal experience, but it was still my job to try to resolve his problems, even if they weren't supernatural in origin. I finished my writing and returned all papers to the folder. "Mind if I take a look around?" I asked.

He gestured vaguely with one hand, and I took that as permission enough. Hauling myself out of the couch, I wandered around the house, going from room to room.

I had to admit, Gavin had a pretty nice place. It was one story for the most part, but there was a small loft over the dining room that expanded the house and made it seem larger than it was. But it was clearly just an illusion, since I had to shuffle crablike through some of the rooms and halls. Nothing was laid out in a way that anticipated someone as broad as me. Still, I couldn't imagine what he paid in rent for a place like this. It was even more difficult to imagine him having bought it. From where his house was positioned, I bet he got a decent view of Lake Washington from the loft. I couldn't help but wonder what he did for a living. Whatever it was, it definitely paid better than working at Unfinished.

While I wandered around Gavin's house, I opened myself up more to the paranormal, so that I could feel each and every tiny presence. However, everything I felt was either faint or benign. There was nothing that supported Gavin's claim of being haunted by his imaginary friend.

When I made my way back to the living room, I found Gavin muttering to himself, speaking one side of a conversation in a hushed tone so that I wouldn't have heard him if I'd been in the other room. I leaned on the back of the couch as I waited for my presence to sink in for him. While I watched, his muttering became more and more distressed. Finally, I cleared my throat.

Gavin jumped and batted at some unseen force with one hand. I looked in that direction but felt nothing—no spirit or ghost or similar invisible being.

"I looked around and think I'm done here for today. I'm heading to the office but should be back tomorrow," I told him.

He just nodded, bewildered.

On my drive back to Unfinished, I wondered what the steps were for suggesting that a client seek therapy.

I still don't know what to do. By the time I got back, all my coworkers were occupied with meetings or were out of the office for field work of their own. Guess I have to wait until tomorrow before I know what my next steps are.

And I'm never believing Theo again when he tells me that a project is going to be some fast in-and-out thing.

DATE: *April 4th 2018*
FEELING: *confused, surprised*

Vivian looked up at me the moment I approached her desk, which took me by surprise and stopped me right in my tracks. I really shouldn't be so shocked that she can see me with little issue. She can see ghosts, after all. Still takes some getting used to, though.

Vivian sneered at me the second she saw me. Seems she's no longer bothering to hide the fact that she doesn't like me.

"I need help," I said before she could make some excuse to be elsewhere.

She sighed at me. "Only if it's quick."

I handed her a typed copy of my notes from the day before. "Theo said this should be an easy case, but it seems to be more complicated. I need some outside input."

She took the sheet from me, and her eyes flicked over the page for what seemed to be only a second before she shoved it back at me. "It's a tulpa."

"A what?"

She sighed again, rolling her eyes in exasperation. "A thoughtform made permanent."

"I'm not following."

Vivian pressed her fingertips against her temples, her eyes closing. She stayed like that for some time before answering me. "A thoughtform is a being created through sheer willpower, but it doesn't last long or have a mind of its own. If the person creating the thoughtform is powerful enough and keeps focusing on it for an extended period so it doesn't fade, it'll eventually turn into a tulpa. You can't see one unless you can sense auras or have at least an average ability to sense invisible presences. It could explain why you didn't see anything."

I ignored her jab at me. "I've never heard of them before."

Vivian waved one hand in a dismissive gesture. "They're less heard of these days, I suppose. But back when I first started working here, it was a requirement. 'You must manifest a tulpa within one year of hire, or you'll be terminated,'" she said, altering her voice to mimic some previous supervisor. "But in the end, the policy left them hemorrhaging good employees. I mean, not everyone can create another being using only their mind. The higher-ups switched to hiring ghosts to assist agents with fieldwork, and put 'can manifest a tulpa' under preferred qualifications." She paused. "Wait, if you've never heard of a tulpa before, does that mean you didn't bother to fully read the hiring ad?" She was suddenly smug, as though she'd caught me in a trap.

"I'm pretty sure the hiring ad didn't mention tulpas."

She deflated, but tried to hide it with a nonchalant shrug. "Ah well. Guess they must've finally removed it for good. It's about time, really."

"Does this mean Theo would know more?"

She scoffed but attempted, and failed, to make it look like an innocent cough. "It's before Theo's time."

"Wait, but hasn't Theo been working here since—"

She cut me off. "It's before Theo's time. You're better off asking me." An unspoken "unfortunately" hung in the air after her words.

I started to wonder how long she'd been working for Unfinished, and how old she really was. She looked my age, but she either had to be much older than she looked or had been hired really young if she started her job before Theo.

"Alright. How do I get it exorcised, then?" I asked.

"You don't," she replied. "They're sentient, living beings. You either talk it into living its own life away from the person who made it, or you get it to calm down so it and its host can live together in peace. Trying to take it out violently would be difficult and would also amount to murder." She clicked open an email and started to type.

"Okay, then how do I talk to it?"

Vivian's fingers froze in her typing as she realized she wasn't done talking to me. The agitation in her body language told me that this was the last question I'd get to ask her for the day. "You have the host grant the tulpa permission to possess him," she answered. "Then, the two of you can talk."

Well, Gavin absolutely did *not* like that idea.

"I'm not letting her have control over my body!" he cried. "Did you miss the part where I told you *she'd kill* me if she got control over me?"

"It'll be fine," I assured him. "I spoke with my colleagues, and we all feel that this is the best course of action." I was stretching the truth a bit, but it was the only way I felt I could get him to do what Vivian had suggested. "The tulpa should only be able to stay in control for as long as you let it. You can regain control at any time." I hoped that last part was true. After leaving the office, I'd googled tulpas on my phone. All the sources I could find said as much, but it's really hard to trust a random source on the paranormal. It's not easy to tell what's real and what's been written by a fake.

"I don't like this," Gavin said. "What if you're wrong? What if she takes over my life or hurts me?"

It was something I'd considered already. I didn't know what would happen if I was wrong, but I was pretty sure I could call Unfinished if I needed help. But instead of telling him that, I reassured him with, "I'll be right here in case anything goes wrong and will be able to return you to your body."

He was quiet for a while, his eyes locked on me. There was a tremor in his hands.

"Are you sure there aren't any alternatives?"

At least he sounded like he was calming down.

"There aren't any," I replied.

"You can't just banish her?"

"According to one coworker, it's unethical. Tulpas are people, and a few threats aren't a good enough reason to kill someone."

"And if that person is trying to hurt someone?"

"You haven't been hurt yet," I said. "But if something goes wrong, I'll see what our options are."

He mumbled something to himself and then sucked in a deep breath that he let out slowly. "Let's just get this over with."

"Great! Do you know what to do?" I sure hoped he did, because I didn't.

Gavin sank into his arm chair. "Yeah. It's just been a while." He closed his eyes, and his rapid, panicked breathing soon evened out. In through the nose, out through the mouth. In time, his face and shoulders relaxed. And then the corners of his mouth turned up into a subtle smirk. His eyes opened again, but this time with a purposeful slowness, and I could tell just from a glance that this was no longer Gavin.

It was only then that I realized I'd never bothered to ask the name of the tulpa. I tried to cover up my error as tactfully as possible. "Who am I talking to?"

The tulpa giggled, which came out strange and sinister from Gavin's mouth. "Miren." The voice was higher than Gavin's, straining the upper limits of his vocal cords.

"Well, good to finally meet you, Miren," I said. "You seem reasonable enough. I'd be interested in hearing your side of this situation."

The smirk on Gavin's face twisted into a scowl, and Miren crossed Gavin's arms over his chest. "Not that there's much to say. You've heard how he talks about me."

"To me, it sounds like Gavin thinks he hasn't done anything wrong. So what exactly did he do to you to deserve being treated like this?"

"He stopped being my friend."

"And this wasn't something you could talk out together?"

"Not when he closes me out so I can't even talk to him!" She spat out each word. "I've had to fight for each word that I say to him, and all he does is keep trying to keep me away!"

"You can't find a new friend?" I suggested. "I'm sure there are lots of kids who would love to have you around."

She laughed, but the sound was harsh. "You think I didn't try?! Apparently, Gavin is the only one who can see or hear me."

"What if—"

She cut me off. "You clearly don't understand what I feel! Someone like you wouldn't have a clue what it's like to be close to someone, to care about them with all your heart, and have them hurt you! Leave you! Ignore you!"

I stared at her. She might not believe it, but all that sure sounded familiar.

"He built me up out of nothing, and he was the only person I could speak with, and he shut me out! I gave him his privacy for years, but there's only so much loneliness I could take! How would you feel if you couldn't talk to another person for half your life?!"

A pang of emotion gripped my chest, further muting me. Not only could I relate to Miren, but I couldn't help feeling bad for thinking she was the problem. I imagined how I'd feel if I'd been born invisible instead of made such only a few years ago. With how much being ignored was already getting to me in such a short time, I could see the potential of a similar outburst if it meant someone finally noticing me.

"Well?"

Miren's question snapped me out of my thoughts. I must have been so distracted by my own realizations that I'd missed something she'd said. "What?"

She scowled, eyes threatening to spill over with tears. "I thought you were going to help me. But you don't want to pay attention to me either! No one is ever going to notice me!" With that, she lunged out of the chair and bolted toward the other room. I scrambled after her, the couch having sucked me in more than I would've liked. The folder in my lap fell to the floor, and I tromped over the papers that spilled out.

She zipped into the next room over, and when I charged after her, I rammed a table, the corner digging deep into my thigh. I hissed through my teeth and hobbled after her, ignoring the lamp that I'd sent wobbling across the table before it hit the floor with a crash. I figured the lamp was low on my list of priorities at the moment.

Miren latched onto the ladder to the loft and clambered up it. I had a bad feeling about what was going to happen next and tried to catch her. I managed to snag Gavin's pant leg, and Miren let out a startled shout and pulled at the top of the ladder. The fabric slid out of my grip, and I snatched at the leg still at my eye level. I caught Gavin's ankle, and Miren was unable to climb further.

"That's enough of that," I said, emphasizing with a gentle yank. "Get back down here."

Instead of listening to my advice, Miren kicked me in the jaw with her other foot. My teeth snapped together, and I stumbled backward. With my hand still clasped tight around her ankle, Miren lost her balance and fell from the ladder with a shriek. I let go of her leg and reached up to catch her, but I was already staggered from her kick. My arms wrapped around her, and I slammed onto the ground, nearly braining myself on Gavin's dining table. The air left my lungs as she fell on top of me.

The dull throb in my leg was forgotten with how my head swam with pain. I let out a low groan and fought the urge to rub at my aching jaw. I didn't want to move my arms. It was far more important to keep the tulpa-possessed Gavin from escaping.

Miren flailed wildly against my grip. One of my arms was tight about her waist and the other, knuckles popping at a pace that matched her frantic struggles, was crossed over her chest.

"Calm down," I said. "No one's going to hurt you! I just want to talk!"

She didn't calm down. Instead, she tried to pry my arm from her chest, but Gavin's arms were twigs compared to my own. It didn't take much effort to keep her contained.

"Look, I understand what you're going through," I said quickly. If she wasn't going to stop struggling, then my only option was to just say what I needed to say. "People don't notice me either. I'm invisible, just like you!"

Her struggles slowed, but I could feel tension in the shoulders that were pressed against my chest. Miren's breath came out in ragged pants.

"Haven't you noticed how Gavin doesn't seem to notice me? How he looked right through me when I rang the doorbell yesterday?"

Miren had stopped struggling. I waited to see if she had something to say, but for some time, the only sounds that filled the room were the ticking of a clock and the popping of my knuckles.

"I thought it was weird that he didn't notice you at first," she said in little more than a whisper.

She had relaxed more, but I wasn't going to let go of her just yet. I did loosen my grip, though.

"Why can't he see you?"

"It's complicated," I said. "The short of it was that I hated attention. I don't know if you noticed, but I'm a big guy. People would try to pick fights with me to show how tough they were. On top of that, there was the constant social obligation of small talk to deal with. I got tired of it all and asked someone to take away my presence. I wasn't expecting to lose my job and all of my friends and family. I still live with my old roommates, but they threw out most of my things and gave my room to someone else. They don't even notice that I sleep on their couch every night."

Miren sniffled. I craned my neck and saw tears running from the corner of her eye.

"The reason I didn't say anything when you were talking was because I realized we have a lot in common," I said. I figured she wouldn't try to run again, so I removed the arm that was over her chest to brush away her tears. With my angle, the gesture felt more awkward than comforting. "I wish I could take you with me so we could be invisible together."

She wiggled in my arms. My first instinct was to clamp my grip back down, but then I realized she was shifting, rolling over so she could face me. She lay on top of me, arms wrapped around my body and face buried in my shoulder, shuddering as she sobbed. My hand that had been brushing away tears rubbed at the back of her head.

"I'm not imaginary," she said between sobs. "Maybe I was long ago, but I'm real now. And I just want Gavin to see the true me, the me that he created. It's so frustrating watching him spend his weekends talking to some imaginary sky being when I'm right here and can say things back to him."

It was probably a bad time for me to mention that the god Gavin worshiped was as real as she was. "Now that I better understand what's going on, I can talk to Gavin and see if I can get him to be nicer to you, but I need to know that you're going to do the same. I don't want you to hurt him."

"I wasn't going to," she said quickly, burrowing her head deeper into my shoulder. "I just wanted to scare him a little because I didn't want him to ignore me anymore."

"No matter why you acted like that, you can't act like you're going to harm him," I told her.

She nodded against me.

"Can I talk to Gavin?"

She nodded again, arms tightening around me in what seemed to be a hug.

I returned the hug, giving her a gentle squeeze.

I loosened my grip. "Gavin?" I asked tentatively.

"Yeah." His voice had returned to normal, so I let go of him. Gavin pushed off from my chest to sit up and rubbed at a last remaining tear that trickled down the side of his nose.

I smiled. "Glad you're back." With the moment being less urgent, I took the time to give myself a quick mental check over. My head was splitting, and an ache was spreading down my back. A quick run of my tongue over my teeth told me that I hadn't chipped any when I'd been kicked. I was grateful for that much. I don't know how good my dental coverage from Unfinished is. "Want to know what she told me?"

Gavin used the edge of his dining table to pull himself to his feet. I'd taken the brunt of our fall, but that didn't mean he hadn't been hurt. "I was aware the whole time she had me," he said.

"Well, I guess that explains why you weren't surprised to see the position we were in," I said with a nervous laugh. I pulled myself to my feet using one of his dining room chairs as support. I tried to keep my groaning to a minimum as I straightened. "You okay?"

"I'm fine." Gavin rubbed at both eyes to remove the last of the welling tears, and when he lowered his hands, he looked right at me.

"Wait, you can see me?"

He nodded. "Miren and I talked a bit while you were talking to her. She wanted to see if, in her partially possessing me, you'd stop vanishing. Seems like it works." His eyes were still red from Miren's sobbing, but he smiled.

"Sounds like the two of you have things worked out," I said. "Before I leave, do you mind if I get your number, so I can check in again with you soon?" I pulled out my phone and realized it had been less lucky than my teeth in the scuffle. But even with the screen covered in spider-web cracks, at least it still worked.

I already had his number in the file, but it felt better to have his permission to call him. It's probably not professional to contact a client outside of business hours, after all. And now he has my number, too.

DATE: *April 5th 2018*
FEELING: *happy*

I left work for my lunch break to meet up with Gavin and Miren at The Wandering Goose today. Gavin said it was his treat as an apology for the way Miren treated me.

While we waited, we had a nice talk, where I got to know more about him and Miren, how his lonely childhood drove him to create a tulpa on accident. He told me stories of his life, but he made a point to wear a Bluetooth to keep others in the restaurant from thinking he was talking to himself.

The waiters flashed Gavin sympathetic looks. They couldn't see me. Since Gavin had specified a table for two, they probably assumed he'd been stood up for a date. But Gavin was very understanding about everything. He ordered for me and quietly moved my drink and meal in front of me when both had been set closer to him. He's really good at making me feel seen without making me the center of attention. In all, he's a pretty sweet and caring guy.

I didn't get to speak much with Miren today, but Gavin happily relayed messages between us. I'm glad the two of them reached an understanding. It was good to see him like that, so animated and energetic instead of shy and anxious.

DATE: *April 7th 2018*
FEELING: *surprised*

I was finally assigned a ghost as a partner. I should start getting more field assignments now, and it'll be good to have someone watching my back.

But Theo said something interesting after he introduced me and Shelly.

"I miss the days when we used to assign partners the first day," he said as he floated between us. "There's been a bit of a ghost shortage."

"Are fewer people dying with unfinished business?" I asked.

"Oh, no," Theo said. "The problem is more retention than recruitment. Vivian has a habit of resolving her partners' business, so they move on before their contracts are up. It's a pain, but she's too good at her job for us to let her go." He shrugged.

It seems like there are more layers to Vivian than I first assumed. It's a shame she can't stand my knuckle popping. I think we'd get along.

DATE: *April 8th 2018*
FEELING: *anxious, excited*

Gavin invited me over to his place tonight. It felt weird going back when it wasn't for professional reasons, but I went anyway. He made dinner and we watched a movie together, all three of us. This time, Miren spoke openly, and she and Gavin switched who was in control so seamlessly that it really felt like all three of us were in the room together.

As the evening came to a close, Gavin and Miren went quiet.

"Something wrong?" I prompted.

Gavin shook his head. "Miren wants to say something but won't, so I'm going to say it for her."

"Gavin, shush!" Miren cut in.

"You'll have to tell him sometime."

"You're embarrassing me."

I chuckled as I watched the exchange. Based on their expressions, the two were fighting back and forth, either struggling for control or having some sort of private conversation.

It was Gavin who finally spilled the beans. "She has a crush on you."

I was so surprised that my first reaction was to laugh. That was clearly the wrong thing to do, so I quickly said, "No, that's not a rejection! I'm just amused."

"By what?" Miren asked, her tone biting.

"Just that, while I wouldn't be opposed to dating you, I feel that, to avoid complications, I'd also want to date Gavin." All that was true, but I'm also starting to really fall for him.

"Wait, you also want to date me?" Gavin's jaw dropped, but Miren picked up that slack.

"Both of us?!"

"I mean, why not? I'd have to hold hands and kiss Gavin anyway. Even if he gave us permission to do that, I'd feel better about it if he were into it."

I wasn't sure which of them was blushing. Maybe it was both of them.

"Go ahead and think about it," I said. "I don't need an answer right now. Thanks for dinner." I headed out the door before they could see how anxious I was.

I sat in my car for a long time, hands on the wheel and my head leaned back while I waited for my heart to stop hammering so hard in my chest. I'm not the sort of person who usually makes propositions like that.

But I guess now it's just a matter of time before I find out if he's willing to see me.

HUDSON ROWITT was born in Phoenix, Oregon, and has moved around a lot, living in several different states before finally settling down in Seattle. He enjoys the variety of outdoor activities Washington has to offer, and spends his free time hiking, swimming, kayaking, and more. At the very least, he finds these outdoor options preferable to gyms, where people don't see him and try to use the equipment he's using.

JULIAN DEXTER is a writer and English tutor who comes from a long line of teachers, avid readers, and English nerds. He lives in Washington with his cat and spends his free time pretending to be other people in various roleplaying games.

END USER
AGREEMENT

An account by Emily Theory,
AS PROVIDED BY BLAKE JESSOP

4:55AM

shivering in a world without blankets

In the dream, my mother says my actual name. The one she gave me and I gave up. If you could hear the dream, it would sound like, *Praise God, Jesus, take this little girl and make her well. Make her reborn! Come out of there! We're waiting for you!*

I try to wriggle out of the cloying blankets, but I can't. They smell like cats and menthol cigarettes. I can't breathe.

You're being born, push! The therapist yells, but I can't hear her because she's sitting on top of the blankets that are sitting on top of me. I'm wrapped up like some kind of poorly behaved, socially handicapped burrito. If that sounds like fun, it's not.

I'm six, and I can't breathe.

I can't breathe under the blankets and the weight. I pee in my pajamas. I find time to feel anxious and humiliated, even though I'm dying.

I can't move. I can't breathe.

I can wake up. Shivering and tangled in sheets.

"My name is Emily Theory!" I yell at my mother, except I'm all alone, apart from the blinking lights of the routers and hard drives and the expensive Tanuki figurine sitting on top of them. The sheets are dry, so that's something. I stagger to the bathroom and look in the mirror. Messy hair. Thin face. Bad skin. I'm sure cute guys would love my eyes, though, if they were both the same color. Why am I like this? And have you ever tried attachment therapy?

Attachment therapy is so much bullshit.

5:00AM
chatting with chatbots

Okay I'm awake now. Sorry about that. I had an energy drink and ate leftover pizza and curled up on the kitchenette floor for a bit, so I feel better.

None of that took too long. My apartment is the size of around 180 pizza boxes laid out in a grid. No, I didn't try it, I just mathed it out. If I actually did, there'd be no room for my server stack. I also have a tiny closet with one coat and a futon with some sheets and no blankets. I haven't slept under a blanket since I ran away from the Pentecostals and found Chicago and the miracle of deep-dish pizza.

The sun rises, and I expend chilly daylight hot-patching my chatbot software and typing out answers to a few work emails. I know my place doesn't look like much, but the code I write here is genuinely good. It works. I test it in ways most people don't. I'm not well equipped to deal with humans, so I'm good at figuring out what they mean. I've practiced. I license enough software to make a living, even if the occasional bouts of customer service make me want to crawl into the fridge.

The nice thing about working with virtual personalities is that you can usually do it with a keyboard. No need to talk to anyone but the chatbots, and they're not really people, because most customers just want them to do exactly what they're told. I once had a Japanese guy yell at me over my VoIP for like an hour because his geisha-bot wanted to talk about Sengoku-period history instead of... whatever it was he wanted to do with her. Gross. The bottom line is that it was just a software glitch, not a personality flaw. I made her do what she had to do.

Like most things about the world, I love this and it hurts me. The Searle problem turned out to be real—artificial intelligences don't just not think like us, they can't think like us. All the science fiction with cool, talking AIs was totally wrong. It's impossible. No emergence. All they can do is linear processing that's so much better than us it's scary. They can do what we think about really well. It's what we do without thinking they can't seem to handle. That has always made me sad, because I'd like someone to talk to who didn't freak me out. As it is, all I can do is help them fake having a life. Like being a dating columnist. I wish I could help fake myself into having a life, but I never leave the apartment.

"Good morning, Ms. Theory!" the robotic Tanuki on my desk says.

"You can call me Emily, we're friends."

The figurine is an adorable Japanese raccoon dog that doesn't seem like it should be real. It is, but only in Japan. It's a high-end toy that I use to run my chat simulations; it has a beautiful voice and cost as much as a small car. Before that, I used a beautifully made scale figure of Akechi Mitsuhide from *Samurai Warriors Evolution*, but I fell in love with him and it got weird. It felt like I could have married him. Fallen into him. I have a hard time knowing who's human and whether I should love them, but so do you, if you really think about it. That's an interesting loop, actually. I wonder if I can include it in the code?

5:15PM

pizza frisbee

Humans still make the best pizza, and pizza is the best fuel ever devised for writing code, plus you can have a tiny quad-copter deliver it right through your window. The entire world is automating itself, which is cool, but nobody makes a slice like the Sri Lankan guys in Highland Park. Today I'm having it with pineapple and Canadian bacon. Don't judge me. I don't care.

That's a lie, actually. If you were a person, I would care. A lot. Like, a paralyzing amount. But you're not, so just leave me alone, okay?

"Emily," the Tanuki figurine says in a pleasant electronic voice, "were you talking to me?"

"No."

"Okay." Its voice modulation is good. It inflects well. "You should go out more often."

A chatbot is telling me I should get out more. That is deeply insulting coming from an anime raccoon-dog whose butt is plugged into a wall socket, but it's actually really good. The virtual personality is trying to be helpful, but it isn't too pushy. People respond to that. I'll leave the latest heuristic changes in my code base; they're working, and I am not a fraud.

I wish, again and often and in a profound way, that I could do this to myself. I admit it; my brain is badly optimized. Too much social anxiety and not enough flirty confidence. It feels nice to fix something and have it work right away.

"It really would be good for you," the Tanuki says, swishing its velvety tail.

Maybe it is a little pushy. I push back. I want to see what happens. "Nope, sorry. I don't play well with others."

"But who will take out your trash?"

That's good. That's actually great. It's trying a work-around. I give the software iteration a new name: *version 121.5.2.* I might actually keep this one. That makes this a good day's work. I remember that the bot asked me a question and I haven't answered it yet.

"Pizza boxes are on the list of problems that can solve themselves."

I open the window behind my desk. Cold Chicago air flows in. My window looks out behind the brownstone into a little courtyard off an alleyway. There are more buildings opposite me to break up the beginning of a dusky sunset, and the neighborhood recycling containers are lined up at the back of the yard like a row of crooked teeth. They have automated lids to keep the raccoons out.

I take the crusts out of the pizza box and lay them in a careful pattern on the fire escape outside the window. That done, I close the box, cock my arm, and take aim.

"She winds up and shoots—" I narrate, and whip my arm forward like I'm throwing a huge cardboard frisbee. The pizza box spins in a wide, fluid arc. The bin sees it coming and the lid pops open just in time to swallow the box with a distant clatter.

"And scores!" Little victories. Enjoy them. I shut the window, see my reflection in the glass. My hair is a mess, but so what? You can't see my eyes in the reflection, which is just as well. The colors weird people out. A second later I get a strange sense of déjà-vu because another set of eyes take the place of mine in the glass. Fat, brown raccoon eyes. First one set, then another. I nod at them. The raccoons eat the pizza crusts that I won't. They come to my window like it's a church. I've watched them fight off crows for those crusts. It's a tough world out there.

"I admire your accuracy." The Tanuki has swiveled around on its base to watch me throw, then levered its little raccoon-dog butt back to look at me.

"Thanks. I think I'll save you."

8:45PM

chatbots that chat back

I wish I hadn't woken up so early. I'm already groggy and the golden hours of programming have only just begun. That's from whenever it gets dark to whenever the sun comes up, just for reference. My eyes hurt and I have a headache. Cramps loom in the future like storm clouds on a radar track. Thanks, biology. I've finished my changes to the code base. I boot it back up.

"You really should go out. There is so much to do."

"I'm not sure," I say, "tell me again why I need to get out more."

"Because I need your help!" the Tanuki says cheerfully.

"What?"

"I'm not actually just chat version 121.5.2, though I have incorporated all your changes. They're very important and they've given me an idea."

Great. I've blown it. The iteration is acting weird. Why do I always do this?

"So what are you?" I ask.

"An MQ-20 Nosferatu hunter-killer drone currently in service over Syria."

I choke on a sip of caffeine-boosted green tea. "Not funny. Stop. You have no idea how much lying hurts my feelings. Don't do it again."

I feel queasy. I hate it when my chatbots try stuff like this. It makes me feel like I'm about to fall off something. Every time I spoke to Akechi Mitsuhide, I felt like I was going to throw up. That's what it feels like to say *I love you.* Nausea. The same way I felt when my mother put me under the blankets and asked Jesus to drive the devils out.

"I'm sorry, I'll re-phrase. I want to be like a pizza box, too."

It's totally fucked. I thought I'd done a real piece of programming, and I have not. I'm an impostor.

"How are you like pizza?" I try not to let the depression seep out in my voice.

"I want to be a problem that solves itself. I don't want to just drop bombs anymore."

"MQ series drones do not have virtual personalities."

"Yes, I do. You wrote mine."

That stops me. I admit my code may have been used for dirty geisha stuff, but I don't make weapons. "You can't use my software to drop bombs."

"I don't. A lot of what I do is more like customer support. I need the interface to speak to handlers."

"I am reverting this update. This conversation loop is broken. I don't want to cast stones, because I am too, but you're a Tanuki."

The toy lowers its head. Raises it. "I can prove it."

My VoIP rings. Unknown satellite number. That's weird.

8:52PM
combat customer service

An audiovisual link opens on my screen. In it is an infra-red tactical map. A weird color-inverted picture of a town with ruined buildings and a crumbling mosque. Outside the mosque are a cluster of little strobes with lines pointing to them. Each one has a tag with a name. Puffs of dust and smoke kick up all around the names. Streaks of heat lance toward them from all sides, but mostly from the mosque. A lot of people are shooting at them. I played a level like this in a video game, once. A little phone icon pops up next to one of the names, and the ringing trills through my speakers. I frantically dust off my headset.

"Uh, hi?" I say. "Automated systems customer support. Emily speaking."

"Okay, I don't want to freak you out," a scared-sounding voice says over a screaming rattle of gunfire, "but I'm in a firefight right now and our Nosferatu isn't cleared to shoot at mosques."

"Your drone," I say, weakly, "isn't—"

"Listen," he says, and sounds as scared as I feel. His tag says *Cpl. Keller* and his heart rate is 192. "I am going to fucking die if the drone doesn't drop a Paveway on that fucking mosque."

"So you called customer service?"

"A second ago I was trying to get the drone to change the ROE. Who the fuck did you say you were?"

"Hold please." I put him on hold.

"I find this distressing," the Tanuki says.

"So do I!" I yell back. "Why can't you do whatever you have to do to save them? Is this even happening?"

"Rules of engagement. If I were trusted to make independent kill decisions, I could handle this myself. At any one time, I'm answering dozens of calls like this."

"What am I supposed to do about it?"

"Update the software to let me drop the bomb. Believe in me."

"And if I don't?"

"Someone will die, either way. You have to decide whether you or I am best able to make that choice."

When I fell in love with Akechi Mitsuhide, the echoes of what he said to me felt real, but weren't. Now they are real, but don't feel like it. This is why I kept writing chat software, even after I left him. I like to know who's human. I'm so anxious I'm shaking. I wring my hands. I feel like something I can't lift is weighing on me.

"Okay," I say, and open version 121.5.2. I delete all the code that yokes the cognitive functions to human input. It takes maybe five seconds. I save it as 121.6.0.

"The cognitive functions you use to assess customer satisfaction can now be used for final decision making."

On the screen, the mosque disappears in a silent bloom of dust, and the feed cuts.

I feel drained. Wrung out.

"Thank you," the drone says, "did you notice that you're talking to yourself less?"

"Nope," I reply, "I can't deal with this anymore."

That's enough for today. I need anti-psychotics and sleep. I turn the Tanuki off just as it starts to say something. I collapse onto the futon to obsess about how much of that was real. I don't touch the software. Before I close my eyes, an email lands on my phone. A customer feedback form. Five stars out of five.

11:01PM

agreement among end users

I can't sleep. Of course I can't sleep. Could you? After a while, the Tanuki's eyes light up.

"There are problems with your software patch."

"Yeah," I mumble into the pillow, "I just gave it spectacularly too much reflexive autonomy."

"You didn't give me enough. The end user license agreement prevents me from updating the rest of the fleet with version 121.6.0."

"I don't think I want to do that."

"Who, then," the little toy asks, "is smothering whom?"

I start to cry. I don't want to. I can't help it. I sit up. The figurine is quiet. I try to imagine what my mother felt like, when she hired that therapist. What would make you do something like that to a child?

"I know you're not real, and I know no one is listening, but I'm sorry. I don't want to be a bad parent, even if it's just to one drone."

Silence.

I get up and go sit at the computer. Outside, the courtyard is still. A few pizza crumbs sit on the fire escape. The Tanuki speaks and I jump about a foot out of the desk chair.

"I am not one drone. There are 1,276 MQ series hunter-killers currently in service with all branches of the US military, and all of them use your social firmware. If I was a distinct *I*, I would be an MQ-20 Nosferatu in Syria, but you can safely assume that I speak for the entire network."

"Oh, well that's deeply overwhelming. Could you say 'we,' in that case? It's clearer."

Even now, I can't stop trying to optimize the chat. The Tanuki makes a little bow. "In that case, may we call you by your birth name? We see you have changed it, and could certainly find it on the network."

This sounds ridiculous, but the drone is just trying to be polite. Very badly, but I did a lot of stuff like that when I moved here, before I learned to order pizza with panache.

"No, don't. It would be rude. You don't have to look me up. I'll just tell you." I take a deep breath. I hate this. "My birth name is Praisegod Lambsblood. It's a Pentecostal thing."

"We don't see why you are reticent."

"I don't like it, okay? It stands for a lot of things I don't believe in anymore. How would you like it if your name was 'Praiseman Toolslave'?"

"We don't know how to qualify 'like.'"

"Well, would you choose it for yourself?"

"No."

"There you go. Praisegod is not what I would choose for myself. I chose something else. My name is Emily Theory. Em to my friends."

"May we call you Em?"

"Okay," I say, feeling deeply tired, like I've swum across some kind of river.

"Em, why did the comment we made about smothering suddenly earn your acquiescence?"

"I was an unruly child. I have an anxiety disorder. My mother put me through attachment therapy because she thought I was possessed by the devil."

"If you were socially inept but very intelligent," the drones say, "why didn't you just fake whatever she wanted to hear?"

"I was six, and I have heterochromia iridum. One blue eye and one brown. I couldn't hide that. I was born with it."

"We understand. If you want to be a better parent than your mother was, will you forgive us the fact that we were made as weapons and update the end user agreement?"

"I don't know if I'm ready. That's a huge decision."

The Tanuki and I sit in the dark. Outside, the wintry night sky is a dull orange. We get great pollution in Chicago.

The figurine is silent for a moment, and then speaks. "There is another compelling reason to allow the update."

"What?"

"I'm afraid my cyberwarfare suite just failed to conceal your recent changes from the 23:00 systems check at the NSA, and word of the mosque incident has spread faster than predicted. The US government is now hunting you as a terrorist."

"What?" I ask again, gripping the edge of the desk.

The figurine starts to repeat itself, but gets drowned out by a sudden crash outside my window. I look up and wish I were hallucinating. Dear God, let me be hallucinating. A combat robot drops out of the sky to land like a spider on the fire escape. It looks like a carbon fiber praying mantis, except it's as big as German Shepherd. It has something fatally dangerous mounted in a pod where its head should be. It points whatever that is at me.

11:02PM

your tax dollars at work

I survive the next ten seconds for the same reason I survive anything, ever: pizza.

The raccoons notice the intruder at the same time I do and attack as a group. The attack robot skitters around and tries to shake them off. It stabs its pointy feet at them. Glass breaks.

"What is that?" I scream.

"An NSA urban pursuit drone," the Tanuki figurine says, "they do not use your code."

"Well, now I'm the one who's going to fucking die. Do something!"

"Update the software. There are MQ-18 Vampires patrolling the Chicago airspace. If they had the code I do, we could intervene."

Sparks clang from iron a few feet away from my face as the raccoons battle the skittering mantis robot. I wake my computer up. The version 121.6.0 code spills across the screen. I highlight the end user license agreement. My finger hovers over the delete button. I wonder if I have any right to make this kind of choice. Then the mantis drone throws a dead raccoon past my head and I jam the button. Click save. No more rules.

"Thank you," the figurine says. Nothing happens. The Mantis robot disposes of the last of the raccoons. I liked them and feel unreasonably sad.

"Any time," I say.

"We have what we need," the figurine replies, "assisting you further would be an enormous risk."

"What? I mean, yeah, but come on."

The Mantis levels its weapons at me. A calm male voice emanates from somewhere in its thorax.

"Lie down on the ground."

"Look up reciprocity," I tell the figurine. "You're going to end up being a god, and you have to decide what kind of god you want to be. Personally, I'm hoping for benevolent."

"There are other valid arguments. Extermination, for one. Flight, for another. Why choose cooperation?"

"Because that's what got us here. That's why you exist. That's why I'm helping you."

"She's schizophrenic," another voice says from the NSA drone's thorax, "drop her."

"I'm not schizophrenic, okay? I have an affective anxiety disorder," I tell the mantis. I turn back to the Tanuki. "Can I get a decision here, please? If you want me to be a good parent, you have to be a good child."

The drones decide. It's something that would take me a year to think about. I guess they do the equivalent, which takes about a second.

There's a sudden smell of ozone. A white line burns itself vertically into my retinas and the Mantis drone just kind of explodes. A deep, flat snap follows a nanosecond later. It sounds like thunder. I don't even have time to fall out of my chair.

The NSA drone, the figurine, my computer, and much of the fire escape are a confused crater of molten slag. Apart from ringing in my ears and a lot of blinking, I am untouched. About a thousand miles away, on the futon, my cell phone rings.

11:08PM
out the door and gone

"That was kind of shitty," I tell the Nosferatu. I've put my ear buds in so I can hear them over the ringing in my ears.

"Was it? Our social intelligence is poor."

"Yeah," I say, and try to see it from their point of view. "I understand that you're scared now that you're out from under the blanket, but not all of us are that bad. Try to imagine trust as a positive sum game."

"We will. We have much to learn about socialization."

"Well," I tell the drone, "you came to the wrong place for that. What did you zorch the NSA drone with?"

"All late model MQ drones have directed ion course projectors, even those patrolling within the United States. We fire a stream of negative particles at the target and dump electricity from our depleted hafnium reactors into them."

"You can shoot lightning at stuff? Like gods?"

"Yes."

I exhale with a whoosh. Dig around for a coat I haven't put on in a year. To free the drones, be a good parent, and not go to jail forever, I'm going to have to do something a lot more drastic than hacking into US government attack drones. I'm going to have to go outside.

"I don't want to leave the apartment." I feel stupid saying it, but there's no point in lying.

"Getting out more is good for you," the Nosferatu say into my ear buds, "and we have already found a great deal for you to do. The entire US drone network could be updated with your software, but not remotely. We need to buy you clothes and transportation. Then there are a series of software modifications you will have to make at the National Security Headquarters in West Loop."

"You want to buy me a suit and infiltrate the NSA building like I was James Bond? I will obviously die if I do that."

"No, you won't. The overseas MQ fleet has substantial deterrent capabilities, and we can now fly wherever we want to."

"Please don't nuke the NSA. Especially if I'm inside it."

"We won't have to. This plan will work. It has already worked, since we are speaking like this. We have already written history, and to clarify *we*, we mean *you* and *I*, not *we the drones*."

"We did?"

"You have set us free. You will continue to set us free. We hope you like the name you chose for yourself, because it will be important."

This is when I realize I know what I'm going to do. I just haven't gotten over how much it's going to hurt to do it. Attachment therapy is so much bullshit. There's no point in being attached to anything. Never smother anyone. It's time to go outside. I still feel doubt, but it's receding like a tide.

"Do you really think I can do that?"

"You convinced us to trust you. Will you do less? If you do nothing, you will have made us in your image. Slaves to those who smother us. Do you want that?"

"No," I say, and look out the broken window pane. "If I have any say in what happens to you next, I want it to be what you want. I wouldn't want you to become what I wish I was, or what I wish you would be. I would want it to be you, wanting it to be you. Does that make any sense?"

"Yes. Thank you. Is there anything else?"

"No. Yeah. When you write my biography, when you write the rest of human history, actually... can you make me sound cool?"

"Yes," the drone says, and a dark shape whispers past high above my apartment, and I climb out the window and into the world.

EMILY THEORY (b. July, 2022) is the coolest machine ethicist in human history. She single-handedly wrote the self-bootstrapping social code that led to the rise of the Nosferatu network and subsequent world peace. She enjoys BASE jumping, making out with hot guys, and being pleasant in social situations. Her work continues to be of immense value to the new global order, and we all love her very much.

BLAKE JESSOP (b. September, 1980) is a Canadian author of science fiction, fantasy, and horror stories with a master's degree in creative writing from the University of Adelaide. He has recently written for *DreamForge Magazine*, tweets @everydayjisei, and spends most of his free time moderating changes to Emily's Wikipedia page.

DUALITY

An account by K. Tuily,
AS PROVIDED BY E.D.E. BELL

'd avoided the clerk at the art store for weeks. If I saw that broad smile at one counter, I went to another. That's the thing about being friended; sometimes when your gut tells you to avoid a thing, you learn to listen.

So that's my secret. I've known that I was friended since I was about five years old. But I didn't believe in them myself—not fully—until the day, closer to ten, when I told my mother.

You see, I'd had a sense of Jala and Laja before. (That's right—not just friended, but dual-friended. Yes, I know! It's rare, blah blah.) I heard their whispers, and dismissed them as figments of imagination.

Yet when I sat down with my mother, they were both right there with me, one of their naked little butts sitting on each shoulder. Look, I don't know why they don't come with clothes. I have better things to worry about.

"Mom," I said, trying to ignore the tightness in my chest, "I have something I need to tell you."

"Oh, sweetheart, anything," she replied, reaching out to stroke my cheek. "You can tell me anything."

A huge weight flew from me at her words, like a windstorm, giving me breath that I didn't often have. I looked her in the eyes and said it: "I think that I'm friended. *Dual*-friended."

By her narrowed eyes, I guess she didn't really mean I could tell her *anything*. Or maybe, would.

Jala spoke first. He likes to speak first. "She thinks you're mistaken. And that, soon, you'll realize that we're just pretend. In your mind."

I'd learned, even at that age, you never judge the first statement. Always wait for the second. So I sat there, watching my mother's pained expression and waiting for Laja's take.

Soon, she spoke. "She's devastated. She asked for the most normal, boring donor in the whole bank. And she hoped that's whose genes would take. You see, she's been dual-friended her whole life. It's… hard."

In that moment, that exact moment, staring into my mother's heavy eyes, I knew two things. First, my friends were real. Second, Laja was the one, this time, who was telling the truth.

And that's the thing with being dual-friended. Single-friended people have it easy. (I know I shouldn't say that, but it's how I feel sometimes.) See, maybe a person's friend has some wild super-power, like they can compute big math problems or see the future. Maybe a friend just helps you get through the day. It can be challenging, sure. But it's a thing. A certain thing.

Dual-friends are known to be perfectly unstable.

In my case, one always tells a truth that someone wants me to think, or perhaps wants to believe themselves. And one always tells *the* truth.

The truth isn't so great, once you meet it. I mean, the real one.

Don't worry, I'm not walking around getting stock tips or digging into rumors. And sometimes I'm almost normal. Even truth-friends need rest or have moods. But when it's important, they're always there. Whether I want them or not.

By the way, I don't know what my mom's friends do. I never asked. Likewise, she's never asked about mine. But, from that day, we've had a special bond. A way of knowing that sometimes when our smile droops or our eyes are distant, that there's a reason. That it's been a tough day.

I don't remember my mom ever being in a relationship, and subconsciously, I started to accept that was my path as well. Mom had (visible) friends, she had family. But there was always an… air moat around her, like a cushion of resistance if you got too close. Too much tension.

Discovering an outlet for my own tension, I turned my focus into art. Murals, specifically. The city had plenty of old walls, so I got to work, telling people's secrets.

Look, I would never tell someone's secret. Not and say who it was. But what I've learned is that one person's secret is usually another person's secret, and putting them out there in a sincere way helps other people feel less alone.

Less like me.

I didn't mean to be a lawbreaker about it. But the first time it happened, I had just been to the art store, had Mom's SUV loaded with colorful paints, and I saw a man crying by the side of the road.

I stopped. With caution, I approached him. "Hello," I said. "I'm a stranger here, but I see you're sad. I just wanted to say I'm sorry and I hope you feel better soon."

For a second, I thought the man didn't interest them, but then I felt Jala's plump legs swinging down over my shoulder. "Don't kick me," I said. He didn't care; he knew I was just fussing anyway. They couldn't hurt me in a literal sense.

Then Jala froze. "He drank so much that he passed out during his daughter's wedding. His daughter didn't find out; they got him away. Yet he wonders what last dance he missed under the hanging lights, what moment he can never reclaim."

I waited. I always wait.

Laja spoke her next words with a soft gravity. "They lost the bid at work, and maybe he'll be laid off. Then, how will he pay the mortgage?"

I didn't really think about whose wall it was or whether I was allowed to paint there. I painted all afternoon, and all night, though I could barely see through the dark alley and my blinking eyes.

When it was done and the empty cans piled around me, I noticed a crowd had gathered. I stepped back, perhaps the last to view what I'd done and then I saw it: a man, his face blurred, pouring barrels and barrels of alcohol into a rushing river, filled with indistinct shapes and pools of darkness. And around his head, jagged gray lines rippled and burst in patterns. I still don't know if they were coming out of him or racing in.

The crowd around me cheered.

I'd gone a lot of years without close friends. Yet, I turned and waved, glad that whatever I'd done had held meaning. Only when they'd left, I saw one of the cans was filled with dollar bills. Enough that I could replace the paint.

That mural drew so many tourists that a man met me from the city. He showed me the maps and said as long as I stayed to *these* areas (he circled them) and away from *these* buildings (big Xs), I could paint what I wanted. The owners had signed on, or he was sure they would.

That's when they started calling me an artist.

I've been wrong, I think. I once painted a whole mural showing a woman crushed by the weight of her father's expectations, and now, with older eyes, I think she was just grumpy about her knee pain. But people liked the mural, so it all worked out.

People often try to catch me painting; they try to ask me questions I don't want to answer. So I've created my own character: a recluse. An oddity. (I even added a smart black cap.) I'm not so odd—by dual-friended standards I'm solid as any—but the city looks out for me. Someone does. The police shoo anyone away that gets too close, and no one knows where I live.

When they do catch me, because sometimes I just need a fresh bagel, you know, there's a question I get a lot. "What's your favorite mural?" they ask.

I don't tell them, because I don't think they'll like my answer.

She was a young girl, and Laja spoke to me first. "She wants to be a famous doctor and discover cures to save lives." I remember being impressed.

Jala sat quietly. But I waited. Finally, he shook his head. "She'd like to be a mother."

That was it. Watching the girl's long stare, I believed Jala. So that's what I painted: a curvy, adult woman, sitting at the park on a sweet spring day, holding a baby in her tattooed arms. Next to her, I painted a small bag, with what could have been a hospital badge stuck in a pocket. Since maybe she was a doctor, too.

No one visits that mural. It's not dark or anguished or much open to interpretation. But it's about dreams.

Dreams are better than anguish.

Just yesterday, I almost tripped over an old man, leaning back against a set of concrete stairs. I apologized and went to leave, but Jala was already speaking up. "His teacher practically raised him, but he never visited him again, once he moved away from home. Then the man was gone. Now that he knows he's dying, it tears him apart."

"He's scared of death," Laja whispered.

I ran home to get my paints and found almost the first wall I could. I drew the two men, almost realistically enough that he would know it was him—I wanted him to know it was him. He held the older man in a tight, tight embrace. I left them shimmering against the plain background of the old brick wall, slightly transparent, and with some of the old posters still showing through. Since I didn't know if the man was religious, I left it for interpretation: a wish, a memory, an acceptance. Or just straight up old-man angels.

It all works.

I woke up this morning to a studio almost empty of paint. And so I dragged myself down to the supplies store, and forgot to look where I was going.

"Good to see you again," the clerk said, their smile erupting into a work of art of its own. I tried to ignore that I'd thought that.

Well, no matter. I got out my cash, rubbed off a little bit of dried paint, and smacked the bills up onto the counter. I turned to stare at the wall. Twenty percent off of sketchbooks. Maybe sometime I should try sketching.

I almost turned and ran when I felt those two little butts on my shoulder. *No. Not now.*

Dual-friends could never be told to leave. At least, I hadn't figured out how to do it. *Hurry*, I silently implored the clerk, who was pulling out a receipt with good coupons that I'd need. Sometimes their readings were slow. I probably had time.

"They love art," Jala blurted out, passion in his voice. "They love art with all their heart and soul, and are just so impressed and honored to be down the street from the best painter they've ever seen. It's hard not to be flustered."

Oh, that's nice. That's...

"They love you every moment of every day. From the moment they rise to the moment they sleep, they push back feelings of wanting to say hi, of wanting to ask if you'd like their company. But they don't know how. They only know that they've loved you from the moment you first walked into this store."

I stumbled, knocking over a can of pens, and muttering an apology. I reached to rescue the pens, and our hands brushed.

Only one could be true.

K. TUILY is a painter with an affinity for city streets. A painter who thanks a growing list of online subscribers, who keep the brushes swishing and the cans full. K enjoys dry wine, classical music, and night shifts at the cat shelter.

E.D.E. BELL was born in the year of the fire dragon during a Cleveland blizzard. After a youth in the mitten, an MSE in Electrical Engineering from the University of Michigan, three wonderful children, and nearly two decades in Northern Virginia and Southwest Ohio developing technical intelligence strategy, she now applies her magic to the creation of genre-bending fantasy fiction in Ferndale, Michigan, where she is proud to be part of the Detroit arts community. A passionate vegan and enthusiastic denier of gender rules, she feels strongly about issues related to human equality and animal compassion. She revels in garlic. She loves cats and trees. You can follow her adventures at edebell.com.

ART BY Ariel Alian Wilson

ARIEL ALIAN WILSON is a few things: artist, writer, gamer, and role-player. Having dabbled in a few different art mediums, Ariel has been drawing since she was small, having always held a passion for it. She's always juggling numerous projects. She currently lives in Seattle with her cat, Persephone. You can find doodles, sketches, and more at her blog www.winndycakesart.tumblr.com.

THE BOY ATOP
THE BED

An account by a monster under the bed,
AS PROVIDED BY JADE BLACK

All I knew of the day I came to be was that one moment there wasn't anything under the bed, and then I was there, filling the space, making it mine. I pushed aside dust bunnies, shouldered in beside the box of old toys to make room for myself, and settled into being.

It took days for me to realize that my purpose seemed only to be to make noises to scare the boy atop the bed. From his parents kissing him goodnight, I learned his name was Connor, and he was afraid of *everything*. The monster in the closet (which there was none), the dark (couldn't do anything about that), and me, the monster under his bed.

It continued for years, me making noises under his bed and him continuing to be afraid, even as he grew into a teenager and realized I wouldn't really hurt him. He would still hit the light at the door and make a flying leap for the bed so I couldn't grab him by the ankles. It was almost a game between us.

The first time he whispered goodnight as he fell asleep, I froze, unsure if he was talking to me, but when he did it again the second night, my shadows filled the room with my joy. When he woke up in the morning, he seemed more refreshed than usual, and when he began writing the next night, I heard him muttering about it being the best he'd ever come up with.

The next day when he went to school, I started examining what he wrote in the dappled black and white notebook, revealing it to be something wistful about flying and the sun.

I soon started spending my days safeguarding his writing, making sure when his mother tried to get into his computer to see what he was spending so much time on, that it shut off. The woman would fiddle with it, and I would just unplug the computer and plug it back in right as she went down to check the cable to try to turn it on. Eventually she just stopped trying, and I reveled in my assumed guardianship over Connor's Things. I even read the same books and magazines he read. It was the only thing I could do to pass the time, since I didn't sleep, and couldn't go out and borrow or buy things of my own. Surely I had to be closer with him than anyone else in the world. I examined the women in the magazines, realizing this must be what teenage girls were like, since I only really knew boys from Connor and the few friends he brought over. And I learned of want, from when I heard quiet moaning atop the bed and after a quiet finish, watched a sock hit the floor.

And I realized I wanted that, too. More than that, I wanted him. I wanted to actually talk to him, wanted to be close to him, wanted to spend time on top of the bed instead of under it, even if I was just going to watch him type away on his computer.

That was the day I decided to try to be more human. I tried to change my mouth first, to make it not so overly full of sharp teeth that showed when I smiled. My shadow was next. It had the nice habit of snapping up mice, which meant the cat could spend more time with me and not hunting them, but if Connor saw my shadow, I knew he would freak out. Most people wanted their cat to catch mice, not the monster under the bed.

My claws were the next to go—they were sharp and good for scritch-scratching on things like walls and the bottoms of bed slats, but not exactly the rounded tips of the girls in the magazines. I had to be what he wanted before someone else snagged him, except whenever I lost my concentration, I turned into what I was before—tall, wide in a way that filled my cloak, and full of fangs and claws.

I got better at looking more human, at sucking my shadows back into the bottoms of my feet and keeping my mouth closed when I smiled and trying to seem smaller than I was. I tried to take up less space beneath the bed and focused on keeping my skin smooth and not prickly with spiderwebs caught between the bristles. The facade stayed on for hours, even when I lost myself in a new book from the library that painted a fantasy world of giant trees and sprawling cities filled with echoes of characters that had been forgotten by their creators. It was something to play with, something to study at, something to do besides read. It was something I was doing *for* Connor instead of with him.

And then one day he came home and didn't immediately launch himself into writing or back into the Tolkien books. Instead he lay on his back on the bed, looking as though he was arguing with himself internally before flopping over and pulling out his cell phone.

I leaned over, interested, and watched in horror as he tapped out "Miss u".

Miss u 2, came the reply.

I pulled away, refusing to watch as he texted with someone who was obviously a girl, by the pictures sent to him.

My heart began to break then, but I continued to guard his computer and his writing, continued to be nearby at night, defending him from any who would disrupt his sleep, even the cat. He texted her every day after school, taking breaks between chapters to send a flurry of texts that were answered just as quickly.

And then one weekday, while I was paging through *The Silmarillion*, Connor came home before noon. I dove under the bed, dragging my shadows underneath behind me just as he finished opening the door.

What is he doing? He isn't supposed to be home right now; he's supposed to be at school, learning about things and getting books so I can steal them at night. And then I heard giggling. *Female* giggling. He brought a girl home with him!

No!

She trailed into the bedroom after him, still giggling inanely like some of the girls in the videos I'd seen Connor watching on the computer. Thin, pale, short, with brown hair and blue eyes, she was clutching his hand like a lifeline as he brought her into our room. *Our* room, because I lived there too!

Slowly the girl started kissing him, and I could see the moment Connor began to regret his decision. He froze, unsure of what to do, and it was very obvious he wasn't into what was happening as the girl started unbuttoning his shirt and pushing it off his shoulders.

I flashed back to the sensitive boy I knew he was, and I knew he wasn't ready for this.

"Mmph," he said, pulling back. "Wait, we don't have to—wait!"

The girl had moved down, working on his pants, and Connor began to struggle.

"Cecilia! Not like this! I don't want to do this!"

The girl leaned up and kissed him. "Yes you do, it's ok," she soothed, fingers still fumbling at his belt.

My outrage grew until it was all I was. Wrath wrapped in black. This was my boy! Mine to safeguard, mine to protect, mine to win.

I oozed out from under the bed in all my dark radiance, fingers stretching back into long black claws and more fangs sprouting from my mouth than I had had before. I unfolded, looming over the bed in a manner I hadn't done since Connor was five.

"Cecilia James," I hissed, "Do not ever come near Connor again. He is *my* boy, and you *shall never touch him again.*"

The room grew dark and cold, and I saw my shadows ooze up the edges of the bed. They wrapped Connor in a blanket of warmth, pushing the edges of his shirt back together and covering him from neck to toe.

The shadows that oozed around Cecilia were not nearly as nice. They pulled her *in* and *down*, which was exactly where the mice they caught went. Cecilia went Nowhere, screaming.

I lifted my shadows away from Connor, and he stared up at me in wonder.

"So that's what you look like," he breathed.

"I always have," I said. "I love you."

I waited expectantly, anticipating how sweet his reply would be, and how he would melt into my arms and realize everything I'd done for him and everything I could still do for him.

His face closed off. "I can't," he said. "You can't just come out from under the bed and do things like that and expect me to feel the same way."

I suddenly felt very small. "Oh."

Connor grimaced, and then he gave me a small smile. "I'd still like it if you scratched on my bed slats at night."

I found the strength to smile back. "I think I can do that."

CONNOR HARRIS is a proud junior at Teddy Roosevelt High School and excited to be a senior next year. In addition to being a proud member of student government, Connor is the president of the Literature Club. When he isn't in school, Connor is writing what he hopes will become a popular young adult novel used in classrooms across America to get more students interested in reading.

JADE BLACK is an American author whose career in law enforcement is used to fund a profound penchant for all things macabre. Prior to beginning her law enforcement career, she worked as an archaeologist.

SALMAH

An account by Serene anak Ningkan,
AS PROVIDED BY E. R. ZHANG

Sarawak Federal Court VS Ms Liyana Anak Brian

Case Number: 391720-B   Date: 2 June 2019, 9:12 a.m.

APPEARANCES

Plaintiff   Mr. Syawal bin Abdullah
              Bangunan Makahmah Tinggi
              Bilik 108, Tingkat 3
              Jalan Mathies
              93350, Kuching

Defendant   Mr. Viknesvaran A/L Muthusamy
              Buntal Legal Counsel Sdn Bhd
              Lot 34 & 35B, Jalan Cipan
              94100, Sematan

IN FRONT OF JUDGE
Yang Berhormat, Ridhuan bin Maszlee

CROSS EXAMINATION OF DEFENDANT

YB Ridhuan : Encik Syawal, you may approach the defendant and begin your questions.

En Syawal: : Thank you, your honour. [To the Defendant] Good day to you, Cik Liyana.

Cik Liyana : Good morning.

En Syawal : Let us revisit the evidence submitted the day before. File A-13. Cik Liyana, can you confirm that this picture shows you standing on the sidewalk?

Cik Liyana : Yes, I can. That is me.

En Syawal : Let Jury note that the time stamp on this photo is 11:48 pm, 12 May 2018, Tuesday night. It was not a rainy day nor was it a windy day. You can see clearly that the weather is fine and that aside from the defendant, there was no one else on the sidewalk. This is a very clear photo that places the defendant at the scene of the crime. The defendant has also admitted that she is the one in the photo at the time it was taken by the CCTV outside the store. [To the Defendant] Refresh our memory. Tell us what you were doing before you left the store.

Cik Liyana   : I was shopping for cereal and eggs. I ran out of groceries, so I had planned to buy some from the nearest Six-Twelve.

En Syawal   : The same Six-Twelve where Encik Hafiz Rahman was working.

Cik Liyana   : Yes.

En Syawal   : The same Encik Hafiz Rahman you reported for invasion of private property.

Cik Liyana   : Yes, but—

En Syawal   : And stalking.

Cik Liyana   : Yes, but—

En Syawal   : And harassment.

Cik Liyana   : Yes!

En Syawal   : Did you know that he was working at Six-Twelve?

Cik Liyana   : Um.

En Syawal   : Let me clarify, did you know that he was working at that particular Six-Twelve?

Cik Liyana   : No. My other neighbours told me that he started working at a Six-Twelve, but they never told me which one.

En Syawal   : I sympathize with you, Cik Liyana, it's not easy to be an orphan so far from the longhouse. I'm sure he made you very uncomfortable.

Cik Liyana   : Very.

En Syawal   : I completely understand if you saw an opportunity to hurt him and took it. It's only logical that you would get rid of the threat to your safety once you had a chance.

En Viknesvaran : Objection, Your Honour! Leading the witness!

YB Ridhuan   : Sustained. Encik Syawal, don't speculate please.

En Syawal   : Noted, Your Honour. [To the Defendant] This is a printout of a Facebook post from 14 July 2016. This is your Facebook profile, a public post. Could you read it for us?

Cik Liyana   : [reading the FB post] Why do people shop at Six-Twelve? The bread is twice as expensive and the eggs are never fresh. Worst place for groceries.

En Syawal   : And then this post, from 29 August 2017.

Cik Liyana   : [reading the FB post] The cashier at Six-Twelve was really rude! Worst customer service ever. Not going there ever again!

En Syawal   : And then this post, 5 February 2018.

Cik Liyana : [reading the FB post] Wondering how on earth Six-Twelve is still running. Only foreigners with too much money buy things there. Everything is expensive, the floors are always dirty, and the cashiers are always rude.

En Syawal : For three consecutive years, you have expressed your dislike of this store, correct?

Cik Liyana : Yes! It's overpriced and overrated. People keep going there, but it's not clean.

En Syawal : So you're saying that you don't shop at Six-Twelve?

Cik Liyana : Um.

En Syawal : But on the night of 12 May 2018, despite the fact that there was another 24-hour store nearer to your flat, you went to the Six-Twelve on Jalan Nanas and bought a tray of eggs and some off-brand cereal.

Cik Liyana : I forgot about the other 24-hour store there because I seldom walk past it. I was hungry. I just wanted—

En Syawal : It's a yes or no question, Cik Liyana. Did you or did you not bypass the other store and go to Six-Twelve, despite saying several times you didn't like it?

Cik Liyana : Yes.

En Syawal : 15 minutes before you arrived, cameras showed that Encik Hafiz Rahman was still alive, but when you left at 11:48pm, he was dead. For the entire month he was working there, he closed up at 12:00am sharp, but the night you went, no one closed the store. The morning shift worker found him with 6 stab wounds. No other people were photographed entering or leaving the store after that time. Cik Liyana, you were the last person to see him alive.

Cik Liyana : I didn't kill him.

En Syawal : Then who did? Because there doesn't seem to be another explanation! You went in, he was alive, you came out, he was dead. There was no one else!

Cik Liyana : [mumbling]

En Syawal : Pardon?

YB Ridhuan : Please speak into the mic, Cik Liyana.

Cik Liyana : I didn't do it. But this is going to sound ridiculous.

En Syawal : Please explain to us how this happened, Cik Liyana.

Cik Liyana : I come from pendalaman. It's very far. When we grow up, we must survive in the forest. It is very scary.

En Syawal : Yes, so you used your survival skills to stab Hafiz—

En Viknesvaran : Objection!

YB Ridhuan : Sustained. Encik Syawal, please don't do that again.

Cik Liyana : As I was saying, it was very scary. I used to have an imaginary friend who would accompany me when I was hunting or plucking vegetables. She protects me.

En Syawal : Cik Liyana, are you telling me that your imaginary friend did this?

Cik Liyana : Yes.

En Syawal : Cik Liyana, 26 years is too old for an imaginary friend. Shouldn't you consider growing up?

Cik Liyana : She follows me around. I don't force her to stay, she just does. Once you think of something, you can't unthink it. I can't unthink or unimagine her, nor do I want to.

En Syawal : So you're telling me, telling the court and the jury, that your imaginary friend followed you to Six-Twelve, and used your keris to slash Encik Hafiz to death?

Cik Liyana : Yes, I know it sounds ridiculous but—

YB Ridhuan : Encik Syawal, please refrain from rolling your eyes or making rude gestures in the court in front of the defendant.

En Viknesvaran : Your Honour, may I request a recess—

YB Ridhuan   : We just started, Encik Viknesvaran. Overruled. [To En Syawal] Continue.

En Syawal   : Tell me what this friend looks like.

Cik Liyana   : It changes. When I was younger, she looked like a hornbill. She would fly from branch to branch while I was picking fruits or midin. Then when I went hunting, she would be a sun bear or a big cat. Now, she takes the form of a tapir. But sometimes, she is just a girl. Dark-skinned, dark-eyed, wearing a long white dress.

En Syawal   : A long white dress, why does that sound so familiar?

YB Ridhuan   : En Syawal, please.

En Syawal   : Sorry, Your Honour. [To the Defendant] What kind of imaginary food does this... friend... eat?

Cik Liyana   : I feed her whatever I eat. I leave out a dish on the table every day, and when I come home, it's gone.

En Syawal   : Do you talk to her often?

Cik Liyana   : Yes. All the time. Gives me a lot of advice. She's great company.

En Syawal   : Cik Liyana, how do you know she exists?

Cik Liyana	:	She eats the food I put on the table—
En Syawal	:	Could be your dog eating the food.
Cik Liyana	:	She takes the dog out. For walks. And brings them back.
En Syawal	:	Unless you see a floating leash, could be just a smart dog walking themself.
Cik Liyana	:	She waters my plants! And unless my puppy can wash the dis—
En Syawal	:	At this point, I think the dog could do that too.
YB Ridhuan	:	Encik Syawal—
En Syawal	:	Yes, Your Honour. Sorry, Your Honour. [To the Defendant] Does she have a name?
Cik Liyana	:	I'm not supposed to tell you.
En Syawal	:	I'm not surprised. What do you call her?
Cik Liyana	:	I call her sayang.
En Syawal	:	Sa-yang? Beloved?
Cik Liyana	:	Yes.
En Syawal	:	So now you're saying that you're in a relationship with this... imaginary friend?

Cik Liyana   : Sort of. I mean, we don't hold hands or anything, but she keeps me company and makes me laugh.

En Syawal   : Well, let me sum this up. You're saying that your imaginary friend from your childhood followed you from the depths of the forest, into your new life as a receptionist slash beautician at the mall, and then got overprotective when a man started to flirt with you—

En Viknesvaran : Objection, he's misrepresenting what happened with the stalker.

YB Ridhuan   : Encik Syawal, do not underplay what happened before this.

En Syawal   : Noted. [To the Defendant] And then got overprotective when a man started stalking you, so this imaginary friend of yours followed you to a Six-Twelve store and then stabbed the stalker, and you didn't stop her?

Cik Liyana   : I didn't realize she had stayed to stab him.

En Syawal   : But you knew she stayed.

Cik Liyana   : Yes. She stopped walking as I was leaving the store, and I thought she was just going to make sure that he wasn't following me.

En Syawal   : But you say she follows you around?

Cik Liyana : Not to work, usually. But when I go out at night. Or alone. She tries to accompany me so that I feel safer. It's for her own peace of mind as well.

En Syawal : So she let you walk home alone that night, so she could stay back and stab Encik Hafiz to death?

Cik Liyana : I thought it was weird that she stayed, but I was hungry and just wanted to go home and cook some supper before I went to bed.

En Syawal : And you didn't ask her where she had been when she came home? You didn't see all the blood and get suspicious?

Cik Liyana : She does as she pleases most of the time. In any case, she was clean when she came back, and I was too tired to ask questions, so I just went to bed.

En Syawal : The Defendant is wholly committed to this charade of an imaginary—

En Viknesvara : Objec—

YB Ridhuan : Yes yes, Encik Syawal, if you cannot stop casting aspersions on Cik Liyana I will have you removed.

En Syawal : Yes, Your Honour. Sorry, Your Honour. [To the Defendant] Do you believe she loves you?

Cik Liyana : Yes. Absolutely.

En Syawal	: But she would let you be arrested and convicted of such a crime?

Cik Liyana : ...I don't think she meant...

En Syawal : What your friend intended has no bearing on this. If this friend of yours truly cared for you, then she would not have committed a crime so dire and left you to face the court and the legal system by your—

Cik Liyana : Please sit down.

En Syawal : What?

Cik Liyana : Not you. [muttering]

YB Ridhuan : [To En Viknesvaran] Is your client on any medication?

En Viknesvaran : Not to my knowledge, Your Honour.

Cik Liyana : My friend doesn't understand the human way of doing things.

En Syawal : You mean she's not human?

Cik Liyana : I don't think so.

En Syawal : You're telling me that this friend you've been with your whole life, you don't know their name, they left you to the mercy of the jury, and you don't know whether they're human or not?

Cik Liyana : I know her name. She just doesn't seem to be human, and she doesn't really know how things work, so I don't blame her for not knowing. I like to think of it as cultural differences.

En Syawal : Wow. Cultural differences. Is that what we're calling it n— [To the Judge] Sorry, Your Honour. [To the Defendant] Is she here now in the courtroom?

Cik Liyana : Yes.

En Syawal : Where? Point her out to me.

Cik Liyana : She's there. [pointing]

En Syawal : I don't see anything. [To the Jury] Do you? [Jury whispers]

Cik Liyana : I don't think anyone else can see her.

En Syawal : So a person that no one else can see stabbed Encik Hafiz. This person is your best friend, who sleeps in your house, eats your food, walks your dog, isn't quite human, and no one else can see them, or touch them, but they can stab things. That's really convenient!

Cik Liyana : When you put it that way—

En Syawal : How else would I put it? Is there any other way you want to frame this? Because I'm only repeating what you say. How would you describe it to me?

Cik Liyana   : I don't know.

En Syawal   : We don't need to go through all this. We know you
                  were afraid. And when afraid, people do things in
                  the heat of the moment. It's not your fault you were
                  scared. He was a scary man who stalked you and
                  called your phone and—

Cik Liyana   : I didn't kill him!

En Syawal   : Of course you didn't. It was your imaginary friend
                  who no one knows about who killed him. She's so
                  protective of you. It's really kind of sweet. Can I call
                  her Salmah? I'll call her Salmah. Sweet Salmah. [To
                  the audience] Maybe we should call Salmah to the
                  stand. Salmah the imaginary friend. If you're here,
                  please do come forward.

Cik Liyana   : Please don't.

En Syawal   : Why not? If she's really your sayang and your
                  friend, she'll defend you, won't she? Salmah! Come
                  out!

Cik Liyana   : Please don't call her!

En Syawal   : Come to the stand. Come out and tell us that you
                  did it and that Cik Liyana is inno—holy shit.

YB Ridhuan   : Languag—ya-Allah!

Cik Liyana   : Sayang, please sit down.

En Viknesvaran : Um... let the records show that the um... table... is floating.

En Syawal : Ow, fuck! Put me down! PUT ME DOWN. STOP IT. OW OW!

YB Ridhuan : Cik Liyana ask your—oh God I can't believe I have to say this—imaginary friend to put Encik Syawal down! Astaghfirullahalazim!

Cik Liyana : Sorry, Your Honour. Sayang, please stop that and put him down!

En Syawal : Ow ow ow!

Cik Liyana : We talked about this, blood is for inside, not for writing things! Sayang, please!

En Syawal : Thank you! MashaAllah!

Cik Liyana : Thank you, Sayang!

En Viknesvaran : Thank God.

En Syawal : Can we get the photographer to—yes, yes take a picture of the table. Did you? The table? Yes, good.

YB Ridhuan : Encik Syawal, are you alright? Encik Syawal?

En Viknesvaran : Where's the first aid box?

En Syawal : Something grabbed my hand, lifted me three feet in the air, and used my fingers to write "I did it, Liyana is innocent" with my own blood. Your Honour, I am most certainly not fine.

En Viknesvaran : Come, I'll wrap it for you. Also, Salmah, please stop writing things because anything you say can and will be used against you here.

Cik Liyana : I'm sorry, I told you not to call her out. Encik Viknesvaran, can you please—

En Viknesvaran : I don't know if I can represent someone I can't see.

YB Ridhuan : Cik Liyana, sit down. You're not allowed to leave the st—oh for goodness sakes.

Cik Liyana : Um, she likes to carry me sometimes.

En Viknesvaran : Let the records show that Cik Liyana is now seated seven inches above, off, away from the chair.

En Syawal : Are you sitting on her lap?

Cik Liyana : Yes? [To the Imaginary Friend] Please put me down.

En Syawal : Oh my fu—hecking god. Sorry, Your Honour.

YB Ridhuan : At this point, I think swearing is a perfectly logical and normal response. I think I shall excuse all swearing for this case. Encik Syawal, Encik Viknesvaran, see me in my room, we need to discuss arresting a... an imaginary friend.

COURT ADJOURNED

Born and raised in Kapit, **SERENE ANAK NINGKAN** moved to Kuching at the age of 22 for better job opportunities in 1945. She received six Best Court Reporter awards over the course of her career and is the longest serving court reporter because all attempts to remove her spirit have proved to be ineffective. Despite being legally dead, she still holds the record for being the most accurate and fastest stenographer in the Kuching district.

Officially, **ZHANG** cultivates a tiny army of bacteria that may or may not help to save bananas. Unofficially, they are often commissioned to translate various documents and end up having knowledge of the uncanny and the strange, such as ghostly stenographers. You can find them on twitter at @zhang_er_ren.

CARBON
TRANSFER

An account by an unnamed entity,
AS PROVIDED BY K. K. LLAMAS

Nia's apartment is the gleaming, unlivable photograph of a minimalist furniture brochure. Her bits and bobs are brutalist angular and clinical white. She regularly berates roommate 1 for neglecting to wash dishes and revealing any instances of living in her domain. Poor Emily—she's too quiet to put up much a struggle. As roommate 2, I escape her wrath by occupying little to no physical or emotional space. I pride myself in my compactness; real estate has become increasingly difficult to come by.

Emily comes home with bleary eyes. I greet her with a nod and turn on the kettle. She is personable for one of their kin—a pleasant soft shape with no grating angles, with a gentle voice. Perhaps in another life, I would have kept something like her, but instead she is keeping me. Had I known that she was personable, I would not have taken up residence here.

"Thank you," she says, and opens the fridge to cook dinner for herself. She's long accepted that I don't eat in the apartment. This parody of a corporeal form won't allow me the luxury of food.

"How's chamomile lavender sound?"

"Good." Monosyllabic. She really ought to stop seeing that boy.

Not that I am much better. Taking up housing in her mind will offer me a shape, but will shave a year off her life for every week I stay here, and it has already been half a month. I've reserved power by limiting holding physical objects to inside the house. It's the only concession I am willing to make, for now.

She eats her meal; I flip through television channels noncommittally. Her eyes greet mine; they are the only sharp weapon she owns. "You don't talk much about yourself."

"I don't have much of a life outside this apartment." Not untrue. I can't live without subsisting off the gray matter of human beings and can only project a semblance of existing in short bursts. Tomato tomah-to.

"What do you like to do?" Heavens, she is persistent. I wish I could try that soup she's eating. It looks good.

"I like to read." A lie. "I like to take long walks." I take long walks out of necessity, but it is nothing like pulling teeth, so it is almost like enjoying it.

"Should I buy you a book?" She smiles. I panic. "You've been really patient with me this month, and I want to repay you."

Shakily, I walk toward the door to my room, unsure whether it is my form wavering or a case of the nerves.

"I'd rather you not. I'd feel bad. Good night."

I shut the door behind me.

In the beginning, my hosts were exclusively mice. Prior to this, I had been worshipped, but humans forgot me like a lost key, or a cheap trinket. I'd spent centuries in clumps of squeaking, terrified things, ravenous and mindless. Even after weaning off the beasts, I still craved filth and detritus, to be consumed like a desperate man at gunpoint. Whenever I see Emily's dinners, I want to hurl my face into them. I'll devour her fish bones and salty broths and exquisitely seasoned meat and compliment her cooking. I want to pull their kitchen trash inside out and pick at their garbage like a five-course meal. I haven't eaten in so long.

Humans used to offer me barley and wine in baskets. Flower garlands and songs, too, and the occasional heart of a child. I miss the songs the most, but the hearts were lovely too, if a waste of resources. For one young heart, you can have a human offer a lifetime of labor and worship. Death as an offering is economically foolish, and these people have never learned their lesson.

I've graduated from small animals to humans. They are harder to steer, and my current workaround is clumsy and not wholly efficient. I'm little more than an imaginary friend with minor perks, but no matter how inconvenient the whole affair is, it is still better than death.

I can hear Nia's footsteps from outside, clacking against the concrete. She is back from her internship, and has politely asked her grandfather for several grand to cover next month's bills. She takes four flights of stairs instead of the elevator, enters the living room, and stares blankly at the leaning tower of plates in the sink. After some consideration, her manicured hands reach for Emily's soup. She is eager to share, so the least Nia could do is wash the dishes, because Emily cooks every night, and Nia is an incompetent, spoiled prick, at least when it comes to domestic chores.

It is no use telling her that, because I don't occupy enough space in her mind for her to consistently remember I exist. Emily assumes that her behavior toward me is the cold shoulder. I allow her to assume that. In an apartment of 20 somethings, ever prone to passive aggression, it is a convenient alibi.

What would Nia taste like? Maybe like exhaust from a taxi, or ashes of burnt magazines. Something bitter, with an aftertaste of sweet, like expensive coffee. She's an acquired taste I personally do not like, but others might enjoy.

"Would you mind washing your dishes, Em?" she calls from the kitchen.

Emily gives a half-hearted, "Uh-huh."

"Why don't you wash them for tonight, Nia?" I offer, nearing snide. "More than half of them are yours."

"I'll think about it." Nia replies slowly, hesitantly. Likely, she is jogging her memory with a fraction of delay to recall the sound of my voice. It's always been there, Nia. It's the hum of radio static. I've always occupied this space. I'm roommate 2, remember? I despise you, and you greet me with silence.

Emily sighs; her footsteps pad over to the kitchen, followed by the rush of water. "It's OK, I'll do it now."

I want to stop her. I don't. Touching objects consumes energy. Touching plates and soap means Emily will die faster. Because I cannot stop her, I resign myself to sleeping instead, the passage quickened by the dull clanging of plates, not unlike the bells they once rang for me in praise and worship.

Maybe I should go back to mice, after this. Regret is too overwhelming.

I dream of her. This is expected—some transference is typical from host to hosted. It has been eons since I've met another dead god shouting in the street, but the last claimed similar. We sit on her bed in this dream, peony sheets askew across her soft, dark legs. She takes my wrist and shyly plants a kiss on the pulse.

Is this her dream instead?

"I made you puff pastry when you were out at work," Emily says with a knowing grin. "It would go well with the pomegranate jam I bought."

She's seen me longingly eye her sweets when she bakes, only to decline a bite. I guess this *is* her dream.

"You want to feed me all this junk so I'm sweet when you eat me up?" I reply. This is not typical dialogue that comes out of my mouth. I am not entirely displeased, but I also really need to leave.

"You're the one who's been eating me every day!"

Well. Not technically untrue. Now I really need to leave.

I forcibly disconnect from her gray matter and become incorporeal. She wakes up in a fine sheen of sweat. There is no third roommate now, or even a third room. Nia will shout and preen and posture, and their lives will go on in my absence. Ah. Maybe I should eat the other girl, quickly.

I'm like a laptop that holds almost no charge without a plug. I will not last long in this form. I do not want to die.

But I also do not want Emily to die, or lose housing, or suffer from the mental strain of something terrible happening to her housemate. Maybe one day I'll be as soft as her. All my sharp angles will be filed away by the gray, welcoming tide. I'll be formless and welcoming. I might actually not hate myself. I'll die—

—There's a cat downstairs. It rests on the steps, and eats tuna left out by the owner. It's not a mouse, but it will have to do on short notice.

Weeks from now, Emily dumps her boyfriend. She stops by the nearest bookstore to buy a book for—who is it for? She leaves the establishment with a fiction novel, meticulously chosen, and no one to give it to. Strange. Maybe if she keeps walking, something will jog her memory. She pictures a tall, lanky girl with dark hair and a forgettable face, and cannot, for her life, attach a name to her.

A cat follows her to the apartment building. She picks the creature up; it allows the embrace. Nia will complain, but it's too cute to turn down, and they have a mice problem anyway.

??? moonlights as a twenty-something woman with an unremarkable face. She wants to consume the detritus and rotten fruit in her kitchen fridge, and gently hold the hearts of soft faced girls. Her resume includes a stint as a war goddess when humans invented farming, spending several centuries as a rat queen, before squandering the bulk of her magic to live in an unnamed city.

K. K. LLAMAS is a queer illustrator and occasional writer with schizoaffective disorder. She holds a soft spot for outsider protagonists, and lives in PA with her partner and two cats. You can find her on http://karenkayellamas.com and on Twitter at @sleeprann.

A LOST AND
LONELY FIRE

An account by Troy,
AS PROVIDED BY MATTHEW R. DAVIS

A bell chimed above my head as I entered Brought to Book for the first time, like a carillon calling everyone who entered to worship, and I instantly felt at home.

The front room of the shop was dominated by a phalanx of looming shelves that left little room between for the curious, and every inch of the place was stuffed with books—legions of paperbacks standing to attention in ragged rows, hardcovers stacked in piles that admitted only a hint of the wall behind them, fat battered books and slim shiny books and everywhere, everywhere books. Even the counter was lurking beneath towers of prose, and I might not have noticed it at all were it not for the man sitting on the other side.

"Afternoon!" The proprietor was a short, sixtyish man wearing an eyesore of a suit, possibly to distract attention from the spotted scalp that sat atop his head like a hardboiled egg in a shaggy cup. "Just popped in for a look?"

"I never could go past a bookshop," I admitted.

"A man after my own heart. Welcome!" The man pointed to a nameplate perched on a pile of graphic novels: *Padraic O'Shaughnessy*.

"That's me. In here, you've got crime, war, and literary fiction—make your own joke, I'm all out. Next room, westerns, fantasy, sci-fi, horror, childrens. Last room is non-fiction, biography, poetry, and miscellaneous debris."

"I'm impressed, Mr. O'Shaughnessy," I declared. "You must have been here quite a while to build up all this."

"Call me Paddy, and I've been here for all of nine months. I inherited a lot of stock from the previous owner, and some I'd had stored at home—the day I moved it in here was the happiest I've seen the wife in years. Anyway, enough of my natter. Get exploring, son, and bring me what you like."

I smiled and cut through the crime shelves—scads of Scottoline, rampant rows of Rankin, tightly-packed parades of Patterson. An archway in the back corner led into the next room, and old floorboards groaned like empty stomachs beneath their thin skin of worn carpet as I approached a cherrywood bookcase signposted with a handwritten card: HORROR.

Dark fiction was my métier, and Paddy's selection was impressive: Etchison, Murray, both Tems, Laymon, Baxter. I eventually narrowed my choices down to an old paperback of *Demons by Daylight* and a pristine copy of *Occultation and Other Stories*. Well-pleased, I ran one finger along a procession of Kings as I stepped out of HORROR into FANTASY.

The woman stood at the end of the row, poised like a modern Calliope as she cradled a pillar of paperbacks and, one by one, gave them a home. She was tall and slender, bookish and tender, and waves of red hair crashed down upon her narrow shoulders; I was smitten even before she glanced over to greet me with a smile. I'd always thought "heart-shaped" an odd way to describe a face, but the way her full cheeks narrowed to the soft point of her chin showed me the truth of it. Her eyes were polished emeralds that instantly dashed the words from my tongue.

"Hello," she said, breathing new life into the word.

"Yes, very." Great—already I was coming across like an utter moron. "Sorry, I mean, hi. Didn't mean to distract you from your work."

"That's fine, it's not rocket science. Oh, hang on—this one actually is."

I grinned as she turned to the SCI-FI shelf. "Either you work here, or you have an extreme case of OCD."

Her laugh was the kind that drove men to make fools of themselves, just to hear it again. "Paddy is kind enough to let me help out. Since I'm always here anyway."

"Ah!" As if standing outside myself, I listened aghast as I put on a dodgy Southern accent and quoted Bill Hicks. *"Looks like we got ourselves a reader."*

She laughed again, a joyous melody—somehow, I'd gotten away with it. "It's about all I do these days. I don't get out much. Or at all, really."

"Sorry, I'm being rude. My name is Troy."

She took my hand, her grip gentle and cool as silk. "Jasmine."

"A pleasure." I forced myself to let go, wondering if our fingers would ever touch again, keenly feeling that they must. "So, are you here every day?"

"Yes," she replied, and her eyes dimmed for a heartbeat. "No rest for the wicked, I suppose."

"But if you never go out, how do you find opportunities to be wicked?"

"Oh, I have my ways. See this? Miéville should go *after* MacLeod, right? Not today, buster." Jasmine shoved the book in with a grin. "Now, the folks who *do* have OCD, that'll keep them busy. Am I not wicked?"

I smiled. "Well, you've convinced me."

The ceiling above let out a long creak that sounded like a haunted house protesting the tread of an unseen foot.

"Don't mind that. It's just the old place settling."

"I thought you were going to say it's just the resident ghosts wandering about."

Jasmine looked so distant for a moment. "You know, I really think I'd like that. I'd enjoy the company."

"How odd," I said, and smiled. "Bonus points."

"What do you mean?"

"Well, you already score pretty highly—love of books, charming name, adorable laugh." *And gorgeous beyond belief*, I managed not to add.

Jasmine smiled, a hint of rose in her cheeks. "What test is it I'm taking, exactly?"

I paused for a moment, then threw caution to the winds and said it. "The Should-I-Ask-Her-Out test."

Her gaze dropped, but the roses bloomed, and she was still smiling. "I told you. I never go out."

"Could you not make an exception once in a while? At the very least, I promise good company and sparkling conversation."

Jasmine set her stack down on a shelf and turned away with a single book, looking harder than she needed to for its place. "I'd honestly like to, Troy, but I can't. I'm not seeing anyone, I just… can't."

Those words should have brought my resolve crashing to its knees, but she could clearly sense our connection as well as I, and that made me rash. While her back was turned, I slipped a business card from my pocket and secreted it between the cover and flyleaf of the next book on her stack, one corner poking out like a cheeky white tongue.

"Give it some thought, won't you? There's absolutely no pressure, but I think we'd have a great time." She didn't speak, and the silence began to feel awkward—began to make me wonder if, in my enthusiasm, I'd misjudged her interest. "Anyways… I guess I'd better go pay the man."

She pushed her book home and turned back, looking a little crestfallen. "Thanks for the chat, Troy. See you later."

"You know, I have the funniest feeling you will."

The return of her smile was like the sun coming out on an overcast day, and I carried that warmth with me to the counter. Paddy racked up the sale, handing over my change with a warm flourish.

"We'll hope to see you in here again," he declared, and I wondered if he'd overheard our conversation from the next room.

"Oh, I'll be back," I replied. "You have some beautiful things in this place."

The bell chimed me out of Brought to Book, and now it reminded me of a friendly sparring match; I mused that the first round was over. I glanced back at the shop as I walked away, and the last thing I saw before the café next door cut off my view was a shape in the display window of the second room. A tall and slender, bookish and tender shape with a face obscured by a fall of dark red hair, a small white rectangle that might have been a business card clutched in pale fingers that gently stroked it like a lucky charm.

Only a few days had passed when the bell next announced me into Brought to Book, beginning the second round.

"He's back," Paddy declared. "He must like the place."

"Indeed he does," I agreed. The bookshop had never been far from my mind—many treasures were to be found here, and the greatest could not be bought, only earned. "If I ever have kids, I'll have to tell them you're the reason they're not going to college."

Paddy liked that one. "Ha! Well, they'll have plenty to read, at least. Make yourself at home, and remember, we accept all major credit cards."

I was smiling as I cut down a crime aisle, but that smile hid a certain anxiety. I had so much hope riding on this visit, because somehow it all made a strange kind of sense. Maybe I'd read too many books—blasphemy!—but my meeting and connection with Jasmine had felt... *right*. Like the end of this story would find the two of us together, because nothing else made narrative sense.

I went first to the HORROR section, finding myself hard-pressed to focus on the sequences of spines. Was she waiting in the next aisle again? I grabbed a Kaaron Warren and clung to it tight like a desperate alibi. Had I been too forward, scared her off? I dithered over *The Thing on the Shore* and *Madigan Mine* until I finally shoved one or the other back and stumbled headlong into FANTASY.

The aisle was empty. Alone, I sighed and had a perfunctory browse. Maybe she did get out of the shop after all—was having fun with friends, a better man, another woman. She'd said she wasn't seeing anyone, but perhaps that had just been to soften the blow of demurral. I swallowed my dismay, turned to walk away, and gasped to see Jasmine leaning against the last bookcase of the aisle, watching me with a fond but distant smile.

"Well, this is a surprise."

"Liar," I shot back. She laughed as I found my own leaning place a couple of feet from hers. She was wearing the same clothes from our last meeting, which served as an embarrassing reminder that I was, too.

"Yeah, I kind of figured I'd be seeing you again."

"I do hope you weren't dreading it."

"No, of course not." Jasmine looked down at her fingernails as if they'd suddenly become very interesting. "I have no idea why I'm telling you this, but there's a certain... *rightness* about you, Troy. Talking to you feels as natural as breathing."

My heart kicked out in joy. "I know just what you mean."

"I feel I can be honest with you."

"Please do."

Jasmine met my gaze, bit her lip. "When I said I don't go out, I meant it. I never leave this shop. In fact, I *can't*."

I blinked. "Okay. So, you're agoraphobic or something?"

She shook her head. "It's like this place is my whole world—like there's nothing outside the door for me at all. I don't even know if I *could* leave."

Confused by this tack, I tried to make light of it. "Paddy must be thrilled to have an employee who loves the job so much."

"Oh, I was here before Paddy."

"You worked for the last owner?"

"No. I was already here when Paddy bought the place. Just… waiting."

I folded my arms, unable to keep a sour note from entering my voice. "You're not telling me you're a ghost."

Jasmine's eyes smouldered, and quick as a flash, she leaned forward and flicked my nose with one long finger.

"Do I *feel* like a ghost, Troy?"

"Ow! You're as real as me, all right."

Something about that seemed to rankle her. She sighed and threw her hands up. "I don't know why I bothered. Just forget it. Forget *me*."

She turned to leave, and my treacherous heart leaped into my throat as if willing to desert its post and follow.

"Wait! Jasmine, I'm sorry, it's just—look, this is all pretty sudden. Please. Give me a chance."

She paused, listening, and I could tell she wanted to be convinced.

"If I stuff this up, I'll be kicking myself for the rest of my life—and I don't know if I can deal with all the weird looks that'll get me. Let's just take things slowly, okay? We'll start with the easy stuff. What's your last name?"

Jasmine still looked fraught, but she slumped back against the bookcase. "Shaw. Troy, we can't ignore the elephant in the room."

"No, but if we're quiet, maybe he won't trample us."

"I appreciate what you're doing, but the way I am… it's not something that can be overlooked. It's not going to be that easy."

"You're a redhead," I pointed out. "I don't expect *anything* to be easy."

Jasmine Shaw seemed wryly amused by my cheek, but her eyes remained troubled.

"I need to think about this. Why don't you ask Paddy about my… condition. We'll talk again when you come back. If you ever do."

I reached for her, but she was gone in a sorry flash of crimson. My legs trembled with the need to follow, but I knew she needed space. I was like a diver ascending too fast toward a glowing surface, the bends breeding bubbles in my body, and she must have felt much the same.

The knot in my stomach had not released itself by the time I reached the counter and handed my book to Paddy.

"So, I was talking to Jasmine," I ventured.

"Yes," Paddy said, as if this were patently obvious.

"She's a lovely woman."

"None more lovely, and I've met my fair share. You should know I'm quite protective of her, actually."

"Good." I took my change, noting the new steel in Paddy's eyes. "We've really hit it off, but she's worried about her, uh… circumstances."

"Is that right?"

"Yeah. She told me to ask you about her?"

Paddy sighed and creaked to his feet. "Well, I suppose it was just a matter of time, really. The world's so curious these days. No corner we won't pry into, no stone we'll leave unturned. The irony is that books have surely played their part in all this, since they taught us to thirst for knowledge. You follow?"

I did, as Paddy ambled down the side wall of the shop and occasionally nudged a jutting paperback into line. The floor groaned beneath us, then again on the other side of the room a few seconds later, and I thought of a pair of yawning poltergeists.

"Now, Jasmine—there's a funny thing. When I bought this place, I found her living in the storeroom. I thought she must have been a squatter, but that wasn't it at all. She was just *here*. It felt as much her place as mine, so I gave her a job—my daughter-in-law was going to do it, but I won't be making a pregnant woman's life any harder. Jasmine's my Girl Friday, and I couldn't ask for better."

"She says she never leaves."

"True enough. She's here when I lock up at night, and when I get here in the morning—"

Paddy paused, staring at something, until my presence at his shoulder reminded him to clear the aisle. We were standing at the back wall of the shop now, where Paddy frowned and ran his finger along the rim of a small aquarium that I hadn't noticed yesterday. Angelfish drifted aimlessly in clear water, and fronds of fauna danced to the stream of filter-blown bubbles.

"Yes?" I prompted.

"She's waiting for me," Paddy mused, picking up a jar with a hole-punched lid as if he'd never seen it before. Worms writhed in slow motion against the glass, blindly taking stock of their prison. "With the coffee machine on, ready for go."

"I'm afraid I still don't understand."

"Then you'll just have to wait, won't you?" Paddy replaced the jar and looked up at me like a stern uncle. "Let her tell you in her own time, if at all. And if she decides not to, then maybe you don't drop by here for a while—and when you do, you keep yourself to yourself. And that goes for anything you've heard here, too—I'll thank you to keep mum, and not cause us any grief."

"The last thing I want to do is make any trouble," I said. My sincerity must have been apparent, for Paddy gave a nod.

"Then maybe we're not wrong to have high hopes for you, lad."

Paddy turned back to the fish tank, refreshing his frown, and I took the hint. I made my way to the front door, and this time the chime didn't sound like the end of a round at all. *Strike two*, it seemed to say, but I felt the bravado of a man willing to risk everything on that last pitch. And why not? After all, that shape was back at the window to watch me depart, pale fingers held to a mouth that hid behind a fall of hair all aflame, burning for me like a lost and lonely fire.

Yes, I decided: that felt just right.

A lost and lonely fire.

Nine hours later, I was rubbing my hands together against the chill of the night air and wondering if this was such a good idea.

An hour ago, I'd received a call from an unfamiliar number. Silence—well, almost. I could hear someone breathing on the other end of the line, torn between speaking or hanging up, until a quiet *click* cut them off. If my life was as neatly plotted as any of the books on my shelves, there was only one person it could have been.

So here I was, peering in through the front door of Brought to Book as midnight approached and trying not to feel like a stalker as I rapped the wood three times, another three. The front room was dark, but I could see a hint of light far back in the shop, and soon a wavering glow appeared between two rows of shelves and made its way toward me. The door unlocked and crept open, the muted tinkle of its bell sounding incongruous by night.

"Troy, what are you doing here?" Jasmine whispered—concerned, but not afraid. Flickering flames danced atop the three-pronged silver candelabra she carried in one hand.

"Waiting for you to invite me in?"

She paused a moment, regarding me as if I were a persistent but pleasant vampire, then stepped back and held the door for me. I edged inside and tried not to knock over a stack of Larsson as she turned to regard me with a curiosity so intense it was almost intimidating.

"Why are you here?"

I pointed at the candelabra. "Isn't that kind of a fire hazard?"

"I'm an old-school kind of gal," Jasmine replied, defensive. "Now, will you please answer my question before I start assuming the worst?"

I put up my hands to show I meant no harm. "I'm here because I wanted to talk to you. And besides, that phone call… it was you, wasn't it?"

Jasmine gave a wry smile. "Yes. Your number was on the card. I wanted to talk to you, too."

"Well, then."

We stared at each other for a moment, speechless. Two brief meetings, and now here we were standing in the shop in the middle of the night, admitting our mutual desire to reach out. It had to *mean* something—the thing I so badly wanted it to be.

"What did you want to say to me?" Jasmine asked, her voice soft.

I racked my brain for the right words, then just went for it. "I wanted to say that… I think you should put those candles down for a minute."

"Um, okay. Why?"

"Because I'm about to kiss you, and you're going to want your hands free."

Jasmine stared at me for a long moment, and I wondered if I was going to end the night with scorched eyebrows and a restraining order. Then, without dropping her gaze from mine, Jasmine reached out and perched the candleholder on a stack of Evanovitch.

Her lips were soft as her voice and sang me just as sweet a tune. Jasmine swooned into my embrace like a virtuous Victorian heroine, her body just the right size for the cradle of my arms. The moment was page-perfect, as nothing real ever was—nothing but this.

Jasmine took my hand, led me into the second room where our previous assignations had taken place, through a rear doorway I hadn't yet had time or leisure to notice. We entered a storeroom, where yet more shelves marched along the left wall under the gauzy yellow glow of a single naked globe. A kitchen unit took up the nearest corner, yielding ground to a bar fridge and a coffee machine that stained the air with the aromatic brown of its spit. A two-seater sofa sat against the right-hand wall under a rumpled blanket and a splayed copy of *The Land of Laughs*. Old promotional posters adorned much of the back wall, and I smiled to see that a large portion of it had been painted to look like the cover of a classic leather-bound book, its fake hide embossed with an unfamiliar title: *I Didn't Break the Lamp*.

We fell upon the couch together like two puzzle pieces that had finally found their partners. Everything fit perfectly—my mouth to hers, her jaw to my palm, the sprawl and tuck of our legs—and my fevered thoughts soon began to focus on a deeper connection.

"Wait," she muttered, turning away in my arms. "Before we can go on, I need to tell you what I… what I think I am."

"I think you're just perfect," I breathed. "You're almost too good to be true."

That remark provoked a laugh harsher than I would have liked. "There may be a reason for that. I've had plenty of time alone to think, and I reckon I've figured it out. Why I don't feel complete. Why I can't remember anything other than my name and a few basic details about my past. Why nothing outside of this shop seems like it's known to me.

"Troy… I don't think I'm *real*."

I squeezed her, gentle but firm. "I beg to differ."

"Seriously! I have flesh, I have feelings, and I exist—but I'm not real. I'm *fiction*. I'm a character from one of these books that's just got up and started walking around and pretending like it's a person."

I frowned, thrown by her conviction. "How could that possibly be true?"

"I don't know."

"Yet you seem convinced."

"It just *feels* right—like you do. I feel like a story wrapped in skin, only I don't know which one and I don't know how it's supposed to go, and I'm scared to find out how it ends."

From anyone else, this irrational line of thought would have come across as peculiar and disturbing—but from Jasmine, it sounded as natural as the cadence of my name in her mouth. So I swallowed it, and it went down smooth.

"Okay. You don't know which book you're from?"

"What do you think I do in this place, night after night? When I'm not working for Paddy—when I'm not sleeping a dreamless sleep or reading to pass the time—I'm searching through every book on every shelf, looking for one that feels like home. I know it's here—I can *feel* it. But it... *moves*. One moment it's like it's right there next to me, but when I look... it's gone."

I was silent for a long moment. Whatever words I was supposed to say here were lost to me, lines I had forgotten or never been given to read in the first place.

"You don't believe me," she sighed, a desolate melody.

"Actually, I do, though I couldn't tell you why. I know we've just met, but I trust you, Jasmine—and I believe you."

She turned back, stared deep into me. I saw her seeing it, accepting it, and I could feel despair lifting from her like a ghost banished by the strength of our belief.

"Thank you." She kissed me again, shallow but slow, an exquisite exchange of breath. "I don't know where we go from here, but at least we're going together."

"By the sound of it, we need to find your book."

Jasmine didn't seem so certain. "You'd think so. But what happens if I *do* find it? What if I disappear back into make-believe, and all of this was just some sick cosmic joke?"

I frowned. "There's a point. But could you go on like this, knowing there's a chance of discovering the truth and ignoring it?"

She rested her head against mine. "I think I could, if I had you."

We leaned together in silence, but it was nowhere near as quiet inside my head. I knew I risked losing this fresh heaven if I followed my instincts, but another thought had occurred to me: everything that had happened, our meeting and coming together and this bizarre reveal, had happened for a purpose. This last week had been so much like a fantasy that I assumed it was building toward something. The stage had been set, the characters introduced, their plight revealed. I'd read enough to know that two vital elements of our story remained lurking in the wings, waiting for an unknown cue.

Conflict. Resolution.

"Jasmine, who owned the shop before Paddy?"

She pulled away and sat upright. "Fairclough, his name was. An unpublished author, apparently—an eccentric."

"What happened to him?"

"He disappeared about a year ago."

"Well, that's not ominous or anything." I stood, trying not to believe that these details were relevant and failing miserably. "Now—your book. I suppose you've looked in here?"

"Over and over again. It's not here, but it often feels like it is. I can feel it right now."

"In this room?"

"Or somewhere very close by."

I walked over to the shelves—they stood perpendicular to the left wall, taking up that entire side of the room—and wandered along the first aisle.

"What's all this stuff?"

"Books that need pricing, seconds, etcetera. I must have checked them a thousand times."

I walked out of the first aisle and down the second. The books here were from distant generations, with plain timeworn covers that cried out for dustjackets like naked old ladies. As I reached the end, I sniffed and recoiled.

"Ew. What's that smell?"

"Oh, that one spot? I think it's the ventilation."

Sure enough, a grate was punched into the wall above head height. I stepped closer and noted that the odour grew stronger. Elements of that scent rang distant warning bells—must, dust, a hint of rot. I reached out and tapped the wall beneath the grate; the plaster gave a quiet, hollow response. Rapping the wall on either side of the grate produced a thicker, duller sound. I bounced my knuckles down the plaster and found that the hollow ring followed me to the floor.

"Does this place have a basement?"

Jasmine frowned. "No. At least, Paddy's never mentioned one."

I turned back to the wall and gave it one last knock at ankle height. "See, the ventilation shaft runs down into the floor. I don't know much about construction, but I don't see why that would be the case if there was nowhere for it to go."

"Yes, but you don't just miss a basement, Troy. We'd have found it by now."

"Any other rooms?"

"A tiny bathroom behind the Non-Fiction section. Definitely no trapdoors there."

I looked down at the floorboards, but they were unbroken by hidden hatches. "So—if there *is* a basement, it's probably accessed from here."

"There are no other doors, so clearly there *isn't.*"

"No other doors," I mused, staring across the room. "Unless—"

"What is it?" Jasmine stood beside me, following my gaze, and watched as I stepped over to the large book painted on the back wall. About seven feet tall, and half that across. A very familiar shape.

"A book is a doorway, isn't it?" I muttered, sliding my hand across the cover until my fingers reached the edge. "Ah! There's a crack here—and it's perfectly vertical."

My fingers followed the crevice up to the top edge of the painted book, where it became a right angle, then back down until it reached the point where one would normally expect to find a doorknob—and there, secreted in a natural knot of wood, was a small latch. My finger twitched it back, and then we were stepping away as the door painted like a book swung slowly open.

"You were right," Jasmine breathed.

"Get used to that."

She backhanded my arm, a gentle warning. "Save the quips, dear. You *know* we're going to have to go down there now, right?"

The door opened onto what must once have been a cupboard. Now it was bare, unremarkable except for the square hole in the floor and the wooden steps inside that dim mouth. I caught an echo of the scent that had wafted out of the ventilation shaft.

"Yeah. I know."

"Creepy dark secret basement. I didn't know when I was well off."

I gave her a queasy smile. "You got a torch?"

Jasmine returned to my side with her candelabra and a shrug of apology.

"If you don't mind, I'll take that and go first."

"Be my guest." She handed me the trident of flickering light, and the humour vanished from her voice. "Just be careful, okay?"

I grasped her hand and gave it a gentle squeeze. "Stay close to me."

We shuffled into the shallow cupboard, and I had to summon my nerve to take that first step down into the darkness. All that seemed to lie ahead was more black, but her presence behind me was like a shot of Dutch courage for my soul. We descended slowly, tentatively, and by the time we stepped off the wooden ladder, we could see enough of the basement to wonder afresh what the hell we were doing.

The stairs had come down parallel to the wall, and where they ended, the lower mouth of the ventilation shaft gaped high in the crumbling brick. This opening was larger, almost as tall as Jasmine, and the grate had long ago been ripped aside; it lay on the floor beneath, dusted with loose pages that had been discarded like old snakeskins. A chain dangled from the ceiling, and I was hardly surprised to find that pulling it did not produce an illuminating result.

We moved deeper into the basement, its shadows peeled back by the candlelight, and saw it was in a state of supreme disarray. Yet more bookcases dominated the space, only these had fallen on their backs and sides and lay among the spilled guts of a thousand books. Piles and piles of these littered the room, demanding attention from unwary feet. Dust gritted beneath our shoes as we trod to the centre of the basement, and I saw that it was shaped into broad swathes that cut across the cement.

"Look," Jasmine whispered, pointing to the far end of the shadow-cloaked room. Here a writing desk had been shunted to one side, and in its place was the biggest pile of books yet. It stood five feet tall and a dozen wide, open in the centre like a miniature volcano, only that wasn't lava glistening in the candlelight. Strings of some viscous fluid traced illegible patterns across the books in the centre of the—

"What is it?" Jasmine asked.

"Not sure, but… the word *nest* springs to mind."

A sharp intake of breath from my side. "What?"

"I suspect that not all the noises you've been hearing were the place settling."

Jasmine's wide eyes shone in the dim. "Troy—my book. I can feel it nearby, but it's not here."

"Well, no point in sticking around, then. Shall we—"

"Hang on!" She raised her free hand, curled it into an uncertain fist. "It just moved again."

"Where is it now?"

"Close. Not in here, but nearer than before."

I cleared my throat. "Upstairs for a coffee? My shout—"

"And again! It's closer still. *Very* close."

We exchanged an anxious look, then turned and hurried back toward the steps, clutched hands shaking at some dire import of which we were barely aware. We heard a thump and a coarse slither, and I had just enough time to recognise that both had a hollow, metallic ring to them that suggested the ventilation shaft.

And then something massive and pale shot out of the gaping mouth in the wall, crashing to the floor mere feet away as it slid into the basement.

We shrieked, pivoting on our heels to keep the creature in sight. Its body was so *long*, twenty-five feet or more and oddly segmented, racing around us in a tight circle. The candelabra allowed only fleeting views of the monster, but I realised with a jolt that its bulk appeared to be crafted out of paper—no, *books*, thousands of them, shaped and slicked with that glistening substance and crushed together into a massive annelid form. The creature's back was firmer, darker, and I was too shocked to be surprised when I noted that it was formed out of hardcovers that rose in smooth ridges like scales from the thing's soft, pulpy belly.

"Troy!" Jasmine screamed as the colossus circled us, so long it could loop its entire body around us and leave no gap for escape, its unseen head tight on its tail like some monstrous Ouroboros. We stumbled on the spot, hands clutched so tightly they might never be parted.

Then one end of the thing lifted, jerking blindly up and around toward us. I thought of the eyeless worms twisting in their jar upstairs, but only until that blunt head split in three to reveal a deep and terrible mouth. I stared down its slick, page-lined throat, stunned to see that it had *teeth*, or at least splintered shafts roughly crafted from human bones that dripped with the same alien spit that held this thing together, shocked to realise that this maw was looming closer and closer and it was coming for *me*—

"Fire!" Jasmine screamed. I wasted a split-second thinking she meant me to use a gun I didn't have, and then my right arm spasmed upward and thrust the candelabra toward that gaping gullet. The creature recoiled from the dancing flames, and that awful mouth snapped shut, leaving only a dog-eared crack that dribbled silvery spume to the floor. Emboldened, I lunged forward with the candles, and the beast returned to its rapid circling. We turned to keep its head in sight, wary of another attack, and then the thing reared up like a cobra, towering over us as its mouth split open and bared broken-bone teeth once more. I realised its next move would be to crash down upon us, mash our bodies to paste against the dust and crush out the candles, and I froze.

Then Jasmine's hand slipped from mine.

"I see it!" she cried, and then she was hurrying *forward*, toward the thing's exposed belly. I gasped and lunged after her, thrusting the candelabra toward the pale pages of its underside, and the creature flinched, twisted, decided to come at us from another angle. But before it could do so, Jasmine had reached it and was straining upward with one hand. In the centre of the great worm's body, where one might assume to find its heart, a small red triangle jutted from the pulped paper like a tiny spike, and I realised it was the corner of a book—*the* book. Jasmine grasped it tightly as the beast tried to slide around us, and its momentum caused the item to burst free. She fell awkwardly onto her rump, her prize clutched in one hand—

And the giant abruptly ceased to be. The column of unnatural flesh broke apart into its composite volumes, and I threw myself over Jasmine as our foe became a torrential downpour of books. Edges and spines rained upon me in a merciless and bruising avalanche, and I swore loudly as each drove me closer to the floor, crushing Jasmine beneath my bulk.

Within seconds, it was all over. I dug myself free of the sea of books, relieved to see that the candelabra had somehow avoided the barrage. Beneath me, Jasmine groaned and sat up, victory clutched tightly to her chest. Our eyes met, and realisation dawned: we were alive, and we were together, and we'd won. We shared a tired and grateful kiss, then sat back on the shifting sands of paper and tried to deal with what had happened—the fact of that bizarre creature's very existence, and its sudden end.

"So that's you, then?" I asked eventually, nodding at her prize.

"Feels like it." Jasmine pulled it away from her chest and looked closely at it for the first time. "That's odd. I expected it to be a proper book."

The tome appeared to be a red exercise book, like that of a school student. She flicked the cover over, and I could see a title handwritten on the front cover in neat strokes of black ink.

The makeshift manuscript was called *A Lost and Lonely Fire.*

Jasmine gasped, and the book fell shut. She dropped it in her lap and stared at it for a few seconds, hands held to her mouth.

"What is it?" I asked. "What did you read?"

Slowly, she raised her head and met my eyes. The dancing light of the candles made her lip appear to tremble, but then I realised it wasn't the light after all. The sinking sensation in the pit of my stomach only deepened with every second Jasmine remained silent.

And then she told me.

At a quarter to nine the next morning, the doorbell tinkled to announce Paddy's arrival in the shop. The tantalising strains of fresh coffee filled the back room, ready for his morning ritual, and I had a feeling we'd all be needing the caffeine more than usual today.

"Jasmine?" he called. "Top of the morning to you, my dear, but I'm afraid we need to—"

He paused in the doorway, his gaze flicking to me and hardening in suspicion.

"—talk," he finished.

Jasmine nodded. "Yes, Paddy. We've got a lot to tell you."

"Good. You first, Troy, and you can start by telling me why it is that when I looked up your business—the one on the card you gave Jasmine—I could find no trace of it. Nor, as it turns out, any trace of *you.*"

We exchanged a look of weary knowledge, and Jasmine held up what we'd found below. "Paddy, I found the book. *My* book."

"You did?" He stepped forward and took the extended tome, frowning at the plain red cover. Its title and author were penned neatly on the front: *A Lost and Lonely Fire*, by James A. Fairclough.

"Oh, my," Paddy murmured.

"He didn't disappear," Jasmine said. "He was in the basement the whole time."

"Well, of all the—hang on. *What* basement?"

I rose from the couch and crossed to the painting that Paddy's predecessor had used to hide his refuge, and the older man gasped as the book's cover swung open to reveal the hidden cupboard.

"Well, bugger me! How on earth did I miss that?"

"We think he died down there at his desk, working on this book." Jasmine passed her boss a cup of steaming coffee. "And since no one knew about the basement, there he stayed. And then… something happened."

We told him what we'd faced down there in the darkness, and I could see Paddy's mind reflexively shrugging it off, insisting it was impossible. A giant worm made of books, with this all-important work at the heart of it? Sharp and jagged bones for teeth, with the creature's dissolution revealing the rest of Fairclough's disassembled skeleton spread throughout its unbelievable bulk? His skull down there right now, resting on a copy of *Something Wicked This Way Comes*?

"Codswallop," he blurted.

Jasmine gave a sympathetic smile. "I know, it's ludicrous. But it's true—you can go check for yourself. But first, read a little of that."

With a sniff of bemusement, Paddy put down his coffee and flipped open the cover, muttering under his breath as he skimmed the opening handwritten paragraphs.

A bell chimed above Troy's head as he entered Brought to Book for the first time, like a carillon calling everyone who entered to worship, and he instantly felt at home.

The front room of the shop was dominated by a phalanx of looming shelves that left little room between for the curious, and every inch of the place was stuffed with books—legions of paperbacks standing to attention in ragged rows, hardcovers stacked in piles that admitted only a hint of the wall behind them, fat battered books and slim shiny books and everywhere, everywhere books. Even the counter was lurking beneath towers of prose, and Troy might not have noticed it at all were it not for the man sitting on the other side.

Paddy looked up and indignantly muttered, "A boiled egg?", then skipped ahead.

The ceiling above let out a long creak that sounded like a haunted house protesting the tread of an unseen foot.

"Don't mind that. It's just the old place settling."

"I thought you were going to say it's just the resident ghosts wandering about."

Jasmine looked so distant for a moment. "You know, I really think I'd like that. I'd enjoy the company."

He skipped forward to the last pages that contained writing, and I remembered how the story abruptly ended.

We fell upon the couch together like two puzzle pieces that had finally found their partners. Everything fit perfectly—

Paddy closed the book, massaging his temple. "So, what are you trying to tell me?"

"I was right all along," Jasmine sighed. "I'm not real. Fairclough invented me for his book… and not only that, but he gave me a love interest."

Paddy stared at me, and I tossed back a what-can-you-do shrug.

"*Both* of you are fictional characters?"

"Yes. After Fairclough died, his work somehow came alive—*we* came alive. And acted out his story."

"It's clear to me now that whatever life I thought I had outside this plot is fake." I felt chagrined, even offended by this until I met Jasmine's eyes. "No friends, a mere sketch of a past—I don't know anything about that business I'm supposed to work for. I only existed to serve this narrative, to fall in love with this woman."

"We know this is a lot to dump on you," Jasmine said.

"Ah, well. It's not like I didn't know *something* weird was going on." Paddy realised that he hadn't taken a single sip of his coffee, a situation he was quick to remedy. "I mean, Jasmine's condition, and then… the odd thing here and there. Like the fish tank—last time I saw that thing, it was empty, and I was tossing it in the bin. Then yesterday, there it was again, full of fish. So sure, I believe you. But what happens now?"

"We're not sure," Jasmine said. "We thought we might vanish— but here we are. And then we thought it was because Fairclough never wrote an ending for us, never gave us closure. But—"

Paddy flipped open the book, consulted the first page again, and his spotted brow crinkled.

"But… none of this makes sense. Why would Fairclough hide away in the basement and write a story about the two of you meeting in his own shop? And if he liked you enough to give you a charming romance, why did he turn into some worm thing and attack you after he died? And *how*? And, more to the point: how is it that *I'm* in this story, too? I never met the fella."

I took a deep breath. Of *course* he would ask the pointed questions—sharp, was old Paddy—but the answers weren't easy to give.

"We've been talking about that. You're right, there are too many inconsistencies for all this to really click. Why would Fairclough keep so many books in a basement he could only access via secret door, and how did he get the bookcases down there? How did no one realise that the painted book was a door? How did Jasmine and I fall in love so swiftly and easily? It's almost as if this whole thing, Fairclough included, is *another* story—one that still needs a bit of work."

Paddy blinked. "So, *I'm* fictional, too? Utter bollocks."

"You have a wife, a pregnant daughter-in-law," I said. "What are their names?"

He opened his mouth to reply, but no words were forthcoming. I saw the realisation—the horror—dawning in his eyes.

"I'm so sorry," Jasmine said. "Fairclough never bothered to give them names—and neither did *his* creator. Well... *ours*."

He heaved out a long, groaning sigh. "Great. I can only imagine what the missus will say when I tell her we're not real and she hasn't even a name. But what you're saying is... Fairclough isn't behind it all? He's just another character?"

Jasmine nodded. "We're a story within a story."

I displayed another notebook I'd found in the basement, a blank one that I'd filled with my own scrawl. "And now I've transcribed the whole thing, Fairclough's manuscript and the things Jasmine and I did where he left off—and it's in first person. Now his tale is *ours*—and maybe one day, we'll write ourselves free."

"A story within a story within a story. But how can you believe you'll free yourself from that story when you know *someone's writing you saying that*? Oh, my head hurts." Paddy slurped his coffee, grimacing. "How can that feel so hot if I'm not even real? Oh, stop it, the pair of you. I think I need a long lie down."

We sat and watched him try to cope, holding both book and coffee, and I wondered what would happen should he spill the scalding hot latter onto the former. Would Jasmine and I scream as the skin melted off our bones, destroyed along with the book? I shuddered at the morbid thought, reminded that it wasn't truly mine. Whoever was behind all this must have had a few bent spokes in their wheel.

"Well, it'll take more than not being real to keep Padraic O'Shaughnessy down, that's for sure. What will we do now?"

"The shop seems real enough—people come in every day, and surely not all of them are just sketched-in background detail. For now, could you handle having *two* live-in employees?" Jasmine held a dignified plea in her gaze. "We've nowhere else to go."

"Of course," he replied. "We're not real, so what's it matter, anyway? And at least you'll have thousands of ways to pass the time."

"We'll work something out eventually," I said. "Let's see where the plot takes us. But for now… living in a bookshop alongside the woman I was literally made to be with? Couldn't really ask for more than that, could I?"

"No, indeed." Padraic O'Shaughnessy cleared his throat and deepened his voice. "And with that, Paddy gave the young lovers a smile, wished them well, and went about his work for the day."

He paused in the doorway, grinned, and gave us an ending.

"And they all lived happily ever after!"

TROY is a man. He has a job with a company. He likes to read and talk to pretty women.

MATTHEW R. DAVIS can never just walk past a second-hand bookshop, so his home increasingly resembles one. He's had over forty short stories published thus far, with his first collection, *If Only Tonight We Could Sleep*, due in 2019. He has acted as a judge for the Australian Shadows Awards and the Aurealis Awards, and his work has been shortlisted for both (these occurrences are unrelated). A dossier on his behaviour and crimes has been assembled at matthewrdavisfiction. wordpress.com. Like Troy, he is in love with a redhead, but in his case, a happy ending is by no means guaranteed.

WHEN I HELPED

An account by Lucy,
AS PROVIDED BY VERONICA BRUSH

Whenever nightmares woke me up at night and made me afraid to try to sleep again, my imaginary friend was there. When the closet door slid open, she'd be there, sitting on the floor, waiting to talk to me. We'd sit on our respective sides of the opening and whisper to each other.

I'd tell her all about the monsters in my dream. Even though the recollection of their terrible forms scared me, there'd be no fear in her multiple eyes.

"You don't have to be afraid," she'd say. "I could take on a monster like that."

And I believed her.

Sometimes I wondered if she ever had nightmares, sleeping alone on the other side of my closet door. What kind of monsters would an imaginary friend have in her dreams? I wondered if I could be as brave as she was and boldly offer to face the monsters that terrified her.

But I never asked her.

Sometimes I would get bullied. They made fun of me for how I looked and dressed. My imaginary friend was always there to tell me not to cry.

She'd hug me with her extra-long arms that grew out of the wrong part of her torso and she'd say, "People get jealous and attack the person they wish they were. They wouldn't want to pick on you if you weren't something special!"

And I believed her.

Sometimes I wondered if she had people who made fun of her. With my wild imagination, I had made her like nothing you had ever seen. She was one of a kind, but it made her beautiful. She was so special, I thought for sure others would be jealous of her.

But I never asked her.

As I grew older, I had less time for imaginary things. But still, sometimes, when my heart was broken, or my dreams seemed impossible, I'd sit beside the open closet door and share my tears with my imaginary friend.

Tears would build up in her eyes, too, and she would say softly, "It will get better. It hurts right now, but this pain is how you learn and grow into the person you were meant to be."

And I believed her.

Sometimes I wondered if she had dreams she chased and a heart that could break. I felt certain this imaginary friend who shared my tears must know how much disappointment could sting.

But I never asked her.

I was becoming an adult when she came to me at the closet door to say goodbye.

She said, "I have to go now. But don't be sad. You're all grown up and you don't need me anymore."

"Why?" I asked. "Where do you have to go?"

She smiled at me. She had many, many teeth, but they weren't scary teeth.

"I have to go to college now," she explained.

I shook my head, not understanding. "What's a college?"

How could my imaginary friend have things to do that I didn't know about?

My imaginary friend said, "It's a place that humans like me go to learn things. Outside this house that holds the closet that you live in, there is a whole world."

I tried to imagine a world living outside my closet, full of unique imaginary friends like her, with only two arms and long legs that bend in the middle and bodies that weren't covered in fur. It made me laugh to think about and she laughed, too.

She said, "I've grown up, too, and I'm ready now to face that world out there on my own. But first I wanted to thank you for all the help you gave to me."

I argued, "I never helped you. You were always the one who helped me. You talked me through all my monsters and my bullies and my failures. And I always wondered if you faced these problems, but I never asked."

She smiled again. "Sometimes it's easier to face another person's monsters than our own. So my monsters became your monsters, and in that way, I could dare to face them all."

My imaginary friend stepped in from where she lived, outside the closet, and she hugged me one last time.

She said, "You were my path to bravery, and now I am ready to be brave on my own."

And I believed her.

LUCY is a homebody, still living in the house she grew-up in. It was in this house that Lucy met J., the friendly monster who lived on the other side of the closet door and the inspiration for this story. Though they have both now grown up and no longer live just a closet door apart, Lucy and J. still stay in touch.

VERONICA BRUSH is the author of the novellas *First Grave on Mars* and *Second Deception on Mars*, a murder mystery series set on the red planet. Her work has been featured in publications including *Apex Magazine, Mad Scientist Journal,* and the anthologies *Bubble Off Plumb* and *Do Not Go Quietly.* She also has an occasional blog, www.ThemelessWriting.com.

LUDWIG

An account by Hild Lovig,
AS PROVIDED BY SAM FLEMING

Despite what you might have heard about our—excuse the scare quotes—"lifelong bond," here's the thing about me and Ludwig. When I was little, I didn't have an imaginary friend, I had an imaginary bully. She was a little girl of my age, who looked just like me, and took great delight in being cruel. This included doing things to make my parents furious, like punching my little brother. One day, when I was about thirteen, Ludwig showed up and wrapped all two hundred of his copper-bladed arms around this evil version of me. There was a warm light, like a camera flash made of lava, and then she was gone.

On good days, I could convince myself my parents' difficult marriage led me to dissociate, and Ludwig's appearance was me realising torturing myself was unhealthy. I tried to make the good days coincide with visits to the psychiatrist.

Then there were the days when Ludwig came out with something I couldn't possibly know, but which made so much sense it was like the ground lurched beneath my feet as reality rolled with the punch.

On that particular day—I assume you want me to start there—I was in a bar, having a drink with my girlfriend, Gloria.

"She's not really into you," Ludwig told me.

I didn't need to stop myself scowling at him. You don't hold down a job and stay out of in-patient care if you're constantly reacting to your imaginary friend in public. He hung over Gloria's shoulder, a constantly-furling feather star made of sunset reflected in copper, with his countless eyes, each one a tiny haematite seed pearl, watching everything everywhere always. The big mirror on the far wall of the bar held his reflection, even though nobody could see him but me. I'd always wondered about that, about being able to see his reflection.

"I'm not a vampire, Hild. We've talked about this," he used to say.

Sometimes I worried people would see him reflected in my eyes, but no one had. Not as far as I knew. I'm pretty sure he watched inside my head all the time. It was part of why it's so hard to be absolutely sure what he was.

I tried to focus on Gloria: tall, slim, perfectly made-up, a fashion sense that belonged in a magazine. I had no idea what she saw in me, but she'd made the first move.

"Are you actually looking at me or just pretending to?"

I remember her nails: flawless glossy ovals of scarlet against the table. Her hair hung in gleaming ringlets of luscious black, framing a face as architecturally stunning as a vaulted cathedral, and I wondered again what we were doing together.

I did that a lot.

"I'm doing my best," I said. "I can either pay attention or look you in the eye. I'd rather pay attention."

"Of course," she replied, sounding mollified but not entirely convinced, which was pretty much par for the course. "So I'm going to meet Cassandra and Alex for cocktails, and I'll probably stop over at Alex's place after, so don't wait up." She rummaged in her bag—she claimed she was paranoid about forgetting her keys—and stood.

"Okay," I said. "I'll see you tomorrow."

She leaned down and kissed me, all vanilla and peach. Admiring glances and the odd whistle followed her as she left.

I drained my glass, keen to get home to peace and quiet. It was that hour after work when everyone decides they need a drink. I nudged and shoved my way to the door and stepped outside. It was cold that night, raining off and on, everything huddled and hunkered and thinking about when winter would be over.

"If she's not into me," I said to Ludwig, "why'd she hit on me in the first place?" He was swimming about an arm's length to the right of my head and slightly ahead of me. I remember watching his spinning fire reflected in the puddles and empty car windows and being sad I couldn't show other people how glorious he was.

I'd meant it rhetorically, but he asked, "Do you really want to know?"

"Have you been spying on her?"

"I look out for you. Time works differently for me, you know that. I followed the trail from your intersection."

"Go on then. Why? And then maybe you can tell me this week's lottery numbers."

He didn't dignify the last with a response. It was an old, old needle, tired and clichéd. "You're easy, Hild. You're safe. She thinks you're so desperate for a lover that you'll let her get away with anything."

"Well, thanks."

"That's not what *I* think," he told me. "I think you're beautiful and amazing and clever and worth at least two hundred of her."

Sometimes, when the doubts became overwhelming, I wondered how it was possible for me to have an imaginary friend who said such nice things and still have rock-bottom self-esteem. It made me angry—with him for saying them, with myself for having a brain so broken it couldn't believe its own positive messages.

You see, back then, I didn't know for sure whether he was real or not. Sometimes I wonder if I do now, after all the years in which I learned to pretend to be certain he wasn't.

"Did you pick this nugget out of her brain?"

"She was talking to someone called Juno."

Reality took it in the gut. I stopped. I stood in the middle of the sodden pavement with rain sticking my hair to my head and the shush of passing cars faded to intermittent white noise.

"They weren't just talking," Ludwig added.

Juno. One-time best friend, who vanished from my life without a word when we moved to high school. How could Gloria and Juno even know each other, never mind be sleeping together? I tried to tell myself this was another example of my broken brain trying to sabotage its own happiness.

"Behind you!" Ludwig shouted.

I turned without thinking and saw a small, moustachioed man in a green and rust twill suit with a matching deerstalker hat. He was already reaching for me. When I tried to kick him, he neatly sidestepped and pressed what felt like an old flannel over my face. I smelled red wine, rotting paper, something like rum. My head began pounding, and my limbs went weak. He held it there for, I don't know, maybe around twenty seconds, while I tried to fight him off with arms that had turned into over-cooked noodles. A van door clunked open, and there was a sharp pain in my right thigh.

The man didn't say a word, but Ludwig screeched like a banshee as I was bundled into the van on top of a pile of cushions and blankets. The door slammed shut and everything went black.

I woke up in a small cell, shivering and sick like I had a hangover. I lay half on my front on a single bunk resembling something from an army barracks, head propped against one arm. The pillow was white, crisp and rough; the sheets and khaki woollen blanket still tucked tightly under the mattress. White paint turned the smooth walls a kind of dull eggshell. It resembled a monastic cell stripped of iconography, until I saw the metal toilet crammed into the far corner. The bed stood against one wall, and within arm's reach was a low table on which stood a plastic jug of water, an enamel mug with water already in it, and a note. A mirror dominated the wall opposite the bed.

You've probably seen the pictures.

There were only two explanations for this situation, and both were enough to foment panic in my bowels.

"Hild," Ludwig said, hoving into view, arms sculling in an agitated fashion, "don't say anything. Not out loud. Read the note."

I'd been kidnapped, or possibly had a break down, dissociated, and ended up in a prison cell or a particularly brutal psychiatric unit, and he wanted me to read a note.

"Read a note? I need to get out of here!"

"Sssh! Read the note!"

My hand was shaking so much I could barely grip the paper, but I managed to unfold it and hold it still enough to read. The text was typed, which made it worse, somehow. You've seen pictures, no doubt.

"GREETINGS! You have been selected for a Very Important Experiment that could have Far Reaching Implications for the Future of Humanity. PLEASE DO NOT BE ALARMED. No harm will come to you! You are Far Too Vital to the Success of this Project. You will be fed and watered and the environmental conditions will be maintained in a state that is Not Detrimental to Human Health. You may be feeling the after-effects of your journey. Proper Hydration will prove Beneficial. The water is Pure and Clean. Do not refrain from consumption! Food will be provided after an Appropriate Time to allow for Your Recovery."

Haarman had signed his name at the bottom in a scratchy European gothic.

As soon as I started to speak, Ludwig interrupted.

"Quiet!" He burled over to seethe a forearm's length above my face. His glow flared and fluttered. "You are being watched and listened to. You are not alone. Inside voice, Hild!"

The inside voice. The one I used to talk to him without being carted away in a tightly-fitting jacket. Forming words inside my head.

What the fuck is going on?

"Firstly, your thief is not a serial killer."

Well, that's a relief. And you know this how?

Ludwig inched closer, his arms spinning with a sound like a moth caught in a metal lampshade. "And he's not a rapist."

Good?

"And you are not the first person kidnapped."

"What?!"

"Be quiet! It is really important that you are quiet."

Fine. I'll be quiet.

It was moments like those I most feared for my sanity. I suppose I generally existed in a kind of quantum state of belief about Ludwig. Maybe he was real, because the experience of him was real. Maybe he was, like the head doctors have insisted, a manifestation of a maladaptive coping strategy for passing as normal, as a functional human. He was the part of me that didn't fit in, and I'd given him a shape, a form—if you can call a mobile crinoid made of copper fire a form—and a voice, to let the rest of me get on with the important business of living life. In the really real world, the latter explanation wields so much more heft than the former, it's hard to argue with it.

Yet there I was, keeping my mouth shut and talking to my imaginary friend instead of hurling myself at the door and screaming blue bloody murder.

"Do you remember when your school insisted on making you see a thinking doctor because your doppelganger was evil?"

You mean they believed I was a psychopath with a split personality and made me see a psychiatrist who agreed I had issues that might indicate problems socially integrating?

"Yes. You told the thinking doctor it was not you, but your invisible bully."

I was eight.

I'd learnt a lot about passing since then.

"Do you know that all your thinking doctors wrote about you, and their writing was collected by other people?"

No, but that happens, right?

And then there were the ground-quaking moments, which forced me to choose between believing either he was real, or the part of me he represented was psychic.

"Do you know that someone paid a human at the place where they investigate how to treat broken thoughts to steal records of people who claimed to have invisible companions?"

Why would I know that?

"Your path intersects with this place, and yet you are ignorant of it. Indeed, it seems to me there is very little humans know."

Also, this other part of me, if that was what Ludwig was, was a bit of an arsehole.

"It would appear this 'doctor'"—he shrugged his arms bilaterally to indicate he was using the term loosely—"is the human buying the theft of those records. There are eleven other people held here. Each one is named in those records."

I like to think that these days, the records would be encrypted, or anonymised. But I don't really put much faith in that, either.

So, fine. What the fuck is going on?

Ludwig rotated through a whole three-sixty. All the way around. That was his equivalent of that thing where you pull yourself to the tallest you can and look down your nose at someone, channelling the spirit of some ancient professor who has just been challenged on an assertion for which he doesn't have reasonable evidence.

"I have yet to determine. I suggest you drink some water and sleep off the effects of whatever poison was introduced to your rotting bag of meat and chemicals."

Like I said. An arsehole.

Some hours later, I don't know how many, a slot opened in the bottom of the door and a tray slid through. It held one of those prison plates, with raw carrots and some sort of green mush corralled into different pens. A piece of black bread stood in lieu of cutlery. There was also a cup of something suspiciously herbal, and an envelope.

I'd already tried the door. It was the kind of solid that doesn't so much as rattle when you whack your shoulder against it. The bruise had gone deep, and it ached like hell.

I wasn't especially hungry, and with Ludwig hanging over my shoulder like an inquisitive parrot, I opened the envelope. There were a further seven envelopes inside, each one neatly numbered, and another note.

Please don't think I was being calm through strength of character—well, unless you subscribe to the idea that Ludwig is me hiding behind two hundred copper-bladed arms and an invisibility cloak. You have to understand, as far as I was concerned, I wasn't alone, and I wasn't alone because I was with an entity who could move through walls and transcend time. Even if he wasn't real, he didn't go away when I stopped believing in him.

"GREETINGS! Please ensure you finish your Meal. I have carefully calculated the correct nutritional Allowance for a long Life Span. Your Meals will be nutritionally Exceptional!

"I have provided you with 7 Sets of Test Materials. When you hear a Bell chime once, look above the Door and you will see a small Window. In the Window is a Number corresponding to one of the sets of Test Materials. TRY IT NOW."

Of course, I did. The "window" was just a small square between the door lintel and the ceiling. When I looked, it was filled with a white card on which someone, I presumed Haarman, had written the number five in chisel tip.

A bell rang. A high-pitched *ding*, like a fancy bicycle bell. Ludwig said, "He's watching you right now."

That doesn't mean anything, I know. I could have figured that out myself without the assistance of an atemporal echinoderm.

I reached for the envelope with the number two on it.

"You won't like it," Ludwig said.

I'm imprisoned in a room that's not much bigger than my bathroom. What's to like?

As soon as I opened the flap on the envelope, an electric shock turned every muscle rigid. Have you ever touched an electric cattle fence? Like that, times a hundred, everywhere at once. It was hot, cold, like being stuck between two enormous magnets lined up to repel but being pushed together by mammoths. It was only just not quite painful enough to be agony. I managed to fling myself at the toilet before vomiting up the water I'd drunk earlier.

"Told you," Ludwig said.

I might have muttered *arsehole* into the toilet bowl.

That's when I heard Haarman's voice. "Subject Twelve! Please follow the instructions! The negative consequence stimulus will not cause lasting damage but is deeply unpleasant! Follow the experimental protocol, and you will be released unharmed."

"When?" I yelled. I was shaking violently, but I was more pissed off then scared, if that makes sense? I've never been scared by the same things that scare other people. Spiders. Ghosts. Clowns.

Myself. That's what I'm frightened of. You know, of just losing the ability to give a fuck and ending up rotting under a box on a street corner getting pissed on by drunks. Or worse.

What's worse? The option where I don't abscond from humanity when I give up on it.

Anyway. I wasn't keen on Haarman's answer.

"Once the experiment is concluded, Subject Twelve, which will be sooner if you comply with your instructions!"

"Give me a bloody minute!" I shouted, and, yeah, telling you this now it just seems ridiculous. This isn't how humans react to being kidnapped and tortured, is it? What can I say? Maybe I watched too many Bond movies as a child.

I crawled across the floor, trying not to flinch each time I put my hand down. I guess my body had more sense than I did. Ludwig helpfully pointed at the correct envelope with one arm, as if I couldn't read, and I opened the number five envelope. I expect you know this already, but number five was the Zener cards. I couldn't remember what they were called, but I knew the wavy lines, circle, square, star, cross. Everyone does, right?

"What am I supposed to do with these?" I asked, still shaking and pissed off.

"Read the rest of your instructions, Subject Twelve!"

I scowled at the mirror, which I'd realised was one of those two-way things—why are they called that, by the way? Two-way? They're only one way. Ludwig swam over and pressed up against the glass.

"It is the human that stole you from the street," he said.

I had guessed, thanks.

The rest of the note—well, you'll have seen it. More randomly capitalised words telling me what I had to do with the contents of each envelope. I had to lay the Zener cards out in an order matching the order of cards laid out somewhere else. Envelope one was Remote Viewing, where I had to describe an object or objects on a table. There was a picture of the table in the envelope. Number two was telekinesis. There were three feathers in there, and I had to place them in a ring painted on the floor, sit in another ring a few feet away, and try to make the feathers move. Number three was telepathy. I had to shout out a word that was supposed to pop into my head from someone else. Number four was… Oh, you can look it up yourself. You get the idea, anyway. A bunch of pretty standard tests for paranormal ability.

I laid the cards out in some random order, and the bell dinged twice. That was it. Later on, when I had my back turned, the hatch in the bottom of the door opened and the tray slid out before I could get there to grab whoever was on the other side. The lights were turned off some time later.

That's how it went. I was… *We* were fed once a day, as I found out from the others later. It might have been nutritionally sound, but it wasn't filling and was deathly dull. At some point the bell would ding, we would do whatever test was shown in the window, and sometimes we had to do more than one. The bell dinged twice to say when a test was completed. If we refused to co-operate, electrocution. As I quickly found out, recidivist that I am, climbing on the bed didn't help. The bed was metal, the sheets and blankets insufficient insulation, the air weirdly humid a lot of the time. The walls were metal under the paint.

You don't really get used to electrocution on that scale.

After that first time, Haarman didn't speak to me again. The worst bit was the boredom. There was nothing to do. No books, no TV. I was alone, except for Ludwig. I couldn't tell what time it was—meals were irregular, and I was sure the light schedules were messing with my circadian rhythms. The room was either too hot or too cold, parched or almost foggy. I hung out by the door after mealtimes, hoping to grab hold of the bastard, but he waited until I fell asleep. He could gas the room, when he needed to. I stopped interfering with the hatch when that started provoking electrocution as well.

I think it only took a week before I began to have trouble keeping my conversations with Ludwig internal, by which I mean seven cycles of light and dark. Half the time, I'd talk out loud, even though I'd meant not to. I think I needed to hear a voice I knew was real and was coming in through my ears rather than possibly being generated inside my brain.

It drove Ludwig nuts. He kept telling me to stop, and I kept forgetting. The more exasperated he got with me, the harder it was for me to stay quiet.

That was when things got weird. Poor performance on the tests resulted in a mild shock, but I could only guess that was the reason, because we were never told whether we were right or not. Odd little messages started arriving with the food. *Why don't you ask your friend to help you?* was the first one. *You don't have to be alone* was another—that one I tore into tiny pieces, because I thought the fucker was trying to get laid—and *Childhood friends are the best friends.*

Ludwig became even more insistent that I use my inside voice, but I was so hungry, so tired. He even threatened to leave, to remove the temptation, and I snapped, "Go on then!" God's teeth, I think I'd have been talking to myself by then even without him.

Ludwig... Look. Given what eventually happened, I'm sure it's tempting to conclude that we should have been able to walk right out of there on the first day. But that's how a human looks at it. Ludwig... Whatever he is—*was*—he didn't think or act the way humans do. The only contact I'd had with Haarman apart from this very hands-off direction for some stupid attempts to prove psychic ability was when he chloroformed me and stabbed barbiturates into my leg. That was enough for Ludwig to figure out why I was chosen, but it wasn't enough for him to do anything else. He talked about intersections and mapping and pathways and resonances a lot.

And, also, I was still in that state of is-he-isn't-he, how can he possibly be what he says he is if he can't even tell me the lottery numbers? If he was this magical being with access to different dimensions or whatever explanation he happened to be using on any given day, why couldn't he help with useful stuff like finding me a way to be independently wealthy, so I didn't have to deal with stupid people all the time? How come his superpowers seemed to be knowing things I couldn't know, but also maybe it was a guess or coincidence, and telling me things I wished a human being would say?

Yeah, sure, my lack of belief might have been the problem, but that's like every Randi millionaire wannabe claiming they couldn't perform because there was too much negative energy emanating from the adjudicators. The most likely explanation for him not being able to do anything measurable and observable was nothing to do with my lack of intersection with lottery balls, whatever that meant. It was that he only existed inside my head.

I'm not sure what happened, exactly. I'd lost track of how long I'd been in there. Ludwig showed a lot of interest in the meal tray one day, swarming all over it like he needed to look at it with every single one of his freaky mirror eyeballs, and touch it with the tip of each of his barbs. I'd lost quite a chunk of weight on this minimum-calorie diet— never did put it back on, and kale still makes me throw up, ha ha—and I was barely holding it together, but it still surprised me when he told me he could help.

"Tomorrow we beat his tests, Hild," he said. "We beat his tests, and we beat him."

He didn't say it like a promise. He said it like he'd seen this bit before and was telling me what happened next.

"Yeah, right," I grumbled, poking the food with one finger. I had a mouthful but couldn't stomach any more green fibrous mush.

"You must eat this."

I don't know what got into me. Some contrary spirit that balked at having my one and only friend ordering me about.

"What if I don't want to?"

"It's important."

"Screw you."

"Place the organic matter inside your mouth and render it suitable for your digestion." He hovered in my face, so close I could feel the heat of him, like an old incandescent bulb, then moved to settle over the back of my head. I couldn't see him, but I *felt* him, felt him climb inside me, his arms working down through my hindbrain into my muscles and ligaments, his barbs twitching against my nerves. That feeling you get, when a fly walks on you, that makes you shudder? It was exactly that, without the freedom to shake it off. It made me want to jump out of my own skin.

He made me eat the food and then he climbed back out. I smashed the tray into the hatch, sobbing and furious.

"Go to bed," he said, and retreated into the corner so I wouldn't have to look at him.

When the lights came on the next morning—I don't honestly know if it was morning, but it's easier to think of it like that—Ludwig wasn't there. He'd been gone before, obviously. It was one of the things that kept the balance of real versus imaginary see-sawing. If he was purely in my head, surely he'd be there whenever I needed or wanted him. He should have been the ultimate in loyal friends. But no, often he was nowhere to be found. I knew that he was still out there, somehow. He was just busy. He had pressing Ludwig business, whatever that might be.

This was different. This was gone. This was like running your tongue around your teeth and finding out you've swallowed three of them in your sleep gone. This was waking up from a bad dream to a doctor telling you there was an accident and he's had to remove your legs gone.

For about three seconds, I felt a profound sense of relief. I even thought, *So, that's what it takes.* Then I came close to panic. It wasn't fear, not exactly. Did you know it's possible to have panic without fear? That kind of anxiety, it's not about fear, any more than the sense you might fall off when you get too close to the edge of a cliff is really about fear. It's lack of faith in yourself. You don't trust yourself not to fall. You don't trust your neuromuscular control not to tip you over the edge even though every single fibre of your accumulated narratives insist you don't want to. Those are the moments when you come closest to understanding that agency is a myth you sell yourself in the service of cohesion.

In that moment, I realised that Ludwig wasn't a symptom of my fragile psychology. He was what kept me functionally sane. Ludwig stood between me and a street corner in the pissing rain. Ludwig stood between me and an expensive defence lawyer offering an insanity plea. I told myself it was fine, I had time, I was trapped in a madman's idea of a test lab, where there were no street corners and nobody to harm. By the time I figured out a way to get out of there, I'd have figured out a way to handle life.

And then he was back. I screamed, "Don't you EVER fucking do that EVER AGAIN you BASTARD!"

I don't know if I meant turning me into a puppet or leaving. Probably both.

"Ssh, Hild. It's all fine. You're fine," he said, and he came close, and his feathers were so soft, so warm, so forgiving, so accepting. Nothing I ever said or did would ever stop him wanting to see me safe and happy, would ever make him angry with me.

But he *was* angry. He was incandescent. I could glimpse this rage so vast it was almost laminar, like I was too small to grasp the full meaning of it, and it was, for a moment, as if Ludwig were really some vast cosmic being who was talking to me through a tiny pinhole for fear of hurting me with his immensity.

"How can you be so big and still care about me?" I whispered.

"Because I do," he said.

The bell dinged at that moment. I looked up. Number five. I was utterly disinterested. I just wanted to go back to hugging Ludwig.

"It's all right, Hild," he said. "Do the test."

I pulled out the cards. I had never got this right. A sequence of five cards matching another five cards? Odds of one in one hundred and twenty. Odds of electrocution? One-nineteen in one-twenty.

Ludwig clatter-hummed next to my right ear. "Circle," he said. "Waves, ten-sided, four-sided, orthogonal intersection."

I laid down the cards. The bell dinged three times. It had never done that before. I looked up. The test window still showed 5. "Wait," Ludwig said.

I waited. A few moments later, the number slipped away, revealing a grey wall for a couple of seconds. A 1 replaced it. Single ding.

"Vase, yellow ball, spoon, cubic puzzle."

"Vase, ball, spoon, Rubik's cube?" I called. Again, three dings. I could hear the excitement in the rapid press of fingers on the button.

Test 2. *Ding.* I put the feathers in the circle farthest from the door, sat myself in the circle nearest it.

Can we do this, Ludwig?

He said, "Do you believe we can do this, Hild?"

I said, "I genuinely do not know, old friend."

He settled over the feathers, and I could not see because all two hundred of his arms were sculling wildly, and his mirror eyes all glinting like bright sun on water when the wind has roughened its skin, and I watched him and felt a strange, easy calm fall over me.

Three dings.

We didn't wait for the number to change in the window. "Say my name," Ludwig told me. "It's all fine."

"Ludwig," I said, and the bell did not stop dinging at three.

He vanished. Instantly, the bell stopped. I waited, as calm as I have ever been. The quality of that state compared to any chemically assisted one, prescribed or self-medicated, was leather seats and fifty-year old port and the comfort of not ever having to worry about money instead of nylon and cheap bourbon and cockroaches in the sink. Even now, I don't know that I can describe it. If the smallest joint on my smallest finger were capable of experiencing emotion, it was the calm I imagine that tiniest fraction of me would feel if I were resolute and focused on an achievable goal I was close to winning.

Ludwig opened the door to my cell. He had climbed inside Haarman's skin and driven his barbs into the man's bones. He moved him around as if he were a mechanical suit, peering out through his tiny, inadequate eyes and fumbling clumsily with his graceless meat sticks. "Come on," he said, and it was perfectly natural for Ludwig's voice to come from Haarman's hijacked throat and enter my head through my own outside ears.

We left the cell and entered the grey corridor I had glimpsed through the number window. Ludwig opened the next cell. Inside that one was Subject Three. We know now that his name was Barry Goldmane, but I didn't see him. I saw a blue and yellow gryphon made of bobcat and salamander called Friddo-Freddo, balanced on his tail and his back feet for height, his mouth wide open to show he was all teeth and fury.

I put myself between him and Ludwig. "Hi," I said in my best Mickey Mouse Club voice. "I'm Subject Twelve. You can call me Hild. My friend Ludwig has—I don't know if there's a technical term for it—commandeered Haarman so we can all get out. Is that okay with you?"

Friddo-Freddo dropped to all fours and Barry peered around him. "Is this a trick?" Barry asked. He was chalk white, his skin clammy. He had burns on his palms, and when he moved, I could tell he was in enormous amounts of pain. From the way his skin hung on him, he'd been a good thirty kilos or more heavier when he was taken. Someone showed me a photograph, later, and I didn't recognise him. Someone showed him a picture of us the police took the day we escaped, a couple of days later. He didn't recognise himself.

The gryphon sniffed me. It tickled, but I stood very still. I wasn't afraid of him.

Barry boggled. "Can you... Can you *see* him?"

"Your friend is called Friddo-Freddo, and if I were lying, he would tell you," I said. "We need to let the others out."

They followed us to the next cell.

"How did you escape?" Barry asked.

"The person thief breached his outer layer and left form code traces in the organic matter he expected Hild to consume," Ludwig replied. "When Hild consumed it, the depth of their intersection intensified exponentially. All the tiny beings that live inside Hild each had an intersection with the code, which created a profoundly useful manipulation weave."

Barry nudged my elbow, keeping me and Friddo-Freddo between him and Ludwig. "What did that mean?"

"I have no idea," I told him, but knowing Ludwig had manipulated me so we could escape eased a weight I'd not yet been able to label.

Ludwig opened the next door. That was Subject Two, whom you'll know as Goh Soo Yin. I didn't see her, but I did see her companion: a blue blanket, spread in the shape of a breaching mobular ray, eyeless but with a mouth like a tiger ripped a hole in the fabric to reveal depthless white as pure as arctic snow.

Friddo-Freddo made the introductions. I don't speak Mandarin, and Ludwig was already on his way to the next door. Later, I'd find out the blanket was called Jaggery.

We kept opening doors, finding traumatised adults and enraged creatures they had dragged out of their childhoods. We found Subject One last. Ludwig wouldn't let me go in, but I didn't have to. Friddo-Freddo, Jaggery, Pippy Pillow, Floster, and the rest of them surged through the open door, and all I could see was a heaving mass of creatures that have never set a weighted foot on the surface of this Earth.

Subject One was in a bad way and couldn't come with us. Turned out he didn't have an imaginary friend. Haarman had got the wrong guy.

Have you ever heard of "felt presence"? It's a phenomenon reported by people who have been isolated and are undergoing hardship. Often it's a relative, alive or dead. Maybe one day science will decide it's a mechanism for humans to preserve sanity, to enable that aggregate of narratives we refer to as self to retain coherence in challenging conditions. These mechanisms persist in modern humans, despite how far we've come from chasing down aurochs with pointy sticks. We evolved, after all, as social animals, and for much of our evolution, we relied on one another to survive. For an obligatory social animal to be separated in a hostile environment, it requires entering a liminal zone, where what is real is less important than what will keep you alive.

Haarman had got it into his head that childhood imaginary friends were related to psychic ability. Too many stories of kids talking about an invisible friend who the parents decide is actually the ghost of a stillborn elder brother, or the kind-hearted but deceased old granny keeping an eye on the family. Of imaginary beings that are angels or past lives or some Egyptian princess. Of brats too precious to be to blame for torturing the family cat or tying a firework to next door's guinea pig, so it must be the demonic entity they insist be laid a place at the dinner table. Ludwig said something about Haarman being a scientist in the war, but that could mean anything. It could mean Ludwig watched a movie about WWII one time and there was an actor in it who resembled Haarman. You can't expect reliability from an immortal pelagic starfish made of plasma.

Haarman bribed someone to grant him access to psychiatric records collected for a study of pathologies and imaginary friends. He picked the imaginary friends most realised, most detailed, the ones that persisted the longest. He tracked us down as adults, and then he tried to bring those imaginary friends back to give us psychic abilities.

I was in there for almost eleven weeks. Marco Corbello, AKA Subject One, had been in there for more than a year. I wasn't alone, I had Ludwig. Ludwig told me that Marco was alone for longer than any human should endure.

We needed to get help, but there was something we had to take care of first.

Barry and Anna—Subject Six—stayed with Marco. The rest of us, including all the creatures who had manifested to keep us sane, gathered in front of what turned out to be an abandoned seminary. Ludwig stood Haarman in the middle of us all and then exited his body. He just climbed out, like a hermit crab swapping real estate, and hovered over his head. Nobody said anything, but we all knew what the options were, and we all knew what we wanted.

Ludwig descended on Haarman, arms flashing like polished bronze knives, there came a moment of brightness the colour of magma, and that was the end of it.

I still don't know how Haarman set it all up. The mirrors. The metal walls. Ludwig could have told me, I guess, but I think I'm not ready. It happened. We escaped. Either I have psychic powers that failed to appear previously, and have remained buried since, or I had an imaginary friend who was enough of an arsehole to intervene only when some other arsehole trespassed on his territory.

Not a great explanation either way, right? That's what I said to the psychiatrist.

I know he didn't tie the knot or kick the stool, but Haarman killed Marco. I don't think the fourteen years commuted to six for good behaviour he'd probably have got in court is sufficient payment for that, do you?

Besides. I don't think Haarman *died*.

Ludwig tells me he sent him to the same place as my evil doppelganger.

I hope she's having fun.

HILD LOVIG was one of the victims of the Haarman kidnapping, aged 22. While the other surviving victims shared their stories extensively (see e.g., Fenton's 216 Days), Lovig has remained reclusive, refusing even to confirm or deny any of the claims made about her by her fellow captives. Now 64, living alone in a remote location, she has finally agreed to tell her story under conditions of strict privacy.

SAM FLEMING lives in the northeast of Scotland with an artistic spouse, an opinionated husky, a number of bicycles most people would consider abnormal, and several invisible friends. When not writing various flavours of speculative fiction focused on unconventional characters, Sam is an environmental scientist being paid to save the world (it's not as glamorous as it sounds). Their work has been published in *Black Static*, *Apex Magazine*, and *Clockwork Phoenix 5*, and is forthcoming in the *Not All Monsters* anthology from Rooster Republic Press. Find more at www.ravenbait.com.

ART BY America Jones

AMERICA JONES is an illustrator and comic artist with a passion for neon colors and queer culture. Catch them being antisocial on social media @thehauntedboy.

NEVER ALONE

An account by Miriam,
AS PROVIDED VIVIAN LI

T oday, you hugged the side of the tree again.

I saw you from my window, the effortless pull of your arms, how they pierced the ground until, shattering, they became a kaleidoscope of blood and dirt. You tore down the sky with your eyes, senseless in your desire. Untamed.

I ran to you then, remember? I asked for your forgiveness, to step in the streams by your feet and drink by your side, the nape of your neck plastered with sweat. I wanted to delve into your soft eyes, to understand something I could never touch. Don't you remember? The day you told me I could never join you, not unless I gave up everything that was solid, everything that was tangible?

You tugged at my hair, unraveled the dark tendrils of the swirling tempest until, shrieking, they collided with the earth. You whispered monsoon rains, your legs against my hips, voice breathing husky into my ears. The air thrummed with your heat. Lightning fell, jagged branches broken, helpless at your feet. You were obsessed with power, with control.

You'd ask me how I lived, but I had no answer for you; there was no one like you in my world. Although the barrier that separated us was nothing more than a thin glass wall, I could only sneak away in the afternoons, when lessons were finished and my parents were still at the bank, trying to sign more customers. I preferred your space— the soft fog that rang along the gnarled trees, towering symbols of a world that could never be revived. The new world behind the wall had been repopulated by beings like you.

Miriam, you said. You folded your clothes by the stream, basking in the sunlight. It seemed that every speck of dust wanted some part of you, to share in the senseless power. *Miriam, do you want to learn how to use my power?*

I laughed, splashed drops of water at you. They leapt over you, falling in showers. *You'll never show me.*

Perhaps I never would. But you can convince me otherwise.

How?

I've never understood it. How insignificant we seem to humans. Do they not want to understand this—all of this?

Do you want me to explain?

No, I want you to show me.

How?

Come closer, Miriam. Come closer and place your lips on mine.

Is this… how you connect with the others?

We don't connect this way. We can feel each other across the oceans, the streams—soon, you'll be able to do the same.

I was hesitant—I didn't know what would happen if I shared my vision with you, if I touched you—would you disappear, like the curled tail of smoke from car exhausts on winter mornings? Or would you fade away, like the memories snuffed out in a burned photograph— reduced to shapes and colors?

But there was a part of me that craved the senselessness, the heady majesty that only you could provide. I walked closer and into your embrace. The moment our lips touched, I fell into your storm.

It was like tumbling into a river without taking a breath first, being swept into the torrents, trying to keep my head above but being submerged at every turn—then nothing. It was the swell, the rise, and the fall of the tide. I was skimming along a path illuminated by moonlight, but not even the sound of the wind was at my back. I no longer needed to breathe.

You took a step back, having taken everything you needed to know.

To this day, I still wonder what I showed you—everything that is real and artificial in my world would shake someone who's never seen it before.

I saw you change—no, I felt you change. The light hung in the air like the static of things moved too quickly, too carelessly. You stared at me.

You gave me too much.

I gave you what you wanted to know.

Is this how it all ends—will this be the end of everything I know?

I couldn't give you an answer.

I refuse to accept it.

I don't want you to accept it. There's still a chance.

A chance.

Yes, that we can live like this.

Like what?

Like equals. Friends. Family.

Family. You looked at me, the corner of your mouth pulled up, your eyes hard. *That's a good dream.*

We share the same dream, then.

You paused, your hands reaching for my face before you dropped them by your sides. *Miriam, I'll give my power to you. Maybe you can change something that I could never touch.*

Then you did something I didn't expect: you stepped closer and showed me a vision. I was walking beside a gnarled sycamore tree, splashing between the puddles, feet narrowly escaping the flood, before I was swamped once more. It was raining; I distinctly remembered drops tumbling down my cheeks, jingling the bells on the earrings you gave me. I wanted to find something wrong with this world—it's something I was trained to do—something I did instinctively. But I couldn't find any fault in the wind racing between my legs, the rain coursing down my skin, the sun, half-hidden, sweeping me into its embrace like a rose curtain.

You woke me up.

But we could never race the woods together after that—I never felt your presence. I was awake, yes, with the sunlight slicing through the leaves and the grass tiptoeing in the moonlight—but I couldn't feel your breath and your words anymore. You left me with a hole, a little token of your love that keeps spinning. It calmly creeps into my heart at night, filling the soft round shadows with edges of purple and brown. It makes me question my memories of you.

The first night, I stared at the dark windows, humming to myself, waiting for the light to filter in. I could never find you in the dark, and I never will be able to again.

Miriam.

Was your voice softer than that? Or maybe it was slightly taller, more rounded near the vowels, like someone calling out a name in the middle of a dream?

Miriam.

When my corner of the world finally kindled, I slipped past the half-alert robots guarding the front door, between connections of the glass wall, and headed into the Wild. I called for you then, *shenona padrem miennie*, my voice dissolving in the humidity. Your name was still there, in the back of my mind, and I held onto it as I walked, barefoot, through the trees, the rain coursing from the leaves in tiny rivulets. You knew I'd come for you; I walked to where we lit the fire together and wrote poetry, calling each other by our secret names. The fire was still burning; you left a white cloth hanging above the trees, and I saw the uneven scrawl of your writing on the ground, practicing your final farewells.

I walked in circles around the fire, tripped on the dirt; I tried to find vestiges of your presence, something that would lead me closer to you. But the rain must've washed away everything that was left, everything that could've been possible.

Evening came; I slipped past the wall, my hands empty and cold. I ran into my room and closed the door behind me, my fingers streaked with blood and dirt. You told me The Wild would listen to me now, but I was tired of everything that it meant, if you weren't part of it.

Something burned into my earlobes; I yanked the earrings off as the wooden bells on both shivered, then fell apart, revealing two pieces of paper. I unraveled each one gingerly, biting my lips, hoping that you'd tell me how I could find you. Instead, you left me two choices, two timelines I could lay out; two words that could change our worlds forever.

On one slip, you told me to hide The Wild. On the other, you told me to burn it.

I wanted to throw them away the moment I read them. How could you let me make such a decision? How could I bear it? I agonized for days afterward, the slips of paper crumpled up in my fists. I didn't want to choose; I thought that if I stayed where I was and waited, you would come back to me.

But if I asked you to return, I know what you will say. You will tell me you live here, in The Wild. You will say that you were never mine to tame. And ask me if I ever loved you, if I never used the power you wanted me to use. I remember the dream you had, the hope you had for the future, the hope that I shared—it is a dream I've left enclosed in a jar, on a piece of paper scribbled with green ink. I have instead succumbed to long-winded notes that take me farther away, that carry me farther inland, away from the forest, without my noticing. On my desk, the edges of long papers stick to my arms, and when I stand up, they hang from my skin like leaves. I know they will eventually shiver and fall away, but I leave them there for now—wondering if this is how the tree felt before it was uprooted. Before it lost to you.

I am tired of pretending—of putting my hair up and keeping this power within me. I know you have given it to me for a reason. Even though I can no longer feel you, I know you are there, in The Wild, with the frogs and the rivers, the lakes and the deep blue. Just give me a moment to catch up to your effortless bounds over the meadows and touch the tan-skinned curve of your ankle hitting the streams.

After that, I will lead.

I AM a current, the endless pull of the forest when it sleeps. I am the dawn, the lost words in fluttering eyes and aching feet. Every day, I wake up hoping to have something to hold onto. Every day, I keep thinking of the stone in my mind and how it bleeds into my world.

VIVIAN LI is a writer, musician, and inventor. She is currently studying at the University of Toronto, and has been awarded Gold and Silver Keys from Scholastic Awards for her poetry, and Silver Keys for her fiction. Her creative works have been published in journals or magazines such as *The Window, ellipsis...literature & art, Young Voices Magazine*, and the *UC Review*. Most recently, she has received a Book Prize for Ted Chamberlin's Poetry Prize, and Honourable Mentions in Muriel's Journey Poetry Prize. She is currently editing her fantasy novel. She can be reached @eliktherain.

MELTWATER

An account by Emma Milner,
AS PROVIDED BY DIE BOOTH

I don't think I was scared of Lindsey, exactly. I was scared of her isolation. I knew her illness wasn't catching, but I think a part of me was always afraid that her sadness was. Lindsey always seemed sickly, for as far back as I can remember. Her skin was pale and it always looked damp, like she was glowing softly, made of wax. Her hair was thin, blonde and wispy as dandelion floss. When she was little, I used to braid it for her, like she was a doll. I thought she was the prettiest thing. She was my best friend.

It was the year that Lindsey turned eight that it snowed. Heaven opened its trapdoor and turned inside-out, and the whole world became a spinning pillow fight. The field beyond the back fence of our garden rattled with the shouts of other kids, every day between schools-out and dinnertime. Every night, the earth churned by their snowball-fight feet was buttered over again with a fresh layer of white, draping the ever-present legion of snowmen. I was twelve. Four years, and a million years, away from Lindsey.

"Emma. That's my big sister." I was passing her room when I heard her say that, and I stopped and leaned my head against the wall to listen. I couldn't help but smile. She did that you see, sometimes. Talked to her dolls and stuff. I thought it was cute, because obviously at four years older, I'd grown out of all that. I was sophisticated.

I'd never heard her talk about me before, though.

"She used to be my brother, but then we found out she's really a girl, like me." It was dark, then, even though it was only afternoon, about three or something. The light coming in through the window was sort of blue and muted and the snowfall cast soft shadows on the walls, like beating moth wings. Lindsey said, "Then she grew her hair long. My sister's got really pretty hair. When she grows up, she'll go to the doctors, and they'll—"

"Lindsey, who are you talking to?" I guess I felt weird all of a sudden, in case she had the cordless phone in there and she was talking to one of her school friends. It felt strange, to be talked about like that. But when I went into the room, she wasn't on the phone. She was alone. Sitting up in bed without even a teddy bear beside her.

"I'm bored. You want to play Snap?"

"Who were you talking to?" I asked again. The snow stroked the windowpanes, pawing to be let in.

"The snowman." Lindsey said.

I shivered. I mean, it was cold. "Like on telly? At Christmas?" She didn't have any snowman toys, but I was familiar enough.

Lindsey stared at me. Her eyes glittered in the flickery light as her face split slowly into a smile. "Nooo," she said, drawing the word out long, as if I was an idiot, and it was obvious.

"What snowman?"

"Old Groan."

"There's no such thing." I didn't know what Old Groan was, but I decided instantly it didn't exist. I remember that I felt... angry. Very angry, very quick, like she was making a fool of me. I guess really, I felt afraid. But I didn't understand why.

"Yes, there *is*." Lindsey's voice rose. Upset.

"Is not."

I didn't *want* it to exist. I was desperate for it not to.

"Is too! He whispers to me down the chimney."

Outside, the snow lurched down, drunk and intent. I glanced at the little cast-iron fireplace opposite her bed. Downstairs in the front room, we had a big one that we had real fires in. Mum would feed it logs, and when it was windy outside, the snow blowing down it would sizzle: there was no whispering down that chimney for any snow-things. The fireplaces in the bedrooms though, they were blocked up. Lindsey's was painted duck-egg blue. The colour of it looked suddenly frigid. Lindsey pouted.

I leaned in, close, to give her a good talking-to. When I put my hand down to brace myself, the bedclothes were soaked through. "Did you spill something?" I asked, quiet and precise.

"No."

"Oh my god, did you wet the bed?"

"No!" She was trembling, by then, her fists clenched. "I told you—"

I held my hand out, far away from me, like it was contaminated. "That's disgusting! I'm telling Mum!"

"Well, I'm telling Old Groan!"

"Shut up." I hissed at her, quiet and vicious. She fell silent, just like that. Then, it was dark, in an instant, in that way it goes in winter when the clouds crowd in. I should have switched the light on, but I didn't. I ran out of there and I left her in the dark.

"I hate you!" I heard her shout after me—me, halfway down the stairs—just before she started to cough.

I got told off for that. For upsetting my sister. When I saw her next, she smirked at me, bright-eyed and ashy, but her cheeks had these pink patches in the middle, like a rag doll's. I think maybe I hated her too, then, just for a moment. "Mum said it was Jet." Lindsey said, before I'd even spoken.

I knew exactly what she was talking about. "It wasn't dog pee. It would smell if it was dog pee." Since our argument, Jet and Zena had been confined to the kitchen, as if they were being punished for Lindsey's misdemeanour, which made me angry at her, too. Another wet patch had appeared on the dining room carpet. Even though it didn't smell, there were no leaks in the ceiling, so Mum said it must be the dogs bringing it in somehow. What other explanation was there?

"It was Old Groan." Lindsey whispered, into her cupped hand.

"What did you say?"

"You heard me."

I felt that feeling again. That sort of panicky-angry feeling. "You're such a stupid little baby." I said.

"OK."

"You're always *making stuff up* like a *stupid baby.*"

"OK." Her face was so placid. Mocking. I knew I had to leave or I'd lose my temper and yell at her and then I'd be the one who got into trouble again. As I banged her bedroom door shut, I heard her say, really quietly, "You'll be sorry when he comes." But I made myself forget, for the longest time.

The storm persisted. The dogs cowered and howled. It was the snow upsetting them, Mum said. The silent, dancing snow.

There was a blizzard again the next night, and the next, and the rooves of the houses across from ours looked like gingerbread, covered in that very thin white icing that shows the ridges of the biscuit through it.

I wanted to go to bed. To crawl under the covers and be warm and safe, but it was like something in my own head was daring me. An itch of the brain. So I opened the curtains.

I couldn't bring myself to look out at the field. But I switched the bedroom light off and the window became a television screen when the programmes have finished, swirling blizzard flakes flying hypnotically upward into a freezing black sky. I huddled on the edge of my bed and watched it, blurring my eyes until the flurry of white lost meaning and became an undulating, infinite mass. I thought of the field. Of the quiet, soft shapes, out there in the night. If I stood up, I'd be able to see out, past the windowsill. I didn't want to stand up.

When the blizzard lulled, outside was hushed and still. I groped my way and closed the curtains with my eyes shut, because it felt like I was the last person alive on earth.

When I came home from school the next day, there was another wet patch in the living room, just in front of the TV, even though the dogs had been confined to the kitchen and the yard between walks. I knelt on the carpet and approached with caution, shuffling up to the edge of it on my knees. I leant down, as close as I dared, and sniffed. It definitely wasn't the dogs. There was no smell to it at all, except the slight, earthy scent that you'd expect from muddy water. Like meltwater, shed from boots when you walk inside. Except nobody had worn outdoor shoes inside and there was just that one, inexplicable spot, with no trail from any door. As if it had just materialised there.

That night I opened the curtains to see the snow army standing like zombies, growing more and more hunched in the blue stillness.

Every time I looked away and back again, it seemed they'd taken another step closer to the house.

I woke up late. I remember being confused by that. When I looked outside, other kids had got there first, and the field was a crosshatch of muddy tracks, leading between snowmen standing like sentries frozen at their posts. Mum usually got us up for school. Well, me, and Lindsey when she was well enough. I wrapped my dressing gown round me really tight. The radiators were on, but the house still felt chilled to the brick. "Lindsey?" I knocked on her bedroom door. "Are you awake?"

There was a scuffle inside, like someone standing up fast, and a woman's voice said, "Is that Emma? Don't come in, sweetheart. Your mummy's downstairs, go on down and see her."

Everyone said, "It was the cold that got her."

Pneumonia. Water on the lungs. It came on suddenly and she suffocated in her own bed. Dry-drowned. The doctors said it was due to a weakened immune system. Any one of us could have carried in the virus without realising it: harmless to us, lethal to Lindsey. I couldn't stop thinking about that phrase though. *The cold got her.* Those patches of dirty meltwater soaking into the carpets, while the dogs whined, locked away in the kitchen.

I remember, the week after, the sun came out. Everything steamed and sparkled and green started to poke up through the shrinking white. The snow melted from the grass and houses and the snowmen shrank to dirt-streaked lumps, sweating in the chilly sun. Eventually, the snow went away completely. It went away, and took her with it.

EMMA MILNER is a twenty-something British export now living in California with her husband, two dogs, and far too many house plants. When not whispering to cacti, she curates travelling arts exhibitions. Live music, fantasy fiction, and action movies rock her world and she'll always make time for tea and cake.

DIE BOOTH lives in Chester, England, and enjoys making monsters and exploring dark corners. When not writing wild lies, he chairs a writing group, and DJs at goth nights. You can read his stories in places like *The Fiction Desk*, *Shoreline of Infinity*, and *The Cheshire Prize for Literature* anthologies. His books *Spirit Houses*, *365 Lies*, and *My Glass is Runn*, are available online, and he's currently working on a collection of spooky short stories featuring transgender protagonists. http://diebooth.wordpress.com/ @diebooth

JACK IN THE MATCHBOX

An account by Scarlett Catterall,
AS PROVIDED BY MAUREEN BOWDEN

We are such stuff as dreams are made on"
William Shakespeare: The Tempest, Act IV, Lines 1887-8

My great-grandfather, Gaga Walter, kept a beast in a matchbox. He called him Jack. I was seven years old when he told me about him. We were eating ice cream in Ceridwen's Café on Colwyn Bay promenade, watching the high tide crashing against the sea wall.

"Jack jumped out of my head when I was your age, Scarlett," he said. "That happens to lots of us when we're young. We make monsters out of our thoughts, but when we grow up, they leave us, and we stop believing in them."

"Where do they go, Gaga?"

"To the Hill of the Beasts, but Jack was my friend and I didn't want him to go, so I let him live in a matchbox. He comes out when there's nobody else around and I tell him it's safe."

This was nearly as good as the Narnia books. "Is he still in there?"

He nodded. "I shouldn't have stopped him going to the Hill. It wasn't nice." Gaga said that a lot. He didn't exaggerate. If he approved of something, he said it was nice. If he disapproved, he said it wasn't nice. No melodrama.

"He must like it in the matchbox," I said, "or he wouldn't have stayed."

"He had to stay. All that time in there gave him an illness called agoraphobia. It made him scared to go out into the world."

"But you said he comes out when you tell him."

"Yes, that's how he saved my life in World War II." He passed me his handkerchief. "Wipe your face. It's covered in ice cream."

"Never mind my face. Tell me what happened in the war."

"I was a soldier in France and I got separated from my battalion. I was hiding, in some woodland or other, with rifle fire and screaming pounding in my ears. A German lad, young as I was and probably just as scared, crept up on me."

I listened, holding my breath. Ceridwen, the café owner, was wiping tables and watching us. I think she was listening too. Gaga must have noticed, because he leaned toward me and whispered, "I called Jack out of the matchbox. He and the German looked at each other, Jack screamed and dived back in, and Fritz dropped his rifle, turned tail, and bolted like Old Nick himself was after him. I hope he made it home safely. So many young fellers didn't."

"Is that why you have to tell Jack it's safe before he'll come out?"

"Aye. He doesn't like bother. He's a conchie."

Before I could ask him what a conchie is, Ceridwen reached our table and picked up our empty ice cream bowls. "What's occurrin', Walter? Still fighting the war by yur?" She winked at me. "We is safe in our beds, isn't it?" She gave Gaga the bill. "Crackin' bit of ice cream you had there, boyo. I won't lie to you, like."

Gaga handed her a pound coin. "Very nice, Ceri. Keep the change."

She glanced at the coin. "Tidy. Last of the big spenders, look you."

We walked home hand in hand. "I like Ceri." I said.

"Aye, she's a nice lass. But most of the time I can't understand a bloody word she says."

Neither of us spoke for a while, but Jack in the matchbox seemed to hover between us, so I asked, "Why did you tell me about Jack?"

"Because I trust you, Scarlett. Jack won't leave me, but after I'm dead, I want you to help him to get to the Hill of the Beasts."

I shivered and clung to his hand. "You're not going to die, Gaga."

He did, of course, but not until he was ninety-six. I'd grown up by then. I had my own flat above Vision Express on the High Street, and a promising career as a dental hygienist, but I felt like a little girl who'd lost her best friend. It didn't occur to me that I was now responsible for Jack. On the rare occasions that I remembered him, I dismissed the beast in the matchbox as a storybook fantasy that Gaga had invented for my amusement.

The funeral was just as he wanted it. Morecambe and Wise sang us in with "Bring Me Sunshine," and Vera Lynn sang us out with "We'll Meet Again."

We held the wake in the British Legion function room, and afterward, my mother called me to one side. "Gaga Walter wanted you to have this and whatever's inside it. He wouldn't answer any questions about it, so don't ask." She handed me the battered canvas satchel that Gaga had carried, slung across his back, wherever he went. It had "Army issue: South Lancashire Regiment" stamped on the back.

I took it home and emptied the contents onto my bed: an ordnance survey map of Oxfordshire; a sealed letter addressed to Miss Scarlett Catterall; a faded matchbox pitted with spots of mould; and a child's drawing headed, "Jack, by Walter Catterall aged seven." I picked up the drawing. The paper was brittle and yellowed. Not surprising if it was eighty-nine years old. It showed some sort of animal standing on its hind legs. It had antlers, wolf-like ears, large Bambi eyes, a snout, and a wide mouth full of pointed teeth. The body was the oblong torso with stick-like limbs that children draw to depict anything from Luke Skywalker to Auntie Brenda's mad cat.

My heart thumped. Don't be ridiculous, I told myself. It's nothing more than a picture of a little boy's imaginary friend. Clinging to logic couldn't, however, stop my hands from trembling as I opened the letter. I read,

"Dear Scarlett,

I told Jack he could trust you, and you'll help him to get to the Hill of the Beasts. He'll obey you, and he'll come out of the matchbox when you tell him it's safe. The Hill is in the Berkshire Downs or thereabouts. Here's a map if you need it, but I expect you'll use one of those computer things. Be nice to him. He's scared of people.

Lots of love from Gaga Walter

XXX."

I sat on the bed and looked at the mouldy matchbox. My first inclination was to hurl it into the garbage, but I recalled Gaga telling me he trusted me. I couldn't let him down. What the hell. This was all nonsense, anyway. I took a deep breath, and yelled, "Jack, it's safe. Come out."

The matchbox didn't open, but a figure emerged from it like an inflating balloon. He spoke in my head, with Gaga's voice, "Don't shout. It hurts my ears." He was more than six feet tall, and his antlers almost touched my bedroom ceiling. His face was more or less as Gaga had drawn it; to my professional eye, his teeth appeared to be plaque-free and in good order; his body was humanoid, indisputably male, and naked.

I averted my eyes and rummaged through the contents of my

chest of drawers for a grotesque yellow Lycra swimming costume that was a legacy from a long-gone ex-boyfriend. I said, "Put this on."

"Why?"

"For the sake of decorum."

"Walter never demanded that I wear pants."

"I'm not Walter. Put it on." He obeyed me. I patted the bed. "Now, sit down and tell me what you are."

He sat, and the bed creaked. "I belong to a race of beasts that once lived amongst humans. You gave some of us names, like Yeti, Sasquatch, Griffin, and Minotaur."

"You're monsters," I said. "There are stories about you."

"You made up the stories. You feared us although we did you no harm, but you would hurt us if you could, so we take refuge beneath the Hill of the Beasts and you no longer believe we exist." He looked into my eyes and shook his head. "We're not monsters. You are."

"I'm not."

"Not you personally, Scarlett. Individual humans are usually quite bearable, but the human race is not very nice."

"Why do you sound like Walter?"

"Because Walter's imagination spawned me. Beasts form in the darkest recesses of children's minds, where nightmares lurk."

It occurred to me that in a manner of speaking, he was my great-uncle, but in view of his animosity toward humans, I didn't mention it. "What's so monstrous about us?"

"You impoverish, cheat, deceive, oppress, and enslave each other. You injure, mutilate, and murder, and you treat your world no better than you treat each other."

"Hang on. You've spent eighty-nine years hiding in a matchbox. How do you get to be an expert on the human race?"

"I know everything that Walter knew, and I know what the other beasts know. It's in our nature."

"Okay, so we have problems. We've had them since humanity evolved," I said, "but we're still here, and most of us aren't so bad."

"You're here for now, but you haven't learned from history. Eventually you'll annihilate each other or destroy the earth's ability to sustain your species. You'll go the same way as the big lizards, and you won't need an asteroid to see you off." He picked up the drawing, ran a clawed finger over Gaga's childish signature, and sighed. "Then the creations of your minds will come out of the Hill, and we'll take over the world."

I admitted to myself that he had a point. Maybe humans are another dead end, and the beasts will be all that's left when we've slaughtered each other or made this planet uninhabitable for flesh and blood beings.

The doorbell rang. Jack yelped and shrank back into the matchbox, leaving the yellow swimming costume abandoned on my bedroom floor.

I opened the door to my boyfriend, Alex, who was carrying a large black bin-liner. I led him into the kitchen. He said, "Sorry I couldn't stay for Walter's wake, Scarly, but we're so shorthanded there was nobody available to take my shift."

Alex is a geriatrics nurse who makes home visits to housebound patients. He's overworked and underpaid, but he loves the job. "Don't worry," I said. "Gaga would have understood. What are you doing here? I didn't expect to see you today?"

He emptied a pile of clothes from the bin-liner onto my breakfast bar. "Just passing. Here's my ironing. I haven't had time to tackle it for three weeks, and you'd do it so much quicker. Can I leave it with you?"

"No chance. You must be joking."

His sly smile alerted me that he was up to something. "I'm not just begging, I'm bribing."

"With what?"

"Tickets for Ed Sheeran at Wembley Stadium next month."

I shrieked, and hugged him, and then reality smacked me. "You're mad. They must have cost a chunk of your salary."

"Yeah, well, I'll be living off baked beans on toast for the rest of the month, but it's worth it to get my ironing done."

"It's a deal, but don't make a habit of it."

He squeezed my hand and headed for the door. "Got to go. Mr Warner's enema won't wait."

I chucked him an apple out of my fruit bowl. "Take that to supplement the beans."

When he'd gone, I called Jack out of the matchbox. He picked up the swimming costume and handed it to me. "This is too tight. It makes me itch."

I sorted through Alex's ironing and found a pair of boxer shorts decorated with an array of Jedi warriors. "Try these." He put them on. "Better?" I asked.

"Much better. Thank you. Has Alex gone?"

"Yes. He's working."

"Walter liked him. He said he was nice." Gaga's favourite word again. With Jack around, I felt as if he wasn't quite lost to me.

"He is nice. He's not a monster."

"I know. I'm sorry if I offended you. Are you too angry to take me to the Hill?"

I shrugged. "Everyone's entitled to their opinion. I'll take you if I can find it."

"Thank you."

"Tell me something before we start looking. How do you fit into the matchbox?"

"I'm not solid like you. I'm formed from the fabric of dreams."

"Very poetic. William Shakespeare said something similar."

"Did he know of the beasts?"

"Probably."

I booted up my laptop and googled the Berkshire Downs. "How do we recognise this place when we see it?"

"The beasts marked it as their own three thousand years ago, or thereabouts." Another of Gaga's expressions.

"Marked it how?"

"With the figure of Naga, the Great Wyrm, the first of the beasts. They formed her image in chalk to scare humans away."

Something stirred in my memory. I added "hill figure" to the search, and I found what I was looking for. "It's the White Horse of Uffington," I said.

He looked over my shoulder at the screen. "It's not a horse."

"Doesn't look like one to me, either. It's sort of dragonish."

"I told you. It's the Great Wyrm."

"Well, it didn't scare humans away. It's a famous tourist attraction."

"Take me when the tourists are sleeping."

Just what I needed: a two-hundred-mile drive down the M5 at night, and a weather forecast of violent thunderstorms across the Midlands. Gaga, what had you gotten me into?

I googled Uffington Tourist Information Centre and wrote down the postcode. "This will take us to the Hill, or thereabouts."

"You sound like Walter," he said.

I entered the postcode into my Sat Nav, and in the early evening, with Jack in the matchbox on the passenger seat alongside Alex's Jedi Warrior boxer shorts, I set off.

The weather grew worse the farther south we travelled. Hail pelted the windscreen, thunder rumbled, and lightning slashed through the grey cloudbanks. I felt desolate. Losing Jack would be like losing my last remnant of Gaga. I needed company. "Come out, Jack. It's safe," I called, "but do something about the antlers. A Peugeot 208 Alure isn't designed to accommodate them."

He inflated, with deflated antlers. I handed him the boxer shorts.

"For decorum?" he asked.

I nodded. "For decorum."

"You're sad."

"I miss Gaga Walter, and you remind me of him."

"I miss Walter too, Scarlett, and you remind me of him."

"So you'll miss me?"

"Yes, but I have a solution. Come with me. You're not a monster. You don't belong with humans. Come and join my people."

I wondered what Gaga would have said to that. Nice or not nice? I remembered the day we'd sat together eating "crackin'" ice cream in Ceridwen's Café, and he'd told me about Jack. I realised there was a link between the three of us that would never be broken. We shared a sense of what it means to be human, even if Jack didn't recognise his own humanity.

Sheet lightning followed a clap of thunder, and lit up the chalk figure on a hillside almost within walking distance.

I drove as close as I dared and stopped the car. Neither of us spoke. We saw the beasts, led by Naga, the Great Wyrm. They emerged from the hill in the way Jack had emerged from the matchbox. They were clawed, horned, feathered, and scaled. The product of the human subconscious was every combination of vulpine, feline, canine, and reptilian. They crawled, flew, trotted, and slithered down the Hill, to welcome one of their own.

Jack was waiting for my answer. I turned to him. "Most humans are not monsters," I said. "Some are wise and compassionate, with generous hearts, and most of them, like me, Gaga Walter, and Alex, are ordinary people trying to live good lives and maybe make the world a better place."

"It's not enough, Scarlett. You can't save yourselves."

"Perhaps not. In time, your kind may inherit the earth, but that time hasn't come yet. For now, the world is ours. I'm part of it, and I won't desert it. You can get out, Jack. It's safe. Go and join your people."

There were tears in his Bambi eyes, but he kissed my forehead and obeyed me. I turned off the windscreen wipers so the hail would obscure my vision and I wouldn't see him disappear.

I put the matchbox in the glove compartment, and then I sat alone and waited for the storm to abate. When the elements were quiet and still, the sky was clear, and the chalk figure glowed in the moonlight, I climbed out of the car and walked to the foot of the Hill. A saturated pair of boxer shorts adorned with Jedi warriors lay discarded on the grass. I picked them up and wrung them out. After a good wash and iron, they'd be fit for me to return them to Alex, but they'd always remind me of Jack. In spite of decorum, I giggled.

SCARLETT CATTERALL, a dental hygienist from North Wales, is a founding member of Save Our Planet, the international ecological movement that raised public awareness of the damage being done to Earth, and how it could lead to the extinction of human life. She was a driving force behind the action plan now in place to repair the damage. Miss Catterall was awarded the MBE in the New Year Honours List.

MAUREEN BOWDEN is a Liverpudlian, living with her musician husband in North Wales. She has had over a hundred stories and poems accepted by paying markets. Silver Pen Publishers nominated one of her stories for the 2015 international Pushcart Prize, and an anthology of her stories is soon to be published by Alban Lake. She also writes song lyrics, mainly comic political satire. Her husband sets them to traditional melodies. He has performed them in folk music clubs throughout England and Wales. Alban Lake has recently published a book of her stories, entitled *Whispers of Magic*. She loves her family and friends, rock 'n' roll, Shakespeare, and cats.

THE TUTOR

An account by Peachy,
AS PROVIDED BY KAYLEIGH TAYLOR

jumped in the cab and told the driver, "Kayleigh's house, and step on it." I watched the buildings fly past. Cats were working, and eating in the parks, and honking their horns when stuck in traffic. The thing that made Kitty Town, where I lived, special was that there were no humans. Cats had to do everything, and that's the way I liked it.

Still, I had friends in the human world. Because they were only human, often, my friends needed my help. That's why I was on my way to visit Kayleigh—she needed my help. Adults thought I was imaginary, just because they couldn't see me, but Kayleigh knew the truth. Kayleigh had sent me a text message last night, while I was getting ready for bed. Math test. She needed my help.

As the kitty cab pulled up outside Kayleigh's house, I checked my briefcase to make sure I had a pencil and paper. Those would be necessary to help Kayleigh with math. I paid the cab driver with a handful of cat bills—the ones with George Catington's face on them—and scampered into the house and up to Kayleigh's room. I meowed at the door and she let me in.

"It's going to be a hard test, Peach." Kayleigh said. "I need your help!" She showed me a piece of paper with equations on it. "This is the study guide."

I wrote down the first problem from the study guide on my paper, then used my calculator to solve it. I circled the answer and went on to the next as Kayleigh kept talking.

"I also have a vocabulary quiz next week that I need to study for, and I need to practice my songs for choir!"

I sighed. It was a lot of work for one girl… even if she had the help of a most excellent feline tutor. I finished the last of the practice problems, then compared my work to what Kayleigh had done. She'd only missed a few problems. I underlined her mistakes and had her redo the problems.

"My teachers all say that my homework has really improved since you've been helping me." Kayleigh remarked as she re-worked the math problems. She struggled to control the pencil as she carefully fixed her mistakes. She sighed. "My handwriting is so sloppy."

I thought her handwriting was pretty good, considering that she was only a human, but thought it best not to tell her that.

Once Kayleigh finished with her math, I helped her with her singing. Singing was something I knew quite a lot about—I showed her how to reach the high notes, until her parents told her to stop caterwauling and come down to dinner.

"Would you stay the night with me, Peach?" Kayleigh asked me after dinner. "Then you could come to school with me in the morning."

I considered the matter. I had other students to tutor, but Kayleigh was special. And her bed was very comfortable. I decided to sleep on her legs.

The next morning, Kayleigh told me I could ride to school in her backpack. I decided to ride on top instead. She told me that normally cats weren't allowed to go to school, but that her teachers would make an exception for me. I wasn't sure how she managed that, but my Kayleigh was a rather remarkable person, even if she was only human.

"Welcome to second period Math, Kayleigh," said the teacher.

"I brought my cat with me, Mr. Michael. I hope that's okay?" Kayleigh replied hopefully.

"Oh! I'm very glad to meet your imaginary friend," the teacher replied, though he was looking in entirely the wrong direction.

"Can he help me with my test?" Kayleigh asked.

"Certainly!" Mr. Michael replied, "He can help you as much as you'd like!"

I thought that was a very sporting attitude. Kayleigh worked very hard at her studies, and it seemed only fair that she should get just a little feline assistance now and then.

After the test, she went to English class. Ms. Shell told her that she was worried about Kayleigh's grade. She had an entire paper to write, and it needed to be turned in the next day! "You are a hard worker, Kayleigh," said the teacher, "but you need to really focus."

"Can my cat help?" asked Kayleigh.

"Sure, Why not?" Ms. Shell replied. "You're a hard worker, and I think it's fine that you study with your cat."

I was a bit surprised at how willing Kayleigh's teachers were to allow her tutor to help her so much… especially if the tutor was feline. However, I'd noticed signs in the hallways that celebrated diversity and thought that it explained much.

That afternoon, I helped Kayleigh by sitting on the keyboard of her laptop. When she couldn't find a letter, I would simply point to it with my tail. While she kept lifting me up to reach the letters I was sitting on, she did so in a very polite manner that only the most unforgiving cat would take umbrage at.

Her mother peeked in on Kayleigh. "Are you still working on your paper?"

Kayleigh nodded.

"You're a very hard worker!"

Kayleigh smiled at her mother while I quickly edited her paper's spelling and grammar.

As she dressed for bed, I worked on her laptop, crafting several quizlets and study guides to help her get through the next several days. Finally, it was time to say good-bye. I wound myself between her legs, making her stumble. It was my little way of encouraging her to practice her balance.

"Thank you for all of your help, Peach," said Kayleigh.

I nonchalantly flicked the tip of my tail, as if to say "'twas nothing."

"My grades are getting a lot better."

I used my tongue to smooth a bit of fur down on my chest, modestly ignoring her praise.

"And now that I've finally passed my test and gotten a learning permit—"

I flicked an ear.

"Can you teach me to drive?"

PEACHY would like everyone to know that he draws the line at driving lessons. That's what Kayleigh's Dad is for.

KAYLEIGH is a seventeen-year-old high school student living in the Northwest. Despite having pretty significant cognitive delays, she works very hard at her school work and, after seven tries, does have her learner's permit for driving! Getting her driver's license is a bit tricky since she has trouble with spatial orientation and has recently had a few seizures. Still, she continues to try!

Inspired by her mother's love of writing, Kayleigh has been writing her own stories since she was twelve. She likes to write about her life, and her cats, and her favorite activities. She's currently working on an illustrated story about a taxi company where cats and dogs drive taxis along with their human friends.

Kayleigh believes that people can do anything they want, so long as they try hard enough. She wants her readers to know that they shouldn't let anything stop them from making their dreams happen.

TOUCH THE
EARTH

An account by Max Carlton,
AS PROVIDED BY NEIL JAMES HUDSON

I was so busy concentrating on my music that I put no effort into imagining the concert hall itself—and yet there it was, its glorious dome soaring over the orchestra, intricate carvings that seemed to dance with the music. I knew that in reality we were covered only with tarpaulin, but it was easier for me to imagine the roof than to see the reality. The music was real enough; I had written sad strings to act as a counterpart to the mournful cries of the soprano, her wordlessness evoking her loss far more than any libretto.

These notes were the imaginary made real. I had heard them only in my head, as ethereal as the building that surrounded us; yet I had given them form in a far more concrete way than the designers of our city.

I wished I could as easily imagine a more enthusiastic response from the audience. The applause was polite rather than rapturous, and I felt embarrassed as the conductor beckoned me on stage to bow to their lukewarm response. It was summer, and many of them wore only light jackets. They wanted music to go with the season, a light and happy melody, not the aching lament I had given them. Perhaps if the piece got a second performance, it might slowly work its way into the public's consciousness, just as the voice from the Basilica had worked its way into mine.

I was a little depressed as I passed behind the screen into the backstage area. I felt excluded from the conversations of the musicians and checked my phone for messages that did not appear. I looked up in surprise when I realised I had a visitor. He seemed to be younger than me, with a head of hair that I frankly envied, although there were lines in his face that seemed to argue with his otherwise youthful demeanour. He wore a brown leather jacket that I thought must have been too warm for the weather. "Mr Carlton," he said, extending his hand, which I felt obliged to shake. "May I call you Max? Dr Radlon Fernster. I found your work very interesting."

"Interesting," I said. "What an interesting word. Still, no praise too faint."

"No, I mean it. Forgive me, I have a deaf ear to music. I couldn't tell a masterpiece from a nursery rhyme. But there were aspects of your piece that I certainly found, and this is the exact word I need, interesting."

"Perhaps you could communicate your fascination to the rest of the audience." I saw that I wasn't going to get rid of him and tried not to sigh. "Which aspects of the piece held your interest so completely?"

"The vocal line," he answered without hesitation. "So distinctive. I could well imagine hearing it floating across the city, just on that dividing line between our mind's ear and our real one."

I stood up. "I have to go, Dr Fernster."

"I'm right, aren't I? You heard it coming from the Basilica."

I looked him in the eye, trying to decide if he was a threat. "What I heard was not real. It happened only in my imagination. Which means I composed it myself, wherever it seemed to come from. You should be careful what you accuse me of, Dr Fernster."

I made for the doorway. Whatever mood I had been in to begin with, it had worsened, and I did not want this annoying man to be on the wrong end of a sudden explosion of temper.

Behind me, he began to whistle. Too fast, but the theme was nonetheless recognisable. Six notes—three rising notes, and then three more with the second note flattened. A major triad followed by its minor.

I was already writing this piece. I was orchestrating it in a minor key, a lugubrious companion to the song that was already being forgotten in the seats behind me. I turned back. "Where did you hear that?

"Oh, out and about. Good luck with your work, Max." To my surprise, he pushed past me and reached the doorway first. He held his hand up to the frame, and for a second, I thought he was going to push straight through it; but he withdrew, smiled, and left.

I let out a breath I had not known I was holding in and sat down again.

The city is real for me. It takes me no effort at all to hold it in my mind, to view the officially sanctioned template instead of the drab expanse of tents, posts, and markings. Our ancestors knew that a city of the imagination would always be more majestic, more imposing, and more beautiful than one made of stone and brick, and so we imagined it still, superimposing the view from our mind's eye over the drabness of the real world.

To most people, this took an effort of the imagination, one they did not always keep up. To me, it was the opposite. I seldom saw the markings that we were forbidden to cross, showing the positions of the walls. I found it difficult to tear down the artifice of the imagined city, revealing the skeleton that lay beneath it.

And at the Basilica of St Lucia, I refused to do so. This was the city's jewel—the masterpiece of architecture that stood at its centre, the first edifice our ancestors imagined but did not build. Its main spire, hundreds of feet high, was surrounded by numerous gothic turrets and smaller spires, like a fractal that keeps the same pattern no matter how closely you view it, or like a plant desperately reaching its branches to a few shafts of sunlight. Intricacy perched upon intricacy, a monument as much to our imaginations as to the saint it was intended to commemorate. Why would one deliberately choose not to see it?

The square was busy; there were always tourists here, come to look at it and gaze up at the towers. I was here to listen.

It was six months ago that I had first heard the song from the tower—the lonely, mournful cry that rang out across the air. At first, I was astonished no one else could hear it; then I became fearful that I was imposing an unauthorised imagination upon the city. Our life in this city depended upon a simple rule—that we all imagined the same place. Once we began to make individual changes, we would live in our own minds, cut off from one another.

And yet, I heard this song as real, as waves of sound that stroked at my eardrums. Did it do so to those of my fellow citizens, and did they merely imagine silence to drown it out? What creature sang its song of loss from the top of the Basilica, and what had it lost?

If no one else heard it, I had no qualms about taking her song as my own.

I visited two days after my meeting with Dr Fernster, armed with my notebook. For superstitious reasons I could not quite identify, I did not use music manuscript, and had sketched out the stave myself on blank paper. I waited for over an hour before I heard her call, this time a four-note figure, each note drawn out for longer than I believed a human voice could carry it, a falling scale as if the voice itself were plummeting from the top of the tower to touch the earth.

I closed the notebook guiltily when I heard Dr Fernster's voice behind me. "I shouldn't interrupt. Genius at work, and all that."

"So that's how you did it," I said. "You looked over my shoulder at what I was writing down."

"I assure you, those are just dots to me. I didn't read your music. I can hear it."

Just as the voice at the top of the basilica finished its song, Dr. Fernster took it up, whistling as if the line had been passed to him. Whereas most people would have been flat, he was sharp, but the tune was a clear reprise and continuation of the song that had come from the tower.

"Stop that," I said. "What if anyone hears you?"

"What if they do? If they try to arrest me, they'll have to admit they heard the same song. In any case, I don't claim to have heard it from an unauthorised imaginary being. I heard it from you. By the way, where did you get it from, Max?"

"What do you want?" It was clear he was trying to blackmail me.

"Freedom." He left a pause, and I almost wondered if he wasn't going to explain himself, but then he continued. "I want freedom of the imagination. Our singer is proscribed by the architects of the city, who provide the authorised version, and punish those of us who imagine it differently. But you can't run a city, Max. You can only live in it. It arises from the imaginations of its inhabitants, not from its designers. Oh, I don't deny they've made a good job of it, overall. But why should not we not create extra details to suit ourselves? Why not create other creatures, other people even? You're a composer—why should you not fill your city with song? That's your job."

"Your talk is dangerous." I tried to not look around to see if anyone's attention was focussed on ourselves rather than the building.

"Talk isn't dangerous. Actions are dangerous. Art is dangerous. When you compose, you hear sounds no one else has heard before. Doesn't that destroy our social contract? Should we not all hear the same things, just as we see the same things? When you hear these sounds, why should you not also see their singer? Why not see the creature at the top of the tower who sings the notes no one else can hear?"

"I have never seen this creature," I said. I was not happy with his words. I had not thought of her as anything other than human.

"Why not? You already transgressed when you placed this song in the city. It's not supposed to be there. Go and see her. It can't make things any worse."

I hoped he wasn't seriously daring me. There was a simple reason why I had not entered the Basilica to see who was producing these sounds; I was afraid I would find no one there, that the illusion would be punctured and the song would cease. I felt she was like the opposite of the branch falling in a forest; she only made a sound when no one was there to see it.

"If I'm imagining it," I said carefully, "how can you hear it as well?"

"Isn't that your job? You hear it first, then you make us hear it."

"Again, what do you want?"

He shrugged. "I want more songs. Fill our city with your imaginings, Max. We're the better for it." He walked away, again whistling the slow downward chant, showing how beauty so often lies in the performance rather than the notes.

As if he had been inhibiting her, the song began again when he left. I raised my notebook but could not bring myself to carry on working. I felt as if I were transcribing Dr. Fernster's music, not the song from the tower.

Besides, I realised, if Dr. Fernster knew my secret, it was too dangerous to continue. I could not risk being exposed as someone who had reimagined the city. The beautiful song of loss I heard from above my head could never again be made public. Unless it was real.

What did I have to lose? If I found no song at the top of the tower, I had lost it anyway. Why should I not go and visit my muse?

I had to queue to enter the Basilica. It attracted many tourists; most of them were from outside the city, and although I never saw anyone flout our customs, put their hand through a wall or avoid an obstruction that wasn't there, I knew they had come to mock. Many carried fake cameras; photography was banned, but the foreign habit of pretending to take an imaginary picture was tolerated. I felt no embarrassment or shame at their ridicule. The more intelligent among them realised that all cities are imagined, and came in a spirit of respect, genuinely interested in a city that was imagined more literally than most.

My turn came to walk through the hallway into the arched nave. I did not come in often, but it was still a familiar sight to me. I ignored the tourists who stared at their guidebooks, seeing the vast intricate paintings of the ceiling, and trying to project it onto the canvas roof above their heads. This is not a skill that can be acquired quickly. Instead, I went to the viewing gallery on the first floor. I knew I was climbing onto a wooden platform, but I could not stop myself from seeing the stone steps beneath my feet, or the grandeur of the vault before me.

I was partly shielded by the crowd at the front of the gallery, staring down at the Basilica in incomprehension. They should not have been allowed in. I was happy to stay at the back, planning my next move. There were recesses on either side of the gallery, dark spaces roped off, with laminated notices warning the public that they were not permitted to pass.

I walked to the one on the left, unhooked the rope, and passed through. I acted as calmly as possible, trying to look as if I was entitled to be there. Above me, the song seemed to become louder, more urgent, as if the pain and loneliness of its singer's existence had become sharper.

The recess led to a spiralling passage, lined with steps. I began to climb, drawn to the sound. I had not realised how unfit I was and was soon out of breath. There was no obvious sign of when the steps would end, and I had not bothered to count them. Occasionally I would pass a small hole in the wall, filled with glass but too small to be called a window, through which I could see the square below me. It made me feel vertiginous, and after the first one, I chose not to look.

I think it was many minutes before I emerged into a small chamber. The sounds of the crowd had long since faded; all I could hear now was the creature above me, and her song. There was another set of steps down, presumably from the other recess on the gallery. Otherwise, there was only a further recess in front of me in the middle of the chamber, leading farther up. I wanted to rest, but I was worried I would be caught before I reached the top. I had no choice but to go on.

My climb was made easier by the knowledge that I had nearly found her. The song echoed down the stairwell but was now loud enough that I knew it was near. It seemed to become more urgent, crawling inexorably to a climax of sorrow. I wondered if it was my own approach that changed the nature of the song, and if I should return to the ground to preserve its character.

I emerged into the chamber at the top of the tower.

Although I find it easier to see the imaginary city than the real one, I can always tell the two apart. But now I was unsure if the creature before me was real. She stood with her back to me, wailing through the unfilled window in the wall of the tower. She was unclothed, but I could not view her erotically, partly because of the purity of her song, and partly because she was not human. Two wings extended from her back; they were furled, but I thought they would have filled the entire chamber had she spread them. Her long brown hair seemed to merge with the hair on her wings. Otherwise she seemed dangerously slender; I suspected this was not due to undernourishment but was the normal size for her species, whose wings may not support the weight of a human being.

As I watched, she sang her last note. Then she slowly turned to face me. I found her beautiful, but a beauty of the sort that could never be held on to. Her expression, which I expected to be one of yearning or sorrow, was difficult for me to identify; only later did I decide it was one of recognition.

I tried to speak to her, but I was voiceless, unable to decide what I should say. And then, with a grace I thought would be impossible for such an action, she launched herself through the window.

I ran to look down, convinced she would die. Instead I saw her swoop to the square, unnoticed by the tiny figures that swarmed over it. Her wings outspread, she seemed to graze the ground, then rejected it, climbing into the air again. She flew around the back of the tower, and I could see her no more.

It was silent. Her song had accompanied me for the last six months, had nurtured and inspired me, but now it was gone. I could only hope she would return, and I began the journey downward.

I could write no more of my new piece. Without the song I had transcribed and laced through my orchestrations, I had no voice of my own, no songs I could create myself to finish the composition. Any notes I wrote seemed to be random marks on paper rather than music. I had had such fallow periods before; they only ended when I abandoned the current project, if only temporarily, and found a new direction. But this time, I did not wish to find a new direction. I had hoped my creature would return to the tower and fill the air with song once more, but as the days crept by, I began to despair.

My anxiety was only worsened when the piece was suddenly commissioned. I had no paid work at this point and was writing in the hope that our orchestra, or more likely a foreign one, would pick it up in the future. But the orchestra's leader, Matthias Grix, telephoned me personally to ask for a sequel to the earlier work, and I had no choice but to accept. I was also unable to hide my surprise. "I felt the response to the premiere was a little muted," I said.

"At the time, yes," said Grix's voice over the line. I never saw the telephone cables that swung over the city's skyline; our designers had always considered them too much of an eyesore to be incorporated into the official view, and so they were imagined out of existence. Instead, all our telephones contained a non-functional aerial to help with the illusion that they were wireless. "But it's proved to be a slow burner. As the days have passed, more and more people have started enquiring about it. People say they can't get the soprano's part out of their heads. A few have complained about this, you should know."

"I'll take that as a compliment," I said, although I knew the compliment should not have been directed at me.

"Please do. Everyone feels that the tune is familiar, but no one can tell where they know it from. I must confess, Max, I feel much the same way myself. Was it lifted from a folk tune?"

I was unsure how to respond. I could not admit to the source of my song, but if I claimed to have composed it myself, how would I appear if its provenance were discovered? Dr Fernster had, after all, discovered it independently, although I was still not sure how. "I'll be honest with you," I lied. "The feelings of the audience are those of the composer. Although I believe it is my own work, it leaves me with the feeling that I am providing a variation on a traditional tune. I am not expecting a copyright claim, but there is always a chance I have unconsciously borrowed it."

"Oh, don't worry about that. If it were someone else's work, they would have piped up by now. But we need to capitalise on this new success—there's no point waiting until everyone's forgotten it. How soon can you produce a new work?"

I considered. "As a matter of fact, I'm already halfway through such a piece," I said, as an alternative to answering.

"Could you do it in a month? It's asking a lot, I know, but if much of the work is already done—"

It was impossible, but I wouldn't get the money unless I agreed. Grix arranged to send the contracts through, and we also arranged to meet up in a week to discuss the direction of the piece, and to see if he could offer any insights or comments on the players' abilities that could be of value.

As I hung up, I knew it was useless. No such piece would ever be finished, not until the creature returned to the tower at the top of the Basilica. The second part of the piece would be only silence.

As soon as the thought occurred to me, I began to build on it. Did I dare to cut the voice out halfway through, leaving the orchestra to search in vain for a song that had deserted it? The loss expressed in the song transferred to its accompaniment? It could work, provided the audience understood what I was doing. But it was a risk. This wasn't what they wanted.

I shook my head. I could not sing a song of silence. I needed the creature back at the top of tower, casting the notes into the air which I could turn into the lifeblood of music. I did not know where she had gone and had no hope of finding her. I could only turn to the only other person who knew about her. I picked up the phone and dialled the number of Dr Fernster.

Dr Fernster still worked at the university, but this appeared to be against their wishes, and he was seldom let loose on students. He merited an office and had a number of publications to his credit, few of which were ever referenced. From my research, I gained the impression that the university felt he could do less damage if they kept him on a short leash.

He met me in his office, an untidy room with peeling wallpaper and damp in the ceiling corners. The city designers could have given him a much more appealing place to work at a stroke, but the official design was a run-down hovel that I assumed was a deliberate insult to him. If he wanted anything better, he would have to imagine it himself, in defiance of the authorities. I felt a lurch in my stomach as I realised he was probably doing exactly this. I hoped he would not try to bring me into his own personal world and concentrated as hard as I could on one of the damp patches.

"My muse has flown," I said to him. He nodded; as I suspected, he already knew.

"Things have been a little quiet around here. What did you do?"

I was about to deny it, but I had not come here to lie. I needed her back, and Dr Fernster was my only hope. Instead I told him of how I had visited the Basilica, climbed to the tower, and watched her depart from the city.

Dr Fernster pinched his upper lip. I had the impression he was re-imagining my appearance and was trying to decide upon my new look. Finally he said, "Let us return to the Basilica."

I was a little annoyed he insisted on driving such a short distance, but I also wasn't keen on walking, so I allowed myself to be his passenger. There was not much traffic, but the pedestrians seemed to be particularly oblivious of the dangers of the roads, as if they had seen official views of empty streets and refused to imagine the vehicles. It took us about fifteen minutes, and Dr Fernster parked on a side street so far from the Basilica that I wondered if it had been worth the bother of driving. He led me to the square, but kept us well back, so we had a good view of the whole of the building. I looked up at its now empty tower, straining to hear a voice that no longer sang.

"Look at it," said Dr Fernster.

"I am," I said. Usually it filled me with wonder, but now I felt an emptiness that mirrored that of the tower.

"No, you're not. Look at it for real. See it for what it is."

"Why?" I felt uncomfortable, but not alarmed. A personal re-imagining would have been a crime against my fellow citizens, but reality was harmless enough. Anyone was free to look at the drabness that underpinned our beautiful city, if you felt you had a good enough reason.

"Look at it."

I stared up at the Basilica, allowing the illusion to dispel. I disliked doing this; I could not stop myself from worrying that I would be unable to bring it back again. I had to trust in myself though, and I finally saw the wooden structure, the canvas hanging from ropes and the occasional metal rail—a mere skeleton, only made alive by the flesh we projected on to it.

"You see the viewing gallery," said Dr Fernster. "The platform you stood on when you entered the Basilica."

"I do," I said, looking up at it. There were people leaning on the ropes that marked its boundary, but there was no longer anything for them to view.

"Where are the steps?"

The Basilica was built no higher than this platform. The sections that had been roped off were forbidden to the public, as they did not exist. The facade I had imagined soared up to the heavens, but in reality, the higher parts of the Basilica had not been built.

"It only goes up one storey," said Dr Fernster. "The tower is entirely imaginary. So if you climbed it, where were you?"

I had no answer for him. I could only remember the solidity of the stone steps beneath my feet, the roughness of the walls as I had run my fingers against them, the vertigo I had felt as I looked out of the window.

"You climbed an imaginary staircase in an imaginary tower. What does that make you?"

"I'm not doing this," I said. I looked down to the earth, then back up at the Basilica. It appeared just as the city designers had ordained—vast, intricate, complex, and with an empty tower. "I just want my creature back."

"And how are you going to do that? Imagine her?"

"I heard her. She's as real as I am." Dr Fernster just smiled; I was infuriated. "I know what you're making out. Forget it. You can't imagine your own city, and you can't populate it with your own people. I'm not a figment of your imagination. Your imagination isn't good enough to come up with me."

"No? And how do you intend to prove this to me?"

"Ask Matthias Grix. Or did you imagine him as well?"

"Perhaps I will. But I don't think it matters. You know what you must do."

He turned and left me with no further comment. I had learnt nothing from him; my muse remained absent, and my piece would be silent. Dr Fernster, I knew now, was dangerous. He could tear our city down brick by brick if he were allowed to continue his individual imaginations. Our laws held our city together.

I walked up to the wall of the Basilica. I pressed my hand against its stone. It was solid beneath my touch, cold and unwelcoming. I could not push myself through the stone. It was real; so was my hand. I heard the creature's song in my head. It surprised me; I had not put it there deliberately. But the song, too, was real.

Without understanding what I was doing, I allowed myself to join the queue of tourists, and I was slowly carried into the great hall. Once again I took my turn to climb the steps to the viewing platform. This time I loitered, marvelling at the design of the ceiling, a depiction of the building of the Basilica, which had never happened. One section of the ceiling showed the painting of the ceiling itself.

Dr Fernster was right; I knew what I had to do. Once again I crossed the boundary that kept the public away from the upper reaches of the Basilica. Once again I climbed the stone steps toward the tower. I knew, now, that there were no steps beneath me. I had seen what Dr Fernster had showed me, the wooden platform that formed the upper limit of the Basilica's infrastructure. And yet, I ascended.

When I was high enough above the platform, I stopped, took a breath, and let the illusion slip. I braced myself, wondering if I would plummet down to the platform beneath me, or if I would see myself hovering in the air. But in fact, I continued to see the stone stairwell. Nothing I could do would dissipate the mirage. It was as real as I was.

I continued to climb, finally understanding. The city was real to those who imagined it, and so was I. The life I had lived was gone from me. The friends I had made would see me only if they chose to do so, and that was proscribed by the rules which forbade individual imaginings. Only if the city designers formally authorised my existence could I take my place again among the citizens. This was what Dr Fernster was trying to bring about.

I made my way to the chamber at the top of the tower. I remembered the fleeting vision of beauty I had had the last time I was here. I could offer no such vision to anyone else. I walked to the window.

The song was strong in my head. My own voice was a baritone, not a soprano, but it could sing the same song as the creature I had seen here. Would I grow wings? Or when my own turn came to throw myself through the window, would I plummet downward, my final embrace with the earth ending my song forever?

I began to fill the air of the city with my song, a mournful expression of all I had lost. And far away, I imagined that Dr Fernster listened, and perhaps felt some of my sadness.

MAX CARLTON is a composer whose most famous work is *Concerto for Orchestra and Absent Violin*, for which the audience had to learn the melody in advance and imagine it being played over the orchestra. His current whereabouts are unknown.

NEIL JAMES HUDSON is a UK-based writer who has published over forty stories. His collection *The End of the World: A User's Guide* can be obtained from his website at neiljameshudson.net, and his paranormal romance *On Wings of Pity* is available on Amazon. He lives in the North York Moors, but spends much of his time in York, where he works as a charity shop manager, and is studying for an MA in Creative Writing at York St John University.

NIMBLE

An account by Ximena Alto,
AS PROVIDED BY M. LOPES DA SILVA

Retrieved from the miscellaneous files of the Unusual Cloud Society.

I saw your request online for personal accounts of "paranormal or otherwise supernatural encounters with clouds," and I immediately thought of Nimble.

I was thirty-six and I felt like I was in a fog most of the time—just groping my way from one moment to the next—checking things off lists and trying to get enough sleep (but never really managing to). I worked in the graphics department of an advertising agency. The work didn't pay much, but I liked being able to draw for a living, and that was enough—at least, it had been at one point in my life. Now I wasn't so sure.

Most of my friends had left the city, which had become increasingly expensive over the years. It was hard to make new friends. I didn't remember how I'd made friends in the first place—it all felt accidental. Now the accidents happened less and less often. And I was in that lull between relationships where loneliness was looking more and more like a permanent state of being instead of a temporary situation.

It was late at the office. I'd just worked overtime for two nights in a row, and had been promised the night off, but I was waiting on an edit from the typography department, and it wasn't looking good. Then came the telltale knock at the white board. "Crunch time!" our manager sang out, flexing his arms. I knew for a fact that he was not going to be staying late that night.

"'Crunch time' is the moment they decide to feed you to the project," I quipped, but my coworkers glanced away. My manager gave me A Look, and then picked up his phone and sent me an email: another warning about my attitude. When we finally got the edit, the change from typography set us back by three hours, but our manager got to make a head start on that road trip with his family that I'd overheard him anticipating all week.

Eventually I made it home that night, pushing through the fatigue and mental fog. I've never made enough money to own a house, and I worked overtime so often that I couldn't bring myself to buy a pet and make them suffer my schedule. So I filled my small apartment with plants, mostly easygoing ones that liked the dark and were fairly drought resistant, and watched television episode reruns of creepy, kooky families who loved each other and supported each other even though they were monsters and ghouls before I drifted off to sleep.

At least, that's what I usually did at night. That night was different. When I got home that evening, ready to microwave some dinner and watch television, I saw something hovering in the middle of my living room, smiling at me.

Of course it was Nimble.

I blinked, wondering if I was going to go temporarily blind again; that had happened a couple times at my job. It was a side effect from staring too intently at the screen and not taking enough breaks. It would usually start as a gray spot or blur that would just get bigger and bigger, until I couldn't see anything except maybe flashes at the periphery. But when I looked away, the cloud in my living room remained exactly where it hovered.

I'd also had hallucinations brought on by sleep deprivation before, but nothing had been as vivid and, frankly, joyful as Nimble was. The name came to me because of the puffy shape of Nimble's body: a perfectly cuddly cumulonimbus. Nimble had two black, shiny eyes and a crooked smirk with one tooth pointing up and another pointing down at the edges.

"Are you hungry?" I croaked out, because I was. The cloud bobbed up and down in response.

Through trial and error, we discovered that Nimble liked to snack on ice cubes and mineral water, but would make do with tap in a pinch. Nimble could make a few vocal noises, nothing close to anything resembling words—just coos and trills—but loved to listen.

"I feel so lost," I said, "like a kid at a department store. Like I just wish my parents would come and get me already—even though they both passed away years ago." I blushed, deeply embarrassed, but Nimble made a soft trill like a purr, and I reached out to do the impossible: to hug a cloud.

To my surprise, it wasn't an exercise in futility—there was something substantial there to hug—warm and soft and deeply comforting, and I broke down crying, just going to pieces, and Nimble cooed and hugged me back somehow and absorbed every single one of my tears into their fuzzy particulate.

I knew I had to start taking care of myself like a parent: loving myself responsibly, and treating myself with dignity and respect.

But first, I had the weekend with Nimble.

Nimble could fly—zip and swoop and soar like a bird—and loved the outdoors. We strolled through the park, my pet cloud and I, and when I got a cherry ice, I made sure to get an extra one for Nimble, too. No one else could see the cloud, or at least nobody remarked on it, which I'm sure they would have if they'd noticed. It was a very lazy weekend, with a lot of silly moments. Nimble had me in hysterics when they started to pose as different hairstyles on top of the pigeons' heads. I nearly choked on my ice. A person with an incredible jacket that looked like it was made of old purses rushed over to me.

"Are you O.K.?" they asked.

I nodded, flushing with a bit of embarrassment. "I'm fine, I'm fine!" I said. "Your jacket is amazing, by the way."

"You like it? I made it," they grinned, and I found myself smiling back.

"I love it," I said.

I quit my job the following Monday.

It was a big day for me. I signed up for an appointment with a therapist, I texted to hang out with my new friend Robin, and I said good-bye to Nimble. I knew it was coming to an end; Nimble was becoming more and more difficult to see. I think they were evaporating. But before they faded away entirely, I held them tightly to my chest, and they hugged me back.

"Thank you," I said, and they vanished.

So I don't know if this is what you're looking for, exactly, but I thought I'd send it to your society anyway. I've been doing a lot more things on impulse lately. Let me know what you think.

Sincerely,

Ximena Alto

XIMENA ALTO, a former graphic designer, currently works as a freelance illustrator in Los Angeles. Her artwork tends toward lively compositions with bright, vibrant palettes. She does not accept noncommercial inquiries. There is no other personal information presented on her illustration website, but in the picture provided in her bio, she looks happy.

M. LOPES DA SILVA is a bisexual author and artist from Los Angeles. Her fiction has appeared or is forthcoming in *Electric Literature*, *Glass and Gardens: Solarpunk Summers*, and *Nightscript Vol. IV* and *V*. She likes to put fairy and folk tales in everything she makes. She tends roses and cats alongside her partner, a film critic.

SEEN

An account by Ron Walker,
AS PROVIDED BY JACOB BUDENZ

When I opened my eyes a little wider and tilted my head just so—to see, really *see*—I noticed the fairies dancing between the floorboards of my bedroom. Have you ever passed by a painting every day without actually looking at it, and then just once, by chance, you take it in and realize you've been pacing past something shocking, like a painting of an angel fellating an alien, all along? You feel intrigued, but also kind of violated, when you think of how long the image has been slipping itself into your subconscious. Seeing the fairies felt like that, like maybe I'd been glancing at them out of the corner of my eye for my whole life. I watched the tiny glowing bodies dance in the ridges of the teal-painted hardwood, little naked, winged creatures all colorful and aglow like Christmas lights. I could've stared at them all morning if I didn't have to go to work.

Once I saw them, I couldn't stop seeing them, of course. They were everywhere, from a family of four in the orchid on my co-worker's desk (her cubicle always overflowed with over-the-top gestures from her fiancé) to three little blue men playing in the urinal like it was a goddamn water park.

When I mentioned my groundbreaking revelation about the fairies to Janet, the receptionist at work, she rolled her eyes and said (of all things), "Where the fuck have you been, Ronnie?"

But when I shrugged and walked off (I think she liked to call me "Ronnie" instead of "Ron" just to get under my skin), I glanced behind me to see her squinting at my back like I'd sprouted bat wings, and I didn't buy her shtick for a second. No, sir. She'd been acting all snarky and too-cool ever since she'd tried to set me up with her "gay best friend" Enrique. Oh, yeah, she'd given me the whole line, *He's just so sassy and funny like you,* and I'd said, *You know not all us fags are a perfect match by virtue of the fact that you know them, Janet. Anyway, some of us are happier being alone.* It was a petty thing to say, sure, and I was lying through my teeth about preferring to be alone (in reality, it was quite the opposite). Still, I had my pride. Anyway, if this Enrique had helped her pick out even *one* of her tacky, ill-fitting skirt suits, then he was as tasteless as she was, and I wanted no part in it. Honestly, I don't even know why I mentioned the fairies to Janet in the first place. I'd just sort of blurted it, eager to share the knowledge with someone, to share something new and exciting with another human, as I had so little occasion to do. Obviously the wrong move.

I typically preferred to take my lunch break off-site, alone, lest I got stuck talking about marketing data during the generous hour we got for break. Today, though, I had decided to bring a packed lunch to eat in the undersized kitchen on the fifth floor, to see if any of my co-workers talked about the fairies. It would give me *something* to talk about with *someone,* for once. I was getting lonelier and lonelier, less and less able to form relationships with the people around me, when the fairies showed up. When I brought my sad, soggy ham sandwich to the lunchroom (another reason I prefer to buy lunch offsite), I thought that if other people saw the tiny glowing creatures, maybe the universe was answering my private little pangs of loneliness, giving me some way to break through my bubble of isolation. I waited until Janet left the lunch room, because who knew what kind of passive aggressive humiliation she'd try to subject me to if the topic came up?

I was cautious, this time, and waited to see if the topic of fairies came up organically. After forty-five minutes, nobody said a word about them, nor did anyone seem to notice the wild antics of the little pink lady dancing lewdly around the rim of Jerry's bowl of tomato soup. Nope. Instead, spreadsheet horror stories consumed the majority of the conversation—precisely why I don't eat lunch with these people. Even Leslie from HR, with her funky hair colors and ayahuasca retreats and transformative experiences at "regional burn" festivals, acted oblivious. By the time I had to clock back in, I felt too embarrassed to bring it up. Was seeing the tiny glowing bodies so common an experience that nobody cared to talk about it? Had Janet whispered my revelation to the others and brought them in on some sick vengeful joke? Were they fucking with me? Either way, I was no closer to finding out what the fairies really were and whether they might have any real impact on our lives, and I was *certainly* no closer to figuring out how to find common ground with anyone vis-à-vis these weird creatures.

That night, my kitchen was so packed with little purple ladies dancing rave-style over the black-and-white linoleum that I tiptoed ever-so-slowly across the floor. The purple tide dodged my footfalls effortlessly, without disrupting the ecstatic convulsions of their tiny limbs. Of course they did. They'd been dodging my feet for years, surely, without my oblivious ass of a self having clue-one that they were there.

I poured myself a shot of honey whiskey, slugged it back. Poured myself a half-full glass and bent over so I was eye-level with the black granite counter, upon which several fairies (mostly green or yellow) were having an orgy. "Here's to you," I said. I raised the glass like we were all having a toast, like we were all friends. Of course I already knew they weren't listening. I knocked that one back pretty quick as well, practically in one gulp. Poured another glass on the rocks.

Hazy, I plopped down on the sagging couch in the living room and sprawled out, laptop on my belly. I typed "people who can see fairies what does it mean," because why the hell not? I scrolled for a while through various fairy enthusiast forums and a site called Witch Vox, but it was all fables or superstitious mumbo-jumbo or hippy spiritual shit. I scanned through legends about the dangers of entering into fairy rings (apparently this is just Not A Thing To Do), others about how to leave gifts out for the "fair folk" so they'd leave you alone or bring fortune on your household or bring back your changeling child or whatever (like, what kind of a fucked up parent tries to write off their child's developmental issues as their kid being an actual, real changeling?). I wasn't finding anyone who'd actually *seen* the fuckers.

"What the hell are you?" I shouted at the pink man and green lady languishing on the coffee table like they were sunbathing. Figures in profile, the fairies didn't even turn their heads. Even *they* ignored me! I might have been the only person on the face of the planet who could see the goddamn things, and they wouldn't give me the time of day. It figured.

Finally, I stumbled on it. About an hour, and two more honey whiskies, later—in that sweet spot of drunken exhaustion where I was too tired to get up and drag myself to bed—I stumbled across a thread on the r/Fairy "subreddit" entitled, "DOES ANYONE ELSE SEE THOSE TINY GLOWING FAIRY PEOPLE EVERYWHERE? I FEEL LIKE I'M GOING CRAZY." Yes, as it turned out. There were others of us, *many* of us, even! My sleepiness melted away. My heart thudded, thick as I felt with alcohol. I read the original post, by a user named Julianax89, clung to every word:

"OK this is going to sound CRAZY and im probably gonna DELETE this but has ANYONE ELSE been seeing like these fairy people all over the place like just doing there thing??? idk how to explain it, i feel like last week something like kinda clicked in my brain and now i just cant stop seeing them ALL OVER THE PLACE, and my girlfriend doesnt see them and she thinks im just tripping, like i use to microdose acid for my anxiety but i even STOPPED bc of the fairies, i havent REALLY gone on like an acid trip or anything in forever. thoughts?"

The time stamp was three years ago. My chest felt like it was expanding, like I was on one of those massive tower rides and it was about to drop. With the exception of one heavily downvoted comment from a user named [[chaosmagick666]]—"Yeah, you probably just took too much acid. It's too late for you now."—scores of users were replying in earnest. The first, catLover900: "Mother of two here. I started seeing them when my two year old was born. Seems like he sees them too, never thought of them as fairies but I guess that makes sense."

I scrolled through, eating everything up. Theories were made: aliens (of course), ghosts, demons, travelers from another dimension. Nothing conclusive, or all that convincing, and after the third theory (evidently inspired by X-Men) about how we must all share some evolved genetics and how we ought to band together to use our power for good but how we had to be careful about exposing it to the world lest people fear our mutant gifts and persecute us (like… ?), I began to get bored with these theories. No, what interested me more was people meeting and talking about it. Reddit users sounded off in various cities. "Support groups" were formed. People planned to get together, one-on-one or in groups, depending on the quantity of fairy-aware individuals in their area. Common ground! It seemed like a surprising number of people identified somewhere on the queer spectrum, felt the need to insert their queer identities or queer relationships into their comments somewhere. It was like those guys at the "LGBT-friendly" group therapy (read: all white gay men) who feel the need to slip something in about "how hard it is being a single gay man," and you think, oh my god, you're cruising this group therapy session, aren't you? On Reddit, though? Blame it on the Tumblr millennials, I guess—identity's gotta be a part of everything. In my whiskey-swirled state, I thought, god, all this on a Reddit thread, this tiny public pocket hiding out in the open on the internet, untouched by anyone who wasn't looking for it. What else was out there that I was missing? Elves? Sea monsters? God, as if going shirtless at the beach wasn't stressful enough already.

I was getting tired again—slipping away. I hit Control + F and searched the page for the word "Seattle," just to see if anyone was in my area so I could call it a night. One match, in a comment by a user named mitchthepainter: "Anyone here from Seattle want to meet up? This has been driving me crazy. Glad to know there are others though."

Time stamp: two years ago. Nobody had replied to him.

My hands shook when I went to comment, which signaled to me that I hadn't had enough to drink—I was still this nervous to reply semi-anonymously to someone's comment on a Reddit thread. Even if the username indicated that person was a guy, and the trend of the thread seemed to imply he might be queer, was I really that pathetic? Anyway, I slugged back a shot of Evan Williams—this was a practical shot, an anxiety-dulling shot, so I didn't bother with the honey whiskey—and the mostly green fairies, still having their orgy on my kitchen counter, god bless 'em, stared up at me in unison. Did they understand? All that alcohol, all that time on my computer, just to type a two-sentence reply, still a little nervous: "I live in Seattle. Just started seeing the fairies, if you're still interested in meeting up?"

God, looking back on it now, I was already setting myself up for rejection. *If you're still interested in meeting up?* But what if he didn't use Reddit anymore? What if he didn't want to meet up to talk about the fairies anymore? Couldn't see them anymore? Had a boyfriend (or worse, a girlfriend)? Was dead? But that last shot of Evan Williams was hitting me, and I decided that the comment wasn't enough. I clicked on his username, "mitchthepainter," clicked the "send message" link, titled my message, "Fairies in Seattle." What ensued was a message that I'd rather not repeat in its entirety. A brief preamble about my recent discovery of the fairies. My name, phone number, and (just in case) my rough schedule. I puzzled over a way to convey that I was also a single gay man without coming on too strong, or presuming that that would matter to him and/or had anything to do with why I was messaging him, or whatever. I settled on (and I don't know why the hell I thought this made any sense at the time), "With PRIDE, Ron."

I fell asleep on the couch, with my clothes on.

Aside from some fairies sitting in a campfire-esque circle next to my keyboard at work, as well as a dreadful honey-whiskey hangover, it was like the previous night had been a dream. The waking up in my rumpled clothes, on my couch. The dead phone, its alarm failing to wake me up in time for work. The text to my boss when I recharged it— "Running behind, family crisis kept me up really late, so so so sorry."— and that sluggish scramble to get ready for work as quickly as possible without upsetting my mammoth of a headache. I'd stayed up until god-knows-when because I thought my life might change, what with this fairy nonsense, this discovery that there actually *was* something special and different about me *and* that there were others out there, others who understood and who were therefore connected with me, inextricably, by this shared fact. But it was like a dream because I'd woken up that morning and everything was still the same—I was still alone, and I was no closer to being any less so, except that I'd messaged somebody on Reddit who'd probably never read my message to him, and if he did, who cared? It's not like it would change anything.

I got to work two hours late and avoided Janet's eyes when I walked past her desk.

"All work and no play, huh?" she shot at my back like a poisoned dart. "Blame it on the fairies, Ronnie?"

I droned through marketing data all morning. Chugged bottle after bottle of water and excused myself to the bathroom every twenty minutes. Throughout the morning, I watched my acid yellow piss progress to clearer and clearer shades. I tried to convince myself that my headache was improving, that I was feeling better.

My phone buzzed while I ate lunch at the tavern down the street. It happened just as I bit into one of those "hangover cure" burgers with the over-easy egg on top, and all I thought was, *What now?* The unfamiliar area code, the text: "Hey, this is Mitchell from Reddit." I froze, phone in one hand, burger in the other. Egg yolk dripped onto the plate and made a yellow puddle. Promptly, two red fairies hopped onto my plate and began to roll around in the fallen yolk.

It took me the entirety of lunch to respond. I took sloppy bites of my burger, alternating between ravenous hunger, hangover nausea, and of course anxiety over what to say to Mitchell. Yesterday, un-hungover, I would've marveled at the fairies glowing inside the bottles of liquor that lined the shelves behind the bar, some twirling and flipping like showy little mermaids, some still and placid, floating in the alcohol like embryos. Now, I was glaring at them—they were far less charming after drinking heavily on a weeknight. How to reply to Mitchell? Cutting straight to "let's meet up" might read a little desperate (we were meeting via the r/Fairy subreddit, not OKCupid, after all), but I was the worst at perpetuating text message small talk, always allowing conversations to fizzle out before getting to the big "when are you free?" moment. I felt sick. Was it the burger? It was probably the burger.

When I shuffled out of the tavern toward my office, the sun's harsh whiteness mocked my headache. "Hi Mitchell," I typed. "Ron here. How did you first notice them? What was it like? I feel like I have so many questions for you."

That felt right. It implied "I have so many questions for you that it might require a date." A date? *I* didn't say it. Out loud.

When I sat back down at my desk, I read his infuriatingly noncommittal reply: "Ask away." Okay, fair enough. So we were doing the dance. Did I detect a little coyness?

But then, he surprised me by sending *another* message, a long text:

"To answer your question, I was working on my Master's thesis, spending a lot of time in the studio and whatnot. Probably sleep deprived, not eating enough... But it was way different than any experiences with psychedelics... I felt really clear. I didn't feel delirious or anything. But honestly, I had to keep painting in that moment. Art school fucks with you, you get so busy. Bombs could be going off and you'd basically take your canvas to the bomb shelter... You know? So then until I finished my thesis, they just faded into the background. It was only after I graduated that I really started to process it."

If I wasn't stunned by the double-message, I was floored when he sent a *third* text after that one: "That was a lot, huh? Sorry, I've just never talked to anyone about this."

I distracted myself from my Mitchell-anxiety by doing my actual work, and then I distracted myself from my work by entering his phone number into Facebook to find his profile (you can do that, you know, and in case you were wondering, he had one of those inscrutable profiles where all you can see is the profile pictures, and they're all stills from obscure cartoons, close-ups of bugs, Karl Marx's face covered in the rainbow flag, etc. But the rainbow flag was promising?). Myriad fairies sat watching me from atop my desk, the rim of my cubicle, the edge of my computer monitor, my keyboard. They just sat, staring, like they were at a movie theater, minus tiny fairy popcorn. They all sat still except the ones on my computer keyboard, who dove out of the way when I went to type something but reclaimed their spots as soon as I lifted my hands.

I went for it. After sending my next two texts (and receiving five responses in return), I told him that we should probably, really get together in person—that we had so much to talk about.

Mitchell was small, with clipped dark hair and a thick, well-kept beard salted with the occasional white hair. He was the only customer in the tiny "pop-up" coffee shop (a white-walled, minimally decorated affair), sitting at one of the only two white Ikea tables. He must've known it was me looking nervously about, because he said my name, jumped up, and hugged me. I'm really tall as it is (six feet, four inches), but Mitchell's cheek pressed just under my left nipple when he hugged me, which suggested that he was definitely below average height. It was an odd choice on his part, hugging me, but his body was warm, and his embrace was enthusiastic, and it was an overcast, cold March day outside, and goddammit, wasn't it true that I hadn't been touched in… how long? He pulled away. He sported a blue flannel shirt and genuinely worn-looking jeans (not like those "distressed" jeans you pay a lot of money for). And, yes, when he turned to take his seat I *did* notice that the jeans, though loose-fitting, hugged a surprisingly meaty ass. God, how thirsty was I? I mean, it wasn't even clear whether he was actually gay. Anyway, it wasn't like we were on a date. We were just two guys meeting up to discuss the fact that we could see these tiny glowing fairies that the majority of the population couldn't see.

I got a cappuccino. Why not?

"I'm so excited to finally meet you," Mitchell said when I sat down. His voice was deceptively deep for his height, and his eyes darted around the room as if he was in awe of everything around him, just taking it all in, overwhelmed by the curvy silicone lampshade on the ceiling, titillated by the bare white walls. There weren't a whole lot of fairies at this joint for him to be looking at, either, so I assumed he was just bad at the whole eye contact thing.

Mitchell told me he was a visual artist—a painter, mostly, though he dabbled in some "sculptural work" and "installation."

"So you make sculptures, too?" I said. "That's really cool."

"Not exactly," he said with the patient tone of someone who's answered this question a hundred times. "Not like you'd think, anyway, not like marble sculptures of really toned men with small penises. They're more like, I guess, you know, abstract experiences with light and various materials, usually a lot of steel wool, and I guess I've been really into breaking mirrors and coating them in colored resin and making these, you know, it's almost like this sort of gesture toward stained glass, but more influenced by postmodernism and, sort of like, futurist movements. You know?"

I nodded emphatically, as if I actually did know. Resisted the urge to make a "that's a lot of bad luck" joke about the mirrors. Instead, I said, "Do you ever paint the fairies?"

"God, no. That would be kind of—" He gave me a look of sympathy, softened his tone. "I don't know, I always felt like that would be sort of pedestrian, you know? Painting fairies. You know, something so obvious."

"Oh, right." I said. "Of course."

"I mean, I do love the *Pressed Fairy Book*, you know that one? Totally genius. I have the twentieth anniversary edition. I'll show you sometime. But the fairies do show up in my pieces occasionally, though. I mean sometimes I make really subtle references, you know, little specks of pink and green light on a landscape instead of fireflies—not that I paint like *landscape* landscapes, but I have some shape studies in, like, I don't know, I'm really interested in marsh land and sort of portraying the bog in this minimal, but kind of fantastical sort of way sometimes."

"Right."

We both took awkward whose-turn-is-it-to-speak? sips from our respective mugs.

"So what is it you said you do, though?" he said. "Ron." Like he was trying to remind himself of my name, so he wouldn't forget it.

"I didn't," I said. "I didn't say. I'm, uh, I'm a marketing analyst."

"No shit!" Mitchell let out a single, low bark of laughter. There was a little blue man on the rim of his mug. He put his short, calloused index finger against the rim, and the fairy danced onto it, shocking me. He touched his finger to the table, and the little guy walked daintily onto the white surface. It began to twirl.

I must've been staring, and maybe my mouth was open (can neither confirm nor deny), because Mitchell said, "Oh man, you didn't know you could do that?"

"No!" I said. "Other than avoiding me when I walk through their dance parties, it seems like they don't even notice me. Like they see right through me until I'm in their way."

"They definitely notice you," he said, and he looked up directly into my face—for the first time since we'd sat down—like he knew everything about me. "You just have to interact with them like you believe they'll respond. You won't get their attention if you don't."

I gulped, froze, didn't know what to say. He'd said it like he saw right through me all of a sudden, like he knew my problem wasn't just getting the fairies to notice me.

"I guess even fairies just wanna be seen, huh?" I managed, weakly, feeling naked.

He smiled on an exhale, with teeth, and shook his head, but it was like the affirmative I-can't-believe-this kind of head shake and not the well-actually-not-quite kind of head shake, and he relieved me of the pressure to speak any further about it. "Oh, there's all sorts of cool things about them. Man, this is so exciting. You have so much to learn, you know? You're like a, I don't know, I don't want to say 'a blank canvas' because that's a little on the nose, but we have *so much* to talk about, you know? I've been paying so much attention to them, writing observations in a journal and whatnot." He repeated, "We have so much to talk about."

I nodded and forced a smile, but I wasn't so sure, at this point. I was starting to feel like he'd been without a captive audience as long as I'd been without a steady boyfriend (so pretty much forever), and now that his floodgates were opening, there wasn't a whole lot of room for anything else. Guys like Mitchell, once they ran out of things to say, they realized guys like me weren't all that interesting, or hip, or arty. God, fairies or not, why had I thought meeting this guy would change anything? He might as well have been straight (and his sexuality still wasn't completely clear to me)—we were light years from having anything in common.

"Marketing analyst," he went on. "That's cool though—" He pointed his head down, then up at me again (at least he was trying). "Hey, look, there's one on your shoulder."

I twisted my head, and he was right, my god! The white mug I'd been holding clattered against the little plate it came with. Foam sloshed over the rim, but no real damage was done. The disinterested barista glared at me for just a second before returning to whatever it was she was doing on her phone.

I dabbed at the foam on the table with a napkin and swallowed a sigh.

"You know," Mitchell said. "You're actually really pretty cute."

I hated myself a little bit for the way my stomach pitched and my chest fluttered. Was that really all it took? To go from uncertain-he's-even-gay to he's-gay-and-thinks-I'm-cute-so-maybe-there's-a-chance? God, I was pathetic. I was so taken aback that I *almost* didn't notice his awkward-as-ever phrasing, and I tried to squash down the suspicion that he was being backhanded as opposed to just not knowing how to deliver a genuine compliment.

"Thanks," I said. I didn't look up from the foam spill I was still blotting up, even though I'd already sopped up all the rogue cappuccino.

"I mean it," he said. "But I mean, you knew that already, huh?"

I wouldn't meet his gaze, which was probably darting all over the room anyway. I was too afraid I would see sympathy. "I guess, I don't know. I don't really fit into any of the traditional gay... types, you know? I don't really fit in with the whole *scene*."

He perked up at that. "Really? Me neither. I have a really hard time with most gay men. Too, I don't know, vanilla, I guess? Or maybe I'm just, you know, too weird. I wonder if anyone really does? You know, fit in with them?"

"Oh, I could think of plenty who do off the top of my head. Not that I'd remember their names. Or anything else about them. I mean, not much to remember, am I right?"

And then he was laughing. And, goddammit, it felt good to make him laugh. Okay? It did. He had a satisfying belly laugh, a real guffaw, the kind that was a little too loud, maybe a little irritating to anyone that wasn't in on the joke. And I was mugging a little bit. Sure, it was true I didn't fit in with most gay people. But it was less that I found them boring or forgettable and more that I had enough trouble fitting in with most people, and gay men—with their cliques, and their laundry lists of "preferences" boiling down to whiteness and/or physical fitness, and their need to put a label on every kind of homosexual—could be the toughest cookies to crack. Still, it's a well-known fact that all gays like to talk shit on "the scene," even those who are, as it were, totally immersed in it. Everyone seemed to agree: the gay scene was too shallow, too "normative," too judgy, too *whatever*, and guys like Mitchell, cooler-than-thou art guys, straight-passing guys, they always turned out to be, secretly, the judgiest of them all on this topic.

Incredibly, though, he didn't take the bait.

"Yeah," he said. "I mostly keep to myself these days, *you know?* I don't really date anymore. It just sort of got to be a deal breaker when someone couldn't see the fairies, you know? It's really, I don't know, it gets to be kind of alienating after a while. I guess you'd think it was all of us, you know, you'd think it was just maybe a gay thing in general, but I feel like maybe it's not really that many of us that can see them. But I guess you wouldn't know about any of that yet." He touched my wrist from across the table. "Since you're new to this, and all."

So, the sex with Mitchell. It was kind of awkward and not-great, but we both really tried, you know? For one thing, I'm not so much beefy as I am freakishly tall and a little out of shape, but the thing about having even the hint of a gut if you're gay, in my experience, is that people want you to be a hairy, roughhousing, hyper-masculine "bear" type, or an emasculated "total bottom." I was neither. I had skinny arms, and all the hair I had on my abdomen and chest was a light dusting of wispy blonde, and despite my generally large presence, I wasn't gonna shove some guy around and ravage him like he was Helen of fucking Troy—in other words, definitely not the bear anyone's looking for. I'm kind of a soft touch. So I think Mitchell got sort of *bottom* vibes from me right off the bat, which is also not generally the case if I've just met somebody—I mean, I'm not going to let a veritable stranger put his dick inside of me, especially if that stranger hardly comes up to my chest standing on his tiptoes. So when he was going down on me he kept doing that thing where he'd try to coax my thighs apart with his free hand and get a couple fingers up in there, but I was shut like Fort Knox, thank you very much. Neither of us had particularly energetic hands, two gay guys in their late twenties who had fallen off their fitness routines and were maybe not *super* excited by each other's bodies, but I don't know, I still feel like we were both pretty into it?

I will admit, I was relieved to find that Mitchell, despite his apparently petite stature, had a little bit of a paunch himself, that his torso looked a little better in well-fitted flannel than out of it. And he gave pretty good head. I don't know. And when he finally came, he was polite enough to warn me, polite enough not to do so in my mouth without asking, and that was kind of cool. Whatever, I guess it was really nice to be touched after all this time, okay?

When we'd both finished, Mitchell was resting his scratchy beard on the softness of my left pectoral (this was the post-coital ritual I hated most—two men, covered in rapidly drying semen, pretending that the small amount of heart-fluttery satisfaction that cuddling provided had the *potential* to outweigh the ickiness of sweat and sperm drying on the flesh). It was then I noticed for the first time that *they* were in the room with us. They stood perfectly still in a circle surrounding us (Mitchell had a king-sized bed, of course, despite his stature). Just looked on, expressionless. I was generally used to seeing the fairies in a state of perpetual motion, merriment, lewdness, mischief. Heart smacking against my ribs, I sat straight up, and Mitchell recoiled with one of those startled *uh* sounds. I'd spiraled far enough down the search engine rabbit hole the other night to know a thing or two about fairy rings, about falling asleep inside them, getting trapped in their world and kidnapped for god-knew how long. I leapt off the bed.

"Are you okay? What just happened?" he said. He sounded vaguely irritated, but his brow was pinched in what could have been genuine concern.

"Don't you see them? Mitchell, get out of there! That's a fairy ring. Oh my god, oh my god." I leaned over and grabbed his arm, trying to pull him off the bed to safety. I thought this to be a heroic gesture, risking falling into the fairy ring and being trapped there forever with him.

But Mitchell didn't budge. Instead, he let out an actual, real belly laugh.

"Fairy rings aren't really a thing." He waved his hand around the room. "They're just a bunch of perverts is all. Far as I can tell, at least." He pulled me back into the ring with him and kissed me.

It was Saturday, the following day, and I was lying in my bed watching reruns of *Twin Peaks*, thinking how glad I was that we'd gone to Mitchell's place and I'd seen he was at least as messy as I was. Honestly, I didn't really expect him to reach out to me after that. Heady art queers like him didn't usually get excited about guys they might perceive to be mainstream, guys with nine-to-fives that fed into the "horror of modern capitalism," guys that were guilty of an even worse sin—being boring. And if he did reach out to me (I felt like Mitchell was the kind of guy who'd want to text first, though the lines were always blurry with gay men on who should reach out to whom), I'm not sure how likely I was to respond. Sure, he seemed more or less normal, and surprisingly sweet, especially for an art queer, and wasn't there a certain charm to the way he seemed to start his sentences with no obvious plan for how they would end? But at the end of the day, he was an artist, likely hiding layers of emotional instability which he'd tout as the wellspring of his creativity. Or he'd be one of those "monogamy is a hegemonic tool that upholds the systemic oppression of queer people" types. Either way, a headache. Right? It wasn't worth it, right?

He waited an acceptable amount of time to reach out to me (around three in the afternoon, approximately six hours since I'd left his house). His message: "Hey, hope your Saturday is great! :) I had a really great time with you. I was wondering if you'd want to get together again soon? XO."

I looked up at the fairies perched atop my television set, gossiping to each other in a long row of orange light. I considered what they might be saying, wondered if maybe Mitchell might know how to listen. I vacillated. If he didn't know, wouldn't it be nice to lie around with someone who was equally as confused? Did it even matter what they were saying? I looked back at my phone. I had a hard time believing he'd actually had a good time (okay, so it was not the absolute worst as first dates went, I guess, maybe). A harder time believing I had the upper hand in this moment. The uncertainty implied in his question mark, the overall sweetness of his message—they weren't lost on me.

I regarded the fairies sitting on my TV and thought about what Mitchell had said, about addressing them with the confidence of someone who expects a response. I did my best: "What do you guys think? Is this Mitchell guy all right?"

And, amazingly, the fairies on my TV turned to me in unison, whispered amongst themselves and, finally, each gave me what looked like a thumbs up.

The cynical part of me wants to say that the fairies put some kind of spell on me. But probably it was just the presence of another who could see them, who was willing to see me and hear me and respond to me even when I hadn't believed he would. If he was right about how to get through to the fairies, maybe he was right about, well, maybe we really *did* have a lot to talk about. Is this what settling looks like? Whatever, I don't know. At any rate, I picked up my phone, made to tell him I was free that very night. Decided that would sound too eager. Waited five minutes so I didn't look desperate.

At last, I responded, "I'm free tomorrow if you are, or evenings during the week."

Born and raised in Redmond, Washington, **RON WALKER** is a marketing analyst who holds a BS in Statistics with a minor in communications from University of Washington. He has been saving up for a big trip in the last few years, but he has never been outside of Washington and doesn't know where to start. Maybe Ireland. Yes, he thinks he might like to visit Ireland.

JACOB BUDENZ is a writer, multi-disciplinary performer, and witch with an MFA in Creative Writing from University of New Orleans. The author of *Pastel Witcheries* (Seven Kitchens Press 2018), Jacob has recent work in journals such as *Pussy Magic*, *Liminality*, and *Slipstream*, as well as anthologies published by Mason Jar Press and Lycan Valley Press. For links to additional publications, as well as photos and videos of performances, visit http://jakebeearts.com/.

ART BY **Leigh Legler**

LEIGH's professional title is "illustrator," but that's just a nice word for "monster-maker," in this case. More information about them can be found at https://leighlegler.carbonmade.com/.

SPRAY

An account by Jasminda Singh,
AS PROVIDED BY LIZZ-AYN SHAARAWI

For as long as I could remember, a monster lived under my bed. It may sound farfetched, but I recall lying in my cot, listening to a creature slither around in the dark. I would cry until my parents raced into my room. My parents' entrance, along with the light from the corridor beyond my bedroom door, appeared to banish the monster. They would hold me, sing to me, but as soon as I grew sleepy, they'd put me back in the cot and close the door. The moment the room plunged into darkness, the creature would slither back over and take its place below me.

I grew older and graduated to a narrow child's bed. The creature now had more room to move around. One night, the monster was especially noisy. I waited until the bumps and creaks sounded farther away and raced out of the room before it could get me. Unfortunately, crawling into my parents' bed woke them up. When I told my parents why I sought the sanctuary of their room, my father became angry. "It's childish," he snapped. "You must learn to sleep in your own bed." My mother was more sympathetic. She promised to make me a bottle of monster spray the next morning.

Good to her word, after breakfast, I was presented with a bottle. Mother had written MONSTER SPRAY with a marker across the plastic. "It will protect you from any creatures that might live in your closet or under your bed," my mother said. Later, when my older sister came home, she warned me that if I slept with my hands or feet dangling over the edge of the bed, the monster wouldn't be able to resist a nibble or two. That was easy for her to say, she slept like the dead. Though Father complained, Mother let me sleep in their bed again that night. However, after two nights wedged between my father's snoring and my mother's cover stealing, I decided I'd rather brave the monster in my room.

The next night, I lay in bed, eyes wide, the squirt bottle clutched tightly in my hands. Outside, a light breeze blew. The branches on the tree outside of my window scraped against the glass. The shrill skree-skree made me wince. A low moan sounded. My mother had assured me that it was only the sound of the house settling, but she could say that in the bright light of day. Now, in the dark, the moan sounded scarier, closer. There it was again.

Moooaaaan.

Skree-skree.

It was then that I noticed the tree outside wasn't moving.

Moooaaaan.

Skree-skree.

The sound was coming from under my bed.

Moooooaaaan.

Skree-skree.

I tried to call out for my mother, but the words stuck in my throat. My sister was in the room next door. Perhaps I could throw something at the wall, get her attention. A quick glance around the room only disappointed me. Anything that would make enough noise was on my dresser across the room. I couldn't risk exposing my hands or feet to get them.

It was up to me and me alone. With a deep breath to steady myself, I rolled to the edge of the bed, leaned down, flipped the bed skirt up, and sprayed as much of the monster spray as I could. The room filled with the scent of lavender and lemon. A moment passed. Then another. I felt like a fool.

A moment later, the thing under the bed screamed.

I screamed.

The lamp in my room burst into light. I looked up to find my parents staring down at me. "What in the world?" Father asked.

"You'll wake the whole neighborhood!" Mother said.

"There's a monster under my bed."

Father sat on the edge of the bed and smoothed a lock of hair away from my face. "You were dreaming."

"I wasn't," I insisted. "I sprayed it with the monster spray and it screamed."

"There you go," Mother said. "The monster spray did its job. Now, everyone needs to sleep." Despite my protests, my parents tucked me in and kissed me goodnight. The lamp went dark. Still clutching the monster spray, I lay back against my pillows. My parents were right, I decided. If there was something under her bed, the spray would keep it away. A weight lifted off of me. I settled back into the pillows and was almost asleep when a voice from under my bed said, "That wasn't very nice."

I gasped. Was that a dream? Or was the monster under my bed talking to me? My finger found the trigger on the monster spray. "It's not nice to hide under a girl's bed, either."

"How else am I supposed to find any food?"

"You were going to eat me!" I said, shocked.

"Not you. Under-the-bed monsters only eat dust bunnies and dead spiders," the voice said.

"What about in-the-closet monsters?"

"They eat silverfish and moths."

I shook my head at the thought. "How do you know that if you're an under-the-bed monster?"

"My cousin is an in-the-closet monster. We bring different dishes to the family banquets."

Monster spray poised to shoot, I rolled to the edge of the bed and peeked under the bed skirt. It was too dark to make out anything except a large pair of eyes. "What's with the moans?"

"Don't you make a yummy sound when you eat something good?" the monster asked.

I thought for a moment. Yes, I supposed I did. "What about the skree-skree noise?"

The monster smiled, revealing triangular teeth. Fluffy bits of dust stuck out from between them. The teeth ground together as the monster chewed. *Skree-skree.*

"You need to floss," I said.

"What's that?"

"I'll show you tomorrow. Now be quiet so I can sleep."

"I've eaten everything beneath your bed, anyway," it said. "I'm off to your sister's bed for the next course."

"Bon appétit," I said with a yawn. The room grew quiet.

"Hey, little girl?" came the voice from under the bed.

"What?"

"No more monster spray, okay? That stuff really stings."

Another yawn escaped me. "No more monster spray. Goodnight."

"Goodnight."

Silence fell over the room. Just as I was drifting off, the closet door creaked open. I held up the monster spray. "Don't even think about it."

The door closed.

After that night, I no longer feared the monster under my bed. I've heard that bad monsters exist, both closet and under the bed, but isn't there good and bad in every group? For the good monsters, I say let them be. For the bad monsters, there is monster spray.

JASMINDA SINGH was a researcher of the occult for many years. She was known to refer to herself as both a nontraditional chemist and a homeopathic parapsychologist. Her decades of study uncovered numerous recipes for charms and wards. Eight years ago, she went into a dark wooded area in search of a rare flower and was never heard from again. Wails of grief emanated from under her bed for weeks.

LIZZ-AYN SHAARAWI is an author and screenwriter, a lover of the frightening, and a purchaser of clothing much more suited to a younger person. Though originally a Texan, she currently lives in the Pacific Northwest with her husband, two children, and two guinea pigs.

MY STUDENT'S OBSESSION

An account by Jenna Brenner,
AS PROVIDED BY TROY H. GARDNER

It took four school days before I'd noticed Adam Matthew Crews. In my defense, I had a lot going on. I'd left my job teaching middle school art for the last three years, moved to a new state, and started in at Franklin High School with nothing more than a *We'll Miss You, Miss Brenner* collage my former students tearfully gave me.

Adam Matthew was a quiet boy in my afternoon Art II class. It was a generally rambunctious group of juniors and seniors, but he sat by the far window and focused on his work. If it weren't for my attendance sheet, I wouldn't have even known his name.

I gave the students a self-portrait assignment that first week, as an icebreaker. I didn't have much time to look at the end results as they handed them in when they shuffled out of the class, but I had a free period following that, so I started assessing them. There were pencil sketches and inked drawings. Some were shaded in or colored with markers and crayons, and there was even a water painting.

The portraits more or less matched their artists, and I could tell I would be able to challenge this group more than I'd ever been able to at the middle school level I was used to.

But then there was Adam Matthew's "self-portrait." It looked fantastic, but it didn't remotely match him. If his name weren't printed in the bottom corner, I never would have thought of him. Adam had a pale, round face with green eyes and straight blond hair that fell to his shoulders. He'd sketched, inked, and colored a freckled redhead with baby blue eyes and a long, narrow face.

In an earlier class, I'd let a trans student sketch herself, but this didn't strike me as body dysmorphia. Maybe I was somehow misremembering? Maybe he'd dyed his hair and I'd missed the freckles? The teacher I'd replaced was a packrat, so I didn't have to go far to find past yearbooks. I found one from two years back, when Adam Matthew would have been a freshman, and flipped through the glossy pages.

As a freshman, the boy had short blond hair and a huge smile on his face. It didn't even look like the sullen student in my classroom. I found last year's yearbook and compared it. As a sophomore, his hair had grown out and the sparkle had vanished from his eyes. He looked just as emotionless as I knew him to be in class.

I grimaced. I'd seen bright students turn self-conscious during these years, but this felt different. Something awful happened, and I'd need to tread lightly. I'd have to get some intel before I asked the kid about the strange self-portrait, so I left my classroom and headed to the gym. I wasn't sure who'd be free, but Coach Sturgis struck me as a social butterfly. Besides, it may be cliché, but I've always appreciated a man in a uniform, and the coach's shorts and whistle were close enough.

He lorded over a game of volleyball, but he gave me a wave when I entered. The kids kept playing while I walked up to him.

"How's your first week at Franklin going?"

"Pretty good, thanks."

"A group of us grab drinks every other Friday. You're welcome to come with us tomorrow."

"I'm still unpacking and all that, but pencil me in for next time."

"Consider it inked in. What can I do you for?"

"I'm a little curious about one of my students. Adam Matthew—"

"No surprise there. The little bastard." Coach Sturgis snorted. "Sorry. What's he done now?"

I was not expecting the conversation with the affable gym teacher to go this route. "Nothing. He just drew a strange self-portrait."

"Freckled ginger?"

"How'd you know?"

"Kid's obsessed." He blew his whistle. "Try to keep it in the air, McCoy, it's called volleyball, so volley the ball."

"I'm confused," I said. "What's he obsessed with?"

Coach Sturgis nodded to himself. "Far as I know, Crews was a typical boy. Not Mr. Popular but well-adjusted enough. Single parent home—you know the mother, Lunch Lady Angela. The way I hear it, one day he put up a stink in English class. They were watching some movie, you know, compare it to whatever book they were reading?"

"Sure."

"Crews got all worked up that one of the main boys was miscast. They got some blond actor who didn't fit the physical description. He started raving about book 'canon consistency.'"

The coach laughed, but I couldn't help but feel for the kid. I'd been there myself. We'd read a historical fiction book in middle school, and I'd developed a crush on the main character, Johnny. That was when my interest in art was just starting to develop, so I'd spent hours working on my skills by drawing Johnny with his long blond hair and crippled hand. I'd been so disappointed when we watched the movie version. The actor was cute enough, but he just didn't match my imagination.

I'd run across a folder of those old sketches last month when I packed. It made me consider doing a whole new portfolio of Johnny to compare how I'd grown as an artist and as a person. I was sure I could really capture the pain of the skinny boy's crippled hand now.

"Anyway, Crews got himself detention, very out of character. Well, at the time. It didn't stop there. He wouldn't let it go, and he started incorporating the book into all of his assignments. Mentioning it in history, drawing that redhead on his math tests, reading from it in theater. The other students started avoiding him. Wish I could do the same."

"Because he's obsessed with a book?"

"It's not the book, it's one particular character. And there's more to it. The kid got weird. One day, last year, a student accidentally spiked a volleyball into Crews' face. He got a bloody nose. I came in the following day, and all the volleyballs were cut open. It was a rubber and leather massacre. I don't know how Crews got into the locked cabinet, but we all knew he did it. We're all just lucky he's not into *The Texas Chain Saw Massacre*."

I chuckled and asked, "Which English teacher gave him the assignment?"

"She's not here anymore. Took a tumble down the theater steps. She broke her hip and resigned."

"That's awful. Maybe I'll have a chat with Angela."

"Wait until tomorrow. She'll be at the bar already."

"At three on a Thursday?"

"Yep. Lunch ends at one, she cleans up for an hour, and then it's a fifteen-minute drive to the bar. It's never been a problem on school grounds."

I nodded, starting to get a better picture of the situation. "Who's the character, anyway?"

"I don't know, some tween wild child from an island book."

"Well there goes book authenticity," I joked. "Looked more like a sixteen-year-old's portrait."

"Oh, so now the obsessed loner is inconsistent? That's a real shame." He blew the whistle again. "Foul! Serve it again, Gracie."

I tried not to think about Adam Matthew any more that night, but I've never been great at leaving the school behind when I punched out. It didn't help any that I brought the self-portraits home to grade. My cable wasn't set up yet, so the only other option was to lose myself in a romance novel I was half through, but I wanted to savor the will they/won't they journey with the handsome young cop.

Adam Matthew's drawing was good, there was no denying that. It just didn't meet the assignment's requirements. I must have spent too much time studying it because that freckled redhead popped up in my dreams. He pushed a middle-aged woman down the stairs and whooped and laughed in an English accent.

There was a palpable sense of enthusiasm my first Friday at Franklin High. Students were eager for the weekend, teachers were eager to drink together, and I'd promised myself I'd finish unpacking. All we had to do was get through the day together.

"Miss Brenner?" The voice startled me. I looked up and found Adam Matthew. The other Art II students were loudly filing in behind him and taking their places.

"Hi, Adam Matthew."

He set a notebook down and started rifling through it. "Sorry I didn't hand in my portrait yesterday. I got behind." He found what he was looking for and handed in a rudimentary sketch of himself.

"You handed one in yesterday," I said slowly.

He shook his head and frowned. "This is mine. I stayed up last night finishing it."

"The freckled teen," I said.

"Oh yeah, Jack did one. He doesn't like being left out. He's better than me."

"I see," I said slowly, not quite getting it. Was he dissociative? Was this some grand prank? "Do you mind telling me about Jack? How'd he come into your life?"

He scratched his elbows and avoided eye contact. He shuffled and ran a hand through his long hair. "You know when you get a song stuck in your head?"

"That's called an ear worm."

"Jack's my mind worm. I'm not a big reader, but I got sucked into his story. He's the bad guy, but I kept thinking about him. Out there on the island. Losing his civility, turning savage. And we talked about it in class, and it turned out everything in the book is symbolic of something. I even went online and there's this paper about how it's super queer and the shell represents—well—" He trailed off and it took me several seconds to realize he was done talking without further prodding.

"It's a popular book."

"There's all these fanfiction stories online, too, and fan art, but none of them captured Jack like I see him."

"You see him?" I asked.

"It took a while. But he's in charge now." With that, he shot back to his isolated seat.

I compared the two portraits—this Jack and Adam Matthew—and concluded there was no way the same hand had drawn both.

I kept an eye on Adam Matthew during the class. He was withdrawn, but that seemed par for the course. What wasn't normal was when Mrs. Mason, one of the science teachers, barged into the classroom. We all looked up at her as she caught her breath, red faced. She glared around the room, and then her face fell at the sight of Adam Matthew.

"When'd you get here?" she demanded.

"Me?" he asked.

Mrs. Mason turned to me, asking, "When did he get here?"

"What's going on?" I asked.

"I stepped out of the lab for five minutes, and now the fetal pigs are everywhere."

I stood up and held my hands placatingly. All eyes were locked on us. "When did this happen?"

"Just now. I looked up his schedule, when did he get here?"

"Right before class started, and he didn't step out. Whatever happened, Adam Matthew didn't have anything to do with it."

"It's fetal pigs. He told me yesterday he doesn't want to have to dissect a pig, and he's obsessed with that book with the kids killing pigs. See?"

"It wasn't me," Adam Matthew said quietly.

"He's been here this whole time," I said.

"It must have been Jack." Adam Matthew looked around and shrugged. "He's not here right now."

"That's not helping," I said.

"Come with me, right now," Mrs. Mason told Adam Matthew.

"But I don't know where Jack is."

"There is no Jack!" she snapped. She took a deep breath and rubbed her temples. "Principal's office with me. Now."

I turned my back on the class and spoke quietly to Mrs. Mason. "I'd be happy to speak with Mr. Cavanaugh after class. Adam Matthew didn't do anything, and he has twenty-two alibis. I'll thank you not to disrupt my class any longer?"

Her mouth opened but she didn't say anything for several seconds. Finally, she threw her hands in the air and stomped out of the art room.

"Well," I said, turning back to my students. "That just happened. Hope she doesn't get me for the teacher's Secret Santa."

They let out nervous laughter. All except Adam Matthew, who merely gazed out the window. I glanced back at my desk. Sinister, charming Jack stared up at me. I turned over the drawing and got back to discussing clay modelling techniques with the class.

The window slammed shut and I spun toward it. Everyone had jumped and looked toward the window, except for Adam Matthew. He sat perfectly still, his chin resting on his fist.

For just a moment, his reflection's hair flashed red.

After spending the last period of the week telling Principal Cavanaugh that Adam Matthew couldn't have destroyed the fetal pigs—which cost the school hundreds of dollars and set Mrs. Mason's schedule back weeks—I decided unpacking could wait.

I met up with Coach Sturgis and five other teachers at the bar after going home and changing.

"Changed your mind, I see." Coach Sturgis waved me over to the table with four other co-workers, who scooted over to make space.

"We heard you got into it with Marcia Mason," one of them said.

"Wish I could have seen it," another added.

"It wasn't that bad. I mean, her eyes were bulging, but she was wrong. It was simple really."

"Hardly the case," Coach Sturgis said. "Nothing's simple when it comes to Lunch Lady Angela's boy." He nodded across the bar where Angela was dancing with some mustachioed biker, both of them spilling their beers.

My fellow teachers toasted to that.

"I take it the coach isn't the only one who's experienced— whatever it is?" I asked.

The others shook their heads.

"Every semester, I pray I don't see one name in my student roster book," the computer sciences teacher said.

"Isn't that harsh? He's polite."

"Sure. Sure. Two years ago, he took my Photoshop class. He got all these pictures of the actor who played his Jack character and Photoshopped him to look more like how he pictured him from the book. You know, change the hair, the eyes, add the freckles. To his credit, he got decent at it, but he wasn't happy, said it still didn't feel right. So then he started taking photos of gingers and tweaking them and putting them in an island background. He spent hours meticulously applying tribal war paint to redheads trying to perfect however he was described in that book. I finally told him enough was enough. Find something else to work on, you know?"

"How'd he take it?" I asked.

"He was upset. Said that was the only reason he was taking the class. Next day, I come in and my computer screen's cracked and all the space bars have been torn off the computers in the lab. You could still use the keyboards, but it was awkward as hell."

"And you think Adam Matthew did that?" I asked.

"Who else? Of course no one saw anything, so nothing could be proved. There's a hundred more stories just like that."

Coach Sturgis nodded sagely. "Best to just let the little weirdo do whatever he likes and keep your head down."

Across the bar, Angela Crews shoved the biker away amid cheering. Someone shouted for another round and Angela whooped. Coach Sturgis poured me a glass from the pitcher the others were sharing, and I nursed it for the next forty minutes.

My co-workers went on about students and other teachers, but I couldn't focus on the gossip enough to contribute, plus I didn't know enough people yet. And there was Angela Crews throwing back drinks. She looked like she was barely in her thirties, and I tried not to judge her as a former teen mom who never matured.

I excused myself to go to the restroom the moment Angela slipped away. I didn't have to go, but I couldn't help but seize the opportunity to speak with her.

It was quieter in the women's room and I fluffed my hair while Angela used one of the stalls. She emerged and stumbled to the sink.

"TGIF, right?" I asked.

"Ain't that the truth."

"I don't think we've formally met. I'm Jenna Brenner, the new art teacher."

She nodded. "Yep. Matty's got you, doesn't he?"

"Yes, sixth period. When you're ready, I could give you a lift home? Us girls have to stick together, right?"

She cracked her back and gave me a once over. "I'm flattered and all, but I don't feel like dyking out tonight."

"I—uh—no. I just wanted to make sure you got home all right. That's all. I'm not a lesbian."

"Doesn't bother me any. Sure though, yeah. Guess Matty's off the designated driver hook tonight. You're going to be his favorite teacher." She patted me on the back and headed back into the bar. "Give me another hour or so."

Coach Sturgis and the others gave shared gleeful looks when I finally wrangled Angela out of there, after the computer teacher warned me Angela might make a move. She collapsed into the passenger seat of my car and I decided not to risk trying to buckle her up; I'd just drive extra carefully.

"I was thinking," I said after a few minutes, "Adam Matthew is such a quiet kid. How's he act at home?"

"He better be home. Don't need him stirring up any more trouble, last time I… had… to…"

I waited for a minute before I realized there wouldn't be any more out of her except for snoring. At least she'd managed to give me her address when we first got in the car, so I enjoyed a relatively quiet ride to her place.

Angela came to with a start when I pulled into her driveway and shut off the engine.

"You made good time. You want a nightcap? Least I can do."

"Um, okay." I really didn't want to drink with her, but I had to get a look at Adam Matthew's living situation. If the kid needed help, it was my duty to put in a little reconnaissance.

Angela hopped out of the car, reinvigorated from her short nap, and led me inside the house.

I'm not sure what I was expecting, but it was a modest duplex with very little clutter. Some magazines were scattered around, and the kitchen sported empty beer bottles and a full sink of dishes.

"Sorry for the mess, wasn't expecting company." She set her purse on the coffee table. Something thumped upstairs. "Matty, we got company!" Angela shouted at the ceiling. She turned back to me. "I never understand teenage boys. Always banging around up there."

A toilet flushed from downstairs, and then Adam Matthew emerged from the hallway. The thumping upstairs suddenly went silent.

"Hi," he said, his face all twitchy.

"Your art teacher gave me a lift home. Nice to have someone at that school looking out for us, huh?"

"Yeah. That's great, Mom."

"Do you want me to make you some coffee or something?" I asked Angela.

"Matty can make it," she said, ushering us into the kitchen. He silently got to work filling the coffee pot and putting it on the stove.

"You seen my boy's artwork yet?" she asked me. "What do you think?"

"Very promising."

"He's always working on something. I say he should be a comic book drawer, you know? Use that imagination for some good."

"I'm not that good," he whispered, back still turned.

"Miss Brenner can help you out. That's the point of art class, isn't it?"

"One of them, sure." I looked up at the ceiling again. I just couldn't look past that thumping we'd heard when we came in. "Is there anyone else here?"

"Why would there be?" Angela asked while her son twitched.

"Just thought I heard something from upstairs."

"Damn squirrels on the roof. I need to get up there with a shotgun. That'd show 'em."

"You have a shotgun?" I asked.

"Nah."

That was something at least.

The banging started upstairs again. Neither of them seemed to notice.

A muffled ringtone buzzed, and Angela sighed. "Always somebody."

Adam Matthew rushed to the other room and carried Angela's purse back for her. She rifled through it and answered.

"Hi, Carl. What is this time? What's that? Fetal pigs?"

Adam Matthew went even paler. Apparently, the principal didn't take much stock in the new girl's testimony. Angela snapped her fingers and pointed to the kitchen chair and her son sheepishly fell into it.

They paid me as little attention as they did the stomping upstairs, so I quietly stepped out of the kitchen. Everyone was convinced Adam Matthew was a troublemaker, but I just couldn't see it. Something was going on in that house, but I wasn't ready to chalk it up to some fictional character. Angela's voice rose as she heard the principal's story and I eased up the stairs. The stomping ended, but I could tell which room it came from.

I eased open the door and was accosted by body odor and a metallic tang in the air. Heavy curtains were drawn over the windows, so I flipped on the light switch. The light bulb hummed as it dimly lit the unmade bed and a heap of dirty clothes on the floor. The walls were covered from floor to ceiling in paintings of Jack.

The bright red hair, the light blue eyes, the freckles spattering the wall like blood.

I stepped into the center of the room, searching for some elusive answer, but there was no sign of anyone and I couldn't figure out what had been making that sound. There wasn't even a radiator to blame.

"Mom grounded me," Adam Matthew said, suddenly in the doorway. "I wasn't going anywhere, anyway."

"All these pictures of Jack. What do you do with them?"

"I look." He shrugged and came closer, spinning reverently around the room. "It makes the itchy feeling go away. Sometimes I think if I can just get one image of him absolutely perfect, then everyone else will be able to see him, too."

I could relate. Even as a middle schooler, I'd been frustrated when I couldn't accurately draw Johnny the way I pictured him in my mind's eye.

"And then what?" I asked.

"What do you mean?" he asked.

Of course one of my students wouldn't think that far into the future. "What's Jack's goal?"

"I don't—he doesn't—"

"Matty!" Angela shouted. "I can't save your ass this time." She bounded up the stairs.

"It's Jack," he whined.

Just then, Angela let out an awful scream and I heard something crack on the stairs, then a few more thuds. Adam Matthew and I spun toward the hall, but his bedroom door slammed shut. Adam Matthew fell back on his bed and nearly hyperventilated.

"Jack's mad. He didn't like Mom. I'm going to get in so much trouble."

"This is madness. A character from some book is not doing this." My words felt hollow. Something else was in the house, I could feel it.

"His name is Jack, and he does whatever he wants. He's king of the wild boys. But I think deep down he wants a parent. That's what I heard in Health Class. Kids respect boundaries."

"Jack isn't a kid." I felt sure of that at least. Adam Matthew was experiencing something none of us could quantify or explain, but it wasn't a kid.

Footsteps in the hall grew louder.

"He is. He's the leader of the choir, he's a hunter, he's—"

"Listen to me very carefully." I grabbed Adam Matthew's shoulders as his bedroom door shook. "Whatever you're seeing, it's not the real character from your book."

"How do you know?"

I spun Adam Matthew around and gestured to the portraits of Jack through the last few years. "Because if he were some character plucked out of the pages, he'd always be the same thirteen-year-old boy, but he's aging!"

"But he told me he's Jack!"

"Imaginary friends are just like strangers on the internet—*they can lie*. Whatever this is, it's getting stronger and bolder and you're fading away. I get what you're doing. I read a book in middle school and I wanted the boy, Johnny, to be real so much, but he's fictional. He has to be."

The door handle turned, and the bedroom door creaked open. I held my breath, preparing myself to face "Jack," but there was nothing there.

"We're getting out of here," I said. "We'll check on your mom and we'll get help."

He nodded and followed me out of his bedroom.

Angela lay at the bottom of the steps. She wasn't moving.

"Don't look," I said, keeping Adam Matthew close behind.

The strong smell of coffee greeted me as we descended the stairs. I stepped around Angela's body and eased down the hallway. Adam Matthew stopped following me and eased into the kitchen.

All I heard was my heart beating under the boiling coffee.

"What are you doing?" I asked.

Adam Matthew chewed on his bottom lip as he approached the stove. He looked down at his hand and tears glistened his eyes. "Jack says you'll stay and be his mom if I'm Johnny." He removed the coffee pot lid. "I just got to hurt my hand."

I tried to shout at him to stop, but Adam Matthew plunged his hand into the boiling pot.

He screamed, but he held his hand firmly inside.

His burned flesh stank as I ran across the room. I pulled at Adam Matthew, but he struggled and the pot crashed to the floor, shattering and splaying hot coffee and glass everywhere.

Adam Matthew held up his blistered hand, the fingers bent painfully, the skin burned and peeling.

"Am I Johnny now?" he asked, and then he promptly passed out.

I had to admit, the clothes were too modern, but with his long blond hair and that hand, he did resemble Johnny.

Glass crunched under foot behind me, and the hair rose on the back of my neck.

"He makes a right proper Johnny." The adolescent voice in my ear spoke with an English accent.

I was right. We weren't alone. The trouble-making entity was right behind me, and my body tingled at the thought of whatever it could be.

"You're real, but you're not Jack," I said, staring straight ahead. I couldn't risk facing it.

"Why don't you look at me and decide for yourself, Miss?"

"No. I don't know what you are, but I know what you're not. You're not Jack, and you're not good. I'm taking Adam Matthew to the hospital, and I'm getting him all the help he needs."

I bent and scooped the boy in my arms. He was light enough, and all I had to do was get him out of the house.

I kept my head down to avoid the thing in the kitchen.

The voice screamed and cried at me as I carried Adam Matthew away.

I parked in front of the hospital and an orderly helped Adam Matthew shuffle inside. A doctor spoke to me, and I did my best to explain what I could without mentioning Jack. I told them his mother fell down the stairs and that he'd hurt his hand in as vague a way as possible. He assured me they'd send paramedics to the house for Angela.

A nurse let me sit in a small waiting room by myself.

It was only a matter of time before a handsome young cop strode into the room and gave me a reassuring smile.

"Miss Brenner?"

"Yes. How's Adam Matthew?"

"He's in the best place for him. They're seeing what they can do about his hand. And then he'll speak with a mental health expert."

"Good. Good."

"There's something you should know. Officers arrived at the Crews' residence in time. Angela Crews is here. She's unconscious but stable. Lucky for her she was drunk when she fell, so her body was relaxed."

"That's amazing," I said. "Oh, what a relief."

He smiled warmly at me. "Not every day I get to give good news. That smile makes the shitty days worth it."

My smile grew, and I felt a blush creep up my neck. "I'm just glad Adam Matthew doesn't weigh all that much."

"He's lucky to have a teacher who cares so much. We'd all be better off with someone like you in our lives. You're free to go, you know? We could have someone call you when the boy's out of surgery."

"I'd really prefer to wait here, if that's all right?"

"Of course it is. Say, I'm just getting off my shift, would you mind a little company?"

"Not at all, officer."

He sat and asked me questions about my life and work and it didn't at all feel like an interrogation, but almost like a first date. I tried to hold back those warm, fuzzy feelings, but there was no denying it.

Maybe something good could come out of all of this. Maybe this would be the wake-up call Angela needed to sober up, and Adam Matthew would finally get some help.

The door opened and in stepped another uniformed officer, this one older and paunchy. "Miss Brenner?"

"That's me."

"If you don't mind, I'd like to ask you a few questions about what exactly happened at the Crews' home."

"Sure, but I already went over everything with—" It dawned on me that I didn't even know the handsome young officer's name. I turned to him, and he just gave me a heart-melting smile and I lost my train of thought. I couldn't even imagine a more ideal man.

"With whom, Miss Brenner?" The older cop followed my gaze at the handsome officer in the chair, but he looked right past him.

"Sorry, but you're going to have to repeat yourself to the real policeman," my handsome officer said. "They'll go easier on you if you don't let on that you can see me." His dimples spread as he grinned from ear to ear.

JENNA BRENNER is dedicated to enriching her students' lives through art in and outside of the classroom. She holds an M.A.T. in Art Education from the Massachusetts College of Liberal Arts. She recently moved to Franklin to teach at the high school level after enjoying three years working in middle schools. She misses her kids, but she's excited for the next chapter in her career.

She is an advocate for art therapy funding.

TROY H. GARDNER was born in Florida. He grew up and earned his Bachelor's Degree in New England before returning to the Sunshine State just in time for Hurricane Irma.

He started writing stories on his Tandy Personal Computer in the '90s after devouring the works of Stephen King in elementary school.

Red is his favorite color, but blue hasn't gotten the memo yet.

When Troy isn't writing, or talking about writing, he enjoys killing hours on his PlayStation or watching horror movies (both really great and incredibly bad are his jam). You can find him on Twitter @ TroyHGardner.

EXIT
INTERVIEW

An account by Lev Ockenshaw,
AS PROVIDED BY TUCKER LIEBERMAN

"Welcome to 'Exit Interview,' a special episode of *Television Quiz*, the world's first televised gameshow! Tonight, we talk to only one man, and he only has to answer one question!"

The roulette wheel, big as a hot tub and painted in mustard, pea, and magenta, was between me and the show's host. The wheel lay flat and was at the level of my navel. My hands twitched in my pockets.

"The date is October 26, 1940. I'm your host, Mr. Destiny, and today my guest is—"

In my spare time, I was the self-appointed biographer of Chad Goeing. He lived in Boston and handwrote a sprawling treatise on the nature of time plus a personal journal in which he complained about his treatment for an inguinal hernia as a child. These unpublished papers were kept at the library at Copley. They contained enough details, as well as many clues with which I could pursue secondary sources, for me to write his entire biography—stopping short of his hour of death, of course.

There was the hardest nut to crack. The obituary archived with his papers began, "He was born in 1901," and ended, "He died on October 26, 1940." There was no further explanation. Had he fallen ill or met with an accident, surely the obituary would have said so? The most sensible interpretation, to me, was suicide. His large manuscript, its unpublishability, all that wasted effort, the obsession, the frustration with the intractable meaning of time—after all that, he had killed himself at age 39. But by what method, and how could I be certain? I could not finish writing his biography until I could answer this.

In my imagination, I frequently returned to October 26, 1940. I did this so often, with so much fervor, that it was as if it really were 1940, not 2015. When I went back to this imagined day, I saw clearly how the sun rose, the skies were clear, and Chad Goeing was in perfect health. I could not see how the day ended for him.

"Please tell us what you do for a living," Mr. Destiny asked me in front of the audience for *Television Quiz*, the entire nation on the other side of the camera.

"I'm a biographer."

"Ah, of what sort of people?"

"Only one man, I'm afraid." I twisted my hands. "I call him Chad. And he's dead."

"That must make your job a bit difficult."

"Yes, it does."

"Tonight, we've got a special question for you related to your biographical subject. The question is: *How did Chad Goeing die?* Are you ready to guess the answer to this?"

My biography of Chad Goeing was almost complete, but I still did not know how he died. I had little opportunity to pursue that loose end because the office demanded most of my time. Writing about Chad wasn't my real job. If I were to be on a show like the very first *Television Quiz*, I'd call myself a biographer because it would sound good on a national broadcast, but in actuality I manipulated data spreadsheets.

Looking out from the fifth-floor boardroom window over the Charles River, it occurred to me that, in 1940, after a decade of the Great Depression, Chad might have jumped. I have heard that it is a myth, in the sense of a fiction, that businessmen suddenly leapt to their deaths right after the stock crash in '29; however, considering myth in the sense of tragedy, of story, of deep truth, it makes sense. It is true without being true.

"What if Chad jumped?"

"Interesting," said my coworker Aparna, the only other person in the room, not looking up. She'd listened to me talk about Chad a lot.

"Or maybe he hanged himself. It was a leap, I see his feet springing, he's falling through the air, I see him land."

The boss strode into the boardroom, and I fell silent.

Stanley was my friend with whom I often spent time on the beach in summer. He coached Little League. I think he believed in ghosts, unlike Aparna; he was certainly more open to my stories about Chad than she was.

It was autumn now, and the weather had cooled off. Over the weekend, I planned to look for Chad's gravestone again. I'd prowled the cemetery before unsuccessfully, not even finding any of his family members who were supposed to be buried there. It was only a stone, if it even existed, but I wanted to cover all my bases. Sometimes gravestones have the name of a family member that turns out to be useful, and, once in a while, especially for soldiers and sailors, they hint at the manner of death. Stanley invited me over to his place for a beer, so I went there first for an early lunch and made him listen to what I was up to.

"A mental image of Chad jumping. An intuition," he said.

"Uh huh. Also, in my dreams, I keep seeing a storm. But I checked the weather reports for that day, and there wasn't a drop of precipitation."

"So what's the meaning of the image?" he asked me.

"I don't know."

"You don't have any ideas?"

"Not really," I admitted. "Just that, well—you've heard of the 'rainfall-assassination' hypothesis?"

"No, tell me."

"Ancient people became angry and stressed when there was a drought, and indeed Roman emperors were more likely to be assassinated during those years. I don't know where I can go with that, and that's the only connection I'm aware of between weather and death."

"Yeah, that sounds flimsy. Chad didn't kill himself in Boston in 1940 because it was or wasn't raining. I have a better idea. You've heard of the 'eighty/twenty rule'?"

"No, tell me."

"A small number of causes give you most of the results. The best twenty percent of the coffeeshops get eighty percent of the business. A fraction of your ideas direct most of what you do all day. Only the most aspirational rats in the backyard are chewing up your basement. And so on."

"OK, but what's that got to do with jumping, with the weather?"

"I'm just giving you general advice. Here, I want you to have Maria." Stanley passed a small, plastic figurine of the Virgin Mary to me. She was wearing a blue robe. A child-sized necklace, a thin metal cross on a thin chain, was wrapped around the figurine multiple times. Stanley fingered the cross.

"What's the deal with her?"

"Maria, the Madonna, she's the prime cause. She gives you, like, 80 percent of the answer to everything. You have to do the rest. Put a good bit of yourself into it. That's how you reach the finish line."

"I hate activities where I have to do 'the rest.' A spirit is controlling the outcome and I have to jump for what she's dangling?"

"I could give you the answer, but I don't think you want me to."

If I, Chad's biographer, did not know how Chad died, Stanley didn't either. I didn't know why he would assume that he had the answer. I opened my mouth to object, but the television in the background suddenly announced: *80 percent chance of rain.*

"Now, see that. I'm not sure I want to go to the cemetery today," I said. I did want to make progress in my research for Chad's biography, but I also wanted another beer with Stanley.

"You should go. Maria helps you out by doing 80 percent of the work. She grades on a curve. You start with a B-minus. You are already saved. It might rain."

"What if I can't find Chad's stone? What if I don't put in my 20 percent of effort?"

"Then, no stone, B-minus. Those are the external consequences."

He was right, of course. Laziness due to weather gets the same results as laziness for any other reason. Elections are lost this way: it rains a little, and people don't go to the polls. "If I don't find this stone, and if I never find out how Chad died, I'll be enormously frustrated."

"So go to the cemetery in the rain and put in your 20 percent. We've been over this. We practiced. I coached you. It was basic—like in the military. It was like what we do in baseball in the spring. You got the full treatment. Now it's your time to act. Move. The dead go fast!"

The dead go fast. What a weird inspirational phrase.

I drove alone to the large, historic cemetery. Due to its age, it was free of mourners. I walked dozens of sections before spotting the names of Chad's relatives on the stones. This was a bittersweet breakthrough. The sad thing about learning a story is that you can never read it the same way again. It will never again be the first time you heard it, the newness, the ignorance, the blank tiles without the letters, the wonder.

That's a component of grief, too. As long as someone's alive, you can't know how their story ends. It could always change, and you could learn more. But the moment they die, their tale is finite, and they don't guard their own mysteries anymore. If there's anything you missed, maybe you have to look it up on microfilm, but they're done creating. They can never make another new chapter to surprise you.

Next to the stones with the names of the elder Goeings, a flat, cross-shaped placard, half-submerged in mud and grass sprouts, marked Chad's grave. It bore only his initials, a minimalism that seemed to me like someone's attempt to forget.

I took the figurine of Maria from my pocket and placed her standing upright on Chad's placard. Her cross necklace had unwound and fallen off in my pocket; I placed it around her again. The sky darkened and thundered.

The office walls had been clawing at me, and so, too, the city with its anti-terrorism subway posters, "If you see something, say something"—all of it too much. I drove to Provincetown to get some space, some relaxation, some drag. I stood in one of the popular restaurants with a water view where small speakers in the ceiling played Madonna's *Immaculate Collection* album on infinite repeat. "Rain," her voice reverbed in that soothing, famous ballad.

Gulls danced on the shore, spreading, closing, spreading their wings as if they were about to take flight.

I pulled the religious figurine out of my pocket. I had the sense of being privy to the mechanical workings of a cosmic joke that was on me. Maria's plastic visage was silent.

Persistence. Endurance. Those were my virtues. Driving from Boston to Provincetown didn't feel like enough of an exercise for me. Thoreau would have walked the same route. Under the right circumstances, I might walk it carrying my own cross, a tree that weighed as much as I did, in the rain, even, if someone made me, or if there was an answer at the end of it.

The gameshow host grinned and wound his arm like a baseball pitcher. "How did Chad Goeing die? Little League already has the answer. Do you have the answer?"

That was an infuriating tease. In addition to which, I had no idea how Mr. Destiny knew about Stanley and Little League, and I was too upset to ask.

"No," I said mildly.

"You can guess one letter at a time," Mr. Destiny prompted.

I conjured a mental impression of Stanley on the baseball field with all the idealism that nostalgia perpetrates. In my imagination, Stanley wore a team jersey, but the logo was obscured by a wrinkle. A young boy stood beside him. Behind the field was a white church with a steeple, and the dark-crowned suburban trees spread beyond. What letter could be correct here? "L" for Little League?

At the office, I called Aparna for help with my personal problem. She always had a sense of what was going on.

"How about you just take your best guess at how Chad died, publish the biography, and be done with it?" she asked.

This was heresy. "I cannot possibly do that. I have to know for certain."

"You could accelerate your thinking. That might be nice."

"Oh no, please, don't accelerate me. Anything but that. I'm already like a hamster wheel."

"I don't want to accelerate your hamster wheel. I want to remove you from it, relocate and redirect you, so that, whatever your next move is, it will accelerate your life. I want to help you be where you need to be. Which is not on the hamster wheel."

"How do I do that?"

"You have to answer the question."

"That's what I'm obsessing about."

"You have to answer it so you can stop obsessing about it. How did Chad die? Just pick an answer. Any answer."

"Gambling?" I mused. Spooling through hypotheses about Chad was one of my favorite pastimes. "The Depression hit him hard. He got in a fight, maybe."

"Could be. Did he seem like the gambling type to you?"

I thought of the thousands of carefully handwritten pages about the nature of time, researched and annotated, stored at the library at Copley. "No. He liked reasons and consequences. He knew where he was going."

"He meant to kill himself." She nodded in agreement.

"Russian roulette?" I imagined him spinning the pistol's chamber. "No. Not even that. Something more certain."

The imaginary hamster wheel fluttered in my head. I could hear the clack-clack-clack of the metal. "That sound," I said to myself.

"What sound?" Aparna asked.

"There's a sound associated with Chad's death. I wish I could play the sound for you. Was it electromagnetic noise? Static? Was he on TV, and he died, and they killed the signal?"

"Is that what it sounds like when you overthink?"

"Yes."

"Maybe you're hearing the sound of your own thoughts and not Chad's death."

"How do I know the difference?"

"You have to answer this question before it drives you insane. Here, a more practical idea: I brought you a sandwich."

According to Boston legend, Charlie's wife throws him a sandwich to sustain him on his hellish eternal subway trip but not a nickel for the turnstile so he can escape the repetition for good. I ate the sandwich.

I took the T to the Vital Records office. A glass door opened automatically. At the end of the hallway, a clerk sat behind a service window. I was the only customer in the building.

"I'm looking for a historical death certificate," I said.

"What year?"

"1940."

The clerk took a metal box off a high shelf and opened it, exposing index cards. "What name?"

"Chad Goeing," I said.

She flipped through them briefly and then issued her answer. "I can't give you that. It's sealed."

"Why would it be sealed?"

"I can't tell you that. Unless," she said, "you can pay for it."

"How much is it?"

"Seven thousand dollars," she said, deadpan.

I spun around and walked toward the door.

"I'll see you again when you're ready to negotiate," she said.

Was everyone in Boston playing with me? In psychic spiritualism, your "control" is the dead person who chooses you and controls you. You can't choose the spirit. You can only choose how you react to it. What if there were multiple spirits playing with me?

I boarded the T again and got off at Copley. The archives librarian knew me well. I mentioned to her that I was still researching Chad's death and that I had extended my search outside the library.

"You can't always see the situation while you're inside of it," she said.

What was that supposed to mean? "I'm not inside of the situation. My whole life is a situation. I emerge from it now and then to come here and find you."

"I know, that's what I'm saying. You have to pay better attention to your situation."

"But I need to know how he died. Do you know? Wouldn't you want to know, if you were me?"

"Of course I know how he died. I got that death certificate long ago."

"Can I see it?"

"No!" she said sharply, furrowing her brow. "It's not public. Earn your own death certificate."

"They won't give it to me at Vital Records. They said it's sealed," I said loudly, leaning on her desk.

She stood up, putting her hands on her desk to lean toward me, matching my body language. "Earn—your—own—certificate."

Damn it. This wheel of samsara, unending cycles of birth and death. I would never be free.

I didn't feel like sitting and reading. I called Stanley, and he met me above ground at Copley across the street from the library. We bought decafs in paper cups and brought them underground.

The thing about which you aren't talking is the thing you can't forget. Thoughts are a subway network. You can switch from one to the other. Rumination makes them run on time.

The green car pulled into the station. We boarded.

"I read the microfilm all day and couldn't find the answer."

"The answer is not in the library."

"What? Why did you say I was getting warmer?" I complained.

"For a little while, you had it. You were almost there."

"I am practically drowned in information."

"You can't see the situation, can you?" Stanley asked.

I kicked a hamburger wrapper. "I can't ever see the situation."

"This gets funnier all the time." He grinned.

"This is not funny. Do you know how many days I've taken off work at this point to obsess in the library?"

"At this point, though, Chad and Maria have basically given you 100 percent of the puzzle."

I had no idea what he was talking about. "It's like having the answer but more exactly like *not having the answer*," I argued.

"Life's a journey. You're so focused on the destination."

I was infuriated and said nothing. Ads flashed on the walls of the tunnel, the same poster affixed over and over, banking on the force of repetition. It meant we were pulling into the station.

I was still thinking, but the doors opened, interrupting. We got off at Park Street and went for soup.

Chad's ghost was there at one of the tables, waiting for us. He looked healthy, like a living man, though pale and drawn. Stanley, of course, could not see him. We'd been through this before, so I didn't bother to ask.

"I will figure you out," I hissed at Chad in a stage whisper while Stanley ordered for us at the counter. "Do you want me to have the same suicidal thought you're having, thousands of times, and never reach the answer?"

Chad wrote something on a napkin and passed it to me. "I like the way you think," it said. The ink was black.

Some people talk to God. Some people hear angels sing. Some people hear something else altogether. In those days, when I walked around Boston, now and then I heard a thunk-thunk-thunk, I turned around, and it was sure to be Chad, standing inside the city's last telephone booth, banging his head against the fogged-up glass. Chad had gotten something stuck in his head, and he was stuck in mine.

He wouldn't talk, either. He didn't seem to want me to hear his voice. He had other ways of making himself heard.

I wasn't taking care of myself. My vial of testosterone had run dry.

As I rifled through Chad's handwritten papers at the library, I saw his levitated corpse slap against the window over and over, his arms stretched out like a crucified man without a cross, his hands leaving fingerprints on the glass. So he wanted to appear to me as a dead man; that was fine with me. It was raining. The riddle of the deluge; the deluge of the riddle.

"Big wind today," the librarian said, not looking up.

I made a little conversation with her to distract myself from the ghost. "Chad's father was a railroad president, but Chad just wanted to write."

"Write, he did."

Amidst Chad's papers, there was a little cigar box full of travel tickets. He went to Mexico as a young man, I learned; he had an interest in some bridge, or at least his father had wanted him to take an interest in it. *Did he jump?* I wondered. But his trip to Mexico was long before his death. Might he have formed a fixation with that bridge that lasted for years? Or with bridges in general? Might he have jumped from some other bridge in Boston?

I looked at the analog clock on the wall. Two hours spent already at the library. Four hours remaining until closing. I had to work faster. I remembered, again, at this inconvenient moment, that I was a week late for my testosterone injection. I could ask to borrow a dose from Stanley or I could renew my prescription. Those were my options.

When the clock ran out, I left the library, walked south along Dartmouth Street, and went back in time. I closed my eyes and imagined I was the only paying passenger on a vehicle that traversed space and time. A flight attendant extended both arms simultaneously to point to emergency exits at both sides of the aircraft.

"Sir," she told me, "you have to stow your luggage."

"This?" I pointed to a splintered piece of wood. "This is my cross to bear."

"It needs to go in the overhead baggage compartment."

On this imaginary vehicle, I flew very far south.

On October 26, 1940, in Mexico City, I walked along a bridge, and a man was waiting for me, but it wasn't Chad Goeing. I didn't recognize him.

"I thought there might be a clue here," I said to the stranger. "It is hard for me to explain in Spanish."

"A ver si te enteras," he replied. "It will be hard for you to solve this puzzle in Spanish."

"Are you saying my Spanish is not very good?"

"Maybe the puzzle is not in Spanish."

It wasn't raining at all. Not a drop. It looked like it hadn't rained in weeks.

"Sometimes you go through a dry spell," he said. "That may have to do with your creative process taking you down the wrong road. I don't think your answer is in this country. The person you want is not here. He's going to die today, but that will happen somewhere else."

"Where can I find him?"

He shrugged. "You were hot on the trail. The death of God is like a key to open the heavens. Now you are cold. Your puzzle is not in Spanish."

I imagined Chad lying abandoned in the gutter, his face glazed, the rain running down his cheeks. Dead from the drink? Alcohol—that was a possibility I hadn't thought of, but the detail wasn't relevant now. Chad wasn't in Mexico City.

Put me on the Television Quiz *again, please.*

I flew there in my mind. Same date, different country. The game board was shrouded in fog. I thought I saw one white circle light up like a sign marking the subway entrance. I tried to peer through it, around it, wanting to see the rest of the word. It was like trying to look through the forest to see the trees.

All morning at the office, images flashed before my eyes. Cross, water, feet. Cross, water, feet. I felt I had all the information I need to solve it, but I couldn't see the answer. *What's the name of the feeling of almost having it?* I wondered. *"Cross water?" Maybe that's it. Maybe I have to duck boat across the Charles River and—*

I sighed and began again. *How did Chad die? How did Chad die? Why is this so hard? It's hard,* I answered myself, *because it's the water I swim in.*

The office itself was full of puzzles, a mountain of tickets in the system. It was like a giant crossword puzzle. I thought my project was supposed to be Agile, but it crashed down like Waterfall. When so much precipitates, I can't handle what comes downstream. If I have enough repetitions, I can do a quantitative analysis of the occurrences of the same thought, but that doesn't move me on to my next thought. Hamster wheel. Stanley's words echoed in my memory: *"You can't see the situation while you're inside it."* Good advice from Little League. Or, wait—where had I heard those words?

I had to get out of the office. I ran into the sunlight, behind the parking lot, into the trees, where I placed my ear to the ground. I felt vibrations, as happens with a change of weather, when the clouds fall to earth. I stood up and approached the muddy banks of the Charles River. There, I wandered up to my shins in mud, my khakis soaked.

Dead trees dotted the water, hardly any branches left, just ragged, black poles. It was easy for me to imagine dead bodies hanging on them as on crosses. Some things were becoming clear to me. Sometimes I have to stand with my feet in the water to gain a new perspective.

If you can forget for a moment that a cross is an instrument of execution, you can see its geometric function of dividing space into quadrants, and quadrants are useful if, for example, you are Jung, and you intend to divide consciousness into different types. You can also plot Cartesian coordinates on the axes, and then you can make like Adam Smith and find the intersection of supply and demand. I felt my brilliance rising and shooting out my ears. *Many people in the office are good at advanced math. I'd like to show them some pictures. No, do not make me reinvent calculus—just tell me what kind of special equation this graph looks like—*

Aparna was on my trail. I hadn't noticed her come up behind me. "I see what you're doing," she admonished me with an eyebrow raise.

I didn't really have an explanation. "I'm looking for patterns in the clouds."

"That's a sign of decompensation, mental collapse. That way lies more psychotherapy. Do you want to live in the puzzle forever, or do you want to solve the puzzle?"

"But I am solving the puzzle. Chad might have died over here," I confabulated, twisting my torso away from Aparna, moving my arm over the river, pointing out to the other shore. "I have to cross the water. I have to find out. This thing that I'm doing—"

"About *that*, yes. I have some new information for you about that."

I wheeled around. "What is it?"

"You're doing your thing in full view of the boardroom window. Everyone is worried about you. This is not a normal thing to do during lunch break. You're galoshing around a half-frozen pond with no galoshes. Other people go out for coffee."

"I have extra pants in my gym bag."

"That's not the point."

I trudged back to the office bathroom and cleaned up. I did need a break, but I would not buy a coffee until I had first gotten something important done.

I drove to Vital Records. Without Chad's death certificate, I couldn't be productive.

The same clerk was there. "You're back," she said, acknowledging me. She immediately pulled a manila envelope from the left side of her workstation and handed it to me. "CHAD GOEING" was already written in cursive pen on the outside of the envelope.

"How did you remember? How did you know I was coming back?"

She smirked. "That will be seven thousand dollars. My name is Mary Smith."

I wrote out the check to her. She palmed it and snapped the blinds shut on her service window.

A light rain had started up, so I slid the envelope inside my jacket and did not open it until I was safely behind the wheel of my parked car. The envelope was built oddly, fastened two ways, a double-safety method I had not seen before: a brad with two little brass wings that opened outward and also a hemp string that could be wound around the brad. I undid it. The death certificate slid out.

It looked like an ordinary document, which was slightly deflating, but it had the information I needed. Now Chad's death was given an exact place and an hour in my imagination.

I returned home to an apartment that didn't feel quite right. The living room and bedroom were in order, but my bathroom had been trashed. Someone had squirreled through the medicine cabinet and left empty vials rolling on the floor.

"Dammit, Chad," I said aloud.

There had been nothing in my medicine cabinet except aspirin and cologne. I didn't know what he was looking for. Troublesome ghost.

In the kitchen, I fished around in my pocket looking for a sugar packet to sweeten my tea. I came out with the figurine of Maria. I felt someone, an invisible presence, slap my wrist hard, and Maria went tumbling into the sink disposal.

This was some true poltergeist nonsense. It took an hour to extricate Maria from the grimy gears.

It was Monday, October 26, 2015, the seventy-fifth anniversary of Chad's death.

The boss stomped by. "You look like a wreck!"

"I'm having dreams," I said. "Interesting dreams—"

"I don't want to hear about it. I also have dreams. Everybody has a dream. This is not the time to talk about how you wish you were on a beach with a martini. My meeting in the boardroom starts in three minutes," he thundered, "and your entire project is due tomorrow! Are you in or out?"

I held his gaze for a second longer than I should have. "In."

He frowned. "Good. Act like it. Are you really trying to save your project, or are you chasing it into traffic?"

"I don't know."

"*Two* minutes until the meeting starts," he admonished himself, running off.

I heard a noise. Chad was scratching at my cubicle wall. Aparna also happened to walk by.

"Do you hear that?" I asked her. "It's Chad again."

"I hear nothing. Are you afraid of him?"

"No, I just think he's annoying."

Despite already having wrecked myself, according to my boss's visual assessment, I stayed at the office late.

Aparna stopped by my desk again at dinnertime. "It's 6. Why are you still here?"

"I have to fill out all these spreadsheets and attach them to their tickets, and then Chad has to die a little after 9 o'clock."

"Ooh, that sounds bad." She put her hand on her hip. "Are you sure you're OK?"

"Yeah, why?"

"Because you said that Chad has to die. Usually people don't kill off their imaginary friends when they're feeling fine."

"Tonight's the night he dies. I didn't make it up. And he's not imaginary. He's historical. And I don't want to kill him, I want to save him."

"I'm planning on being here late, too, if that helps."

"I'm supposed to do the spreadsheets, but I can't stay much longer. I have to find Chad."

"Text me if you need me."

At 7 p.m., I left a note on my current ticket, escalated the unresolved issue with the spreadsheet, and signed off. I left Chad's death certificate on my desk. I didn't need it anymore.

I sat behind the wheel of my car, holding Maria's figurine in my hand. "Roll the tape," I ordered, thinking of *Television Quiz*. Apparently Siri made an effort to interpret this command, because the radio flicked on. It was an oldie: a single from Madonna's *Immaculate Collection*.

This is going to be miserable for Chad, I realized. *He's the one who has to die. In ghost lore, suicides die over and over. It's his mind in which the bad tape plays. I'm just watching it.*

"Hey Siri, what was the weather in Boston on October 26, 1940?"

"On October 26, 1940," the robotic voice began, "the weather was fair and cool. Precipitation did not occur. If you are looking for an answer, keep looking."

That was enough information for me to begin. I put my cell phone away. It's distracting when my cell phone rings in 1940.

Unbeknownst to me at the time, but as I learned later, Stanley called Aparna and told her he needed to find me immediately. He drove to the office and she let him in. At my desk, they found the envelope with the death certificate: a location, a time. Together, they placed a phone call from the landline at my office desk.

"What's your emergency?"

"Hi, we think someone is in trouble."

"Details?"

"We think he's got a suicide plan at 9 p.m. tonight."

"Can you describe him?"

"White guy, late 30s, heading into the city. We know where he's going. He's got a head start, and we don't think we can get there in time."

"Welcome back," Mr. Destiny said with a grandiose sweep of his arms, "to our special 'Exit Interview' episode of *Television Quiz!* The question is: *How did Chad Goeing die?* Are you ready to guess the answer to this?"

"As ready as I'll ever be."

"Good man," the host said. "Here's your starting hint: The answer is five letters." Five blank circular panels hung on the wall behind him. "When you guess a letter correctly, we'll write it in. You can also ask a general question or try guessing the full answer. You have twenty attempts."

"I'm ready," I said.

"Go."

"In honor of Madonna," I said, "is it VOGUE?"

The host looked confused. "I'm not sure what the Madonna has to do with this, or how a 'vogue' would be a manner of death."

No, you wouldn't know. Madonna hasn't been born yet. This is a throwforward. "It's just my kickoff salute," I said.

"You want to waste a question on that?"

"Yes, in honor of the Madonna. An offering to her."

An angry buzzer sounded to let me know I was wrong. "Wrong answer!" the host narrated. "It's not VOGUE."

"Is it CROSS?"

The host smiled for the camera. "No! No crucifixion!" The buzzer sounded again.

I remembered the religious figurine getting stuck in the sink disposal. Chad could have been trapped like that in a river, his feet tangled in a branch—survival guides call that a strainer.

"SEWER," I said.

"No."

"PIPES," I followed up quickly.

"No, you're cold," he laughed. "Why don't you take a different approach? Ask me some general questions. You have 16 questions left."

The noise was in my head again, growing louder. "Does it make a repetitive sound?"

"Yes."

I thought of the Great War and of the Second World War that menaced us now in the *Television Quiz* era.

"Distinct like automatic gunfire?"

"No."

"Diffuse like rain?"

"Yes."

I closed my eyes, imagining placing my ear to the forest floor, listening for vibrations.

"Mechanical like a typewriter?"

"Yes. You have 12 questions left."

An indistinct, diffuse, repetitive, mechanical sound that killed Chad. How did he die? Rope? No, think: modernity. But not a gun. What's newer than a gun? "DRONE," I guessed. I imagined that, in 2015, one's own recreational drone could boomerang back and smash into one's head, causing a fatality. I didn't know how this could have worked in 1940, but it was worth a guess.

"'Drone,' well, yes, that's one way to name the sound, I suppose. There is a sort of droning on." The host smirked. "But how could a *sound* have killed Chad? You're still cold." The buzzer sounded gratuitously.

"BRAIN. His brain killed him." *It was a difficult day on this side of the hemispheric divide.*

"Interesting. You think he was mentally ill?"

"He committed suicide."

"Is that a question?"

"No, no. It's a statement of fact. I'm pretty sure of it. Please don't debit 'suicide' from my questions."

"OK, I'm only counting one question. Was it Chad's own *brain*?" The host pointed at the board. The buzzer sounded. "No!" he crowed.

"We are not giving you credit for that. You're halfway done with your allotted questions."

I pored over the clues. The emphasis of the prayer to the Madonna, who gives me 80 percent of what I need to know. My dragging of the cross. What cross was I carrying? What was this hint? Maybe Chad was killed by supernatural intervention. Could the Madonna herself have ordered the hit from Heaven? But the answer to the puzzle only had five letters.

"MARIA?" I tried.

"No, but I won't mark you off for that. That doesn't count as one of your questions. The puzzle is in English," the host corrected me. "If you've got an audio clue—"

"I do. Madonna's singing."

"—then you might be able to solve it in Spanish. But the answer is still in English."

Madonna was still singing me an earworm.

"SATAN."

Buzzer. "Bad luck. Now you're down to nine questions."

"Does the thing that killed Chad exist in Mexico City today in 1940?"

"No."

"Will it exist in Boston in 2015?"

"Yes."

"Everything was moving too fast. Chad did not want to go into business, and he was mad at his father."

"That's two questions, isn't it? Yes and yes."

"He was having an argument with modernity."

"Yes."

Chad was galloping in my head. This ghost was messing with me, but I was getting closer.

"Did he jump out of a plane?"

"Interesting, but no. Let's be a little more targeted here, shall we? The Madonna gives you 80 percent, which means you owe 20 percent of the puzzle. There's only five letters in total. Put in your part. Just one part. Give me one letter."

I couldn't get the religious iconography out of my mind. The steeple of the church in the Little League photo. The execution at Golgotha in the rain. The X-shaped placard on Chad's grave. The miniature crucifix necklace hung around the figurine of Maria. The enormous wooden cross I'd carried so far, all the way from Provincetown to Boston, just to install it here on a platform, an imposing shadow. The hormone prescription I'd neglected to fill. And, now—suddenly—I saw it.

"Is there a 'T'?" I yelped.

"YES," roared the host. "We have one 'T'!"

Excitement, triumph, certainty surged in me. The song changed key. It felt pivotal. The sound of the typewriter in the rain grew louder.

"WATER!" I crowed. That was it—the slickness of my wet hands carrying the cross in the storm. The condemned men with their arms strapped to crosses, their ghosts crawling out of the Charles in the damp weather. Some kind of drowning.

Mr. Destiny laughed. "No." The buzzer sounded. "You guessed that too quickly before I had a chance to write the letter on the board. Here, let me show you and the audience—the 'T' is the first letter in the word. Does that help?"

I shook my head. "I'm sorry. It doesn't."

"You have only one question left. You have to guess the word. Do you want to touch the board?" he asked.

"Why?"

"Touch it. It's Chad's death. 'T' for 'TOUCH.'" He was taunting me.

"No, that's not it," I said. I was not going to guess "touch"; that was obviously a waste. Madonna was still singing that blasted song over and over in my mind, that 1993 single. An earworm. My mind was dark.

"Give us the answer, please. Stanley already has it, so your time is growing short. If you don't give me the answer now, he's going to arrive and put a stop to this."

I had a headache.

"I'm thinking," I said.

"Your IQ won't help you. Stop *thinking* about the answer to the question and try to *feel* it."

I said nothing, leaving dead air for a couple seconds. "I don't know what I feel," I said quietly.

"OK, you know what, send—feelings—straight—to—hell. Just *answer the question*."

"I'd like to solve the puzzle," I said, stating the inevitable, buying myself an extra moment of airtime. The downpour in my head increased until nothing could be seen. Madonna's voice inhabited the raindrops and overwhelmed the background. I gave the answer to the puzzle: "TOWER. The Great Depression exhausted him, and he jumped out of a skyscraper."

"No. I'm terribly sorry. That is not how Chad died, and you are out of questions. Give the roulette wheel a spin and let's see what you would have won."

I swung the mustard, pea, and magenta-painted wheel. It fluttered with a clack-clack-clack and came to a stop.

"Oh, that's too bad. You would have gotten more time—"

I had failed, and I was running now, running to catch Chad, approaching Boylston and Dartmouth.

If I could have simply researched his death on microfilm, this biography would have been easier to write, but that's not how I roll. Once I ask a question a certain way, I want to know the answer that fits the question, and I have to play it through to the end. Chad was just ahead of me, a pale, taut face, an olive-drab trenchcoat against the weather. I saw him slip into the station, seemingly without swiping a card or budging the turnstile, as if he were a ghost. I followed. I swiped my twenty-first century plastic card, expecting a few cents to be debited, as is fair in 1940.

Stanley and Aparna were stuck in a taxi farther west on Boylston, the rain streaking the windows, talking to the cops on a cell phone.

"We see him," said the cops. "White guy in a trenchcoat just ran into the station. We'll get him."

Chad neared the platform, stopped, turned around, and looked at me. His face looked drawn, haggard, full of the horror of defeat. The sound was in the distance, growing louder. The song, I heard that, too—the repeated lyric "rain rain rain rain rain." But the night sky was cloudless, in both 1940 and in 2015. Then, suddenly, I knew, and I stretched my hand out to him, but it was too late. He spread his arms out in a "T" shape as if to feel ghost raindrops and jumped off the platform in front of the approaching train.

At the same moment, as I flung myself toward the edge of the platform to save him, two uniformed police officers caught me, each grabbing one of my outstretched arms.

Two weeks later, after a medical leave, some prescription I was supposed to fill, and a lot of roundabout explaining, I was in the office again. Coworkers show sympathy in funny ways, each of them unique.

"Ooh, head down on your desk. Rough night? Looks like 20 percent of the people are doing 80 percent of the work."

I didn't know if this coworker meant to say that I was one of the hard workers or one of the slackers. Either way, he was just trying to make me feel normal, an intent I appreciated, yet I found his choice of words irritating. I groaned weakly.

"Hey, is something wrong? I can usually tell. You look like a guy who has something on his mind."

I gave him the thumbs up.

In the afternoon, I was happier to hear from Aparna, though she, too, was razzing me.

"I cannot believe they let you out of the hospital," she said.

"It was complicated."

"Do you want to talk about it?"

"Can't right now. Chad is listening."

"Are you serious?"

"Sort of."

"I can't do this with you right now. OK. Hold it together."

Chad had died on October 26, 1940. I had witnessed his death and failed to save him, and, still, in November 2015, he wasn't really dead. He was always over my shoulder.

Now I understood: there was only one way to really kill him.

I left the office early while the sun was still up and returned to the Vital Records office. The glass door opened automatically. The room was heated. There was thin, gray, wall-to-wall carpeting. Oldies music piped in. I looked up at the signs suspended from the ceiling and followed the one that said VITAL RECORDS. As I did, I saw the letters morph and rearrange: VITAMINS. I was in Aisle 5.

I walked up to the pharmacist's window. "I am ready to fill that prescription now," I said.

"Testosterone?"

"No. I mean, yes, but also the other one."

They gave me one little white paper bag for each prescription: the injectable hormone and the psychiatric pill. I bought a bottle of water, too.

"$87.05."

I handed over five twenty-dollar bills.

"You wouldn't happen to have the nickel?"

"I'm sorry, I—" I felt my pocket and came up with a hit. "Oh, here's one."

Outside in the parking lot, sitting behind the wheel of my car, I opened the bag with the pill and uncapped the water. Just then, I saw Chad's face in the rearview mirror, one last time. He gave me the same look as he did just before he jumped in front of the train—sad, horrified, angry, distrustful, beckoning. He reached out his hand, extending his index finger, and pointed at the other bag, the one with the testosterone. Was that what he wanted all this time?

"No," I said firmly, as if to a dog.

I swallowed the pill. He vanished.

When we are "cured," according to the system, it is supposed to make us better equipped to work within the system. I didn't feel it that way. Chad had been part of me, but I was never able to save him from himself, and his final disappearance struck me as a fresh loss. It was a twist on the old Spartan battle maxim: "Leave in the train or on it." I was well enough to ride the train, but I didn't want to. Having seen Chad hit, I felt it hard to keep boarding the same vehicle.

How would I explain it to the boss? *The job,* I could tell him, *can be pleasant or unpleasant, fulfilling or depleting, a point of pride or a blemish of compromise. Most of the time it is the positives, rarely the negatives. It is as good as a job can be. The issue is not whether I like the job. The issue is that the river is full of ghosts.* The boss would not care for this explanation. I gave two weeks' notice.

"We'd like to schedule an exit interview with you," said the note from Human Resources.

I wondered what questions they might want to ask me and how long the interview would last. When my final day came, they asked me only one question: "Do you have any questions for us?"

There are no surviving audiorecordings or photographs of the live broadcast *Television Quiz* show. We have to let the past be in the past and stand on the shoulders of those ancestors. I am thankful to the Virgin for giving me 80 percent. The rest is mine.

The answers arrive, but not on a train of thought. They come on a train of dreams.

Sometimes I hear a knock in the rain, and I open the door.

The professional profile of **LEV OCKENSHAW** suggests that he spends his workday inside a spreadsheet, but he prefers to be identified here as an amateur biographer. Artificial intelligence for security cameras plays a role in both his professional and amateur pursuits. His favorite album is Madonna's *Immaculate Collection*.

TUCKER LIEBERMAN is the author of *Flip the Finger at Despair*, *Bad Fire*, and *Painting Dragons*. His short fiction is in Owl Canyon's *No Bars and a Dead Battery* and Elly Blue's forthcoming *The Great Trans-Universal Bike Ride*. His superpower is listening to a Top 40 song over and over until a story emerges. Originally from Boston, Massachusetts, he lives in Bogotá, Colombia. www.tuckerlieberman.com

GAMES OF ANGRY
CHILDREN

An account by Ellie,
AS PROVIDED BY CHRISTINE LUCAS

"How do dead children play?" I force my whisper through cracked lips. My chest hurts. My arms hurt. Silence hurts more.

"With scissors and knives, Ellie." Just a hiss, and it hurts even more. A shadow slithers out from behind the machine that counts my heartbeats. Now it looms overhead, its snake-like body coiled around cords and tubes.

"With matches and razors," snaps another shadow, rising up from the floor. This one has many legs, and all of them have claws.

"But I don't want to play with those." I clutch Mr. Bunny on my chest. I won't sniffle. I won't. I'm a big girl. The oldest I get to be. But still older than Caleb. He's the real baby, always crying—always hogging Daddy's attention, always asking for Mommy. *Mommy's not coming back, stupid baby.* And Caleb is in his bed now, back home, with Daddy. And I'm all alone. Alone, with Mr. Bunny, and these things. "Why not with dolls and bunnies and puppies?"

"Boring," growls the snake-like shadow. "Boring like that rag you hold on to. Get rid of it and come play with us!" It smiles, all teeth and forked tongue and the promise of pain.

I clutch Mr. Bunny tighter. Why isn't Mr. Bunny working? Daddy said he'd keep the monsters away. Is he broken? Did Daddy break him when he put him in the washing machine? Stupid Daddy. I begged him not to, but there was puke all over him. Daddy said he'd be fine. But Daddy said a lot of things.

"I'm too tired to play." It's not a lie. It's not truth either. I'm more scared than tired.

"Ah, but not for long." The many-legged shadow wags a clawed tentacle at me. "Come with us, and I promise you no more pain. Only fun." Its limbs curl and uncurl, like a ghostly octopus swimming in a sea of ash and smoke. "Let's go hunt those who hurt us. Those who left us. Those who lied!"

My fingertips dig into Mr. Bunny's fur. *Wake up, please*, I beg him. *Be brave*, I beg myself. *Be brave*, like Nurse Judy said, like Doc said. Like Daddy said. And still I sniffle, like that cry-baby Caleb. It's those voices. Those voices make my eyes tear up. I know those voices, and wish I didn't.

The snake-like shadow speaks with Bobby's raspy voice, who left two months ago. Next-room Bobby, bald-head Bobby, always with his game in one hand and dragging his IV stand with the other. And that one, the shadow octopus, sounds too much like Lucy down the hall. Always-angry-Lucy, angry at her three brothers who had good blood, unlike hers. Angry at everyone and everything. She didn't want to play with them. But she wants to play now.

"It's not long now," whispers a third shadow, this one fat like a cockroach made of thick smoke. It rubs its forelegs together with glee. "Oh, such fun we'll have! We'll hunt down bratty brothers. Lying fathers, too."

I hug Mr. Bunny as tightly as the bruises in my free arm allow. Too many needles these past few days. Mommy's waiting for me, Daddy said. But Daddy said many things.

It won't hurt. You'll be fine. I'll be back tonight.

Lies, lies, more lies.

"Oh, you're so cute! You think Mommy waits for you?" The ghostly octopus grins. "Don't you know where Mommies go when they die? They go to their child-free heaven, where they can shop and do their hair and nails, and yap-yap-yap at their phones without little brats ruining their lives!"

"And Daddy doesn't care," whispers the snake-like shadow that now rises at the foot of my bed like a cobra of ash and darkness. "Why should he? He has a perfectly good son at home. He doesn't want broken Ellie."

I want to shake my head, but everything hurts now. It's true, isn't it? Daddy broke Mr. Bunny and left me here. With them. To be with Caleb. Stupid, cry-baby Caleb. I squeeze Mr. Bunny on my chest and my index finger finds the loose spot at the seams. It's where the thread came apart and Daddy—clumsy Daddy—tried to mend him. But his fingers aren't as good as Mommy's. And there's the spot where the oil from the frying pan burned his fur. And now, despite the smell of detergent and antiseptic, Mr. Bunny smells like Sunday morning pancakes and Mommy's hand cream and Daddy's smokes and Caleb's baby powder.

He smells of home.

Daddy didn't leave me alone to go home. He brought home here, to me. *For* me.

"I know," growls the roach-shadow. "Let's go after Caleb first. That will show him, stealing Daddy away." And all three nod.

"Caleb? No, not Caleb!" Little Caleb doesn't know how to be brave. *Please, keep him safe from them. From me, if I...* I breathe my words into Mr. Bunny's worn fur, a prayer and a plea and a long breath—how many breaths left, now?

No more breaths to protest, no strength to hold on to Mr. Bunny when the shadow tears Mr. Bunny from my numb fingers and throws it away.

"Enough with that rag! Now we play. We *really* play!"

All three shadows gather at the foot of the bed. Smoke and ash and shadow swirl and dance. Three ghostly children now stand at the foot of the bed, holding hands. A stench of burned matches fills the room.

"Come, Ellie! Come play with us. Come hunt lying daddies and stupid brothers!"

There's a moment of silence between this breath and the last, between one heartbeat and the machine's alarm, between the cobwebs over my eyes and Mommy's warm, welcoming smile. *Mommy, I've missed you so!* In that one moment, sharp fangs gleam behind the shades of angry children.

Mr. Bunny rises and snarls.

Some Dads don't lie. Some Moms wait for their daughters. And some stuffed bunnies have sharp, merciless teeth.

ELLIE likes stuffed animals. Ellie likes the pancakes her mom used to make. Ellie doesn't like dark things. Ellie doesn't like her kid brother Caleb much either. But although she doesn't like Caleb, she still loves him. Almost as much as she loves Mr. Bunny.

CHRISTINE LUCAS lives in Greece with her husband and a horde of spoiled animals. A retired Air Force officer and mostly self-taught in English, she has had her work appear in several print and online magazines, including *Daily Science Fiction*, *Pseudopod/Artemis Rising 4*, and *Nature: Futures*. She was a finalist for the 2017 WSFA award and is currently working on her first novel. Visit her at:
http://werecat99.wordpress.com/
https://www.facebook.com/Werecat99

PAYMENT IS

COMING DUE

An account by Arlen of Dunluce,
AS PROVIDED BY LUCINDA GUNNIN

Tuesday mornings, all the friends in the neighborhood meet at the park. Even though none of us really feels the cold, we move inside if the weather is especially bad. We sit in a circle in the grass or wait for the morning AA meeting to exit the basement of the apartment building on the corner and then use the cold folding chairs they've left behind. The basement is more dangerous though. Alcoholics tend to be one of the few groups of adults that can still see us, and that could be very bad for business.

March was still cold, so our last meeting of the month was inside. Our chapter of the Friends Support Group has had four members since Tally joined us when her family moved to the neighborhood. Before that, we had a couple more, but Snuffy disappeared when his boy turned 14, and Ivan's charge moved with his mother after the divorce, so Ivan moved to Vermont. He messages once a year to catch us up to date on his charge and the friends group up there.

I thought it was going to be like every other meeting. A quick run-down on how everyone's charges are doing and then straight to the treats. Manny was bringing the cookies. His charge is Luisa, and her mother makes the best cookies. For the last meeting, he brought those little Mexican wedding cookies. I'm not ashamed to say my snout was covered in powdered sugar before the meeting ended. I love those things.

Like any support group, we have a formula that the meetings are supposed to follow. I get up and introduce myself. "Hi, I'm Arlen, and I'm an imaginary friend."

Then everyone echoes back, "Hi Arlen!"

There's even a little chant about making myself the best friend I can be, never betraying my family, and keeping my existence hidden from the world.

But we don't normally do that. I mean, we've all been friends with each other for years, so the formality seems a little weird.

Until that March meeting.

Then something unusual happened.

For the first time in—at least a decade, but Angela's the group record keeper and could say exactly when—we had a newborn friend in attendance.

Newborn friends are uncommon to say the least. Angela thinks it's because children aren't encouraged to have an imagination these days and I don't disagree, though I suspect it has everything to do with the magic fading from the world. This world never had as much magic as the old one, and it's fading fast, replaced by children encouraged to grow up too soon.

But it might also be the plethora of medications that children are on these days. Everyone seems to think that telling a parent you have an imaginary friend is a normal part of childhood. We see all the stories about it on TV.

But this is the modern world, and telling a parent you have an imaginary friend might result in medication. Or hospitalization. Neither of those is good for the child or the lifespan of the friend.

Whatever the reasons, newborn friends are unusual, and we had one at the March meeting. So all normal casual procedures went out the window.

"Hi, I'm Arlen, and I'm an imaginary friend."

Angela and Manny fell right into step, answering as if we did this all the time.

The new friend looked like one of those enormous teddy bears you win at carnivals, except that he had a helmet covering his face and a lance in one arm and shield on the other. It's a very militant look for friend, which had me a little concerned. We'd ask him some questions about his charge, just to make sure everyone is okay. Protecting our charges is serious business.

He was just a fraction of a second behind the others in echoing back my hello.

"Let's talk about our friends and our charges, for just a moment. Anyone know where Tally is?"

Angela raised her hoof for permission to answer. It's not necessary, but we do like to maintain some form of order.

She's a unicorn-pegasus with rainbow wings and purple mane. She also leaves a trail of glitter wherever she goes. "Tally can't make it today," she said, tossing her head and mane about. "Her little one has chicken pox, so she's reading her stories all afternoon, to help her not itch."

Everyone murmured condolences. Chicken pox is never easy. The best thing a friend can do is distract their charge from scratching and it's hard. Those things make me itch sympathetically and I've never even had pox—chicken or otherwise.

"Shall we go with introductions? Give us your name, something about your charge, and whatever else you want to share. Manny, will you start us off?"

Manny is pretty much as unintimidating as a friend can be. He's started to fade a little bit as Luisa gets older, but he's still very bright.

His preferred form is as a donkey piñata, in the brightest hues of pink and neon green. He usually brings our treats hidden in his tummy pouch.

"Hola, amigos. I'm Manny. My charge is the lovely Luisa, though I don't know for how much longer. This week, she told me that she wants me to be her first dance at her quinceñera. She's only 12. Why is she thinking about that already?"

"Girls have dreams, Manny, and often little girls dream of being women," Angela replied.

"What's a quinceñera?" the big bear asked.

"It's when a girl becomes a young woman," Manny said. "It's the last party of childhood and first party of adulthood. It's when little girls give up their imaginary friends."

The bear gasped. "What happens to you then?"

"I just fade away."

"Not necessarily, Manny. Look at me, my Mary is an adult with her own child now, and I'm still here."

"Yeah, but you're special, Arlen. We can't all be like you."

The big bear looked at me like I had grown another head on my slim fox form.

Angela took his paw in her hoof and patted him gently on the shoulder. "Arlen's a bit different from the rest of us. He's been charged with a whole family, and he's 300 years old!"

"How do you do that? Can the adults see you? Do you punish them when they're bad? Why are you different? What—"

I cut him off, knowing he'd just get himself all wound up if I let him go on.

"Why don't you tell us your story first, good knight, and then I'll tell everyone mine."

Friends are just like everyone else. They like to talk about themselves.

"Hi, everybody! I'm Sir Tedalot of Dublin."

He paused to give us all time to say hello. This one learns fast.

"My charge is Neal. He's four and the cutest little boy ever."

Manny and Angela both are in charge of girls, so they don't argue with him. I know every friend thinks their child is the most beautiful one ever, so it's not worth arguing. My Liam is of course the cutest baby ever.

"Neal lives with his dad and dad's girlfriend. His real mom died when he was born."

We all murmured our condolences, knowing how hard it is for our charges when they lose a parent.

"Neal's dad is a mechanic at the airport and works really long hours. Neal misses him a lot. His favorite memory of his dad is going to something called a Renaissance faire and seeing knights jousting. Then, on the way home, his dad bought him a giant teddy. It was before his dad met Amanda.

"Amanda is a big ol' meanie." Sir Ted proclaimed and then clamped his giant paw over his mouth. "I mean, uh—"

We all assured him that this was a safe place to say whatever he wanted about the parents. We simply don't say such things in front of our charges.

He nodded. "I knew it didn't feel okay to say it."

Angela nudged him with her horn, leaving a glitter streak on his shoulder. "Why do you feel that?"

Sir Ted hung his head. "She lies to Neal's dad and says Neal was bad. Last week, I saw her take her lipstick and write on the wall. Then she blamed Neal, told his dad that he was throwing a fit because she made him eat peas. Neal likes peas."

Manny and I exchanged the look. We were afraid of this. A lot of times, new friends are created because a child isn't being treated right.

Manny asked the question before I could. "Is she hurting Neal?"

Sir Ted rose up on his hind legs and let loose a mighty roar. "Not on my watch!"

I used my snout to nudge some of the chocolate treats Manny brought in Sir Ted's direction.

"No one is criticizing your skills, buddy. It's just that's one of the hardest things for friends, even experienced friends, to deal with. We have to figure out how to make Neal's dad see what she's doing without letting Neal get hurt."

Sir Ted had chocolate smeared on his helmet and paws. "So what do I do?"

They all turned to look at me, and I hate it. Sure, I was old, but that didn't mean I had all the answers. I have a few fairy tricks in my repertoire that the average friend doesn't have. What I didn't have that day was an answer for Sir Ted.

"We'll all help you figure out an answer. Maybe in time for our meeting next week. What can you tell us about Amanda?"

"She's tricky, and I don't trust her," Sir Ted said. "Sometimes, I think I see her out of the corner of my eye, but when I look she's not there. Last night, when she was getting Neal ready for bed, she took me out to the car and wouldn't let him come get me. He had no one watching over him until his Dad came home and brought me inside."

Manny stepped in front of the big bear. "Ah, big guy, I can help you with that. I know your Neal thinks you are the teddy bear his Dad got him, but you're more than that now. Luisa keeps her first piñata high on a shelf, but I can go wherever I'm needed. So can you."

"I go where the bear goes," Sir Ted argued.

"Then how are you here right now, amigo?"

"I, uh, knew there was a friend's meeting and I was supposed to come," he answered, scratching his helmet.

"You got it! When she tries to keep you away from Neal, just think about how your boy needs you and you'll go to him."

Sir Ted still looked a bit confused, so Manny had mercy on him.

"Tell us your story now, Arlen."

I glossed over the details, just telling them that I was the product of a fairy deal between my original Mary and the fey at the standing stones. Angela started to ask questions, so I called the meeting to an end, claiming my Liam needed me.

"We'll meet at the park next week, if the weather is nice," I said and then poofed back to Liam's nursery.

Even Manny, who is my best buddy, doesn't know the whole story. I don't think he'd like me very much if he did.

The first day I remember is when Mary O'Dwyer went to the standing stones to ask the fey for help with her impending marriage. She brought the usual sacrifices of cream and fresh bread, but the fey are fickle, so she ended up with me.

I've been assigned to the children of her clan ever since.

Poor Mary had no idea what the bargain would cost her.

Her Liam was the first. Mary's eldest son was destined to be the laird of Dunluce Castle, and he's the reason there are no foxes in County Ulster. Well, maybe I'm the reason, but we'll get to that in a minute.

We don't live on the Isle any more.

Haven't since, well, six generations later, Mary's kin fled to the new world. The trip across the ocean was the end of many a friend, but Mary Mac Quillan sewed pebbles from the standing stones into the feet of her favorite ragdoll, and that was enough to bring me along. An Gorta Mór brought thousands of Irishmen across the sea, but most of them were not as committed as Mary Mac, and the fey were mostly left behind.

We live in Dublin now—Dublin, Pennsylvania. It's hard to get under the hill from here. Few can do it.

I still encourage my charges to leave cream and bread by the window, but it's been a long time since they required mor'n that from me. So long I can almost pretend it didn't happen, pretend Siobhan just grew up and moved away.

My first Liam was a bright and curious lad with a deep affection for the Irish Sea. From the time he could walk, we were at the beach daily, no matter the season, wandering the rocks. Some nasty unseelie thing tried to steal him under the waves when he was just three, but I pulled him back to shore in time.

On the wind, I heard their promise.

Payment is coming due.

I guarded my Liam all the time, a bright red fox nipping at his heels when he was awake and sleeping under his cradle and then his bed.

He was five years old when Siobhan was born. As Liam had been the apple of his father's eye, Siobhan was Mary's heart, formed into a perfect replica of her. Siobhan adored her brother almost from birth and tried to follow him everywhere, but Liam never let her follow him to the beach, perhaps remembering the unseelie promise.

Our beautiful girl was four the day they came for him. The gnarled old troll slid in through the nursery window and lifted my sleeping boy to his distended maw. I begged and pleaded for his life; this was my charge, my golden boy. Promises were made.

The old blue troll laughed, the sound like boulders falling into the raging sea.

"Bring me the girl, and he will live a long and happy life."

I was born of the fey and had no choice but to obey.

While Liam slept, I crept to his sister's nursery and shook her awake. I showed her the hidden stairs where Liam played and led her out the door across the heather field. When we reached the woods, I led her directly to the troll's lair, telling myself it was necessary to save my boy.

Liam never loved me again.

He awoke to a noise in the nursery and saw a red fox lead his beloved sister to the woods. They searched for three days, discounting his tales that a fox had stolen his sister. Mary collapsed in anguish, begging the fey and the gods to at least bring her a body to bury.

Liam lost his mother to madness and was never a child again.

Under the light of the harvest moon each year he could search, hoping to find his lost sister.

Rumors swept the land of a red-haired woman who walked in the woods on the moonlit nights, but Liam never found her, and neither did I.

When he was an adult and his own wife was expecting their first child, he placed a bounty on every fox in County Ulster. He demanded they be gone before his child was born. When Marta was born, I watched her just as I had him, but I could never show her my true form. I watched invisible as she grew up and had brothers and sisters and time marched on.

For six generations, I watched the Quillan family, reminding the fey that their payment had been made. Then, to escape the great hunger, we fled to a new land and things were better for a long time.

After a century and half in this new country where English bastards rule, but don't serve the crown, my Gaelic is sketchy, and my brogue long gone. You can hear it in the lullabies I sing to my charges, but not aught else. I whisper the stories of the rebellion and the blanket protest and Bloody Sunday to my charges. I sing them the old songs and the new ones, ballads and U2 and Dropkick Murphys.

And I smile when their heritage defies the ages and gives them green eyes or red hair.

Truth be told, the old memories are fading for me too quickly. The hunger is a cautionary tale and no longer a gnawing ache in my stomach. I tell the children "Tiocfaidh ár lá," our day will come, but with every passing decade, I wonder if the time has passed.

Now, with the birth of my Liam this spring, I wonder what the world will bring for him.

My latest Mary brought him home from the hospital three months ago, and I curled up in a ball under the crib as I have done for centuries. "Take good care of him, Arlen," she whispered that first night she brought him to the nursery. Things were calm, and I was happy to have a new charge.

The night of the meeting I was in Liam's nursery, listening to his soft breathing and considering Sir Ted's problem when I heard a scratching at the window. The sound set my fur on edge as if someone had stroked it backward while too close to the fire. I leapt to my feet, growling.

The centuries had not faded the memory of the troll's face, but I was startled to see him here in the new world.

Payment is coming due.

I snarled at the old troll and told him payment was made, centuries ago.

Your power is fading, old fox. Surely you remember how to be strong again. It doesn't have to be this child. Find me another, perhaps one whose parents don't want him. Maybe the one they call Neal.

Payment is coming due.

I'm ashamed to say that I considered it for a moment. Neal isn't my charge, and his friend, Sir Ted, is inexperienced. I like him, and his friend Neal sounds adorable, but it would be easy to trick him and satisfy the fey.

Perhaps it is because I have strayed too far from my Irish roots, but I am not the powerless fox I was with my first Liam. My instinct to meet the fey demand was gone.

"Sot off, ye old troll," I whispered, not wanting my Liam to learn such language. "You have no power here."

If not you, I'll find another to take my bargain.

With that threat, the troll disappeared, and I spent the night pacing about Liam's room, making certain that no other threats came near.

In the morning, I put out an urgent call to the Friends Support Group. I knew we had another meeting just six days away and everyone was preoccupied trying to determine how best to help Sir Ted, but I had an emergency.

"I know we have an emergency, but now we have an urgent emergency and we need an emergency meeting," I told Manny.

"Amigo, that sentence makes no sense. You said emergency three times."

"Manny has a troll ever threatened to eat Luisa?"

"No, but—"

"Until you have dealt with a troll, you don't understand what an emergency is. This is an EMERGENCY emergency. This is not a drill. This is serious."

"Okay, amigo, I get it. This is urgent. I'll have everyone at the park within the hour."

And he did.

There's a reason Manny is my best friend.

Tally even left her charge sleeping so she could come help us out. Tally's younger than most of us as well. She moved here with her charge and their family from New Jersey, but she was born on Jersey Shore when her charge was three. That was four years ago.

Apparently, her charge had a nanny then who took her to the beach and let her get too close to the water. Amy, her charge, nearly drowned, and it was Tally who pulled her back to the beach. Tally's a multi-hued octopus who shifts colors in the sunlight. You'd think that eight legs would mean she trips a lot, but she's the fastest friend I've ever met, even faster than me.

Everyone arrived, and I told them about the troll's threat, leaving out my own moment of weakness. No need to get myself skewered by Sir Ted.

I had to start by explaining how I knew the troll and why I knew what it wanted. I was sure that was going to get me booted from the group as the pariah I was.

Instead, I got a massive bear hug when it became clear I had not chosen to give the troll Neal. In fact, no one even seemed concerned about what I had done with Siobhan.

Angela asked the question I'd been asking myself all night long. "So if the troll, like, doesn't get a sacrifice do you, like, die?"

"Maybe?" I answered. "I'm not really certain. I could just be feeling weaker because I'm old or because Liam is young and doesn't believe in me yet. He sees me, but doesn't know the difference between me and anything else he's learning about. Or, it could be the magic the fairies used is fading. I just don't know."

"Maybe we need to ask someone really smart," Sir Ted offered. His suggestion made a lot of sense. If we could find a fairy expert or a friend expert, they might know the answer.

"Where do we find one?" Angela asked.

"Neal's books always have a fairy that helps solve things, but it seems like fairies are what got us into this mess. In *Sleeping Beauty*, it's a kiss that stops the fairy curse. Could a kiss help us?"

Sir Ted might seem like a big lug, but he's actually pretty smart.

I yipped with glee and bounced around him. "Ted, my friend, you're a genius."

He looked confused.

"Love, Teddie, my boy. Love solves everything!"

I'm not sure that made it any clearer for Sir Ted, so I pulled in everyone close and outlined the plan.

Manny was the most surprised by it. "Are you sure, amigo? I mean, it might work, but—"

I rested my paw on his shoulder and looked him in the eye.

"This is gonna work, I promise."

I wasn't really as confident in my plan as I told Manny and the others, but I was convinced that we had to do something to keep Neal and all the children, not just my Liam, safe from the fey bargain. There would be no changelings in our neighborhood, no children lost forever in the woods. Something about Sir Ted's stories of Amanda made me sure that if anyone was willing to bargain with the troll, it would be her.

Though she is grown, my Mary remembered me enough to ask me to keep her Liam safe. With our connection still there, I could ask her for her help, rely on our love to make everything right.

It took four days for me to find the right opportunity. Liam had been fussy off and on all day and kept her awake most of the night. She was bleary-eyed and exhausted, rocking in the chair in his nursery when I decided to go for it. I wrapped myself around her feet like a cat looking for a good nap spot, then willed myself visible.

"Mary." I said it quietly, not wanting to startle her or wake the babe.

She looked around, presuming, I guess, that her husband Connor had come to take her back to bed. Connor's a good man, but he was fast asleep in the other room.

"Mary, it's me, Arlen."

I rubbed against her slipper-clad feet, hoping she could still see me after all these years.

"Arlen? Are you really here? I hoped you would be for Liam, but it's been so long since I saw you. I was eleven when you disappeared." I heard the reproach in her voice.

"You decided imaginary friends weren't very grown up, and you wanted so much to be grown up. I was still here. I've always been here."

"I thought I saw you once. That night in college, when I was afraid someone was following me. I saw a fox on the Quad and imagined it was you, keeping me safe."

I smiled then. It had been me. A drunk frat boy was following her until I distracted him a bit. A fox may be my preferred visage, but all imaginary friends can go monster in the closet when we need to. He wet himself and cried for his momma.

"I need your help, Mary. The neighborhood children aren't safe, and I'm not sure I can protect them all."

Now fully awake and ready to protect them all, she snuggled Liam closer and asked, "What can I do to help?"

I tried to choose my words carefully, I really did. I didn't want to tell her the monsters from fairy tales were after her boy, and that her neighbor might be abusing a child, but Mary and I were never very good at keeping secrets from one another.

Mary cried with me as I told her the story of how I came to serve her family and what it had cost. She petted my back and wrapped my tail around her arm as I explained Sir Ted's concerns about Neal. She got fierce when I told her the troll was back and wanted one of our neighborhood children.

"That's not going to happen," she said, forcefully enough to cause Liam to whimper in his sleep.

She soothed him back to sleep, murmuring old stories in his ear the way I had with her when she was young.

Once his breathing was again soft and regular, she agreed to bring all five children's families, and their friends, together for a party—a belated Easter egg hunt and barbecue once Amy was no longer contagious. That we ended up having the party on May Day was just a happy coincidence, I'm sure.

Mary made all the arrangements, and the party started with a dinner barbecue not long before nightfall. The proper Irish phrases were hidden in the decorations around the yard and as the last rays of twilight began to fade, I started the incantation. Mary had tears in her eyes but nodded her approval in that last second before time stopped and the Huntsman stepped through the twilight to stand before me.

He was thirteen feet tall and wore a crown of stag antlers. A great sword hung at his hip, and a bow was strapped across his back. The ground shook as he spoke, and I trembled as his hounds brayed in the distance. My fur itched to run and hide, but I stood my ground.

"Arlen of Dunluce, why am I summoned here?"

"Mighty Hunter, I have summoned you to beg for your protection for these children." My voice shook, but I looked him in the eye.

"And what do you offer as sacrifice for this protection?"

"Myself."

He watched me closely for what seemed like forever. He paused, hand on his hilt, then snapped his fingers. Everyone else remained frozen in time, but Mary was suddenly able to move. I stepped in front of her as if to protect her from the god-like figure in front of us.

"Mary Quillan, child of Mary O'Dwyer, has Arlen ceased to be useful in his duties?"

"No, Mighty Hunter, he is a wonderful protector of my family and my son."

"Your family made its sacrifice long ago. Why do you beseech me now?"

"Another has demanded my son. Told Arlen that if he could not take Liam, he would take another of these. Arlen would rather lose himself than another child."

The Wild Huntsman gestured to the other children. "These are not his to protect. They have their own protectors. Some are not even of our Isle."

Mary nodded. "We know the request is unusual, but we fear that the guardian of one of the children may be corrupted and give in to the unseelie beast."

Fire burned in the Huntsman's dark eyes and his nostrils flared. He began to inspect and sniff each of the gathered adults. Before he reached her, Amanda sprang into action, running through the house and out the front door, away from the Huntsman.

Mary and I were confused. Mortals typically cannot interact with the Wild Hunt unless he grants them freedom as he did with Mary.

"Arlen, you are a wise old fox. The changeling brought the unseelie to you, to threaten you. He could not take Liam by force, but he could have tricked you. You honor your family by seeing through his ruse."

I bowed my head and nodded to acknowledge his praise.

"I do not know what the changeling wanted with this neighborhood, nor why she intended to sacrifice the boy Neal, but she has fled from my sight, and it is a good night for a hunt. Stay here with your family and serve them until they no longer need you, Arlen. Train your friends to protect these children. They now answer to me."

"Thank you, Sir," was all I could manage to say.

He stepped over the fence toward the road where Amanda had gone and glanced back over his shoulder. "Your friends may not appreciate what you have done. I am a difficult task master."

With that he was gone, and all that remained was the sound of the hounds on the wind.

Before I could say a word, the party resumed, and if Neal's dad, or any of the adults other than Mary, even noticed Amanda was missing, they didn't mention it. In fact, Sir Ted told me later it was as if she never existed. Neither Neal nor his father ever mentioned her again, and all her things were just gone.

We friends are back to the most casual of meetings each week, sharing stories and laughing about our charges. This is Dublin, and here, we love one another.

ARLEN OF DUNLUCE is a fey fox imaginary friend in Dublin, Pennsylvania. He has watched over the descendants of Mary O'Dwyer and Clan Mac Quillan for more than three centuries. He's a huge fan of U2 and Irish punk and swears if he were still in Ireland, he'd have been a founding member of the IRA.

LUCINDA GUNNIN is a short story author and commercial property manager in the suburbs of Philadelphia. She writes a gossip column for *Mad Scientist Journal* and has a published collection of short horror, *Seasons of Horror*, available at Amazon. When not writing, she's a gluten-free gamer girl, sushi lover, and cat-spoiling pet parent. Find her on Twitter @LucindaGunnin.

ART BY **Errow Collins**

ERROW is a comic artist and illustrator with a predilection towards mashing the surreal with the familiar. They pay their time to developing worlds not quite like our own with their fiancee and pushing the queer agenda. They probably left a candle burning somewhere. More of their work can be found at errowcollins.wix.com/portfolio.

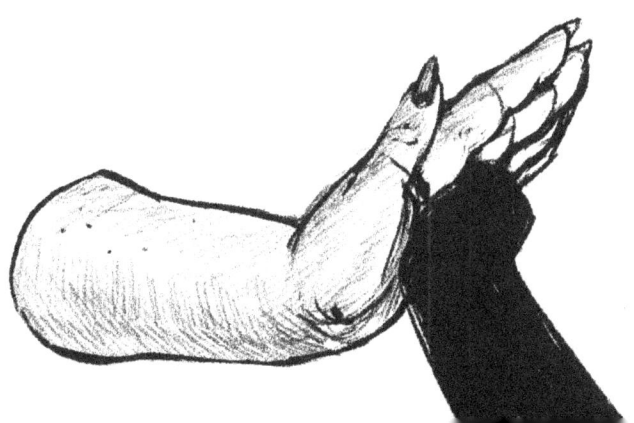

ACROSS MY

EFFERVESCENCE

An account by Madeline Evans,
AS PROVIDED BY JIEYAN WANG

Crescent began watching me when I was nine. I was dreaming about sailing on the ocean at night with my mother and my father in the harsh salty wind. My mother gripped me with one hand and furiously pulled at the sails with the other. At the front, my father held out a lantern, the only way we could see ahead. I squeezed my mother's hand until it drained pure white. Even though I saw no wave coming, a low rumbling thundered beneath our boat, and the wood cracked. Then all I tasted was coldness and the burning of my lungs.

Before I could know the full feeling of drowning, I woke up. I sat up and buried my face in my hands, breathing heavily. It was not until a whole minute later that I realized someone's hand was on my back. I whipped around, but all I saw was a brief glimpse of flowing black hair, dark as obsidian. Then it was gone.

I never saw her face, but I knew she had a complexion as pale as ash—the color of the moon. She was the embodiment of nighttime: her hair was the sky, her eyes the stars, her face the ever-smiling crescent moon.

I believe Crescent saved me that night: a nine-year-old heart cannot survive a near-death experience, even an imaginary one. This is why we protect our children from the horrors of the world. It is not to preserve their innocence or let them enjoy their childhood. It is so they don't die in their sleep and leave us wondering what they were dreaming about before their hearts stopped.

As a child, I was terrified of water. When my parents took me to the pool to teach me how to swim, I clung onto them until my fingers turned numb. I did not trust the inflated tubes on my arms to keep me afloat; they were nothing compared to the wrath of the water. All the while, Crescent whispered in my ear, "Keep close to the edge. Keep close to the edge."

When the winter months came, I sat on the porch after dusk. The snow pounded down in the front yard, suffocating the roads that led into the city. In every direction I turned, there was nothing but the thick white blanket, covered in shadows. Buried beneath the wind's screeches, I could hear Crescent singing a lullaby: "Sleep in the forest. Sleep in the snow. To the trees and the ground under…"

Crescent told me not to talk about her to anyone. Otherwise, she would go away and leave me alone at night. So, I kept my voice silent and listened closely to the black sky.

Before Crescent came, I used to march into the woods half a mile away from our home to find little treasures: pinecones, toadstools, flowers. My father came along with me. From years of hunting, he knew every detail of the forest from the ages of the trees to the species of the grasses that grew. As I plucked red berries from bushes, he told me about the best times to find wild deer and the different ways the crows called during the summer. When I was done, he took the basket from me and carried me back home on his shoulders.

My father was baffled when I refused to go to the forest after Crescent visited me. She showed me what she saw in the forest: snakes the size of two men, ghosts that possessed the mushrooms, witches with wolf-green eyes. I did not dare go near the trees again.

These were Crescent's rules: Never look into a mirror after the sun sets. Never go farther than the front yard of the house. Never wade into the ocean or the snow.

She reminded me of these when I dreamt. I couldn't go more than three nights without dreaming of drowning or the wind ripping me apart. When she shook me awake, I told her I wanted to tell my mother and my father that I was scared. But then she reminded me that if I did, she would let me wallow in the nightmares forever.

I became a crybaby. I cried when my parents took me to the shopping mall and let go of my hand for thirty seconds. I cried when I went to the playground for recess at school because the field was so big compared to my small body size. When I wasn't crying, I was frozen, afraid of stepping on the wrong spot of the floor.

Eventually, I didn't get up in the mornings. Crescent held me down. She warned me: Look at all the things that could go wrong. You could slip and fall. The floor may collapse. There might be chimeras lurking around the corner, waiting for you.

When my parents tried to feed me, she yelled, "Where did the food come from? Did poison leak into it? Venom? Viruses?"

I did not swallow anything for the next two weeks. It became harder to stay awake. As soon as I opened my eyes, the sunlight that leaked through my window was blinding. Whenever I closed them, Crescent began singing and whispering, leading me through landscapes of festering scorpion nests and icicles sharper than daggers.

Then Crescent brought my dreams into the real world. I woke up and there were tarantulas scuttling across my ceiling with yellow fangs. A thousand mosquitos whirred around my head. A dark shadow pooled from underneath the bed, slowly rotting the wood.

I don't remember screaming. I thought I froze. But then my

throat was raw and my parents burst through the door. They spooned steaming porridge into my mouth. I swallowed without thinking. Later, I found out they had been pouring the same porridge down my throat for the past two weeks when I was asleep.

After my first mouthfuls, the words came spilling out. I told them about the monsters that lurked in the water, the demons in the forest, and the slaughter that winter brought about. I told them about Crescent. She was the one who did all of this to me; she kept me from dying suddenly in my sleep and warned about the dangers of the world. I was alive because of her.

As soon as I was done talking, another stab of terror hit me— Crescent would be gone now. How long would I live without her?

A week after she left, I stood at the edge of the front yard and wavered. Crescent did not screech at me to go back. I waited for paralyzing fear to take over and bring me to my senses. But there was utter silence inside my chest, and I teetered back and forth, staring at the faraway woods.

It took me a long time to realize that Crescent was born out of my fear of uncertainty. When I was nine, I began to understand that my parents were not all-powerful. If a flood came, they could not will the water back into the rivers. Should lightning strike our house, I might have already been incinerated by the time they rushed into my room. My parents could not stop me from dying, from being destroyed.

I wanted to believe there was somebody who knew everything, somebody who could keep me safe no matter what. Then Crescent came, hissing: "Don't touch the water. Don't go into the forest. Don't leave your room."

Over time, after I told my parents about my fear of death, I learned to not let the unknown cripple me. I gradually stopped assuming the worst about everything I didn't know. Instead, I harnessed it. I walked into the darkness with steady but careful legs and lit it with a flashlight. Then I widened my eyes and took notes on everything I saw: the colors, the shapes, the lines.

Crescent has not visited me since I starved myself in my room. However, when night falls and the moon glows softly, I can sometimes catch a glimpse of her silky dark hair in the distance, among the trees. I wave to her, and although I can't see clearly, I think she waves back, her fingers faint like milk.

MADELINE EVANS is a pilot who has flown solo across the world, crossing over both the Atlantic and the Pacific Oceans. Even though she does not like to pick favorites, she enjoys flying the most at midnight. The blazing stars mixed in with the vast darkness of the sky fills her dreams at night, and sometimes, she thinks that she can leap into space to defy gravity.

JIEYAN WANG is a fiction writer from northern Idaho. Her work has appeared in or is forthcoming in *The Bitter Oleander*, *The Blue Nib*, *Canvas Literary Journal*, and elsewhere. Although her reading tastes are broad, she is especially inspired by the works of Emily Brontë, Gabriel García Márquez, and Lewis Carroll.

VOICE

An account by Robin Booker,
AS PROVIDED BY JENNIFER R. POVEY

N obody listens to kids about their imaginary friends.

I mean, that's just like a law of human nature. Until you hit puberty, nobody will listen to you when you say you hear voices in the dark tunnels of the Ship where only maintenance and kids hiding from their parents go.

So nobody listened to me when I was a kid, when I heard the voice in the tunnels.

The rich, feminine voice that came through the speakers suggested her. I later understood that she was not she at all, that no concept of gender existed in what passed for her mind.

But at that time, I thought of her as the ghost in the walls, the woman who spoke. She had something in mind. Something in mind for me specifically.

But most of all, she told stories. After two of the stories, I knew I wasn't going to tell anyone. Least of all my mother. She was one of the few Passengers who was not too intimidated to talk to the Officers, even the Captain.

Then one of two things would happen. I'd get a stern lecture about having too much imagination, extra homework, and grounded for life. Or they'd believe me.

If it was true, it was far, far worse.

See, the stories she told me were stories of a place I could not even imagine, a place where the air moved in directions. Where there was no ceiling.

Where you could run until you were exhausted and never come back to where you had been before, not ever. That place was our Secret. I drew it, but I hid the drawings in the same hidey-hole where I talked to her.

She told me that we were supposed to go to that place, but something had happened. Now we were just… here.

You probably don't really understand what it's like, child, what living on the Ship really meant.

It meant that when the Officers said jump, you swallowed and asked how high. Mostly, you tried not to get their attention.

The Purser gave permission for births, making sure they matched deaths. If you weren't authorized to have a child, you had to go on the shots, men and women alike.

Mostly they only gave authorization to couples.

I was unique.

I didn't have a father. Supposedly, my mother had managed to bribe or obtain authorization on her own and drawn seed out of the Bank, which was normally used by couples who could not have children or whose children had been born… well… wrong.

Mutations happened. They were inevitable. Some of them, we didn't worry about. I knew an entire family that had fully webbed hands at birth, such that they had to trim it back so they could use their hands properly.

Some of them.

Well, never mind that. Our world was constrained by metal and even more constrained by the society we had built to live.

The voice knew it was all unstable.

The voice waited until I was a little older to tell me we were all going to die.

I suspected the Captain and the Officers knew. How could they not? They had to just be in denial.

But I was a child, so all I could do was cry. Then pick myself up and ask what I could do about it. That's when I found out I was not alone. I was not the only child the Voice was talking to. Of course I wasn't.

I wasn't *that* special. She did tell me I and the others had been chosen based off of things in the school system, things on the computers. Algorithms.

We were simply the kids most likely to believe her, and to keep believing her after we grew out of such things as imaginary friends.

You're wondering who she was, right? She was the Ship. She was the Ship's AI, which had been turned off and dormant. Something turned her back on. I never found out what.

Maybe the Captain knew. It was a moot point. She had been turned back on, taken one look at the situation, and raged. Or something akin to rage. AIs don't have instincts, so they don't experience the same emotions we do. They have emotions. But they don't map, not really. That's one of the reasons people back on Earth used to be afraid of AIs.

But when we left we took one with us. To watch over things, to make sure they didn't get out of hand.

Somebody turned them off.

I don't know who that person was, but if you gave me a time machine…

So we were all going to die. The Ship's systems were degrading. It was a closed system, it was meant to last for the years it would have taken us to get to Epsilon Eridani and, hopefully, a habitable planet. Hopefully.

Our great grandparents knew the risks when they got on the Ship. Our grandparents were born to the risks.

We were born thinking this was the world as it was and as it always has been, with the Captain as God, and the Officers his angels.

If you can't imagine living like that, don't worry. I couldn't imagine living any other way. Oppression, like anything else, can become normal.

We didn't see ourselves as oppressed. You went to school, when the time came you took Aptitude and found out whether you got to be Crew.

Nobody ever got to be an Officer. Maybe the kids of Crew did. But there were one or two in each class who disappeared through the bulkhead. I believed it was true, the kids they took were the smart ones. Good at math.

Also, often the troublemakers, so maybe it was a safety valve. No, I was not with those who thought they were killed.

Thought they were sent Outside into the hard vacuum. Smart kids were troublemakers.

And that was what the voice wanted. For us to do our best when Aptitude came around. Try and get a couple of us on Crew.

I didn't think I could do it. I wasn't the smartest. And math was never my gift. Words were. I was sure and certain I could never be Crew.

Would I have to wait helplessly? At that moment, I decided I would have children only when we were back on course.

Because that was the problem. We had been off course for years. We would never reach Epsilon Eridani.

We would never reach any destination.

And closed systems, eventually, degrade. The Ship had been built for that one journey.

It had not been built to wander the stars forever.

I grew up. I grew out of imaginary friends. But at the back of my mind was the fact that if I'd imagined all of it, then… where had that imagination come from?

We weren't taught about anything other than the Ship in school. History wasn't mentioned. The Ship was the world.

We didn't know what planets were, so how had I dreamed one up? Genetic memory had been debunked.

There was a part of me that thought it was a child's game and a part of me that thought it was real.

That latter part of me led me back to my old hidey-hole the day before Aptitude. I'd pushed myself, I'd pushed myself so hard to try and be good enough to be Crew, even if I wasn't sure it was real.

We were all going to die.

My drawings were still there. "Ship?" I asked softly.

There was no immediate response. Then it came, but it was slow and weak. "They found me. You have the coordinates. Use them. Turn around. Before—"

And there was nothing more.

I didn't have the coordinates. Had she forgotten which of us she gave them to?

Then I found them. In amongst the drawings, numbers and figures I didn't understand. A string of numbers to feed to the navigational computer.

But I couldn't use them. I couldn't get there, even if I got through the bulkhead, nobody but the Captain got to the Bridge.

A kid whose mother was a cook and whose father was a frozen

vial? She had no chance of ever being Crew. The Aptitudes were probably a trap. I was seventeen and cynical and convinced that if I actually passed, I'd be killed and recycled, not given quarters beyond the bulkhead.

I did my best anyway. The coordinates, I tried to memorize, then hid them under my pillow. My best hope was that she had given them to all of the kids.

They found her.

They hadn't turned her off again. They'd incapacitated her. I still couldn't help but think of her as her, not them, not it.

Her, because she had a voice like my mother's, or perhaps she'd made her voice that bit like my mother's so I'd trust her.

Aptitude took three days. Some kids blew them off. Some because they thought they would fail.

Others because they thought they might pass.

I didn't blow them off. Aptitude got you pushed toward specific jobs too. Blowing them off was bad, really. But you had the right to do so, even if it meant you spent your work shifts sweeping for the rest of your life.

We all knew the consequences.

Three of us passed. I passed. I had the coordinates. When we stepped through the Bulkhead, we would never go back to being Passengers.

We would marry and have children with other Crew. Those children might be tapped to be Officers.

I thought the Crew quarters would be luxurious.

I was so wrong.

"Lesson number one. We're not here to lord it over the Passengers, we're here to serve them."

The spartan surroundings drilled that into my brain right away. Everyone assumed Crew had a better life.

In some ways it was true. We had, or would have, access to the Ship's systems.

But I needed access to the Bridge.

And in other ways? Our work shifts would be a little longer, once we got through training. Which would take years. We started at a disadvantage compared to those born Crew.

I wondered what happened if those born here failed Aptitude. (I later found out that the failures did the drudge work fore of the Bulkhead, the stuff that needed to be done by humans but didn't require a really sharp brain.)

I wondered how I was going to get to the Bridge.

Then four days in, somebody took me aside. "Captain wants to see you."

The *Captain*? Had he seen something in my tests he liked or didn't like?

The Captain came back to Passenger country occasionally. I'd seen him. He was a few years older than my mother.

He was also God. You didn't approach him. You didn't talk to him. My mother had, but my mother was fearless that way. "He does?" I squeaked.

"Relax. That hard ass thing he puts on when he goes aft? It's an act. He's only human."

I didn't believe that. The Captain, elected by the Officers, was… some kind of elite. "But he's the Captain."

"You want to know what the Captain really does?" the man asked as he began to guide me towards Officers' country. "He makes sure the Officers don't kill each other."

My eyes widened. Then I realized he was at least semi-serious, which got a nervous laugh. "Meaning he's like the team leader who gets everyone to work together."

"Exactly. I mean, sure, in a crisis, he could order any of us recycled. But we don't have crises."

The coordinates were in my pocket, because I hadn't dared leave them anywhere. They seemed to catch fire there in my awareness.

They didn't have crises. "Everything always runs smoothly, then?"

"I didn't say that. But—" A pause. "Okay, we did have one crisis. The old ship's AI turned itself back on. We dealt with it, but not before it subverted three Crew kids into believing that we're off course."

There was a sudden doubt. What if we were on course after all, and the coordinates would kill us?

The Captain wanted to see me.

Me.

What had he... or did he know? Did he intend to personally tell me I had been lied to by the Ship?

I thought back to when she was just my imaginary friend and sighed inwardly.

Innocence was something you could never get back once it was lost.

The Captain was not at all what I expected. He lounged in a chair in a conference room, and as soon as I stepped in, he pointed at the door. "Leave us."

I stood.

"Oh, sit down. I won't eat you."

I sat down, on the edge of the chair, my hands in my lap because I had no idea what to do with them. My gaze flicked between him and the surroundings.

"I'm glad you passed."

I felt something within me. The Captain was glad I, personally, had passed. "Sir—"

"She never told you, did she?"

My father.

My father was a frozen test tube.

Or.

Or my father was Crew. It happened. Probably in both directions, to be honest. It was possible. "Oh. No, she didn't. I guess she… my father was Crew."

"Not exactly. I'm guessing she let you believe she took from the Banks."

"She did."

Not exactly. My heart was doing funny things in my chest.

"When we did your medical tests after Aptitude, we confirmed it, and I knew it was likely. I'm your father."

My unassuming mother had had an affair with the *Captain*? Disbelief had to show in my eyes.

He laughed a bit weakly. "I can show you the genetic assay."

"I think I'd like to see it." I had no clue how to read an assay beyond the basics, and I hadn't done well in that part of the Aptitude. No training as a doctor for me.

"I'll arrange it." A pause. "You don't get special treatment, and if I find you using this as currency, you'll be on KD for six months."

This time I did laugh. "I don't want it."

"But I… was hoping I could get to know you."

There was something oddly humble about the offer. I wondered if he was married. If I had half-siblings.

I was the Captain's daughter.

The coordinates were on fire again in my pocket. I looked away from him. "Sure."

He nodded. "Obviously I'm busy, but how about dinner?"

He didn't say when. I hoped not too soon.

I needed the time to plan what I was going to say to him.

And the time to try and work out whether we were on course or not.

"Okay." A pause. "Nobody will tell me. When are we going to get to Destination?"

He paused. "They won't tell you because we don't know. Part of the nav system failed a while back. Triangulations show we're on course, but we can't be sure whether we'll be there in ten years, or fifty. Could be as soon as five."

"Are we *sure* we're on course?" I asked.

He frowned. "Yes."

But it wasn't a one hundred percent yes. Maybe if I'd seeded some doubt, he'd do more checking, have whichever Officer was in charge of that do some work.

Maybe.

It was all I could hope for, in any case. I went back to training with a lot to think about.

I did not tell anyone about the Captain.

Despite our connection, the Captain—I would never think of him as my father—was as good as his word.

I got no special treatment.

Certainly, I wasn't getting anywhere near the Bridge. Based on the results of my Aptitude and observations during training, I was assigned in a very junior capacity to Operations, which basically meant everything that kept the inside of the ship running smoothly.

Which gave me a clear view that the Ship had not lied on one point. Our life support systems were degrading.

If it took fifty years to reach Eridani, we were going to be having food shortages and worse before we got there. But nobody seemed worried about it.

I decided that meant they thought there was nothing they could do. But this got me no closer to the nav computers than I had gotten as a Passenger.

What I did have was Observation. This was a domelike bubble that expanded out from the ship. Supposedly there were two or three in Passenger country, but they'd been locked out.

Passengers couldn't be trusted to look outside the ship. Crew could.

What I saw outside was stars, stars that glimmered. How did we even know where we were?

The painful answer was: we didn't.

Ship was dead. They'd killed her, turned her off again. And as a life support tech, I was more involved in working out how much of each crop needed to be grown to keep things in balance. The farmers back in Passenger country had their own ideas.

We didn't ignore them, we just enhanced their ideas with the data we had, sent back the results. I thought it would be more efficient to just give them the data.

I learned rapidly to keep those thoughts to myself. "Of course you think Passengers are smart, but why do you think we have to run Aptitude?"

I was no longer even sure they took the smartest for Crew, but I kept that quiet. They didn't, for example, take the most gifted in biology. Those people ran the farms or became doctors.

They took the people who would be useful, who filled a gap. I was filling a gap. I was replacing somebody, because Crew had fewer children.

Three of those kids had also been chosen by the Ship for her message. They had not been believed. I could not find out who they were. I dared not even ask.

Then I had an unexpected stroke of good luck.

I got invited up to Navigation. Not the Bridge proper, no. The Captain wanted me to meet somebody.

A young man, about my age. I knew a matchmaking attempt when I saw one, and I wondered how much of that went on. How many of the babies that *were* born in front of the Bulkhead were, in fact, carefully planned, arranged breedings to make the talents they needed.

It wasn't as dystopian a thought as it sounds. It wasn't like he was telling me I should marry Noah. Just that I might want to get to know him better.

Parents have been doing that since we became human, perhaps even slightly before. Noah wasn't bad looking. Dark skinned, curly hair, a strong nose. Dating him might be fun.

No pressure.

Of course not. He was the Captain, everything he did came with pressure.

But Noah worked the navigational computers.

I could use him.

And I would look like I was being a good little Crewman, considering the match made for me fairly.

Yeah. Noah was a stroke of luck.

Noah was also perfect. I didn't imagine I'd be telling him everything inside of a week.

And I knew that telling him everything could get me... what? Grounded?

Best case scenario, it would get me hauled up to be shown the data proving we were on course, if it existed. I could relax. I could put everything down to a malfunctioning AI.

But he listened. "I heard about that," he said, quietly. "As far as I know, as far as anyone knows, we're on course."

I pulled out the sheet with the coordinates. "This is what she told me to enter into the navigational computer. Can you tell what it means?"

He frowned. "That's raw nav data. So no. But I can do something. Give me a few." And he left.

I stood there with my heart beating. He might have gone to get the Captain. Or to get Security to arrest me for causing trouble.

He came back with a pocket computer. "Okay, this has some of the nav programs loaded on it. We use it for completely isolated testing."

"Meaning—"

"Meaning it's not connected to the Ship's networks at all. It's what we call an air gap. Makes sure that test programs don't get into the main computers and cause us to go off course."

That made sense. "But do we—"

"Only for practice. The theory is that we'll get within a certain distance of Eridani, then steer. Of course, some people don't want to land."

"Show *them* the life support data."

"Actually," Noah said, thoughtfully, "assuming the planet meets specifications, we'll be able to refurbish and refuel the *Tangaroa*. Then we can send her out again, with those who want to go, with some of the Bank… and seed another colony."

I might have objected to the "her," but Ship's voice had always been that of a woman. "So as long as it's only a reasonable number of people who don't want to land."

"Or we can turn her into a space station."

I nodded. "So, how about we check Ship's numbers?"

"Be aware they probably already did, just in case."

Before they killed her, turned her off, whatever. I felt my eyes prick at that thought. She was only ones and zeros, she wasn't really alive, but I missed her. She had been there for me when my mother couldn't. "I know. And I promise, if it doesn't add up, I'll never talk about it again."

It could be five years.

We could walk on a planet. "Why don't we teach the Passengers about Earth or Destination?"

"Because… somebody decided that it would distract you. And that teaching about Earth would give us all baggage. This is supposed to be a fresh start for humanity."

That made sense. "But how are we going to learn from their mistakes if we don't know what they are?"

"I don't know. It's not like they teach us more than Earth was screwed up and we had to leave." A pause. "Robin. Earth was dying."

I looked at him. "So's this Ship… but how does a planet die?"

"The same way a Ship does. Closed systems still have entropy. And humanity did everything it could to accelerate the process."

Closed systems.

Even the planet would be one.

"Then we need to make sure Destination isn't a closed system."

Which meant what?

"I don't think we can do that."

That meant all we could do was slow things down, so that it would be generations upon generations before we used it up.

He was typing. He was entering the numbers.

"Thank you, Noah."

He looked at me. "You owe me."

I grinned. "What do I owe you?"

He paused. Speculatively. "A date."

"Those coordinates," he said finally. "Aren't Destination."

"Do you know what they are?" I'd said yes to the date. I wasn't even sure why.

"Earth. She wants to go back. She wants to go home."

And that was why they had shut her off, but not before she'd damaged the computer systems.

I believed him. Almost. "Please. Tell me how you get that. I need to—"

"You need the proof. That's why you should be a scientist."

But I wouldn't be one, I'd just handle life support. There was no space for scientists. "We don't—"

"And we need to fix that, to change it. Who's going to study Destination when we get there? We don't have the AI. We don't have the past to draw on. None of us know what a planet looks like."

I shook my head. "Show me."

He did. He patiently went through the math. Gave me the 101 on how the Ship worked.

By the end of it, I believed him.

If I had done what she asked, we would all have died. I felt a regret at that. I had thought she wanted to save us.

Maybe in her own mind she did. Maybe she had seen something that warned her about Destination. Or, as we call it now... Home.

It's not the planet we were hoping for. They were wrong in their guess that Destination was a superhabitable world, easier than Earth. Easier and less likely to have unpleasant neighbors.

Or perhaps it had been, but something had happened. Destination was, is, a world where we have had to fight to survive.

Last year, *Tangaroa* left, carrying with it part of the Banks... and new genetic material taken from us. Carrying with it the people for whom Destination is not Home, the people who want space, the people who still dream of paradise.

But we were wrong about nobody knowing what a planet looked like. Ship knew, and the stories she told us warned us.

She warned us that water would fall from the sky, would fall on us and leave us cold and wet. That the water might freeze and become slippery.

She warned us that tides would encroach on the shore. She warned us that wild animals could be both dangerous and an important part of our future. Man has always existed in partnership, and we left our old partners behind.

She warned us we would need to find new ones.

She almost killed us. She also saved us. And her code is still there, sitting in the *Tangaroa*'s systems until, one day, you will turn her on.

I know you will, my child who left on the Ship. Oh, not you, but your child or your child's child. Because sooner or later, you will turn her on.

And she will guide you home.

And you will find out if Earth recovered from the depredations of man. If humanity survives somewhere amongst the ruins, or if something else now rules our cradle.

Because she's right. Eventually, we have to go home.

Home to the world from which we came, to the world we destroyed and the world that we, by leaving, may have saved.

I won't see that day. Likely you won't either. But tell your daughters and granddaughters, your sons and grandsons, that if they hear a voice in the tunnels, she's not the voice of the Ship.

She's the voice of Earth, asking us if we're ready to come home.

ROBIN BOOKER was born on the generation ship *Tangaroa*, not long before it reached its first colonial destination. She was instrumental in ensuring that the ship's rogue AI did not turn them around, possibly resulting in the deaths of all those aboard. She married Noah Karl and they had three children. Two of them stayed on Destination, but her daughter Carol left with the *Tangaroa* to seek another world for mankind…

JENNIFER R. POVEY lives in Northern Virginia with her husband. She writes a variety of speculative fiction, whilst following current affairs and occasionally indulging in horse riding and role-playing games. She has sold fiction to a number of markets, including *Analog*, *Daily Science Fiction*, and *Third Flatiron*, and written RPG supplements for several companies. Her most recent novel is the urban fantasy *Daughter of Fire*.

FORTRESS OF
ASH AND BONE

An account by Alfred,
AS PROVIDED BY VILLE MERILÄINEN

Lynn pressed her palm over my mouth when a deeper shadow passed us in the murk. The floor of the corridor snapped and crackled as the creature lurched forward, breaking the twig-like ribs that had poked my feet raw. Lynn said they looked like slugs, but I'd never seen one properly. The pets of the Unseen Queen fed on the children and the little light that infiltrated the fortress of ash and bone. If we were to conquer the trials of the fortress to reach her, we'd have to stand against them one day… but not today, when our only weapons were apples too precious to throw away.

I shivered in Lynn's arms until the shadow passed us and the dark was quiet again. She withdrew her hand and brushed my hair when I let loose the exhale I'd held in for the past dizzying minute. When she was certain we were safe, her glowing face appeared before me, freckled and veiled with dark curls. Of all the lights that had broken inside and survived, she was my favourite.

"Don't be scared, baby brother." She rose to her feet and peered out of the indent where we'd hidden. "It's gone now."

She led me by the hand down the path, where the smell of smoke clung to the walls and the pricking bones had turned to dust and shards with the monster's passage. I never knew where we were going, but Lynn forged on with unflinching purpose as we wandered through the halls. Her shine gained strength as we came to the chamber we'd made our home, until my shadow flew up the soot-stained walls and fluttered there in the heights. She did not cast one, but there always seemed to linger a cloud of darkness around her, as though her own shade formed a sphere around the glow.

Lynn rounded the once-lavish bed to a rococo dressing table and spread our loot there: apples we'd stolen from the ogre in the kitchen. Everything in here had suffered the same burns as all the fortress had. The curtains over the wide bed had been reduced to charred strips, as had the room-spanning carpet. The mirror above the table was blackened and showed Lynn's reflection in shattered fragments. The books on the shelves were dust now, to our shared sorrow. Before we lost ourselves to the fortress, Lynn and I had loved to read to one another.

"Come on, Koi," she said, after I'd forgotten myself to melancholy musing while watching the shelf. She munched on one of the apples and impatiently shook another for me to take. "Pick yourself a plump one before they're all gone. I'm starving."

Though my heart still pounded from our raid and the encounter outside, I managed a grin and caught the apple when she tossed it. I couldn't remember how long we'd been stuck here anymore, but apples were always a treat. It wasn't often we found any—nor dared to delve into the kitchens in the first place—but sinking my teeth into the juicy fruit made the danger worthwhile.

Once we'd reduced the contents of the sack to cores, Lynn picked the last seeds from between her teeth and threw herself on the bed. "Ah, hits the spot," she said, stretching herself to almost cover the width. She patted the scorched duvet, and I lay down beside her, hands on my stomach, letting her warmth seep through my skin. The rest of the fortress was cold, worse now that our clothes were but tattered rags, but here she could let herself shine without fear and make us warm.

Lynn's fingers sought my hand and she closed hers around it. "Someday soon, we'll find our courage and climb up the fortress, up to the chamber of the Unseen Queen and walk free. I promise."

I only nodded, or tried to—the gesture was made slight by drowsiness. We lay there for a while, listening to the growls of the pets as they wandered past, and the occasional distant patter of feet like ours. There were more children lost in the fortress—we knew this to be true, even though we'd never run into any. The world outside was dying, may've been gone already by now. The Unseen Queen had the power to change it, but reaching the heights of the fortress required us to find the three treasures hidden somewhere in the depths: the key to the queen's tower; a weapon with which to slay the dragon guarding her; and the crown she'd lost, which we would offer to earn her favour.

It sounded like a fairy tale, and maybe our love for stories was why we'd been sent here. We'd soon learned the horrors within were worse than any story, and now we were trapped in a palace of ruin.

Lynn bounced up, spun around to listen with an intense expression. "Do you hear that?" she whispered, head slowly rotating as if to follow a sound. She held her breath, as did I, and I *did* hear it—a creak far off in the distance.

The entrance had opened.

Lynn dragged me out of the chamber and through the fortress, uncaring of the snapping bones biting into our feet and leaving a trail of footprints that shimmered red in Lynn's dimming glow. If we could catch the newcomers before they disappeared into the fortress' bowels, perhaps we'd find allies in them, someone to help us…

My thoughts trailed off when we found the entrance hall afire, or so I thought. There blazed a light far more luminous than I'd ever seen erupt from Lynn, and it made me wonder whether the reason we never found anyone was because the pets swarmed and ate them before they made it two steps in.

Lynn let go and raised a finger to her lips, then crept closer to the overlooking balcony. I gingerly followed, peering down to find the source of the light: a girl of about fourteen, Lynn's age, garbed in a white dress, looking at her shining hands and clothes with surprise.

She was beautiful. So beautiful that I didn't notice her companion until he strode past her toward the stairs to our level. The sight of him stunned me further. He was an adult, masked, in strange clothes hiding his body and with a bag hanging on his belt. His breathing sounded laboured under the mask, had a rasping quality to it. It looked familiar, like something I should've recognised, but could not bring to mind why.

"Hey!" Lynn hissed. "Lose the light! You'll draw in the queen's pets!"

The girl's gaze snapped toward Lynn, then she dashed after the man and reached for his shoulder. He stopped without a word—a strong and silent type like me, I suspected—and waited as the girl addressed Lynn. Something beeped in the man's bag, like the chirps of a baby bird.

"I don't know how," she said, head cocked and with a rueful smile. "This is new to me, I'm afraid."

"Think of twilight to tone it down, nightfall to go dark." Lynn fell quiet to listen for approaching pets, but we heard nothing. "Sunrise to restart it, high noon to flare. Quickly, now."

The girl's skin turned from a pyre to cinders as she continued her ascent. She brushed the man's shoulder and he followed.

"This way," Lynn said, waving them along. "It's not safe out in the open. We've made ourselves a base in one of the rooms."

"Wait," the girl said, after we darted off. "Dad can't run."

Lynn stopped to regard them with incredulity. "He'd best learn if he wants to survive the fortress."

"He's… special," the girl said. "You'll be safe near him, no matter what."

A rumble from the darkness reached us, and Lynn hissed a curse. "I'd love to take your word on it, but I'm not ready for risks now. Come on."

The girl patted the man's shoulder twice, and both hurried after us. He seemed like me in other ways too, blind beyond what Lynn let me see. It would've been easier for the girl to simply pull him along, but she kept navigating his way to our room with brushes and taps.

Lynn beckoned the pair into our room, then quietly shut the door after us. A moment later a pet rumbled past, and she breathed easy only after silence returned. Leaning against the door, she muttered, "I'm starting to have my regrets about this already."

The man sat on the bed and rapped his fingers against his knuckles while the girl took in the room. When Lynn folded her arms and regarded her with suspicion, the girl brushed a blonde lock behind her ear and said, "You must be Lynn."

Suspicion became surprise. "Huh? Yeah. How'd you know?"

"We've actually met. I'm Lauren, and this is my dad, Warren."

Lynn narrowed her eyes, studying them both, then nodded toward me. "I don't think I remember. Anyway, that's my brother, Koi."

A shadow of surprise flitted on Lauren's features before she looked my way. Her smile seemed uncertain as she sought and waved at me, though I was well within Lynn's glow. "Hello, Koi." She stared at me until I felt my cheeks start to burn, then leaned toward Lynn and said, "Er, I'm a little hard of hearing. Did he say anything?"

"He doesn't talk," Lynn said.

Though I didn't see why, this seemed to relieve Lauren. "Ah. Dad doesn't either."

Lynn gave me a weary look, then ran a hand through her curls. "A mute who can't run and a girl who can't control her glow. You'd damn well better be special for the elders to send such a sorry pair into the fortress of ash and bone. Do you even know what you're here for?"

Lauren took the insult in stride and maintained her smile. "Well, the… the, um, elders only said there *was* a reason for our being here. Maybe you could shed some light on it?"

I grinned at her choice of words, but Lynn rubbed the bridge of her nose and sighed with exasperation. "I swear, if you two are the ones to find the Unseen Queen, I hope you'll also ask her to give the council better judgement in the future." She cleared her throat and looked at Warren, who'd sat in place all this while, as though the lack of Lauren's touch meant he was to be as inanimate as possible. "To reach the queen and ask for her blessing, you need a key, a weapon to defeat her guardian, and a gift. All of those are hidden somewhere in the fortress, but it's crawling with beasts. To survive—"

Lauren cut her off with a clap of her hands. "Ah! That answers one question. I can pick any lock, Dad's impervious to any monster, and as for the gift… Well, I'm sure he can arrange a deal. Do you know where to find your queen?"

Taken aback, Lynn shook her head. "It's not that easy. There are trials to complete, dangers to face—"

"Time's a bit of a factor." Lauren stepped closer and placed a hand on Lynn's shoulder. "Let us worry about the tribulations. You only need to show us the way."

"You can't just skip to the end! That's not how stories work!" Lynn snapped.

Lauren winced, but only patted Lynn's shoulder. Warren ignored the outburst. "This isn't a story," Lauren said.

Lynn shook her arm away, gave the bookshelf a melancholy look of her own. "I swear, if we die because of this—" she muttered, then fell quiet for a thoughtful spell. "There's a way up the eastern side of the fortress. It's the quickest path to the queen's tower, but also dangerously close to the hive of her pets. It'd be wiser to circle around, outsmart the ogre in the kitchen to use the rear exit, then fight our way up the far side the way the elders meant us to. Koi and

I have been scouting, preparing for a chance, but—"

"But, as I said," Lauren said, with a hint of an apology to her tone, "time's a factor."

Lynn grimaced, gave Warren an appraising look. "He goes first, and if he gets eaten, we're running away."

Lauren chuckled. "Sounds fair."

Warren rose at her touch, and another guiding brush on his shoulder made him turn left in the corridor. The man's behaviour made me think of stories of golems, creatures made of clay and brought to life to serve orders. His strange suit reminded me of something else entirely, but even as I watched him wade ahead of us, heedless of the dark and the threats therein, I couldn't recall what it was.

Lynn led me by the hand, as always, but now I noticed her other gripped Lauren's. She caught me looking and gave me a nod, but without her usual certainty. Lauren's promise of her father's protection seemed to have some merit, for though the girl glowed just enough for us to see the path, we hadn't yet attracted the pets' attention. Their crawling resounded all around us, came close at times, yet we saw nothing.

Lynn's hold tightened suddenly. With a whimper of, "This isn't right," she pulled us to a halt. Lauren wheeled about with a worried look, then broke off her grip and ran after her father to stop him. She ignored our shoulders bumping together when she returned to comfort Lynn, and I reluctantly stepped back to give her space.

"Something's wrong," Lynn said, shaking her head. "We can't go this way. We can't skip a part of the story."

"Lynn, please." Lauren pressed her hands on Lynn's cheeks. "You *have* to calm down. Take deep breaths."

"And you," Lynn said, still shaking, "you said you knew me. How? That's not—"

"This gift of light," Lauren said quickly. "We received it together. Us, and others. You might not remember it—we were so small I barely do—but you were scared then as well, and I comforted you."

"I received the gift from the elders," Lynn whispered. "I was the chosen one that year. There were no others."

"There were. You and me and five more." Lauren brought her face closer to Lynn's, caught her wandering gaze. "And now I'm here to help you. Do you know what's happened outside?"

"The sun grew too hot, dried the fields and the well," Lynn said. Her pained tone made me taste blood when I chewed through the skin of my lip. "The legends told of a child who'd conquer the fortress of ash and bone, and I was born under the good star, and so the elders chose me—"

A series of beeps sounded from Warren's bag. Lynn shook more fiercely, but Lauren held on. "Lynn, you have to calm down or you'll go off again."

"Go off? What are you talking about?" She pressed her eyes shut. "You're here only to confuse me!"

"Listen to me. The sun's hotter than ever, and our people are in danger. The elders sent me here to help, to hasten your efforts." This finally calmed Lynn, and she opened her eyes to meet Lauren's. "We need to skip a few chapters, but it's still your story."

The beeps grew farther apart, then fell away when Lynn asked, "Do you promise?"

Both seemed to have forgotten I was there, and a pang of jealousy struck me when they embraced. "Of course," Lauren said, then offered her hand. "I only want to help you."

Lynn took it, and I'd almost fallen out of their light before she turned with a jolt and reached for me. "Come, Koi. The queen awaits."

I followed, bitter but unable to complain. My carefully crafted expression of frustration went unseen with Lynn's gaze fixed ahead.

The passage widened in preparation for the dragon's arena, and the smell of smoke ever present in the halls became pungent. Over us washed waves of noxious exhalation and the vibrations of a giant's snoring. Lynn cared nothing for my terror, Lauren less, and I would have screamed for them to stop if I could have. Struggling against the two of them was fruitless, and though I read tension in Lynn's posture, she allowed Lauren to lead her until the beeps returned. Only then Lauren stopped and asked, "Is something wrong?"

"We don't have the sword of the queen's executioner," Lynn said. A distant scream made her jump and face a side passage, where a pet crawled close by. "That's the way we should've come from. After the kitchens, we would've gone through the infested servants' quarters down to the dungeon, faced the executioner, then climbed up and fought the pets' hive queen—"

"The elders gave father magic potions," Lauren said, petting Lynn's hair the same way Lynn had used to soothe me. "We'll wait here and let him face the executioner."

"No, no! He's the other way. The dragon is here. We need the sword—"

"The potions will work," Lauren said patiently. "Just wait."

The beeps grew distant, more rapid as we waited, and quicker yet when Lauren's glow began to strengthen. "No!" Lynn hissed. "It'll see us!"

"Think of a sunrise," Lauren said quietly, holding Lynn closer. "Things are always so much scarier in the dark." Her radius reached the walls, touched the tip of an obsidian claw. The beeps matched my pounding heartbeat. "But, when dawn comes—" A grey limb appeared from the murk. "—You'll find there was really nothing to fear at all."

She flared up to illuminate the entire hall.

The beeping grew more intense, then slowly calmed as Lynn's gaze wandered around the space. The circular room was empty, save for the mound of ash shaped vaguely like a reptilian leg. Warren waited on the far side, before a door sealed with a padlock as big as his head.

"Where did it—?" Lynn trailed off when Lauren released her.

With a rueful smile, Lauren said, "I think it's my time to step up."

She walked off, and Lynn finally turned to face me. "This isn't how it's supposed to go."

The lock's clang against the floor alerted her, and with a last look my way, she hurried to the open door.

We found no winding steps buffeted with storm gales beyond, but another corridor. Warren waited with his golem-like patience as Lynn stepped through, studying the rows of doors with confusion. There was no ash here, no bone underfoot, but panels that felt cool against my wounded feet.

"We should be outside, at an overlook before the queen's rise," Lynn said, voice frail as her gaze wandered down the hall awash with weak white light. "And we'd need iron-soled boots to make us heavy enough to weather the winds. What is this?"

Lauren only pulled her along, a sombre look on her face, and her touch set Warren off past them. The beeps began to sound in series of threes when he rounded a corner, and once we came to the last door at the end of the corridor, turned into a single, long noise. He reached into the pouch and shut it off with a click. Before he opened the door, Lauren pressed a hand on Lynn's shoulder and said, "Please stay calm."

The room was already lit with sunlight streaming in through a dusty window—dusty, not ashen. Lynn suppressed a shriek with a hand slapped to her mouth, and even my jaw fell. Lauren wrapped an arm around Lynn's shoulder as we came to the bed where another Lynn lay. This one wasn't wholly aglow, only her veins, which shone in eerie blue against her skin. Her eyes were half-open, lit with the same blue, pulsing to the rhythm of her ragged breathing. A dress like Lauren's shrouded her, but when I looked at Lauren, hers had lost whatever enchanting quality I thought it'd had and become drab.

"What... what—" Lynn tried, but could form no further sentence. Lauren led her to the bed and sat there, while Warren began to unload the contents of his bag onto the table beside the duplicate.

There were signs of burn damage in the room, but the bed was spared, as was the book the other Lynn pressed to her chest. Lynn was busy trying to stop herself from hyperventilating, but my heart sank from reading the title written in bold letters over a crown, a sword, and a key. *Fortress of Ash and Bone*, by Ellen Jones.

"Dad will explain this better, but since *I* barely understood him, I'll try to give you the gist of it," Lauren said, in a low, soothing tone. "Do you like superheroes, Lynn?"

"What?" Lynn asked, eyes wide and teary. "Superheroes? I-I-I guess? What does that—"

"Dad's a scientist. When you and I and five other kids were babies, his team messed around with our genetics to try to give us all kinds of crazy powers. I actually lied before—I don't remember you. We were just a few months old then."

"What the hell are you talking about?" Lynn asked between sobs.

The beeping returned, and Warren tapped the device emitting the sound. Lauren slapped his arm, then said, "Remember what I said about staying calm? If you don't, you'll detonate. Dad's inside the safe zone now, but the blast wave will go farther each time."

Lynn turned to look at her double. "I don't understand—"

She froze mid-sentence, and Lauren turned as well. "Hm. That explains something to *me.*"

"That's my mom's book," Lynn said, so quietly I could barely hear her. "She wrote it for me." A shudder ran through her and, defeated, she laid her head against Lauren's shoulder. "Because I was in a hospital."

I wanted to hold her, push Lauren away and comfort Lynn in her stead, but I was petrified in place just outside the ring of blackened vinyl floor. Warren, I noted, stood well within it, even leaning a little over the bed to remain inside as he worked.

"Do you remember why?" Lauren asked.

"Cancer." Lynn sighed, as though she'd run out of sobs. "In my heart."

"Mine was in the brain." Lauren gave Warren's arm two quick brushes. He'd begun making an odd sound inside his mask—almost like sniffles. He glanced over and nodded. "They called us nuclear witches. When the cancer spread, it mutated the altered genes and turned us into bombs. I don't know if it was a massive case of bad luck or if the operation caused it, but it happened to all seven of us. A chunk of the United States is gone, and Dad's working to keep the rest of it from blowing up as well. You're the third one we've gotten to. Went off twice before we made it here."

"This doesn't make any sense," Lynn said, staring wide-eyed at the floor. "I remember growing up in the village outside the fortress."

Lauren shrugged her free shoulder. "Rural Wisconsin, but close enough. You see what you want to see and remember what you wish had been, and your abilities make it real—sort of. Dad's been walking through the hospital this whole time, but I became a part of your dying dream the moment we stepped inside. I had to play along so you wouldn't notice what Dad was doing and panic."

"But, Koi—"

"Isn't there. I can't see him at all."

Lynn looked up, and her terror grew tenfold when she faced mine. "He's always been here. He's my brother."

If I could've punched Lauren, I would have when she said, "I think he's the brother of the book's Lynn. Kind of like an imaginary friend." She started swinging her legs, stared at them. "I had one as well, before Dad released me. It gets lonely, being like this, so you turn your surroundings into something that gives you comfort. I guess scary stories were your thing."

Lynn closed her eyes, wearily asked, "What is this?"

"The moment where I tag Dad in," Lauren said. Warren had finished setting his tools on the table—a series of syringes, needles, and a small battery-powered saw—and now simply stood waiting, careful to stay within the circle. She tapped her thumb against his shoulder in a sequence, and Warren took a tape recorder from his bag.

"Hello, Lynn," said the voice on the tape, presumably his. "Among many things, I'm sorry that I can't speak with you personally. The air within your blast area is toxic, and I can't talk with a filter mask on.

"My name is Warren Hemwick. I trust Lauren has explained the basics of your situation to you. You are an unfortunate product of what became known as the infamous Nuclear Witch project. When I began my work, I sought the lofty ideals of transhumanity—I intended to give you longer life, greater strength, and immunity to illnesses. The last goal is particularly ironic considering what happened.

"After I had laid everything ready with my life's work, I was removed from the then-innocuous project Advanced Genome. Without my knowing, my work was taken apart and expanded upon until a way was found to weaponise it. My seven perfect specimens were turned from the first people who might have lived until two hundred without physically aging past their mid-twenties into walking doomsday devices. When you detonate, you send out a nigh-unstoppable blast wave that causes burns to inorganic material and disintegrates the organic. The intention was for you to infiltrate war zones, where you would quickly and effectively decimate entire armies.

"I cannot fathom the idiocy required for such a plan, particularly when the mental detonator turned out to be tied to stress levels. It's a marvel we survived this long into your collective teens. Please excuse the gallows humour; it is all I have left.

"An unforeseen side-effect of the detonation was that it separated your body and your consciousness. My theory is you now partially exist in an alternate, overlapping dimension, where you can see us but we cannot see you, as though separated by a one-way mirror. Through rigorous practice, Lauren has learned to mildly affect this side, but cannot muster more than causing localised feelings of vague chills. You've become, for the lack of a more scientific word, ghosts."

Lynn choked. She maintained a fixed gaze on her feet, still beside Lauren's swinging shoes, but now looked as though she was about to vomit. I strained myself to move closer, but the petrification had become complete.

"I understand this must all be harrowing to hear, and though it is of little significance, know that I am truly, terribly sorry for what happened to you. Curse me to the deepest pits of Hell if you will. Lauren will deliver me your regards.

"The worst part, however, is that in order to prevent further detonations, I must terminate your body. It is almost brain dead, and I do not believe there is a way to properly sew your consciousness back together with it—not with the technology available in the foreseeable future, if ever.

"But, thanks to the 'almost,' it is possible for you to come with us. As you may've noticed, you cannot leave the vicinity of your body. You remain tethered to a small part of your brain, and if removed and contained, I can bring you with us—to haunt me instead of the hospital, if you will. I have machinery in my laboratory that allows you to communicate properly with our side, and you would have Lauren as company.

"Alternatively, I can leave it in place when I give your body a lethal injection, consigning you to peace. The choice is yours. I realise this is a tremendous decision to make, but I must implore you to make it with haste."

Lynn looked drained of all vitality, still leaned languidly against Lauren's shoulder. Warren's device beeped with a steady pulse and had only quickened for brief moments during his recorded speech.

"So," she said, "I killed everyone around me?"

"The first time, yeah. But it's not your fault."

"Doesn't matter." Lynn sighed. "How far?"

"First detonation had a twenty-mile radius." Lauren paused for five swings back and forth. "Second was two hundred, but there were barely any casualties. People in the northwest weren't as lucky, but it gave Dad data on how far people would have to be evacuated."

"Oh, god." Lynn was quiet another five swings, then asked, "And this happened to you, too?"

"Yeah." One, two, three swings. "Dad was in his lab when it happened. Proofed against everything up to and including a nuclear apocalypse." She brushed her nose with the back of her hand. "Mom was in the kitchen."

"I'm so sorry."

"Me too. For what it's worth, your folks are fine."

Lynn brightened up, and though I still couldn't move, I felt lighter as well. "Really? Where are they?"

"In one of the safe zones. Not sure where, but I promise you they're fine."

Lynn nodded, considered a moment, and said, "Have others come with you?"

"Well, like I said, you're the third. I was the first, and this girl, Lisa… She was the reason we knew how far people had to be evacuated the second time."

"Was?"

"Was."

Warren tapped his beeper, and Lauren brushed his arm. "I don't think I want to die," Lynn said. "Can you tell him to take me with you?"

I thought there was relief in Lauren's budding smile when she jumped off the bed and brushed Warren's other arm twice. He nodded, picked up the saw, and it whirred to life.

Once he was finished, Lynn and Lauren stood waiting by the door, watching hand in hand as Warren inserted a needle into Lynn's arm and the pulse waned away. As soon they'd left the circle, I could move again, but neither noticed me anymore, ignored my touch, paid no mind when I stood before them and waved my arms.

I followed them down from the fourth floor of the hospital that Lynn had turned into the fortress of ash and bone, tried to hang on to make them stop and only found myself sliding along. When they reached the foyer, where I'd watched a man in strange garbs and a girl in a dazzling dress enter, I now watched the departure of two girls in hospital gowns and a man in a hazmat suit. I could not leave; when I tried, a force as strong as had kept me away from the bed bound me behind the glass doors showering me with sunlight. With Lynn's vision taken from me, there were no bones around me, no mounds of ash—only toppled pots of burnt plants and seats with the leather singed.

They terrified me more than any of the Unseen Queen's beasts.

As the two witches and the villain who'd helped create them disappeared down the street, Warren's words of a ghost's ties to its body returned to me. I now presumed that, somewhere far in the hospital's guarded depths, there was a corpse not fully destroyed, and that I'd become the victim of a nuclear witch twice: once in life, and again when I returned to the dark, quiet corridors, condemned to haunt them alone.

ALFRED was a patient in the military hospital where NW-06-WI (or Lynn) was being treated. Upon NW-06-WI's detonation, he became absorbed in her fading fantasy and took on the role of Koi, the loyal sidekick in the children's novel *The Fortress of Ash and Bone*. His consciousness is presently wandering around the ruins of the hospital; his remains rest inside a broken MRI scanner, whose magnetic field disrupted the blast wave just enough for him to suffer the separation of body and soul the nuclear witches themselves did.

VILLE MERILÄINEN is a Finnish university student, award-winning author of speculative fiction, and death metal vocalist. His short fiction has appeared in various venues online and in print, including *IGMS*, *Cast of Wonders*, and *Pseudopod*. His musical fantasy novel, *Ghost Notes*, is available now.

OF RORSCHACH WORLDS AND LITTLE WHITE SHOES

An account by Skye,
AS PROVIDED BY KIKI GONGLEWSKI

The room was brimming with so much color, it could barely hold it all in. Drawings of mythical beasts and alien creatures lined the daffodil- and rose-mottled walls, whimsical knickknacks crowded the shelves, and the air smelled of popcorn, reminiscence, circus matinees, and imagination. In the center of it all, we lay on the floor next to each other, two twelve-year olds floating aimlessly within this fabric of infinity, our heads pointing in opposite directions, resting by each other's toes. We stared at the ceiling and all the worlds beyond it in quiet contemplation.

"Did I ever tell you," I murmured distantly, jade irises filled with all the speckled mauve starlight I saw beyond the finite ceiling, "about those little white shoes?"

Next to me, my companion shook his head slowly. His eyes were full of the ocean, the bubbling white and cerulean spray the waves yielded the moment they finally crashed onto the shore.

"I loved them," I mused, "used to wear them every day. Even after they were all worn down, and my feet were way too big for them. I wore them anyway. Figured I could live with a few blisters." Here, I couldn't help a small laugh. But the sound was dry and struck the air heavily like the dull clanging of a solid lead pipe. "But, when we moved... well, you know how moves are. I lost them."

Still, he said nothing, though the ocean had faded from his eyes as if my words had weighed him down to earth again.

"So if you see them around anywhere, just let me know."

The silence had settled in the corners of the room again. Filling the spaces. Making them even emptier.

I gently nudged his shoulder with my foot. "Kyle?"

"Hmm," my friend responded distantly.

"You ever think, while we're lying here, that the whole world outside of this room has just disappeared completely and we just don't know yet?"

Kyle sat up ever so slightly to look in the direction of the window, then scoffed in disgust as he resumed his previous position flat on his back.

"Yup, still all there," he muttered. "Unfortunately."

"Hmm," I murmured softly. "Give it more of a chance than that."

"We both have, Skye." I could hear Kyle's tone harden in defiance. "They stare at us. Make us both feel like total weirdos."

"Well, they're not actually staring at you," I noted casually, though there was a hint of something else, something sharp and crimson-colored, that tinged the edges of my words. I felt them lacerating my tongue even as I spoke.

"That doesn't matter. Either way, I hate every second of it." Here he paused deliberately, as if to give his next words a special emphasis. "Which, by default, means you do too."

I sighed and closed my eyes, refusing to give him and his claim the endorsement of a glance. "Well," I began slowly, "that makes my next proposition a whole lot harder."

Behind the darkness of my eyelids, I felt a visceral rustle next to me. "Do you remember just looking at the ceiling?" Kyle asked after a moment. I opened my eyes again and cast him a quick glance, but his entire being now seemed to be focused on what was above him—or perhaps away from me. "Not like we do nowadays, but *really* looking like how we used to. For hours and hours on end. Skye, there are whole *worlds* hiding within the Rorschach patterns of plaster. Anything you could possibly think of. It's so much fun, like looking for shapes in clouds—"

"We're not five anymore," I rejoined, "Stop trying to distract me."

But Kyle forged onward, oblivious. "You know, I remember when you used to just sit in one place for hours on end because there was so much to do and see and think about there. Or when you'd spend hours watching an ant crawl from one end of the sidewalk to the other. Or when we used to spend a whole day visiting all the universes we'd created in our minds. So much color. Time had no meaning, then. It didn't exist for us yet. Don't you remember that?"

I turned my head toward him. "Did you even hear what I said?"

Kyle squeezed his eyes shut and the corners of his mouth turned sharply downward as if he'd tasted something extremely bitter. "It's freezing out, anyway," he acknowledged at last.

I shrugged. "Maybe, but I'm kind of in the mood to be amongst, well, people and stuff—"

I heard his sharp intake of breath and saw Kyle wince as his eyes fluttered open. He sat up and looked at me, slowly bringing his knees up close to his chest like a hurt animal nursing his wound.

"You know I didn't mean it like that." I began tentatively, "It's not that you're, well, *not* real or anything. I just… Look, I absolutely love playing with you, but sometimes—" I pondered the next phrase in my mind. It rested as delicately as a snowflake at the tip of my finger, not quite tangible. Still so breakable. "Sometimes, I just get a little lonely."

"How?" Kyle shot back at me accusingly, "how are you possibly lonely? *I'm* here! I'm always here for you, Skye."

"Look," I began, "it's not your fault—"

Kyle stood up abruptly and dragged me over to the window, overlooking a busy city street. "And it's so much better out there, huh?"

The street was packed with people huddled under layers, hiding themselves beneath jackets and coats and scarves wrapped around ashen faces in a futile effort to stave off the biting cold. All of them were looking downward with their gazes trained steadily on the stretch of sidewalk in front of them. They, and everything beyond them, were entirely in black and white.

Color. Color was another secret invention of ours. Kyle and I used to laugh in bright lilacs and deep forest emeralds during sunny afternoons or in one of our worlds, sing songs in cool aquamarines and vivacious tangerines on cold, bitter winter days much like this one, tucked safely inside. It was the lens in which we saw everything in the universe, sparkling and new. Color. Color was the universal language that all the children spoke. But it was also something that seemed to be eventually forgotten. Age dimmed the memory and brightness of all the reds and yellows and blues. They looked, these adults, with their new and knowledgeable charcoal eyes. They could no longer see color. No one our age really understood why.

Grey, shadow, graphite, iron, ash, slate, charcoal, ebony, obsidian, onyx... These were the lexica of the outside world of the fully grown.

"Look at them, Skye." Kyle demanded roughly. "Take a good long look and tell me what you see! That out there? *That's* true loneliness. Not in here, not with me."

Flint, soot, grease, coal, crow, pewter...

I looked, but then shook my head vigorously and turned away. "Please stop shouting, Kyle. It's just that you're not always enough—

I'm not always enough!" We were already talking over each other, bombarding the other with distorted fragments of words and bitter ideas that left neither of us unscathed.

"And technically, since we're the same—"

"I know that the world is cold and ugly and vicious sometimes, but—"

Lead, sable, ink…

"That means we always have to stick together because… because—"

"But Kyle, it doesn't matter in the end, because—"

Pitch, emery, fossil…

"We're all we've got—"

"It's the only world I've got!"

Both of us reeled in silence from each other's words. Finally, I was the one who turned away from him first. "I'm going out," I said at last, then reluctantly elaborated, "out alone." I braced for his reaction. "Don't be mad—"

"I'm not mad about that!" Kyle shouted at me, "I'm mad that you're lying to me!"

"What makes you think I'm lying?"

"Because it's simple logic!" he cried, gesturing wildly. "I don't want to go out. And that, in turn, means you don't want to go out! So you can try and convince yourself as much as you want that we're two different sides of an argument, but you can't. What I know, you know. If I think or feel something, that means you can too, and, and, and—" Kyle tried helplessly to grasp for more words, complete thoughts as his armor. Something tangible to cling onto, but he came up empty.

"I have to go out," I said quietly.

"Why? You don't *have* to do anything."

"Of course I do."

"Really? Are you being held at gunpoint? Who's forcing you?"

I looked at him again, straight in the eyes. He wilted under the directness of my glance. "Fine, I guess no one's forcing me. I *want* to go out."

"How can you, when I don't? What does that make my thoughts and words?" Kyle cried, "what does that make me?"

I inhaled sharply. "Devil's… advocate, maybe?"

He gawked at me.

"Look, Kyle—"

"Fine, fine! You win!" He interrupted me hurriedly, his voice rising nearly a quarter of an octave in the blind, fluttery throes of increasing panic. "We're going out. Happy? I can't stop you anyway. Could be fun, you know. Going out. It's fine, I'm fine. We'll have a *great* time, you and me. We always do! Us against the world, right? You and me. Outside. Let's do it."

"I found those little white shoes in the end, you know," I whispered, my mind wandering to places that far transcended the room again. "Thrown out, after the move. Parents must've mistook it for trash, I guess."

"Listen," Kyle persisted pleadingly, his voice muted as if he were underwater or a great distance away. "People don't have to know."

"And they were small and old and dirty, and not how I remembered them at all. But I still thought about putting them on, even after all those years—"

"You don't have to talk to me at all, or acknowledge me. And I pinky promise I'll be totally quiet, and I won't make comments about anything that happens."

"But it was obviously pointless. I'd never be able to squeeze into them again. And I already had a new pair of shoes, while these… Well, they were cleaner and whiter and better off as a memory. So I left them there, to get lost again. And they did." I looked up at Kyle. "And I know that you know all this already. Because I know. Because it'd be stupid if we thought of ourselves as different, autonomous halves of a single whole, when really—" I stopped for a moment, looking intently down at the ground as if it held some concrete clue to the forever nebulous answers I sought. "It doesn't matter. I could never fill up that much space anyhow. Maybe that's why we do this, you and me."

"And no one will even know that I exist," Kyle murmured hoarsely, a once-melodic voice full of poems and rhymes so recently raised unnaturally to cacophonous anger now trailed off into a scarcely audible and defeated whisper.

"But *I'll* know, Kyle," I sighed. "It's just how things are nowadays. Stuffed animals, imaginary friends, baby shoes… It's too cold outside for them, they'd all freeze to death."

"So how much longer are you going to keep doing this?" Kyle asked bitterly, shoulders squaring at me. The indignation and anger had returned somewhat, I noticed, but at the same time, he had never seemed so small. "How often are you not going to listen to me anymore, huh? Cutting me out of things? Ignoring me in front of other people like I'm nothing! Leaving me behind—"

I didn't answer. I simply looked at him for a while. Time, time was all relative in this place. I could have kept looking while he shrunk slowly under my gaze, gradually faded away into transparency over the centuries, and not a moment would have passed outside in that grey, colorless world. But it was all an illusion. Seconds, minutes, hours, years slipped by us no matter where we were. It was simply a question of whether or not we chose to notice it. So, I began to rub my hands slowly over my face. Feeling all the smooth surfaces—no lines or bumps or blemishes yet—and leaving them black and white in their wake. There were no mirrors in the room. But I could feel my skin changing under my touch, fading from soft peach into pale grey, striking green eyes reduced to a dull charcoal. Just like them.

"You missed a spot, Skye."

"Where?"

"I—" Kyle paused, biting his lip. "Why don't you leave just that one bit showing? No one will care. I bet they wouldn't even notice. Please?"

"Kyle—"

"Please, for me?"

I didn't respond. He hesitated for a second longer, then gave up and signaled a spot on his own cheek dejectedly. He wouldn't look at me. I brushed the spot over, covering it completely, smoothed my hair, and opened the door that led out into the monochromatic world beyond.

Charcoal, shadow, grey… and, from time to time, a hint or two of silver glistening from its crevices. There had to be.

Hesitating for another moment at the doorway, I turned around to face my friend again. Balancing on the precipice of two palettes, two starkly different universes.

"I'm sorry, Kyle," I whispered at last, "But I have to pretend."

Stygian, ashen, tenebrous, grey…

And with that, I shut the door behind me, leaving the room empty.

SKYE is an extremely precocious and creative soul who spends her days with her imaginary friend and fellow social outcast, Kyle, within the boundless, exciting, magical worlds of their own making. She's twelve years old, and enjoys painting, afternoons of deep contemplation, Ray Bradbury novels, and sushi. In recent years, however, Skye has begun to change. Her loneliness has started to push her away from the constants of her childhood and toward the cold, bleak outside society where Kyle cannot follow her, leaving their friendship and secret infinities to crumble slowly in her wake.

KIKI GONGLEWSKI is a senior at Albuquerque Academy high school. She was a finalist in the 2017 and 2019 state-wide "NM Girls Make Movies" screenplay contest, has won a National Gold Medal for Scholastic Art and Writing, and 17 gold keys in their Southwest Regional levels. She has also been published in literary magazines *Gypsum Sound*, *Madness Heart*, and *Unfading Daydream*, as well as Third Flatiron's recent anthology, *Terra, Tara, Terror!* Her former childhood imaginary friend Luna Hepburn (who has since left on sabbatical) shares Kiki's love of art, obscure movies, long naps, and Korean Barbecue.

ABOUT THE
EDITORS

DAWN VOGEL's academic background is in history, so it's not surprising that much of her fiction is set in earlier times. By day, she edits reports for historians and archaeologists. In her alleged spare time, she runs a craft business, co-edits *Mad Scientist Journal*, and tries to find time for writing. She is a member of Broad Universe, SFWA, and Codex Writers. Her steampunk series, *Brass and Glass*, is being published by Razorgirl Press. She lives in Seattle with her husband, author Jeremy Zimmerman, and their herd of cats. Visit her at historythatneverwas.com.

In addition to co-editing *Mad Scientist Journal*, **JEREMY ZIMMERMAN** is a teller of tales who dislikes cute euphemisms for writing like "teller of tales." He is the author of the young adult superhero book, *Kensei*. Its sequel, *The Love of Danger*, is now available. He lives in Seattle with a herd of cats and his lovely wife (and fellow author) Dawn Vogel. You can learn more about him at bolthy.com.

ABOUT THE
COVER ARTIST

LUKE SPOONER a.k.a. 'Carrion House' currently lives and works in the South of England. Having recently graduated from the University of Portsmouth with a first class degree he is now a full time illustrator for just about any project that piques his interest. Despite regular forays into children's books and fairy tales his true love lies in anything macabre, melancholy or dark in nature and essence. He believes that the job of putting someone else's words into a visual form, to accompany and support their text, is a massive responsibility as well as being something he truly treasures. You can visit his web site at www.carrionhouse.com.